The
Last
Debate

The
Last
Debate

Jim Lehrer

Random House
New York

Library of Congress Cataloging-in-Publication
data is available.
ISBN 679-44159-X

Manufactured in the United States of America
on acid-free paper
Book design by Tanya M. Pérez
9 8 7 6 5 4 3 2
First Edition

To Bob Compton, Lew Harris, and Bob Miller

Those are the facts. Deal with them as you will.
—Sophocles, *Antigone*

Author's Note

I was in Colonial Williamsburg for the Meredith-Greene presidential debate on an assignment from *The New American Tatler* magazine. I was compelled to stay full-time on the story for the next eighteen months by my passionate belief that it was an event that changed forever the practice of journalism in America.

I have tried in this book to re-create in fullest possible detail the circumstances, environment, and process surrounding what happened that night. Some people are certain those four journalists—famous now and forevermore as the Williamsburg Four—committed American journalism's most heroic act. Others charge with equal fervor and certainty that they perpetrated American journalism's most heinous crime. I offer my own conclusions at the end of the book, but I do so with the full and humble acknowledgment that in matters of this magnitude all opinions and impressions are mostly equal.

The reporting and writing route I traveled was the traditional one charted by the six basics of journalism—Who, What, When, Where, Why, and How. I was fortunate in that I had access to the recollections and perspectives of most of the principal players. Three of the four journalist-panelists cooperated fully. The fourth, debate moderator Michael J. Howley, followed a stonewall strategy toward me. That was unfortunate, because he emerged clearly and cleanly from my reporting as the central figure of the story. But I had only one restricted and unpleasant interview session with him. He later asked for the right to submit a written response once my work was finished. I agreed, and you will find Howley's unedited and unabridged words as an appendix at the end of the book. I urge you to read them carefully.

Howley was one of 178 persons I interviewed at least once. Many of the interviews were recorded on audiotape, and I intend to turn over the tapes as well as my notes to a suitable academic depository for use by scholars at some future date—probably no sooner than fifty years from now.

There are only a few instances in the text—mostly involving differing memories and versions of what happened—where I have tied individuals directly to specific quotes or pieces of information. There are also no footnotes or endnotes in which sources are identified. I avoided specific attributions wherever possible to protect my sources—for now, at least—but it was also a matter of technique. I chose to present the story of the Williamsburg Debate in a narrative form rather than in the more traditional journalistic style. I thought the needs of story flow and of delving into the more difficult and complex areas of mind and thought, character and motive, required that method. James Atlas, writing recently in *The New York Times,* described such hybrid forms of reporting as "Journalism as Novel, the Novel as Journalism." Whatever the label, I am prepared for the criticism my approach may bring.

I am also reconciled to coping with the attacks of Michael Howley. In his closing statement, he already accuses me of several journalistic sins—the worst and most absurd being the outright invention of people and events. Coming as it does from a man who could go down in history as American journalism's most notable sinner, this may give new meaning to the old look-who's-calling-the-kettle-black line.

But that, of course, is only one of many things that each of you readers must decide for yourself.

—Tom Chapman
New York

Part 1
Who, When, Where

1
First Light

It had a quiet beginning.

Six people were present, the most important being the two campaign managers—Brad Lilly for Democratic nominee Paul L. Greene and Jack Turpin for David Donald Meredith, the Republican nominee. Each came, as agreed, with another campaign official. General counsel Calvin Anderson was there for Greene; deputy campaign manager Freddy J. Hill was the second Meredith person. The other two participants were Chuck Hammond and Nancy Dewey, the director and assistant director/executive producer, respectively, of the National Commission on Presidential Debates.

They were in the K Street Washington offices of the debate commission behind the closed doors of a conference room decorated with large colored photographs of scenes from past presidential debates. Turpin and Hill sat on one side of a large dark-wood table, Lilly and Anderson directly across on the other. Hammond and Dewey sat side by side at one end.

It was shortly after two P.M., October 7—eight days and four hours before the debate was scheduled to begin in Williamsburg, Virginia.

They first took a vow of silence. Never would any of the six talk publicly about what was said over the next few minutes or hours it took to pick the four journalists who would be on the debate panel.

Then Nancy Dewey passed out two pieces of white typing paper clipped together. The first page had four names typed on it. There were at least fifty other names on the second page.

"We recommend the four there on the top page," she said. "On any slots we can't agree, there is a pool on page two from which we can draw."

Lilly looked at the four names, consulted in whispers with Anderson, and said: "They look fine to us."

All attention moved to Turpin. After a few tight, silent seconds in which he gazed only at the first page and did no consulting with Hill, Turpin slammed the papers down on the table and said: "This is an outrage!"

Nancy Dewey took a breath and held it and her tongue.

"What's the problem?" Hammond said.

"There's no diversity!" Turpin shouted.

"Bullshit. There are two women, a black, and a Hispanic," Hammond said. "I don't know how much more diverse it is possible to be."

Lilly, Anderson, Dewey, and Hammond say Turpin then stuck his right hand out in front of him, let his wrist go limp, and said effeminately, "Like where are *they*?"

Turpin and Hill deny it happened.

They also deny what the others say happened next. Turpin made his right hand into a fist and pumped it against his mouth and said: "There are none of them redskins either. Whoop, whoop, tom, tom, scalp, scalp." Then he squinted his eyes and said: "And what about some slants? They're 11.2 percent of the electorate in California, you know. Chop, chop, chink, chink, jap, jap."

Turpin, while denying it happened, claims that if he had said or done anything along these lines it would have been meant as good-humored satire, designed to make fun of the excesses sometimes found these days in the area of political correctness.

Everyone remembers Turpin saying: "Just kidding. Don't turn me in to the thought police." There was a round of smiles and laughs. No one remembers anyone speaking up to protest Turpin's conduct.

Turpin came to the meeting prepared for the serious business that followed. He and Hill brought with them a two-inch-thick loose-leaf notebook of background reports and other material on most of the leading journalists in Washington.

"He's a Democrat," Turpin said of Don Beard, the CNS News anchorman whose name appeared first on the commission's paper. "There is no way we are going to sit still for him moderating this debate."

Lilly said: "Don Beard's no Democrat. He's spreading one helluva lot more crap on us than he is on you every night at six-thirty Eastern Time."

"Maybe there's more of it to spread every night at six-thirty Eastern Time," Turpin said. Then reading from a page in his notebook, he said: "Beard's mother and father have always registered as Democrats in Arizona. He is a personal friend of Mo Udall. Beard's wife worked as a volunteer in the Kennedy, Johnson, McGovern, Carter, and Mondale campaigns. The poor soul even labored for Dukakis. His daughter is engaged to a young lawyer who works in the Manatt law firm in Los Angeles. He has lunch regularly in New York with Moynihan. He has never had lunch with D'Amato."

"OK, OK," Lilly said. "Scratch Beard." Lilly resisted the temptation to say passing up lunch with D'Amato was a provable act of nonpartisanship.

Dewey and Hammond nodded their agreement on Beard.

"I hereby move that we also scratch Jessica Mueller," Turpin said. Jessica Mueller was the second name on the top list of four. She was White House correspondent for *World News* magazine. "She's a lib, through and through."

"She does straight reporting for the magazine," said Nancy Dewey.

"I assume you have seen her on *Washington Talk-Talk-Talk*?"

"Certainly. My God, yes. It's the best of the TV food-fight shows. Yes . . ."

"She's the house lib on that show, pure and simple. She expresses her opinion, she attacks." Looking down at his book again, Turpin said: "In seventy-three separate statements she has made on *Talk-Talk-Talk* about my candidate during this campaign, only fourteen were positive. All of the others—all fifty-nine—were negative. So, please."

"They used to not let straight reporters also give their opinions like that," Lilly said. "It started with Broder, then Eleanor Clift and that clown from the San Francisco paper—I've already forgotten his name—and then the other bureau chiefs and newsmagazine types. Now it's any- and everybody. You can't tell the reporters from the commentators and comedians anymore. The clownalists, as they're called . . ."

Turpin said: "Broder's different, but I know what you mean. Nobody knows about it more than me and my man and my campaign. Can we agree to scratch her is the question."

Lilly and the others, each in his or her own way, put a line through the name of Jessica Mueller.

"Now to the two dark ones," Turpin said, in what can only be interpreted as a reference to the fact that the last two of the four names on the commission's top list were those of a black and a Hispanic. Ray Adair, a political reporter for *The Washington Post,* was the black. Maria Chavez-Jones, National Public Radio's chief congressional correspondent, was the Hispanic. Turpin told me he did not remember saying "dark ones," but that if he did he did not mean it in a racial way.

"Ray Adair's father signed an ad in the *New Orleans Times-Picayune* calling my candidate 'a modern-day Klansman,' " Turpin said. "Adair the kid has written nothing but negative stories about the impact the election of my man would have on the so-called African American community."

"All he's been doing is telling the truth," Lilly said. "You can't keep a person off this panel for telling the truth."

"I'm also not sure what someone's parents do is relevant," Chuck Hammond said.

"Relevance is in the eye of the beholder," Turpin said. "I am the beholder in this case, Chuck, not you."

Lilly appealed to Dewey. "Nancy, I do not approve of this way of doing things. It's right out of the fraternity blackball system."

"All we can do is recommend," Hammond said. "We cannot force either of you to accept anybody on the panel."

"That is exactly right," Turpin said. "You force, we walk—there's no debate."

"Let's not talk about force," Lilly said to Turpin. "If you are going to treat each one of these four panelist slots as if they're nominations to the Supreme Court, then we are never ever going to get this done."

Turpin, using words and phrases he had worked out in advance, said: "Let's review the situation we are involved in here, Brad. Negotiations for debates between you and me and our respective brethren went nowhere for weeks. You accused us of being the stumbling block, of not wanting to debate. We denied that, accusing you of wanting only the most rigid, controlled kind of joint appearance—not a real debate. That argument aside, the end result is this one event. Only one debate. It is impossible to overstate the potential impact that debate could have on the outcome of this election. You know that. I know that. So let's not play games about it. I care very much about who the four people on the panel are going to be. So do you. You must. I want Ray Adair off this panel."

Brad Lilly, distracted by a myriad of problems in his faltering campaign, truly had not seen the selection of the Williamsburg Debate panelists as being that important. It wasn't until Turpin made his little speech that he realized the explosive potential for this particular exercise. By then it was too late. He acceded to Turpin's complaint. Ray Adair was history.

Next!

Turpin's notebook identified Maria Chavez-Jones as a "typical anti-Republican leftist NPR reporter" who had come out of a strong labor-union background. Her father had been a paid organizer in the San Diego area for the retail clerks' union. Her mother worked as a caseworker for the California Department of Public Welfare. She had a brother who was a Democratic member of the California Assembly and a sister who taught English to recent immigrants from Mexico and other Latin American countries. Good-bye, Maria Chavez-Jones.

And over the course of the next forty-five minutes it was also good-bye to scores of others on the Hammond and Dewey second page, the B-list. They included for moderator all of the principal anchorpeople for the commercial networks, cable and public television, the morning and magazine programs, as well as the nightlies. Turpin gleefully shot the anchors down one at a time with anti-Meredith news-story counts from their newscasts, complaints about an anti-Meredith tone in their interviews, and tidbits of family or personal history that marked them unacceptable as liberals, Democrats, or hostiles. Not only was Lilly unprepared to offer any resistance, but so were Hammond and Dewey. Chuck Hammond did not think it was the commission's job or right to do screening investigations of potential panelists. "We compiled our list from our own long experience with and observations of various journalists in Washington," he said. "It was a subjective list, I will admit."

The turning point, known at the time only to Turpin and Hill, came when Turpin offered no objections to Joan Naylor, the CNS News weekend anchor, serving as one of the panelists. He had rejected her earlier as moderator.

"She's OK for the panel," said Turpin. "She'd be in over her head as moderator. She's no Barbara Walters."

"I don't think women should be compared only to women," said Nancy Dewey.

She was left out there by herself. Lilly was so grateful by then to have someone agreed to he signed off on Joan Naylor without any further discussion.

Henry Ramirez and Barbara Manning, despite being in their late twenties, also passed quick and easy muster with Turpin. The quickness and easiness should have raised warning flags to the others, but apparently it did not.

Lilly's primary interest by then was, in his words, "finding four live humans." He was only vaguely aware of Barbara Manning because of some pieces she had written for *This Week*. He had never even heard of Henry Ramirez and considered his employer, Continental Radio, to be a "third- or fourth-tier" media outlet. But. She was black, he was brown, so fine. Yes, they were young. But she was black, he was brown.

Hammond and Dewey, too, knew of both only because of their respective races. They were put on the list because of the need to have a good representation of black and Hispanic candidates. Manning's name was one of twelve submitted at the commission's request by the National Association of Black Journalists. Ramirez was on the National Association of Hispanic Journalists' list of twelve.

Now it was three down, one to go. The one was the important job of moderator. By the time Turpin got through, only Mike Howley of *The Washington Morning News* remained on the list. Lilly voiced some objection before he said OK.

"The sunavabitch has done nothing but trash my man's campaign," Lilly said.

"He's trashing you, in other words, if he's trashing the campaign," Turpin said. "I don't blame you for not wanting him as moderator."

"That's not the point," Lilly said.

"It's always the point," Turpin said.

Turpin assumed everyone in the room knew what he meant by that, i.e., that many professional political campaign managers—the best ones, mostly—eventually saw all of their campaigns as contests between them and the opposing professional campaign manager. That was always the point.

The point of the meeting had also been reached. They had four panelists—four live human beings. Mission accomplished, meeting over.

Quiet beginning over.

★

The next morning in a suite at the Holiday Inn in Rapid City, South Dakota, Brad Lilly tried his best to make it all look good to Governor Greene. Or at least not as bad as he was so afraid it really was.

First, there was the NBS–*Wall Street Journal* poll. Lilly told Greene that he had heard it was coming and that the news was apparently not going to be great.

"He's caught us, is that it?" the candidate asked his campaign manager.

"Yes, sir—and then some," the campaign manager replied. "But it could be a blip, an air bubble, a quirk, a bad batch."

"Batch? A bad batch of what?"

"Voters, poll respondents."

To Lilly and the others in the room it appeared for a split second that Governor Paul L. Greene of Nebraska was going to break out—or down—into laughter. But it passed and instead he stuck it right back and into Lilly. He said: "Maybe the stories will say the candidate of the great Brad Lilly, the Democratic party's political-consultant prince, has fallen seventeen points in the polls in seven months. Maybe they'll leave me out of it altogether."

Lilly was overcome with a marrow-deep disgust for his candidate for the first time since the campaign began. All he wanted at that moment was out of there. Out of this room, this Holiday Inn, this Rapid City, this world. He moved on to the next piece of business, the debate panel, feeling it would only take a few seconds.

It didn't work because of Joan Naylor.

"She is unacceptable to me," Greene said. "That is it and that is final."

"I really am sorry, Governor, but we did not realize you had such a huge problem with her," said Lilly. "She's not any worse than the others—"

Greene interrupted: "You heard her the other night, Brad. You heard her call me 'the man who is rapidly writing his name in the political histories as the single worst campaigner of all time.' "

"Those weren't her words. She was quoting somebody."

"She lied about that the way they all do. They were her words. She said they were spoken by a 'veteran Democratic mover and shaker who asked to remain anonymous,' but I do not believe that. They were her words. She spoke them to the American people. And she did not even have the guts to say they were her own words. She ducked. She is a coward. She is not somebody I want on this debate panel."

"Yes, sir."

"I will not answer any questions asked by her during the debate or on any other occasion ever as long as the both of us shall live."

"I hear you."

Brad Lilly was a campaign pro who had worked in the Udall, Carter, Mondale, Dukakis, Kerrey, and Clinton campaigns. He was not close enough to Greene to say what his new disgust led him to want to say, which was: Oh, knock it off, please. You're going to lose anyhow, so what difference does it make who is on this goddamn panel?

Almost as if he had been reading Lilly's mind, Greene said: "If the new poll is right, it may mean I might lose this election, possibly by a landslide that will make Goldwater, McGovern, Mondale, and Dukakis look like winners. So somebody could reasonably ask, What the hell difference does one woman on a debate panel matter? Well, the answer is that it makes a difference to me."

Yeah, and that is really some tough, smart answer, thought Lilly.

Lilly reminded himself that the election was now less than a month away and looked around the hotel suite for some help. Anderson and four other campaign operatives were there, each in his own way trying his best to make himself invisible. Lilly claims most everyone in the campaign at this particular time was trying to be invisible.

Lilly looked right at Marvin Al Garrison, the campaign press secretary. "Tell the governor, Marvin Al, what kind of shit would hit the fan if we go back to the debate commission now and try to get Joan Naylor scrubbed from the panel. Tell him, Marvin Al, please, sir."

Marvin Al, a man from Alabama already not happy in his work, stepped forward to say: "They would kill us, Governor. I mean kill."

"Who would?" Greene asked.

"Everybody. The women, the networks, the editorials, the talk shows, the polls, the carrier boys, the truck drivers, the Ph.D.'s, the R.N.'s, the shrinks, the skunks, the punks, the clownalists. Everybody."

"So? How much deader can I get than I already am? You can't kill a dead man, Marvin Al. He's already dead."

Now, there is wisdom for you, thought Lilly. He said: "Marvin Al is right, Governor. It would probably even get the debate itself canceled. The other side would raise hell and pull out. If they didn't, the other three panelists—you know how these pompous asses hang together in moments of public phoniness—would probably refuse to participate if Naylor is dropped. Nobody would come forward to replace them. . . ."

"Why didn't you run these names by me beforehand?"

"There were so many other matters on the plate, it just slipped through the cracks. I didn't see any serious problems with any of them except for Howley, whom I detest, as you know. But the chances of getting anybody better were doubtful. But, at any rate, I did not want to bother you with such details. You have so much more important things to do. But clearly that was a mistake."

"I thought the arrangement was that we had an opportunity to vet the panel," Greene said. "I thought nobody got on without our approval."

"True. I did the approving at a meeting yesterday with Turpin and the commission's people. Turpin came with a lot of information about the possible panelists. I meant to get some together, but there simply wasn't time. I blew that, too, I regret to say."

Greene was sitting in an overstuffed chair in the center of the room. He swiveled it halfway around to the right and then back around to the left.

"Maybe Joan Naylor is right when she says I am the worst candidate there has ever been for president of the United States," he said quietly. "I guess it is only appropriate then that I have a campaign staff that is a perfect match. Isn't that what Mike Howley wrote about you-all a few days ago, Brad? Didn't he say something about the only thing worse in my campaign than the candidate might very well be the campaign staff?"

"He said something like that, yes, sir."

"It was exactly like that, Brad."

★

The three men and one woman around the large Sunday-school classroom table stood when David Donald Meredith came in. That was what they always did every morning at the First Light staff meeting, at the beginning of their workday at the highest levels of the Take It Back With Meredith For President campaign.

"Let us pray," said Meredith after arriving at the table. "Here we are again, dear Lord of us all. Here we are again asking for your guidance as we go about the business of making decisions on behalf of bringing honest, spiritual, and right government to the people of the United States of America. Help us bring love and compassion and justice and mercy to our thinking, our talking, our deciding. Help us to do right in Your name. It is in Your name that we pray. Ahhh-men."

"Ahhh-men," said the others. Meredith sat down, and then the others sat down. Having their daily First Light staff meetings in a church was a practice that had begun almost by accident during the primaries. Meredith had agreed to speak to a sunrise prayer breakfast in Concord, New Hampshire, and asked his staff to join him afterward for a meeting at the church. There was some press attention, followed by some praise and appreciation from the leaders of the American Christian Families Coalition, one of the most important backers of Meredith's candidacy. Jack Turpin suggested that Meredith, only an occasional churchgoing Methodist before the campaign, develop some praying skills, and the First Light meeting-always-in-a-church was born.

This morning it was in the First Baptist Church of Cleve

"The debate panel for Williamsburg is before us first,"
He had held top positions in every Republican presidentia
since Nixon. The Jack Kemp campaign was the only losing one he had
run.

"There will be four. They, the commission, put forward four names.
As could have been expected, they met all Democratic party and liberal
tests. We managed over the course of the meeting to replace their one
white male, one white female, one Hispanic male, and one black female
with our own."

"You don't mean our own politically?" Meredith asked.

"No, sir. There are no four such things in the press corps of this country."

"I didn't think so. They all hate me."

"Our four are four with some insurance possibilities," Turpin said.
"Mike Howley is the moderator. He's . . . well, he's Mike Howley. He's
been harsh in his criticism of everybody connected with this campaign.
Not only you and me, but also the other side. Particularly of Lilly's operation. Howley's about as good as it was possible to get. All of the straight
television types would have been much worse."

"They all hate me," Meredith said.

"Joan Naylor is one of the panelists. She is of television, you know
her," said Turpin. "The other two, the black and the Mexican, you do not
know. Nobody knows them because they are nobodies themselves, both
kids in their late twenties. If they were white, they wouldn't have the jobs
they have, much less be on this panel."

"I have promised to rid our society of the kind of reverse discrimination that has given birth to that very kind of thing," Meredith said. "It is
one promise I promise you I will keep."

"I say amen to that, sir."

"All four of these people are opponents of ours and our cause, I
assume?"

"Of course, yes, sir." Turpin handed a packet of papers across the
table to Meredith. "Here is what Nelson's checks turned up on each of
the four." Nelson was Sid Nelson, a former FBI agent who was the campaign's director of security. The Secret Service did the regular protection

work on the campaign. The campaign's pre-Williamsburg line was that Nelson and a group of other former FBI agents who worked with him did only discreet investigative work that included background checks on potential employees.

Meredith flipped from page to page.

"Can't the abortion of Naylor's sister be confirmed?" he said, without looking up.

Turpin said: "No, not one hundred percent. She was sixteen. Her boyfriend paid for it. Her parents knew all about it."

"Has it ever been in the public print?"

"Not according to our checks. The press does a poor job of reporting on the frailties of its own."

"Yes, indeed. Fine. It could come in handy if something turns nasty on the abortion issue. 'You have asked me about abortion, Ms. Naylor. Does the fact that your sister had an abortion at the age of sixteen present for you a journalistic conflict of interest?' That might cause some commotion."

"Yes, sir, it sure would. That was the idea, the insurance."

"The Mexican? His mother is his problem?"

"Yes. She is a widow who runs a café in a small town in the Rio Grande Valley of Texas. She's been cited for liquor-law and several health-department violations, but none were serious."

"Serving alcohol to minors and filthy food to anyone is always serious to ordinary people, Jack."

"I realize that. That's why he is on the panel."

"Isn't Howley also from Texas?"

"Yes, sir."

"Two Texans on a panel of four. How come?"

"A conspiracy, obviously, sir."

"Obviously. The black girl?"

"Major insurance paydirt. First, her uncle is a Black Muslim, having moved to Chicago from a small town in Georgia some years ago. Two, she rooms with a woman member of the Paul L. Greene campaign staff."

"Are they lesbians?"

"No, sir."

"Too bad."

"Yes, sir. But it's still paydirt."

"You're right," said Meredith. He looked up and over at the woman at the table. She was Joanne Windsor, the campaign press secretary. "What do you think about this?"

"I think she should not be on the panel," said Joanne Windsor. "She's a kid, a lightweight, a standard black, as well as a close friend of the enemy."

The three other men at the table either grunted or smiled their agreement.

"I went for her, among the weakest of the blacks, because I believed we had to have one on the panel," said Jack Turpin. "It would surely be leaked that we had kept off all blacks."

"How could that hurt us?" said Will Hodges, one of the other men. He was the campaign's pollster. "The numbers show that we may not get more than two percent of the black vote anyhow. So we lose a few more?"

Turpin shook his head. "No, I think we should look upon her as serious insurance. If something goes wrong for us during the debate, we then toss out the charge that we just discovered the panel was tainted by the fact that one of the panelists lived with an official of the Greene campaign. Insurance, insurance, insurance."

David Donald Meredith stopped reading the papers and smiled at Turpin, who went on with his self-praise.

"I wanted as many vulnerabilities as possible as insurance on all of them. Naylor and her sister's abortion. On the Mexican, there's not only the mother and her dirt and drunks. Nelson's check showed him to be too young, too ambitious. He thinks he's a brown Donaldson or Wallace, and the chances are he'll go too far trying to nail you and make a fool of himself."

Meredith said: "You are the best, Jack, you really are. Between you and Jesus I have the best campaign management in the history of American politics."

"We'll all say amen to that," Will Hodges said.

"Howley? What about Howley?" Meredith asked. "Does he have insurance possibilities?"

"Not really. He's a widower, no girlfriend at present. He served and was honorably discharged from the navy in the fifties."

"Children with drug problems?"

"No children of any kind."

"I see a reference to a bankruptcy. What is that all about?"

"His uncle ran a Western Auto store in Van Alstyne, Texas, that went belly-up."

"Could be useful, who knows. Ordinary people don't like people who file for bankruptcy. Why did you take him as moderator?"

"He's part of a deal I made with CNS News. They came to me through a deeply covered third-party intermediary asking if there was anything we could do to make sure one of their anchors was the moderator. Their news programs are running third, and it might give them some much needed visibility. I told them that there was no way we would ever agree to Don Beard."

"Amen, amen. He spits and fires with venom for me every evening. Every evening."

"Exactly. They offered Naylor as a backup. I said no, but maybe as a panelist. They said, fine, as long as no other network anchor moderated. So we had to go with a print guy. Howley seemed the safest of them because he's about the only one left from the old school of journalism. He's been as bad to them as he's been to us."

"What do we get in exchange for this from CNS?"

"Their balls."

"What?"

"All I have to do is simply squeeze a hint that I might tell somebody about our little transaction and we get what we want. The ultimate insurance, is the way I see it. I'm not sure anybody has had a network in that position before. When it could really come in handy is after we're in the White House."

"Praise you, Jack Turpin. Praise you," said David Donald Meredith. "You really are the very best."

It was the perfect setup for Jack Turpin. He had saved the best for last.

"I certainly can't take any credit for it, sir," he said, "but it is all finally coming into focus, into place."

He handed Meredith a copy of the summary of the coming NBS–*Wall*

Street Journal poll. "Nelson acquired this from a friendly source within the *Journal*," Turpin said.

Meredith read the news that he had pulled ahead of Paul L. Greene. Then he stood and bowed his head. Turpin and the others stood and bowed their heads.

"Dear Savior," said Meredith in a near whisper. "You said, Follow Me and I will show you the way to glory. We did and You have. Thank You, Lord. Thank You for me, for us, and for the people of the United States of America. Ahhh-men."

Turpin and the others repeated the ahhh-men.

David Donald Meredith had learned how to pray for the good of the campaign. Turpin and the others had learned how to say ahhh-men.

★

Nancy Dewey and Chuck Hammond had stayed in their conference room after the others left. They immediately placed a call to the bipartisan commission's two co-chairmen, former Republican national chairman Paul Clancy and former Democratic national chairman Frank Durkette. They found Clancy at his law office in Minneapolis. Durkette was at his home in Bethesda, Maryland, a Washington suburb. They were all quickly hooked together on a conference line and a speakerphone.

"So what exactly have we ended up with?" Durkette asked after Hammond reported the names of the four panelists and how they were decided.

"Yeah," said Clancy. "Is it going to work?"

Chuck Hammond said he could not guarantee anything. He said he had no problems with Mike Howley and Joan Naylor, but the other two were truly blind flying in the night. Not because they were minorities, of course, he said, but because they were so young and inexperienced.

Of course, said Clancy.

"Being on a presidential-debate panel should be a kind of reward for supreme and long service as a journalist," Durkette said.

They asked Nancy Dewey, the person who was going to actually put the debate on the air from Williamsburg, what she thought.

She told them she was worried. "There was something about the way

Turpin came in here with his black book and took over that was not right," she said. "Lilly was not prepared. Neither were we, really."

Chuck Hammond disagreed. "We have limits, Nancy. We do not have the authority to push anything down their throats. It's a stupid system."

"We have been through that too many times already," Clancy said. "We almost didn't even have a debate this time."

"It's got to be required by law," Durkette said. "Tie it to federal funding. If you take federal matching funds, you have to agree to at least three debates. . . ."

"Frank, for crissakes, save it for another time," Clancy said. "The question, the *only* question before our house right now, is What we do about this?"

"That's not a question. We have no choice."

"Yes, we do. We could decide to scrub the debate. We could take the position that the selection process for the panelists did not meet our standards or criteria or something and we are pulling out."

"Get serious, please. We'd look like fools."

"I am not suggesting we do it. I am merely making the point that there are options."

Chuck Hammond, after a second or two of silence, said: "We proceed? We contact the four selectees and get on with it?"

"I say yes," Durkette said. "What about you, Paul?"

"The same."

Chuck Hammond told me that he was the last to speak before the conference-call connections were cut. He said he said to all: "I have a feeling we are all going to regret having decided to go ahead with this thing."

None of the others recalls Hammond saying anything at all, much less delivering such a doomful warning. I am not prepared to call Hammond a liar over something as trivial as this. But I am prepared to at least suggest it was possible he wished so badly afterward that he *had* said it that it began to seem to him as if he really did.

Whatever, he and Nancy Dewey went back to their respective offices to place the calls to the four selected panelists. Dewey called Naylor and Ramirez. Hammond notified Howley and Manning.

2

The Williamsburg Four

Barbara Manning never even had a glimpse of a daydream about being on the Meredith-Greene debate panel. "I was still way, way back there in the back of the bus for those kinds of fantasies" was the way she described her state of professional mind at the time.

She was twenty-nine years old, ten months into her job at *This Week*, still into the trauma of matching news with coherent words and sentences under what she heard somebody once call "everybody pressure"— meaning doing it for a huge national readership rather than a small local one. She had worked her way to Washington and the magazine from the South Bend, Indiana, *Journal* and the Chicago *Sun-Times*, where she had learned the basics of making real what she had learned at Northwestern University's Medill School of Journalism's special fast-track graduate program for minority journalists. But she was still getting her footing on the weekly newsmagazine track.

So when the call did come from Chuck Hammond, she was not only not expecting it, she almost didn't take it.

"An important person named Hammond on line two for you, Barbara!"

"No calls!" said Barbara.

"He said it was urgent!"

"Nothing is more urgent than this piece!" she said.

The man she was shouting with was Mel Renfro, her boss, the political editor of *This Week* magazine. It was almost five P.M., which meant she had less than thirty minutes to get her story about the way poor blacks were afraid of what might happen to them under a Meredith administration, a case she had already made ten or twelve times in print before, but it could not be said often enough. Her desk and computer were part of the politics cluster in the center of *This Week*'s Washington bureau office. Renfro sat in the center and shouted at people.

"This is!" he shouted at her now.

Barbara was terrorized by him and by deadlines, the coming of which in her weekly life everybody said she would eventually either get used to or perish from. She remained uncertain which was going to happen first.

"Barbara Manning," she said into the phone.

"Chuck Hammond, Barbara," said the male voice on the line. Barbara? she thought. Why are you calling me Barbara? I don't know you.

"I'm director of the National Commission on Presidential Debates," said Chuck Hammond.

"Yeah, right?"

"We would like for you to be one of the four press panelists at Williamsburg next Sunday. What do you say?"

"Me? This is Barbara Manning."

"I know who you are."

"You want me?"

"Yes, ma'am."

"Man, you must really be into affirmative action at your place."

Chuck Hammond was tempted then to respond honestly to her honest response but decided against it. He did not think it would have been helpful for him to say what he really believed, i.e., It is the height of stupid affirmative action to have you, kid, on the panel. He said nothing.

Barbara was truly confused by the call, the invitation. She took a few breaths. It made no sense. Me? You want me? Little old Barbara Manning, granddaughter of Maude Frederick Manning of Perrin, Georgia? You want me? Twenty-nine-year-old me?

"Mr. Hammond, you have thrown me across the room. . . ."

"Chuck. I was Carter's deputy chief of staff." He hated the fact that he had to even identify himself. How could anybody covering politics in America today not know who he was?

"Let me talk to my bosses and think about it some and I'll get back. This is really something, man. Believe me. I am floored. I really am hit by this. I really am. . . ."

Hammond gave her his phone number and she promised to call him within two hours, by seven P.M.

She hung up the phone and shouted: "Me! They want me on the Williamsburg panel!"

Mel smiled at her. He already knew that, Barbara thought. Chuck Hammond must have talked to him first. Mel Renfro already knew that. He shouldn't have. I should have known first. My new friend Chuck should have told me first.

Oh, hell, what difference does it make?

She stood up and threw her fists into the air. "Me! They want me! Gramma Maude, look at me now!"

It was only at that moment that she realized that Mel and her five other colleagues on the political staff of *This Week* magazine were in fact looking at her. All were white men of various ages, all were senior to her in reporting time and in time at *This Week*.

All six were smiling at her, and some even seemed to be mouthing words like, Great, Congratulations, Right on.

But she knew what they were thinking. She knew they were thinking that the only reason she was chosen was because she was an African American, a black person, a person of color, a minority, an affirmative action, a political correct, a face.

Well, white boys, that's what you get for not having any slaves in your background. And isn't that too bad?

Gramma Maude, look at me! Listen to me!

Gramma Maude could not hear her because she was dead. But her daughter—Barbara's mother—was very much alive and living in Pittsburgh. She was very much beside herself a few minutes later when Barbara called her and gave her the news. So was Barbara's father when she reached him at his law office downtown, and her sister in Cambridge and her brother in Chicago and Lilly Owen Mills, her old mentor-tutor at Northwestern.

Barbara talked so fast and so frantically and so excitedly to so many people so quickly that it wasn't until she got on the Metro for home that she got scared. Really to the bone and soul scared.

She saw herself trying to speak at the debate and her mouth freezing open. Wide-open. Exposing the fact that her teeth were mud dirty. Exposing the fact that she had no tongue. Exposing the fact that there were green things on her vocal cords. Then she saw herself throwing up there in front of the whole world, trying to ask a question of Meredith and Greene. "Is it true?" she would say with her mouth full of poorly digested pastrami and chili and mayonnaise and blue-cheese-flavored popcorn. "Is what true?" Meredith and Greene would respond. "Anything," she would respond. She saw Mel Renfro calling her while the debate was still on and firing her. "You little pickaninny piece of baby shit, you fold up your laptop and your floppy disks and your Rolodex and go back to the slave market from where you came," he would say. And she saw Gramma Maude calling in on the other line from heaven saying: "Why didn't you have the brains Jesus is God gave you to say to the man, 'Not right now, Mr. Chuck. Get back to me in a couple of centuries when I'm ready, Mr. Chuck. Not quite yet now, Mr. Chuck'?"

Not quite yet now.

Barbara Manning also had a problem that she did not have to imagine. It was the Barbara Hayes problem. It was real and right there.

They had first met at a meeting of the Black Journalists and Writers Club at Northwestern and had run into each other again when they had come to Washington in search of work. They were now roommates, having rented a basement apartment together in the Dupont Circle section of Washington.

The problem for Barbara Manning was that Barbara Hayes was on the press staff of the Paul L. Greene presidential campaign. Her job was minority press relations, which meant, in both Barbaras' words, sucking up to people like Barbara Manning of *This Week* magazine. To head off any awkwardness, they had agreed never to discuss the campaign or politics of any kind at home, but it hadn't held. Barbara Manning, like most every other sane person she knew in the press or anywhere else, detested and feared David Donald Meredith.

But this was different. This was awful. Being on a presidential-debate panel was different, was awful. There had to be no contact, no loose talk, no real problems, no appearance of problems, no nothing.

There she was. Barbara Hayes was there in the apartment. Barbara Manning opened the front door and there she was. Normally Barbara Hayes was still at her office this time of evening. Or on a plane. Wasn't she supposed to go off to Florida or Georgia or someplace this weekend? This evening?

"Hey, proud to know you," Barbara Hayes said. "I figured you for the big time and here you are already, already in the big time."

"They needed a black face, they got a black face. That's all you ought to figure. I'm scared to death about it. I mean scared. Really scared. But that's it. I am saying not one more word to you about it. And you are saying not one more word to me about it."

"This may be the most important thing you ever do, roommate."

"I thought you were going off somewhere this weekend," Barbara Manning said.

"Change in plans. I needed some clean clothes."

"Oh, yeah. I forgot Washington was the only place with laundries and cleaners."

They were in the small kitchen of their small place on Nineteenth Street, NW. Barbara Hayes had been calmly sipping a caffeine-free Diet Coke when Barbara Manning walked in.

"Don't say another word to me about Williamsburg," said Barbara Manning. "Not one word."

"Have I said a real word? Have I?"

"You came home to say one. Admit it. You came here to say some words to me, didn't you?"

"I live here, remember?"

"The campaign assigned you to do this, didn't they? Well, do not say one word. Not one word. Nothing. I want to be able to say to Mean Mel Renfro or anyone else without breaking my Gramma Maude's lying mirror that I had no conversations with my roommate Barbara Hayes of the

Greene campaign. So forget saying a word. Not a word about anything, and I mean anything, and I mean it."

Barbara Hayes followed Barbara Manning out into the large room where they did everything except sleep, cook, and go to the bathroom. The room had a large sofa, two chairs, and a small dinette table over in one corner. All the pieces were mostly shabby and mostly borrowed from friends or bought at yard sales in the neighborhood.

Barbara Hayes said: "OK, OK. You're right. I came to talk to you. I came to tell you that we are desperate, that America is desperate. That unless something happens in Williamsburg this election, maybe this country is over. If that scumball Meredith is elected, every person in this country, particularly everyone that looks like you and me, is going to suffer, every—"

"I am a journalist! Shut up! Shut up! Shut up!" screamed Barbara Manning as she put her hands up to her ears so she would not hear any more.

Barbara Hayes handed Barbara Manning a piece of paper. It was an advance copy of a press release about the coming NBS–*Wall Street Journal* poll.

Across the top of the page in capital letters was the headline: MERE-DITH ROARS AHEAD.

"A source at NBS slipped this to us ahead of time," said Barbara Hayes. "They're running it in two days."

Barbara Manning read the awful story. In a preference poll of 1,047 probable voters, David Donald Meredith, the Republican nominee, had for the first time surged ahead of the Democratic nominee, Governor Paul L. Greene. The numbers were 51 for Meredith, 44 for Greene, with the rest undecided. The most stunning part was the fact that the numbers had been 47 Greene, 43 Meredith, only two weeks before, and probably even more stunning was it marked a 17-point Meredith jump in the seven weeks since Labor Day.

"The racist bastard is going to be elected president of the United States," Barbara Hayes said to Barbara Manning.

"I do not believe that the people of this country would do that to their country," said Barbara Manning.

"Well, the time has come for you to maybe start."

"Not another word!"

"They're ready for a tough guy. He's a tough guy. They're ready for some order. He's an order guy. They're ready for somebody to do something about all 'them minorities.' He's a do-something-about-them-minorities guy—"

"Shut up," said Barbara Manning. "Shut up, shut up, shut up."

"I can't shut up. Neither can you."

"Watch me."

"I'm going to."

★

Henry Ramirez had had vivid panelist-plus fantasies from the moment the one and only Meredith-Greene debate was announced. He felt spirits moving out there that would move him into one of those four Williamsburg slots. He saw himself clearly and proudly sitting there at a table decorated in red, white, and blue ribbons, exchanging clever, smart words with the candidates and his fellow superjournalists. He moved on from there with the spirits and his fantasies to a black-tie dinner where he received a plaque for being the first Hispanic American to be a presidential-debate panelist, then to standing behind one of the Williamsburg podiums himself as the first Hispanic American to be a nominee for president of the United States, and finally to becoming the first Hispanic president, sending several U.S. Army divisions off to defend Mexico from an attack by leftist or rightist hordes from Guatemala or some other evil force to the south.

His fantasies of political grandeur were fed and encouraged by Paul L. Greene, the Democratic nominee for president. If this gringo dumbbell could make it, then there was certainly hope for the likes of this little brown Mescan dumbbell, as Henry saw it.

Right now he really saw it, too. Right now while listening to Greene make a speech at a campaign rally in a football stadium in Rapid City, South Dakota. Greene stumbled over simple policy-concern words like "deficit" and "Mubarak," raised his voice when he should have whispered, whispered when he should have shouted, mispronounced the names of half the people on the stage with him, and generally lived up to his growing reputation as the single worst major-party candidate for president in the history of the game.

The conventional wisdom among everyone Henry talked to in the traveling press corps was simply that Greene was probably a good man, a sound and honest human being, who would probably make a pretty fair president. But he was not capable of getting elected under any circumstances, much less against a flawless performer like David Donald Meredith, the magic new man of American politics who had swept in from national popularity as a radio/TV political guru to get the Republican nomination.

"How did Greene ever get elected governor of Nebraska is the question, is the question, is the question, is the question, is the question," Henry said to Jones of UPI under his breath. They were sitting side by side on bleachers in the press section off to the right of the stage.

"He retailed it," said Jones. "There are only 1.6 million people in Nebraska and he sought out each one of them, kissed them on a cheek of their choice, shook a hand of their choice, and talked them into voting for him much like a guy talks somebody into buying a used Chevy pickup. He's great retail, lousy wholesale."

"The Democrats have no sense," said Henry.

"They also have a death wish," said Jones. "I understand the new *Wall Street Journal* poll is going to show that creep Meredith ahead. It's hard to believe. Until you see this guy Greene."

"I think I'll run next time," Henry said. "If Greene can do it, anybody can do it, I can do it. Even if I am just a poor little brown-skinned Mescan from Falfurrias. The first child of illegal immigrants to make it to the very top of the American dream."

"There's nothing worse than a reporter who thinks he should be president. . . ."

"Henry, this came in for you from the communications center," said one of the campaign press aides who appeared from behind the bleachers. He handed Henry a note.

Henry immediately returned the call to Nancy Dewey on his company-owned cellular phone, which he wore in a holster on his belt as if it were a 9mm pistol. This is Henry Ramirez of Continental Radio News! Stick 'em up!

A sudden feeling of light-headedness swept over him as he listened to Nancy Dewey identify herself and then deliver the invitation to join three colleagues on the Williamsburg panel. He was unable to catch his breath for a second. And then he said: "I knew it was going to be you. I knew it. I really knew. I accept, I accept. I will do it. I will do it. Do you believe in spirits?"

"The kind you drink, yes," Nancy Dewey replied.

"What about the kind who move in mysterious ways?"

"Not really."

"I do. I really do. They made you call me. They did it. They got this done. They heard me dreaming and they got it done. They got me done."

Nancy Dewey was very concerned when she hung up the phone that evening. She told Chuck Hammond that Henry Ramirez sounded as if he might be slightly off the wall, and if she was right they and the rest of America could have a very long evening in Williamsburg.

Henry, after causing a small scene in the press bleachers, immediately made two telephone calls on his cellular phone. One was to his mother in Falfurrias, Texas. The other was to his boss in Washington.

Henry told his mother that her son was going to be the first child of illegal immigrants ever to be a panelist in a presidential debate.

"*You* should be president," she said. "They should ask *you* questions, not you ask them. You listen to me about this."

That was what she always said and it was what he always did. She told him to listen and he listened. It was his mother's energy and drive that got Henry out of the apple and peach orchards of the Rio Grande Valley to college, to another life. Listening to her was one of the natural things of his life.

"You ask that awful talk-man Meredith why he wants to keep our people out of this country. You ask him why we are not as good Americans as his people, gringo people. You ask him why he wants a wall and soldiers around America.

"You ask them both about the immigration law already here. You ask them. You ask them why they are already treating us like we are not real Americans. You ask them why I have to prove I am American because I am brown, but nobody who are other colors have to prove anything. Those people with the shiny black skin who kill each other on the streets and shoot drugs on the streets and who make their babies have more babies don't have to. Tell me why they look more American than I do. Tell me, you say to them. You ask those two men, those two famous men, that Meredith talk-man of hate and that Greene fool, what they are going to do about this. If you do not ask them, then I will not talk to you for two weeks afterward. I will talk to you only on the day after two weeks have gone by. That will be your punishment. Unless you do not want to be punished like that, you ask those people what I say to ask them."

Henry had placed the call, so that meant his mother, Mama Luisa to the people who came to her café in Falfurrias, would feel free to talk endlessly. It was only when she initiated the call, which was seldom, that she was careful about the time.

"I am afraid people would think I was talking like a special interest if I did that, Mama," Henry said. "I must ask big-league, general questions about war and peace and NATO and other big things so they won't think I am only a special interest."

"We are not special interest. We are not NATOs. We are Americans."

"I must go now, Mama."

"You ask my question or I will not talk to you until the day after two weeks go by."

"Oh, come on now. You won't tell me right afterward how proud you were of me? You won't tell me how proud you are that it is your son who was the first son of illegal immigrants to be a panelist on a debate for president of the United States? I cannot believe you will wait two weeks and one day to tell me that."

"OK, OK. I will tell you that right after, but that is all I will tell you."

"That is all I want to hear, Mama."

"I will tell you you were the best."

"How do you know I will be?"

"I know because I am your mama."

Henry's second call, to Jim Weaver, the president of Continental Radio News, followed a similar theme. Weaver talked like he was not only Henry's mama, but also his daddy and his God. At least, according to Henry he did.

"You had no authority to accept the invitation without consulting us first," Henry later said Weaver said.

"How come?"

"Because you work for us."

"I am not your illegal migrant worker. I am not your picker."

"You were asked because you work for Continental Radio. That is it. Whether you go on that panel is our call, not yours," Henry claims Weaver said.

"I am the one they called. I am the one who makes the call," Henry responded.

"They only asked you because they needed a brown face."

"It's *my* brown face."

"It's *our* brown face."

"Who do you think you are?"

"I am the one who signs your paychecks."

"You should be proud of me."

"If you go out there and screw it up in front of all of the world?"

"Screw it up?"

"You're a kid, Henry. You aren't ready for the big leagues right now. It's that simple. I'm going to call the commission and tell them we will send somebody else from our shop. You're not our only minority, you know. Mathis is black. He's been around. We have Chan in L.A. So has he. We can even give them a woman. Maggie Tobin. She's been around for years."

"They want my kind of minority."

"Well, they ain't getting you."

Henry Ramirez did not see himself as a kid. He was twenty-eight years old, a graduate of Texas A&I in Kingsville, just up the road from Falfurrias, with a B.A. in journalism. He had worked for three years as a radio reporter for KFVL in Harlingen and KMAC in McAllen before being hired as the city-hall reporter for KTRH in Houston, where he won many awards and much attention for his stories on the hard-nosed Houston police. The attention got him the job in the Washington bureau of Continental. In his six months with Continental, he had already made it to be the primary substitute for the two regular reporters covering the Meredith and Greene campaigns. He was in no mind to take seriously "You're a kid, Henry" from anybody.

"You can't stop me from doing this," he said to Weaver.

"Goddamn it, Henry, you work for me!"

"You can't stop me from doing this."

"I am going to hang up now and call the commission," said Weaver. "I am going to tell them I am calling on your behalf and that you have decided you are unable to accept the invitation. I will offer them one of our more experienced reporters of any color or sex they wish."

"You cannot do this! I just talked to my mama!"

"You should have thought about that sooner. Henry, believe me, I am doing you a favor. Someday your day will come. But not now. It's way, way too early. OK?"

Henry did not answer immediately. Henry knew that he had come to what his mama called "a river with no bridge." He reminded himself about himself. He was the real and spiritual child of two people who had the guts and the courage and the bravery to wade through the shallow waters of the Rio Grande River to find a better life. Not just once but, for his father, twelve times. Twelve times he came across illegally. Eleven times he was caught by the border patrol and returned to Mexico. His mother did it seven times before they both became legal through the 1987 amnesty law. They would not be proud of a son who folded forever the first time some immigration cop–like person put the cuffs on.

Henry, trying to imagine he was on the radio, went to the steadiest and deepest voice that was in him. He said: "Jim Weaver, I think you should think about what it would sound like if I told people what you have just said to me and what you have just said you are now going to do to me. It would not be good for you or for the network."

"You can't blackmail me, Henry!"

"I am not blackmailing you, Jim Weaver. I am telling you something. I am telling you this would not look or sound good. If you do not want to look or sound good, then you go right ahead. If you have the convictions of what you believe, then you go right ahead. But when you do, you should know what might happen."

"I forbid you to talk about this to anyone inside or outside our shop!"

"You can forbid nothing. I know the Constitution of my country."

"You're fired!"

"Add that to what this would look and sound like, Jim Weaver."

"You bastard! You kid bastard!"

"You are wrong about that, too. My mother and father had been married in a church for three years when I was born."

Henry's cellular phone went dead. He assumed it was because Jim Weaver had hung up on him.

Jim Weaver, in writing through a lawyer, denied most of Henry's account.

But as a practical matter, the blackmail worked. Nobody—not Chuck Hammond, Nancy Dewey, or anyone else—at the commission ever received a call from Jim Weaver or anyone else at Continental Radio about the Ramirez selection.

And Henry Ramirez, with a spirit and bravado that would have made any set of any kind of parents proud, went on with his daily job in the Washington bureau of Continental Radio and his plans to go to Williamsburg as if nothing had happened.

★

It had not been a happy twenty-six minutes and forty-two seconds for Joan Naylor in the Saturday night *CNS Evening News* anchor chair. A tape operator had missed the roll cue on a piece from Berlin about where all of the Cold War prostitutes had gone, and the TelePrompTer got stuck in the middle of a nine-second intro to a soft closer about the relationship between crime and being a second child.

She also felt that makeup never got her hair quite right tonight and she hated herself for even caring.

Now here she was alone in the office of Carol Reynolds, the Washington bureau chief. Carol had closed the door behind them, something she rarely did.

"You're going to be getting a call in a few minutes from Nancy Dewey at the debate commission," said Carol Reynolds.

"Hey, hey, it happened!" Joan said. She threw her hands up in the air and then came a feeling of well-being warmth that started in her stomach and shot right up through her body to her eyes, which immediately filled with tears.

"Well, not exactly," said Carol Reynolds. "They want you on the panel only—"

"I thought I was going to moderate!"

"Well, we lost that one. Mike Howley's going to do that."

"Lost it with whom?"

"I don't know for sure."

"Did you-all push me?"

"Sure."

"Beard. You went for Don Beard."

"We had to at first. He's our main guy, like it or not. You were our fallback and they wouldn't buy it."

"Who wouldn't buy it?"

"I can't say."

"Because you don't know or because you can't say?"

"I can't say."

"Damn it, Carol. Damn it."

"I agree. Damn it."

"Howley? He's mainly print. And he's already done everything. Isn't it time to start spreading it around a little bit?"

"That was exactly the argument we made. But they wouldn't budge."

"I had my heart set on this. I really did. It . . . Well, I don't have to tell you what it could have meant."

"That's true."

"Is this some kind of message being sent some kind of crazy way from the network?"

"No! Don't go anchorperson paranoid on me now."

Joan stood to leave. The feeling of happy warmth had been replaced with fury heat. "Well, count me out. I am an anchorwoman. It's either moderate or nothing. I will not be just another panelist."

"Sit down, please, Joan."

"No."

"All right. Have it standing up. I will join you." Carol stood. "Number one, dear friend and colleague, let's not lose sight of what is going on here. We are talking about the one and only debate of this campaign between the candidates for president of the United States." She handed Joan a piece of paper. It contained the advance word on next week's poll showing Meredith moving out ahead of Greene. "This is what it is about."

Joan glanced at it and said: "I do not believe the country is going to elect that guy. I don't care what the polls say. In the privacy of the voting booth they will not vote for Meredith. But what's your point?"

"This is not about Joan Naylor or Mike Howley or anybody else who goes out there and asks questions."

"It's about network-news politics. That is what this is about," Joan said.

"I'll ignore that. The really important point is the deal is done. We already told them you would do it."

"You had no right to do that!"

"Oh, please. Let's not go into rights. The fact is that this was worked out on a slot level. A slot for CNS News on the panel. All of the networks wanted one. We are the only one that got one. The other three slots are going one to radio, two to print. We are the only television. We won. We got it. We being CNS News, not you Joan Naylor. It's that simple."

"That is not simple. That is awful. Who did we make the slot deal with?"

"Oh, shit, Joan, just do it. One hundred million or so of your closest friends and fans will be watching. It is good for you and for the network."

"I want to know who we dealt with."

"Drop it."

"Tell me or I will not be a party to this, thank you."

"Yes you will, thank you."

The phone on Carol Reynolds's desk rang at that moment. Within a few more moments Joan was talking to Nancy Dewey. With Carol Reynolds staring at her, she listened to the official invitation. And when Dewey finished Joan Naylor said, Fine, OK, I accept, I will be one of the panelists at the Williamsburg Debate.

She then walked out of Carol Reynolds's office without saying another word. She was angry at Carol and the network and the gods and devils of television. But she was also not proud of herself. She wished even then that she had merely declined the invitation politely. She didn't because in the final few seconds she had to think before replying to Nancy Dewey, she realized that the decision to decline was also probably the decision to walk. Good-bye CNS News, good-bye chance to be the first sole principal woman anchor in the history of network television. At the age of forty-two, her opportunities for bigger and better things were here and most likely only here. CNS had spotted her on KFAA in Cincinnati twenty-two years ago and had brought her along and to national prominence. She was theirs, they were hers. There had even been a story in a recent *TV Guide* that the competition for viewers in the new multioutlet media world might cause the networks to scrap their perky women who were always there under what was known as the Doris Day Always Lives Here rule and go exclusively to what the article called "slink, slim, and cerebral" in their women anchor and correspondent corps. ABS had already done that with its prime-time newsmagazines. All four of them were anchored or co-anchored by women clearly chosen according to what Russell Baker in *The New York Times* called "their Bedroom Fantasy Quotient, hereafter and forever to be referred to only as their B.F.Q."

Joan told me that if she had known her network had made a deal with "that devil Meredith" for its slot on the panel, she would have definitely declined *and* walked. There is no way for me to evaluate such a hypothetical declaration.

Joan Naylor did not go home from the CNS studio on Wisconsin Avenue, NW. She had a network car and driver take her directly and late to a dinner party for twelve at the Cleveland Park home of Lyle Willard and Marge Chambers-Willard on Highland Park Place, NW. Willard was a law partner of Joan's husband, Jeff. Marge was trained as a lawyer but had spent a few years as a reporter for the *Chicago Tribune* and then CNN before becoming what she was now, the executive director of Women in Communications and the Arts, an international study and lobbying organization.

Joan was able to say only a brief hello to Jeff, who was already there, before Marge took her over to meet the special guest for the evening, South African novelist and activist Nadine Gordimer. Joan had wanted to tell Jeff about the debate things, but it was not possible. He was not only her husband and the father of her children, he was also her number one adviser on all professional things that really mattered. Normally she would have called and consulted with him before deciding on Williamsburg. But that had not been a normal situation in Carol Reynolds's office just now.

A while later at the table, and by her own account and admission, Joan did something really stupid. She told her dinner companion on the right, Senator Lewis of Missouri, about the debate invitation. The senator, without a word of reaction to her, tapped his glass for attention.

"Ladies and gentlemen, if I may stop proceedings here for a quick moment for a special announcement," he said. When everyone was quiet, he said: "It is with great pleasure that I announce that my distinguished and esteemed and charming dinner companion on my left, the one and only Joan Naylor, has been selected to be one of the panelists of the one and only presidential debate coming up at Williamsburg."

Joan looked across the table at Jeff, whose face was nothing but a huge smile. "Madam moderator, I salute you," he said. If Joan had been sitting next to him she would have slugged him. If she had had a 9mm pistol she would have shot him. If she had had a baseball bat she would have hit him and his head out of Cleveland Park.

"Here, here," somebody else said.

"I'll drink to that," said another, and there was nice noise around the table. When it died down Joan, in great pain, said: "As a matter of fact, I am not the moderator. I'm one of the three panelists. Mike Howley's going to moderate."

Jeff's smile disappeared. It was replaced by a deep color of red.

Joan Allison Naylor and Jeffrey Alan Grayson had met at a cocktail party fifteen years earlier. She had just come from Cincinnati to Washington as a general-assignment reporter for CNS; he had just joined Wilmer, Cutler & Pickering, a prestigious Washington law firm. He had graduated fifth in his law-school class at Harvard and clerked for a federal judge in his hometown, St. Joseph, Missouri. Jeff proposed marriage six months to the day after they met and they married six months to the day after that. Joan had kept her own name when they married, a natural thing to do at the time. Joan Naylor told me the only problem it caused now was with their twelve-year-old twin girls. They carried Grayson as their last name, which meant nobody knew Joan Naylor was their mother until they were told. And then that usually only confused things. Jeff very much wanted Joan to change her last name to Grayson but also very much understood why professionally it made no sense. Joan Naylor was Joan Naylor. Joan Grayson would be nobody.

I'll never take your last name now! was the message she was transmitting with her eyes across the Willards' dinner table at this moment.

"Well, well, what difference does it make?" said Lyle Willard, the perfect host. "Moderator or panelist or whatever, our Joan will be the one and only star of that one and only night."

"I agree," somebody else said.

"It's an honor, no matter," said another.

"It *does* matter," Marge said sternly, taking charge. "It matters a lot."

Joan said, "Please, Marge," wanting desperately to keep this from going on. She knew Marge Willard.

It was too late. Marge Willard said: "I think it is outrageous that you were not chosen to moderate and I will say so publicly and loudly."

"Good for you," said the senator, which came out sounding condescending and drew a stern frown from Marge Willard.

"Please don't, Marge," Joan said. "It will only make it worse."

"I disagree. These people should not be allowed to get away with this kind of crap anymore."

Jeff said: "Marge is right, honey."

That drew a sharp shut-up stare from Joan. Shut up! was what she wanted to shout to Marge and to everyone else.

"What is your network going to do about this?" Marge asked. "They should be raising the real hell."

Joan just shook her head. Maybe if she refused to talk, the whole thing would peter out on its own. She was wrong again. Mary Beth Riley, the chair of the President's Council of Economic Advisers, was sitting on Jeff's right. She was a former Wimbledon tennis champ who had gone on to a second stardom as a Stanford economist. She was known as someone who took no prisoners. She said now in a rising voice to Joan:

"I think it is outrageous that the CNS network is not prepared to defend the right of its premier woman anchor to moderate this debate rather than just be a panelist. You should be moderating, and the fact that you are not is a clear case of discrimination and you know it."

Joan, still determined to control the damage, said only: "It's more complicated than that, Mary Beth." She gave Willard a pleading look. Please move it on to something else! Help!

Willard read it and said: "The real question about Williamsburg is Meredith. Is this country really going to follow that talking buffoon over the cliff into extremism, isolationism, racism, and many other forms of fanaticism?"

Everyone had an opinion and they carried the rest of the evening through to the dinner party's conclusion promptly at 11:10.

Joan and Jeff were the first to leave and thus the first to have at each other in the privacy of an automobile.

★

Michael J. Howley was on an airplane thinking strange things when he received the first contact about the Williamsburg Debate.

He was thinking about the very early morning during the 1980 campaign when somebody—probably Mashek or Dickenson—asked everybody on the press bus to write the lead for his or her own obit. They were about to get back on their snake-bit chartered jet to follow Jimmy Carter from Atlanta to Kansas City, Chicago, Des Moines, Minneapolis, Denver, Los Angeles, and finally to San Francisco. The plane, a United 727, had had a series of disconcerting mechanical problems, the latest having been a tire blowing out on landing just the night before. The idea, which not everyone thought of as a complete joke, was that it would be a thoughtful parting gesture to have some copy standing by for their respective employers when the plane went down.

Mike Howley wrote and recited out loud on the bus:

"The most prominent person aboard the fallen press plane was Michael J. Howley, America's premier political reporter. His only youthful ambitions had been to be William Faulkner and to be the first boy in his high-school class to run off to Durant, Oklahoma, to get married.

"He was thirty-four."

Mary McGrory topped him and everyone else with:

"Mary McGrory, the most beautiful columnist in the world, had been a Las Vegas showgirl before falling back on a career in journalism.

"She was twenty-three."

That occasion and that campaign came back to him as he looked out the window of this other jet, a regular-schedule American Airlines 757 still on its initial ascent from the Dallas–Fort Worth airport on its way to Washington National. Howley strained his eyes and his imagination off and down to the left to see Denison, Texas, the place he would have run from to Durant, the marriage capital of that very small part of the world. Nobody he loved or even knew well lived in Denison anymore, not even May Ann Brinkman, the girl he would have run off with if she would have gone, which she most surely would not have done.

He was most likely struck by the one singeing similarity between 1980 and this election. No thoughtful person he knew, most particularly in the press, believed then that Ronald Reagan should be president of the United States, but they were all sure he was going to be. All rational people in the country as well as the thoughtful ones were now certain David Donald Meredith should not be president and were terrified by the prospect that he was going to be. The upcoming NBS–*Wall Street Journal* poll the office had just told Mike Howley about made that more than just a prospect.

Howley was one of the many political reporters who had chronicled Meredith's rise from being a small-time political-science professor to being the Republican candidate for president of the United States. Stops along the way included creation of the Take It Back Foundation, a spectacularly successful information enterprise that included book and pamphlet publishing and electronic productions. All of the enterprises—including his various radio call-in and television programs—promoted the Take It Back political philosophy for angry Americans. Take it back—the streets, the schools, the borders, the city halls, the state-houses, and, now, the White House.

Howley had just come from an evening in San Antonio, his favorite Texas city. It was a paid lecture-series appearance before more than a thousand people in the downtown Majestic Theater, which had recently been restored perfectly and elegantly to its early-1900s Victorian presence. After he gave his standard forty-minute "Beltway Blues" speech about Washington, government, politics, and the press, he fielded questions and comments from the audience for twenty minutes. The election was all anyone was interested in, and the more he talked about it the harder it was to hide his real opinion about the disaster the election of Meredith would be for the United States of America.

He didn't even try to hide his increasing self-hate for the way he and his colleagues in the press had contributed not only to Meredith's rise from the radio-talk-show fringes to the mainstream of American politics, but to most psychological, confidence, and other failings of current American society. "We have sold out to a higher purpose than keeping you informed," he told the San Antonio people. "We now are slaves to our own glory, our own lecture fees, our own faces, our own snideness, our own bank accounts." And I believe he meant Me. He meant himself. He was sick and tired of himself.

Now, on the plane headed back to Washington, he thought also of his second youthful ambition. To be William Faulkner. Success in journalism had come fast and easy to Howley, maybe too fast and easy. He had always wanted to turn his mind and his typewriter and his energy from the phony fiction of Washington and the rest of the so-called real world to the real fiction of novels and short stories and maybe even plays. But there had never been time. Hemingway or somebody said only those who have to write fiction or die do it, because it's too hard otherwise. Clearly Mike Howley hadn't had to or die. Did he now?

"Mr. Howley?" said a stewardess, leaning across the man in the aisle seat.

Howley smiled in the affirmative. Yes indeed, he was the famous Mr. Howley. Do you want me to autograph your manifest?

"I sometimes see you on ABS in the morning," she said. "I think you are really great, but I don't know how you remember all of that the way you do. I love your stories in *The New York Herald.*"

Mike Howley continued to smile, deciding it was not worth correcting her to say that if she ever saw him in the morning it was on NBS, not ABS, and that it was *The Washington Morning News,* not *The New York Herald,* that ran his stories, the best political reporting done in America today. He could hardly wait to tell T. R. (Teddy) Lemmon, Jr., of the *Herald,* who did the nation's second-best political reporting, that the stewardesses of American were mistaking him for him, and probably vice versa.

"Here, the captain asked me to give this to you," said the stewardess. "It came on his radio, I think."

Howley thanked her, took the note (must have felt extremely important), and read:

"Urgent that you call Mr. Hammond at 202-555-5498. I appreciate your work. The Captain."

Mike Howley knew Mr. Hammond. Chuck Hammond, the former Carter and Mondale guy who ran the National Commission on Presidential Debates. And Mike Howley immediately assumed Hammond wanted him for Williamsburg—most likely as the moderator.

Howley says his first reaction was an absolute, unequivocal no. There was no way he was going to go on that Williamsburg panel. It was all showbiz, all surface, all preening, and all wrong. Journalists should not participate in debates where the candidates have any say-so at all in selecting the panelists. No, no, no. A thousand times, no. It was against *Washington Morning News* policy anyhow. No.

That absolute, unequivocal no clearly changed to a probable yes after another hour or so in the air. It must have been his thinking through his real and serious fears about the election of David Donald Meredith that caused the change.

He got off that American Airlines 757 at National Airport and went directly to the *Morning News* office to confront the obstacle to his going to Williamsburg.

That obstacle was Jerry Rhome, the executive editor of *The Washington Morning News.*

"Let's go for a walk" were the scariest words a reporter or editor could hear from Rhome, who had a passion for walking. He claimed it cleansed the mind, rejuvenated the spirit, exercised the heart, and enhanced the sex drive. But it was on walks that he also did his major firing, promoting, chewing out, and praising.

He spoke the magic words to Mike Howley a few minutes into their friendly shouting match that followed Howley's brief telephone conversation with Hammond, confirming what he had suspected about their wanting him to moderate the Williamsburg Debate. Friendly shouting matches were Howley and Rhome's favorite method of communication.

"It's too goddamn cold out there, Jerry," Howley said to Rhome's invitation to walk.

"Bundle up, bundle up, you'll be fine."

"I'm busy."

"Busy talking to me, right. You can be busy talking to me walking around the block."

So Mike Howley bundled up and they went outside on K Street and started walking west toward Sixteenth.

"It's against our policy, you know that," Rhome said. "You helped make the policy."

"Change the policy."

"I don't want to."

They turned left at Sixteenth toward Lafayette Square. The White House was visible through the trees on the other side of the park, the Pennsylvania Avenue side.

"I think our policy is too cute, too elitist, too arrogant, too stupid," Howley said.

"That's not what you thought when you signed off on it four years ago. I can remember your high-and-mighty words now. Didn't you say it was 'journalistic malpractice'—yes, 'journalistic malpractice'—to participate in a debate where the candidates had a say-so in choosing the panel? Yes, yes, indeed. I remember your words so well. You really do have a way with words, Mr. Howley."

"I was wrong. You were wrong. We were all wrong. Pompous Perfect Mulvane was right."

Pompous Perfect Mulvane was Douglas Mulvane, the ANC anchorman and former *Los Angeles Times* political editor who had retired last year and now wrote magazine essays, made speeches, and taught graduate seminars on what he called "the downfalling of the American press." He was the one who invented the word "clownalist" in describing Mark Southern, the then Washington bureau chief for a Chicago newspaper whose attempts to be funny on the talk-fight shows were especially ridiculous and embarrassing. The term caught on as a way of referring to a whole new class of what Mulvane called "pseudo-journalist-commentator-clowns who see and use the news as an entertainment vehicle." Mulvane had moderated the most important of the debates four years before and had publicly argued with the *News* and several other news organizations who would not allow their people to participate in the debates. He claimed journalists could not divorce themselves from responsibility as citizens. Doctors and lawyers had obligations to contribute their professional services to the good of society and so did journalists. "We journalists have become the New Arrogants of American society," Mulvane had said over and over again. It was a New Arrogant question, in fact, that had triggered Howley's own attack on the press the other night in San Antonio.

"Look what happened with that Caperton bitch," Mike said to Rhome. "Pompous Perfect said if we New Arrogants stay on our high horses it'll be the talk-show dandies who'll take over, and he was absolutely right." Angela Caperton, a daytime talk-show host on TTCN— Talk Talk Cable News—moderated one of the three debates in the last presidential election.

"Mulvane, I regret to report, may be right for once," Rhome said. "But I also regret to report that all I remember about that Ann Arbor debate was that skirt she had on. It was the shortest I had ever seen off a prostitute picket line. Every time she crossed her legs I lost track of the question, the answer, and even who was running for president and what day it was."

"You have just made my point."

They were approaching the Hay-Adams Hotel.

"How about ducking in here for a cup of coffee or something?" Mike Howley asked.

"Nope. You're a candy ass, Howley. The only one worse is Tubbs."

Tubbs. Pat Tubbs, the *News*'s legendary investigative reporter who now wrote mostly nonfiction inside-Washington exposé books that were made into movies starring people like Tom Cruise and Richard Gere as legendary investigative reporters. He and Howley, the *News*'s biggest stars, had co-authored a "straight" book on the 1976 presidential campaign and were known to be friends and equally untouchable by Rhome and the *News* management.

Howley and Rhome went on to the corner, to the light, and crossed over to Lafayette Park and kept walking.

"These debates are nothing but television spectaculars, so why not leave it to the television spectaculars like Angela Caper-cunt, or whatever her name is, to run them?" Rhome said.

Michael J. Howley, the man who'd wanted nothing more in life than to be William Faulkner or to run away to Oklahoma with May Ann Brinkman, saw before him a target of opportunity.

"Stop a second, Jerry, and look at what lies before you."

Jerry Rhome did as he was told. "I see the White House before me."

"Who lives there, Jerry?"

"A jerk named Gilliam, who thanks to the Twenty-second Amendment to the Constitution of the United States can't hold his job more than the two terms he already has."

"Are there any jobs in the world more important than the one he has?"

Rhome looked to his left and to his right and then to the sidewalk and up to the sky.

"What are you doing?" Howley asked.

"I hear the Marine Band, I think it is, playing 'The Stars and Stripes Forever.' I wondered where you had them stashed."

"Look, goddamn it, isn't a debate—in this case, the one and only debate—between the two candidates for most powerful job in the world something more than a goddamn television spectacular?"

"I have about decided that all politics, all government, all wars, all news, is now nothing but one huge goddamn television spectacular. That's why Meredith, a talking spectacular, is doing so well."

Rhome turned back toward K Street and the *News* office, and Howley, gratefully, followed his lead.

"You may not have been listening," Howley said, "but even in that awful Ann Arbor thing some important things got said. Maybe at Williamsburg we can get Meredith to admit once and for all that he really does believe only his kind of Christians are going to heaven. Something like that . . ."

"I don't understand why nobody has drawn any more blood on that so far."

"Meredith doesn't bleed."

"Everybody bleeds. It's the fourth rule of journalism."

Jerry Rhome was famous for making up fourth rules of journalism. He used to say his first three were: When in doubt write around it, When in doubt leave it out, When in doubt lie. He quit saying that after some people hearing him in a C-SPAN "American Profile" interview thought he was serious, and it turned up in a lot of I-told-you-so letters and articles about the awfulness of the press.

In a few minutes they were back to K Street and a block from the office.

"What do I say about the policy if I let you do this?" Jerry Rhome said.

"If I let you do this" were not words that Michael J. Howley enjoyed hearing from anybody. He and Jerry Rhome were both in their late fifties, both powers in their own right. They were known as friends, but there may have been too much of all the rest for them to be real friends, the kind Howley and Tubbs were, the kind who exchanged secrets and longings or even simple pleasantries. I was able to confirm that neither Howley nor Rhome had ever been in the other's home except for large cocktail parties or small dinner parties held for business reasons by one or the other.

"Tell them the truth," Mike Howley said. "Tell them that after much consultation and experience you have now decided the no-debates policy was wrong. People appreciate people who are big enough to admit they were wrong."

They were at the *News* building's front door.

"I assume you will say the same thing," Rhome said.

"Absolutely. I was wrong, but now I am right."

" 'I was wrong, but now I am right.' You are indeed a man of words, a smith of words. No wonder you have come so far in this, the most noble of all professions in the great democratic society we call America the Beautiful."

After several seconds of awkward and tense silence, Rhome said: "Why have you really changed your mind on debates, Mike? I'd really like to know."

"I already said, I think our policy is elite, stupid . . ."

"All right, all right. Go be Mr. Moderator," Jerry Rhome said. "Only promise me one thing. Promise me you'll make sure Meredith loses his ass. I am not sure the country could survive that take-it-back crap of his. He's the one who needs taking back—to the armpit of hell where he came from."

"I'll do my best," Mike Howley said.

And they both laughed. And they both swore to me it was all meant to be laughed at because it was clearly a joke.

A few minutes later Mike's sister, Janet, said almost the same thing about what Mike should do to Meredith in the debate. Only she was definitely not joking.

"Make me really proud, little brother, and do God's real work," she said to Howley from Santa Fe, New Mexico, where she had gone ten years ago with her husband to co-author the successful "Cowboy Jake" detective novels set in Houston. "Make sure that awful man does not become president."

"I can't do anything about that," he said. "Don't even joke about something like that."

"You're too serious, Mike, and you always have been."

There weren't any other loved ones for him to call about his moderating. His mother and father were both dead, and Janet was his only sibling. His first and only wife, his second and only love after May Ann Brinkman, had suffered from a rare blood disease since she was twenty-six years old. It prevented them from having children and it finally killed her five weeks after the 1988 election. Her name was Sylvia, and Mike loved her and had missed her very much every single day since she died.

He also must have known for a fact that she, too, would have wanted him to figure out a way to keep David Donald Meredith from becoming president. Sylvia lived with him for twenty-seven years, but she never understood why journalists like him could never ever take sides, could never ever be partisan. He and Sylvia had had some particularly tough discussions about the subject in 1980 when the polls showed Reagan, a man she thought to be an empty-headed movie actor, was about to win.

But Sylvia was gone. And no one had replaced her in any way whatsoever—including that of intense adviser on how Mike Howley should cover and deal with the politics and politicians of America.

The news of his Williamsburg invitation traveled fast within his work world. Several *Morning News* people, mostly those he worked with covering politics, came by or called within minutes to offer congratulations. A few accompanied their good wishes with some regret over the *News* changing its no-debates policy, but as far as I was able to determine, there was no major protest made to Rhome or anyone else in management.

Whatever Mike Howley wanted, Mike Howley got.

3
Mock-ups

There were some press reports after the debate that alleged the four panelists had a "secret" meeting somewhere in Washington right after their selection to plot the strategy and tactics for what they did at the debate. I am convinced that did not happen. As best I can determine, there was no communication at all between any of the panelists before they arrived in Williamsburg the Saturday evening prior to the debate on Sunday. Nobody called anybody else to talk logistics or concerns beforehand. Nobody knew any of the others well enough for personal exchanges, and nobody felt compelled to make introduction calls. Mike Howley was the only one who even considered such a thing. He thought about transmitting in notes or on the phone "Welcome to the foxhole" messages to the other three but got busy and didn't get it done.

So they came to Williamsburg mostly as strangers and mostly ignored by their reporting colleagues. The candidates were the story then. Nobody in the working press—including me—paid any attention as the panelists had their first meeting at five o'clock Saturday in Longsworth D, one of many small conference rooms in the Williamsburg Lodge. There were also Longsworths A, B, and C. I had assumed at first that Longsworth must have been some obscure figure in Williamsburg's Colonial past, but that was not so. The rooms were named for Charles Longsworth, a man from Williamsburg's present who had only recently retired as president and chairman of the Colonial Williamsburg Foundation.

The meeting had been Howley's idea. He mentioned it to Chuck Hammond, who got it organized. Hammond reserved the room and passed the word to the others to be there at five o'clock—if it was convenient. Hammond agreed that it might be good for all to say hello and discuss any logistics concerns before the four panelists went into private session for talk and for dinner. Then after dinner, he said, maybe they might want to walk over to the other side of the Lodge complex to the auditorium where the debate itself would take place the next night.

Longsworth D was on the lower basement floor of the Lodge, one of two major hotel facilities run by Colonial Williamsburg within the historic area. The room had a small conference table in the center with eight upholstered chairs around it. Williamsburg Lodge memo pads and green lead pencils were on the table in front of every place. A smaller table off in a corner was set for dinner for four.

Mike Howley had met Joan Naylor a few times when she was her network's White House correspondent. He also had a vague sense that he might have seen this kid Henry Ramirez somewhere before but did not remember exactly.

He was certain he had never laid eyes on Barbara Manning before. "I am scared to death," she said almost immediately to him after being introduced. "I hope to all of my gods in all of my heavens that you are not."

"Bad news," Howley said. "I am."

"Oh, please, Mike," said Joan Naylor. "You have done this before."

"I've been a panelist, yes. Not a moderator. I don't have to tell you that there is a difference."

No, Mr. Howley, you do not have to tell me, she thought. Was he digging me? she wondered but could not resolve because she did not know what Howley knew about what had happened. She also did not know him well enough to know if it was his style.

"I admire everything you do, Mr. Howley, both in print and on the screen," Henry Ramirez said. "We are in the best of hands."

"Please, call me Mike. I am Mike. Didn't I read somewhere this morning that you are from Texas?" Mike asked.

"Yes, sir."

"Me, too. Denison, up on the Red River just this side of Oklahoma."

"I'm from south Texas, just this side of Mexico."

"Where?"

"Falfurrias."

"I've been there."

"Hey, two Texans," said Barbara. "Aren't we over quota on that?"

Everybody laughed.

Henry did not remind Mike Howley that they had met twice out in the country on campaign trips and had, in fact, had a similar aren't-you-from-Texas? conversation. Why say anything about it? Michael J. Howley of *The Washington Morning News* was an important man who met hundreds—thousands, millions—of new people every day. How could he be expected to remember every little Latino radio reporter he ran into?

Said Henry: "I saw that they're now estimating an audience of more than eighty million people. Can that be anywhere near right?"

"Don't think of it that way," Joan said. "Do what I do every Saturday night. I see the faces of everyone in the world who loves me and I imagine that I am talking only to them."

Barbara said: "What if when my turn comes my mouth freezes? I sit there and I smile and then I giggle and then I cry and then I run off the stage."

Henry said: "My mother and the guys in my newsroom—all six of them—are certain I am going to steal the show. Not only from all of you but probably from the candidates, too. So please consider yourselves warned that you are about to be outshone by the first son of illegal-immigrant parents ever to do anything before a television audience of eighty million people."

"What they say around my newsroom is that if I and the rest of the people who do it for a living on the air at CNS can do it, then anybody can do it," Joan said.

"That's exactly how I feel about running for president," Henry said.

Nobody seemed to understand what that meant, but it served as a clear signal to Chuck Hammond that it was time to get this show on the road.

Hammond, a gray-haired guy with a crew cut, was known for having been a Marine infantry officer in the Korean War and having not quite gotten over it. There were several of his former-Marine kind in the Washington political and journalistic world, and together they formed a mutual-aid society for themselves and a group of boring storytellers for most everyone else.

"I trust your rooms are up to snuff," Hammond said, after having guided the other four to join him around the large table.

Mike, Joan, Henry, and Barbara expressed happiness and satisfaction with their rooms, which were across a road in the main Williamsburg Inn, which provided the most luxurious and most expensive accommodations in the area.

Hammond told them about the cars and drivers that would take them tomorrow afternoon from the Inn back to the Lodge for the debate. The cars and drivers would also be available to chauffeur them anywhere else they might want to go between now and then. And he gave them maps of the restored area at Colonial Williamsburg and passes to get them into any of the buildings, museums, and other attractions.

"Feel free to wander," he said. "Anything you need?"

"Yeah," said Barbara Manning. "You got some Valium?"

They all laughed.

"When you're ready to order chow, dial 2-3," Hammond said. "The menus are over there on the other table."

And he left them alone.

To Barbara Manning the sound of the closing of the door behind Chuck Hammond that night was the loudest, most jarring noise she had ever heard up to that point in her life. In the six days from the invitation call till now she had worked herself up into a state of self-doubt that she said was of Shakespearean and Greek-tragedy proportions. She was way beyond the simple fears of having a locked jaw, a frozen tongue, or even throwing up on national television. She was seriously ill with doubt and fear. So seriously ill that several times during the week she came close to calling somebody and dropping out. Wait for another day, another time. Wait those few more centuries until you are ready, little girl. But each time she backed off. Nobody in her achiever family would understand. Nobody else would either. Take it, do it. And be sick. Here she was. And she *was* talking almost like a normal person.

Henry Ramirez spent the week working hard on questions for the candidates and waiting for the summons from Jim Weaver that never came. Was he really prepared to go public if Weaver tried to keep him off the debate? I believe he was. Doubt was not something the kid Henry Ramirez shared with the kid Barbara Manning.

Joan Naylor also threw herself into preparing for the debate, reading stacks of position papers, articles, book chapters, and other things that were relevant to Meredith and Greene and the issues of the campaign. She had no more conversations with Carol Reynolds or anyone else except Marge Willard about not moderating. In a long and painful phone call after the dinner party she had talked Marge out of going public. In return, she had to promise to moderate a panel on "Women Journalists Covering the Military" that Marge's group was planning for next spring at West Point. Everyone always had an angle, a deal, Joan realized. It wasn't just her network. In this case it was she who was trading her time, body, and mind for some peace and quiet—for the deal.

Mike Howley, unlike the other three, declined Chuck Hammond's offer to be driven to Williamsburg from Washington. Howley drove down from Washington in his own car, listening to some of his own CDs. Was he a country-music man? Classical? Opera? Or was he listening to recorded versions of books? If so, what books?

A split second after Hammond left them alone in Longsworth D, Howley put a finger to his lips. Hush, please, the gesture said to his three fellow panelists. They watched in silence as he stalked about the room, stuck his right hand inside a bowl of flowers on a credenza, then peered down into the tops of lamps.

"Hey, Mike, what's going on?" Joan said.

"Call it a little prevention sweep operation," said Howley, still moving and peering and checking.

"Bugs," Henry said. "This man is looking for bugs."

"You got it."

Joan and Barbara exchanged this-is-crazy grimaces with Henry, who then said: "Mr. Howley, this is Colonial Williamsburg. People do not bug rooms in Colonial Williamsburg. . . ."

"Mike. My name is Mike. The hotel people put us on the schedule board in the lobby. 'Presidential Debate Press Panel—Longsworth D,' it said for the whole world to see."

He got down on his knees and ran his hands along the downside edges of tables and chairs.

"If you are saying you think either one or both of the campaigns might bug us," said Barbara, "then I am saying, forget it. Neither side is quite that stupid, although one of them, which shall remain nameless, is damned close."

"I could actually imagine those fools in the Greene campaign doing something that stupid," Henry said. "I really could."

"You mean that smart," Mike Howley said, finishing his job by running a finger up and over the doorsills. "Knowing what was going to be asked would be ever so helpful, particularly to the Greene people."

"Yeah, but it's the Meredith people who would be sleazy enough to actually do it," Henry said.

"And competent enough to actually pull it off," Mike said. "The Greene staff would probably end up putting the bug in the wrong room or something."

"Well, well," said Barbara. "Here I am in the big time of American journalism, and I am watching the biggest of the big-time journalists going around like . . . well, you know . . ."

Joan's hand signal caused her not to finish the sentence. Joan said to Mike: "OK, you checked it out. The room is clean. We have some work to do here now."

"Only twenty-three hours twelve minutes until airtime," Henry said.

Howley said: "With that in mind, I hope that you-all don't mind if I assume a kind of chairman's role here. A very informal one, just to get things moving."

"You're the moderator," Joan said.

"You've done this before," Barbara said.

"You are our hero," Henry said.

Mike Howley bowed his head as if he had just been crowned king of something and said: "All right, then, thanks. First, I think we should establish some ground rules for our talking here now, tomorrow, or whenever, until this thing is over with."

Howley laid out a proposal that, interestingly enough, was identical to the one that opened that original panel-selection meeting back at the commission offices in Washington. He proposed silence.

"I would like for us to agree to keep confidential now and forevermore everything we say to each other as we go about preparing for this debate. We do not write about it or report about it for our respective newspapers, magazines, or networks. We do not gossip about it in our respective newsrooms or at our respective dinner parties. We do not include it in any of our respective memoirs."

Howley paused for a beat. Nobody said anything. They were listening.

Howley said: "I believe all of us must feel free to say anything that we wish to say without worrying about reading it tomorrow or any other tomorrow. . . ."

"What are you worried about?" Joan asked. In light of subsequent events it reads like an amazingly prescient question. But she assured me that nothing like that was involved. She had no hints, no signs, of anything to come. It was simply an automatic knee-jerk response.

"I'm not worried about anything in particular," Howley replied. "But let's say one of us floats an idea for a question or an approach that is truly off the wall. Something that is in bad taste, inappropriate, idiotic. I would not be keen on hearing you report on CNS something like 'Mike Howley of *The Washington Morning News* suggested asking Paul L. Greene if he had ever had sex with a farm animal. He was talked out of it by the other panelists.' "

"You are asking us, journalists all, to agree beforehand not to report on what might happen in something as important as this presidential debate," Barbara said. "I am not sure I am comfortable with that."

Barbara was very proud of what she said. She remembers it as the moment she became coherent. She thought straight and actually said what she thought in a way that was clean and understandable.

"I think Mike may be right, Barbara," Joan said. "We ought to feel free to say anything here among the four of us."

"Right," Henry said. "But so is Barbara."

"This must be what it's like when four thieves get together," Barbara said.

"All right, all right," said Howley. "I won't press the point any further now."

Howley had had some early misgivings about what he called "the hand he was dealt." He meant the fact that the black and the Hispanic were really kids who had no business on this panel. Affirmative action run amuck was the way he saw it. He was fine with Joan Naylor, although he could tell she was pissed about something. He considered the possibility that she had wanted to moderate this debate and was still sore about being passed over.

Joan Naylor, too, was not overjoyed by the presence of Henry Ramirez and Barbara Manning. Those two don't have two weeks' experience between them, she thought. The whole world knows why they are here. But being on a presidential-debate panel ought to be only for people who have been at this awhile, no matter what.

Barbara Manning, though happy she was out of her coma, knew she had to be careful or she'd go too far the other way. Come on too loud, too much. Sometimes she couldn't stop herself. It was the way she got through tough things in her life, and it always worked, and, God knows, this qualified as a tough thing in her life. White boy Howley and white girl Naylor certainly got their noses and their tails in the air over this. But why not? This is a high-nose-and-tail affair. Relax, Barbara, she told herself over and over. Relax. Everything is going to be all right. Poor old Henry Ramirez. It's too bad they couldn't come up with one with a little more age and experience and smarts. Hey, look who's talking! I'll bet that's what the others are thinking about me right now! Well, so what? Here I am! Here he is!

Henry Ramirez was wondering when they were going to start talking about the questions they would ask Greene and Meredith. That's what this is all about, he thought. All of this preliminary stuff is just wasting time. Mike Howley is certainly an impressive guy. Just the way he ought to be. It's too bad he didn't remember me. When I get to be in his shoes I probably won't remember every little gringo reporter from Texas who comes along to kiss my ring either. Where did they get this black lady? African American, sorry. She's so hyper she's about to come out of that shiny black skin of hers. It's not that black, really. In fact, hers is lighter

than mine. Hers and my skin, side by side, wouldn't probably look that different. It's in the eyes. And the nose and the lips. That's where we are different. And in the brain, of course. When are we going to get down to business?

"Shouldn't we decide who is going to ask the first question?" Henry said.

Howley said: "Well, as a matter of fact, the moderator asks the first question. That is in the rules that the candidates' representatives and the commission people worked out."

And he explained the format, which was the most traditional and most controlled of those available. The Greene camp had insisted on the journalists' panel. The Meredith people had argued for a single moderator with a town-hall citizens-audience call-in approach—similar to the Take It Back, America one their candidate had used for seven dramatically successful years before millions on live radio and national television. Turpin—and everyone else—knew his man would "wipe the floor" with Greene in such a free-flowing format. That was why Lilly adamantly opposed its use.

But in many ways the format was considered irrelevant. It was generally believed—and stated repeatedly on every morning, noon, and night, weekday and weekend, talk, food-fight, call-in, analysis, and clownalist show—that Greene would have a problem if he was debating an empty chair. The only unique thing about the final agreed-to setup for Williamsburg was that for the first time there would be no live audience and thus no applause, cheering, or other noise to deal with. The only people in the auditorium with the candidates and the panelists would be the television-camera people and other technicians needed to get it on the air.

Mike Howley went through the details. The four panelists rotated asking questions. Candidate A got two minutes to answer, Candidate B a minute to respond or rebut. Then came the next question to Candidate B for a two-minute answer, Candidate A for a one-minute rebuttal, and on and on in precise rotation for some eighty-two minutes. Then each candidate had two minutes for a closing statement directly to camera. The order of everything would be determined by a drawing.

"What if one of them says something outrageous—namely Meredith—and Greene wants to jump and slap him back?" Barbara asked.

"Can't happen," Mike responded.

"We can't ask follow-ups?" Henry asked.

"Nope. One of you could follow up another's question in the next round, but that is it."

There was a moment of annoyance.

"Well, this is a stupid way to do things," Henry said. "I do not like these rules at all."

"I don't either," Barbara said, looking right at Mike Howley. "Let's just ignore 'em. What if we go out there tomorrow night and you say to those two candidates, 'Mr. Meredith . . . Mr. Greene, we are going to get out of your way. For the next ninety minutes you can talk spontaneously about the issues confronting this country today and how you differ in your approaches to them. You can do it in any way and under any rules or guidelines you like. The four of us on this distinguished panel, us distinguished New Arrogants, are going to just sit back with the rest of the American people and just watch and listen.' "

"Great idea, but no way," Joan said.

Henry said: "Good, no way. I came here to ask some questions. I want to ask some questions."

Barbara said: "I guess Meredith would just start talking and preening and lying, and the governor would be made to look like a stupid ass again, as always."

Howley said: "Some might argue also that there's an issue of credibility and integrity here for *us*. We all are here as invited guests, as professionals willing to contribute our services on behalf of voter education and edification. We accepted the terms, the rules of the debate, when we accepted the invitation. It would be professionally irresponsible to pull a stunt like that."

Then he said: "How about we look at the menus and order some dinner?"

There was an immediate consensus in favor of doing so.

★

I came to my Williamsburg reporting assignment in a four-door Toyota Corolla rented from Avis at the Newport News–Williamsburg International Airport. So what? you (and Howley in the Appendix) might say. Under normal circumstances I would agree that this kind of I-was-there information from a reporter is irrelevant. The problem is that as much as I abhor it, my movements and methods became a minor story within the so-called Media Critics' world in the course of my reporting. Some unfair and nasty charges were leveled at me and they began with that rent-a-car.

The New American Tatler magazine paid for the car. I have my Nations Bank, USAir, Visa, and other receipts—including the frequent-flyer-miles credit form—to prove it. The charge that I was brought into Williamsburg on a private jet by some sinister person or group of sinister persons and then chauffeured around in the company of armed security people affiliated with the private security firm working for Meredith is absurd, ridiculous, a lie. The snide fantasy suggestions, for instance, that appeared in *Fortune,* a once reputable publication, that I was part of a "still shadowy and unknown conspiracy" or "possibly the journalistic front man for an effort to subvert democratic systems" would be laughable if not so potentially damaging to me and my career. *Fortune* refused to print a correction and I still am not sure where all of that came from and why. But I am sure of my movements and actions in those hours leading up to the debate itself.

I came to Virginia from Bloomington, Indiana, where I had gone in pursuit of a story we at the *Tatler* had preslugged "The Violence Teachers." I had gone into it already incensed and appalled by the emotional cripples who coach big-time college basketball, the grown men who throw towels and chairs and vulgarisms at referees, fans, opposition coaches, and even their own players and members of their own families. My blood was now at a full boil over what I had found out about those foul-mouthed bully showoffs and the school administrators and alumni who tolerated and encouraged them. I hated to interrupt my boil, but I also had my obligations to my editor, Jonathan Angel, and the magazine. And the idea of going behind the scenes of a presidential debate was intriguing. The call from Jonathan about Williamsburg was a last-minute affair. He had other writers on the presidential campaign itself, but he wanted me— "somebody with your touch for irony and the personal" is the flattering way he put it, frankly—to go with an idea of doing a "behind-the-faces-and-the-postures" piece about this important event. Another rationalization for me was that a brief respite from my anger at the imbecile coaches and what they were doing to encourage and foster violence and disrespect among the young people of this country might be good for my blood pressure—and thus my health.

The Newport News–Williamsburg airport was a pleasant surprise. It turned out to be a small architectural jewel of a place with a feel and ambience that was more like that of a museum of modern art than of an airport. There were Windsor-style chairs in the phone booths and an atrium in the center that brought the sun down on the waiting-room area filled with wooden garden benches. Across the ceiling in the main ticketing hallway hung eight-feet-tall colored banners with the arty, shadowed portraits and signatures of great Americans/Virginians of history—George and Martha Washington, Thomas Jefferson, James Madison, George Wythe, George Mason, Patrick Henry, John Marshall, and even Pocahontas, among others. The building itself—a brick base with silver support beams and glass halfway up and across the top—bore the mark of a famous architect. I did not take the time to check, but it would not surprise me to find that it was the work of a Pei, Johnson, Jacobsen, Venturi, or one of the other great ones. The only things lacking were customers and flights. United, American, and USAir each had only a handful of small-plane commuter flights from the three Washington airports and places like Philadelphia and Raleigh-Durham.

I came in from Pittsburgh on a USAir 737, one of the few big-plane flights into Newport News–Williamsburg. I arrived just after five P.M. on Saturday. (Yes, I plead guilty to having flown first-class, which was in my contract with the *Tatler*. It is business-class for foreign flights.) I rented the Toyota and drove less than ten minutes east on Interstate 64 to the Omni–Newport News Hotel, where the Meredith campaign was headquartered. The Greene campaign entourage was only a few blocks away on the other side of the interstate in a Ramada Inn. The plan was for the candidates to come to Williamsburg, less than thirty minutes west, on Sunday evening shortly before the debate.

A postdebate story in *The Washington Morning News* (Howley's paper, please remember) claimed I was taken immediately "like royalty" to Meredith's suite at the Omni, where I was "massaged and messaged" and otherwise set up to do a flattering piece about Meredith, a rarity thus far in the entire national press coverage of the campaign. Not true. I went to the ninth-floor suite of Jack Turpin, a man I had never met before, and asked permission to be present when Meredith rehearsed for the debate that evening. I had been told there was going to be a full-scale rehearsal in a ballroom down on the basement level of the hotel. I knew access would be restricted and limited, but I also knew it would be a great place to begin my story, a great place to start looking for what was happening behind the faces and the postures. A reminder, please, that my predebate focus was solely on the candidates.

Turpin not only said no, he said it forcefully, profanely, leaving little doubt that the decision was final. He also reminded me of the trouble the columnist George Will got into by participating in one of Ronald Reagan's debate rehearsals. I told him I did not want to play a part, I only wanted to watch. No, he said again.

But, as a reporter, I did not often take no for the final answer on a matter this important. I saw bearing witness to that rehearsal as a monumentally important thing to do for my story. So I arranged through other means to have access to what happened at that rehearsal. What other means? I will not say. I cannot say. The person or persons who assisted me did so only on the condition that I never reveal their involvement. I gave them my word. My word is good. Did money change hands? Yes, it did. How much? Barely four figures. Again, I was reimbursed by the *Tatler*. (No frequent-flyer miles were awarded on this one.) So the postdebate charge in *The Washington Morning News* that I "paid sources for information and for access into chambers and sanctums" is technically correct. And I would do it again tomorrow if confronted with the same option: pay and get in—don't pay and stay out. The public has a right to know what happened in that hotel ballroom. If the public's right to know is the overriding energy behind journalism, what difference does it make whether the sources of the information come free or for a fee? In my opinion, it is a question from an argument that I believe is no longer relevant to the practice of journalism in this country.

What happened that evening during the rehearsal was critically revealing, particularly in light of what happened barely twenty-four hours later at the real thing.

Rusty Washburn, the former New York congressman and housing secretary, played the rehearsal part of the opponent. He had done so in the rehearsals for debates during the primaries, and although everyone, including Turpin, had thought he got a bit carried away, good luck required that he do it again for the one and only debate of the general-election campaign.

It was a mistake. He got carried away even more this time.

Washburn, well known as a man who saw himself as president more clearly than he did Meredith, played Greene as a candidate a lot better than Greene did.

"You asked me about the federal budget deficit," he said to one of four campaign aides playing the panelists. "That is important and I will address it, but I must first say that the most important issue the American people should be focusing on tonight is one of bigotry and division. The real question of this election is whether this nation can afford the divide-and-conquer politics of fear that my talk-show-meister opponent is dishing out. Fear of fellow Americans and immigrants who look different than us Euro-Caucasian whites. I say no. That is my answer to that question. And on Election Day, I believe that will be the answer of an overwhelming majority of the American people."

He stood behind a podium on a stage against a far wall of the room, the Rainbow Ballroom. Meredith stood at another podium some forty feet away, and the four fake reporters were behind a table facing them. It was a good mock-up replica of what the stage would be like Sunday night in the Williamsburg Lodge auditorium. The main difference was the color scheme. The Rainbow Ballroom was mostly beige, orange, and gold. Beige carpet, orange walls, and gold light fixtures.

"Mr. Washburn," Jack Turpin said, walking up to a spot between the mock-panelists and Washburn, "we appreciate your desire to make some points of your own, if that is what you are doing—"

"What I am doing, my friend, is trying to be helpful by making this as realistic as possible. That is what I am doing."

Meredith, clearly annoyed with Washburn, said: "Realism in the case of my real opponent, Rusty, would require that you fall mute, dumb, or incoherent. If, on the other hand, you are speaking for yourself when you purport to be speaking for mock-candidate Greene, then I would suggest you speak for yourself only to yourself. The wisdom of electing me president of the United States is now in the hands of the American people. If you and your like-minds in my party do not believe in my candidacy on behalf of my party, then I would suggest that it is you who have a problem, not me. Now, if we can proceed without any more of your silly and quite offensive attacks on me."

Turpin backed away and another of the mock-journalists asked another mock-question. Rusty Washburn ignored it and said directly to Meredith: "One can only hope that some of the things you have said during this campaign are not, in fact, a truthful measure or indication of your real beliefs and intentions. One can only hope that once you are in the White House—which the polls now show is an increasingly likely possibility—that you will return to sanity and unity and common sense for the purposes of governing."

"Get this man out of here!" Meredith screamed. His face was red and his hands were grabbing the air as if in search of something he might throw at his Republican colleague/mock-opponent behind the other podium.

Turpin led Washburn out of the ballroom. And in a few minutes the rehearsal continued with a deputy press secretary in the role of the mock-Greene.

I wrote in my notes after witnessing the episode: "This man Meredith has a temper."

They were prophetic words indeed.

But on that Saturday evening my principal concern was trying to be in two places at more or less the same time. The Greene campaign had taken over most of the Ramada, just a few minutes away. It was already almost nine o'clock when I arrived. I was afraid I was going to have missed the Greene rehearsal, but I had given the Meredith run-through top priority, mostly on the calculated grounds that it looked like he was going to win the election. Thus what lay behind his winner's face and postures would make a more relevant story than what lay behind those of the loser. I also thought it was possible that I could get lucky. The Greene schedule called for a later start. Maybe I could do both.

I did get lucky. I did not have to argue with anyone or offer anyone money to get what I wanted. It came easy and it came free.

The Greene debate mock-up operation was in a large meeting room on the first floor that was named after George Mason, one of the men on the banners at the airport. He was a Virginian friend of George Washington and a signer of the Declaration of Independence. Brad Lilly, whom I found having a drink in the bar when I arrived, said I could not come to the rehearsal. "No press allowed," he said, shaking his head and waving me away.

But a few minutes later—it was now 9:15 P.M.—I simply fell in behind him and a few of his assistants for the walk to the rehearsal room. He looked at me and shrugged as we entered the room, and I found a seat off in a corner way, way out of sight and, hopefully, out of mind.

The first thing that struck me sitting there was the vast class difference in how these two campaigns operated. There were the Meredith people living down the road in a nine-story multistar luxury hotel hidden among trees bordering the upscale shopping and business area called Oyster Point. They were doing their rehearsal in a real, fully outfitted replica of the debate scene. Here were the Greene folks in a nice, modest Ramada Inn sprawled on a busy four-lane road, the kind of place usually identified with station wagons full of vacationing families. Their mock-debate setup was only a few chairs and two speaker's podiums set around a room where events such as regional insurance sales breakfasts and lunches were usually held.

I sat there for twenty minutes before Greene appeared, accompanied by a two-man Secret Service detail. Meredith had been dressed in a dark suit with a dark burgundy tie and white shirt, exactly what he would wear at the debate itself. Greene wore slacks and a sweater.

Greene immediately motioned for Lilly to come with him away from the others, the group of aides and others who would play the various mock-parts. Where they went was very close to where I was trying to make myself invisible by sinking farther and farther down into my aluminum and black vinyl chair.

Neither Greene nor Lilly paid any attention to me.

I heard Greene say: "This is ridiculous, Brad."

"What exactly is ridiculous, sir?" Lilly replied.

"That debate tomorrow night is going to be absolute misery for me. Why go through it twice? Why have this rehearsal?"

"In order to keep it—the real one tomorrow night—from being misery."

"There is no way to prevent that. I have my briefing books. I will read them again tonight."

Lilly said nothing and Greene then said: "I realize you might think, and I might even agree, the problem isn't briefing books. But even if we're both right, there is nothing I can do about all of that now. It is too late to have a personality transplant, which is what most everyone seems to think I need."

"Sir, may I be blunt?" Lilly said.

"I never knew you needed permission for that. Have you given any further thought to what you might do after the campaign? I know about the book, of course. And maybe your becoming a commentator—I hope not a clownalist."

"Governor, please! Goddamn it, sir, this thing is not over yet. It really is not. You really could go out there tomorrow night, land some blows, throw it open, and still pull this out. That talk-show con man Meredith is not only not qualified to be president, he is a menace to this country. He is evil, sir. He would seal off our borders and turn us inward and on each other. He would divide this country up into little pieces and turn us into a form of the Balkans. He has no unifying vision for this country. He looks out at a crowd of people and he sees different interests, different races, different everything. He is evil, I promise you, he is evil. He must not be the next president of the United States. You are the only one who can stop that from happening. Please, go out there and take him on. Call him evil, call him a menace. Challenge him on that stupid goddamn Take It Back shit!"

Paul L. Greene was shaking his head.

"You are shaking your head," Brad Lilly said. "Please don't shake your head. Please, sir. Please!"

"Brad, the decision on who is the next president will be made by the voters. They know all there is to know about Meredith. If they want a talk-show con man to run their government, if they want to turn their country into an island, there is not one thing I can do about it. Attacking him, calling him names on national television tomorrow night, is not going to change anything. He is what he is, but they already know it."

"But they might . . . well, get to know more about you, sir."

"I am not somebody who makes personal attacks on people. That is not me, that is not the person I am, so it is not the person I want people to know."

"There is no other way. You take him on or he's got it."

"I know that."

"If you know that, then why . . . Well, how can you not do something more than what you have done?"

"I do not want to be president that badly, Brad."

"The issue is the country, sir, not you!"

"Scrub the rehearsal. Why don't you meet me for breakfast in my suite in the morning?"

Brad Lilly gave Paul L. Greene a kind of salute with his right hand and they said good night.

Greene walked away and out of the room.

Lilly then saw me. "You didn't hear any of that."

"Was that a question?"

"No, a statement of fact."

"It's too late for that," I said.

"It's too late for everything," he said.

4

Saturday Night Live

It was after eleven-thirty by the time I finally arrived at Colonial Williamsburg itself and checked into my reserved and guaranteed-late-arrival (I have my Visa receipt) room at the Williamsburg Lodge. If I had been an all-knowing reader of fortunes and futures, that's where I would have been all evening, of course, hovering mostly around Longsworth D in search of morsels, hints, and signs of what was to come.

What happened in that room and elsewhere among the four panelists that Saturday night is difficult to parse specifically as to how it influenced the final decisions and results. But, if nothing else, that time together clearly helped develop the relationships and set the stage for what was to happen at their pivotal Sunday meeting and thus in the debate itself. Of that, I am certain.

While they ate dinner at the small round table, Henry Ramirez tried a couple of times to get into a discussion of the specific questions they would ask Sunday night. The other three deflected him. They wanted to eat in relative peace. There was time, there was time, Howley said.

So they talked about other things, journalism things, mostly.

Joan asked Howley if Jerry Rhome was really as obsessively nuts about walking as he was reported to be. Yes, indeed, said Howley. But he offered no details and used careful phrasing. Joan told me she suspected Howley had been burned a few times by an innocent remark about Rhome or someone else at the paper coming back to him a few days or weeks later as something very different—and critical. She said she, also the victim of rumors and lousy reporting, very much sympathized with Howley. "Every reporter should be the subject of at least one negative story to see how it feels," Joan Naylor said to me. "I think journalism schools should require students to write hatchet jobs on each other as part of their training."

Mike Howley asked Barbara Manning about the rumor that *This Week* was thinking about turning itself into a daily from a weekly to compete head-on with *USA Today*. She said she was stunned and appalled at the thought, which was completely new to her.

Henry Ramirez then opened up a journalistic can of worms that Mike Howley probably could have done without.

"How does your appearing on *NBS This Morning* work?" Henry said to Howley. "You really do swing from both sides. Print and TV. Straight reporting and commentary. I like that and I would like to do that myself someday. How does that work?"

Howley's face said more than his words. And the message was that of embarrassment, uneasiness. He answered it straight: "I have an arrangement to come on every Wednesday morning through the course of the campaign, and I am on-call, depending on my schedule, to do so on other mornings following a special event or unscheduled news event."

"There must be good money in that."

"Not bad."

"Who picks the other two people who are on there with you?"

"The network people. Producers."

"I notice you give your opinion a lot more on TV than you do in your newspaper stories. How's that work?"

Howley answered: "Well, it just seems that way because it's television. It seems more dramatic and different and opinionated, I guess, than it really is."

Barbara said: "You really let it rip on that Saturday-night program you do, *Marv and Company*. That is some food fight."

Henry said: "It sure is. That looks like fun the way you-all toss your insults back and forth. Now that is a real show. How does that work?"

Joan was enjoying watching Howley squirm a bit. Print journalists make a lot of weather criticizing television while making a lot of money appearing on it. Howley surprised her by telling the truth. "I do it for the money," he said to Henry. "Pure and simple. That is why I do it. That is how it works. I am not only not proud of that, I am often ashamed of it. Now, we probably should wrap this up and move back to the other table. . . ."

"What kind of laptop do you travel with?" Henry asked.

"I have a Dell, but I'm thinking about getting one of those little Gateway HandBooks," Mike Howley replied with what was probably absolute delight in having the subject changed.

Henry said: "One of the guys in our office has one. They are terrific. Two-point-nine-four pounds, two-fifty-MB hard drive, eight-MB RAM. It's got a backlit seven-point-six double-scan VGA screen. MS-DOS is preinstalled. So is Microsoft Word software, but my friend put in his own WordPerfect six. I'm going to get one as soon as I get to be rich and famous. . . ."

"Enough about this," Mike Howley said. "If everyone is about finished, what do you say we move back to the big table and get to work?"

Joan could not remember the last time she'd had such a good time. She was beginning to really love that Henry Ramirez, that radio kid from Texas.

This brown boy ain't bad, thought Barbara. Ain't bad at all. He's got a set of 'em on him, that is for sure. But Mike Howley bothered her. He shouldn't be able to have it both ways, to play Mr. On The Other Hand in print and then go be Mr. Opinion on television. *This Week* magazine would never let me do that. But, of course, who am I? I ain't no big-cheese white man.

Henry was loving being Henry in that room. Here he was in high cotton, as they said in the Valley, sitting here eating a big dinner—he had ordered the Grilled Black Angus Rib Eye Steak with Fresh Mashed Potatoes and Ale Battered Onion Rings—and talking shop with two of the biggest names in American journalism, Mike Howley and Joan Naylor.

The black-girl-who-wasn't-really-black was even making a contribution or two.

★

Back at the large table, in front of their Williamsburg Lodge pads and pencils, Mike Howley said:

"I am taking the attitude that we are all in this together. And that means that we should as far as possible work out our approach, our strategy and our questions, together. No secrets, no surprises. Do our best to act as one. Do our best not to compete with one another. Do our best not to see this as the great journalism ask-off. Do our best to cooperate, coordinate, conglomerate, coagulate, collude, conspire."

Collude? Conspire? Joan and Henry say Howley was smiling when he said all of that. Barbara didn't notice any smile.

Howley said: "So, in that spirit, I hereby open the nominations for an opening question. I will ask it, but I want your help in deciding what it might be, what it should be. OK?"

Henry did not like what was happening, and Howley clearly read that in Henry's face. Howley said: "What's the matter, Henry?"

Henry, thought Henry. Mike Howley finally called me by my name. Henry. He knows my name now. He said: "Well, Mike, you are the man of experience here and all of that, but I have spent a lot of time, I mean a *lot* of time, working on some real zinger questions. I thought that we were each to do our own thing and let the chips fall where they may. I have absolutely no problem telling you-all what I am going to ask, but giving one of mine away for one of you to ask . . . well, I am not sure that is what I had in mind. But, like I say, you are the boss."

"Nobody's the boss here," Howley said.

"What if we just tossed out possible subjects for a first question?" Joan said. "Would that be a problem for you, Henry?"

"Oh, no. Certainly not. In fact, I am not sure the other is. I'm just trying to do what Mike said we should at the very beginning, which is talk straight and open."

Joan said: "Well, I don't mind getting things started. I don't see how you can start with anything other than the deficit. And what he—either he—really plans to do about it. That creep Meredith—sorry, I know I shouldn't talk that way—has said the only way to really do something is to eliminate whole federal agencies and departments and start over again to rebuild the government from scratch on a need basis. The problem is he will not say which whole agencies and departments he would eliminate."

Mike Howley lowered his voice, put it into preacher velvet, and said à la Meredith: "Certainly, my lady-reporter friend, I will be delighted to lay out the departments and agencies I would eliminate. First and foremost, in Jesus' name, would be the Immigration and Naturalization Service. There won't be any immigrating or naturalizing in the Meredith administration. Number two, the Congress of the United States. We could certainly do without them. All they do is take God's name in vain and drink alcoholic beverages and have sex with their employees of all sexes, most of whom are political hacks and hackers with terrorist or transvestite backgrounds. Number three would be the Supreme Court. All they do is take God out of our government and our lives. We sure as the Lord is everywhere do not need the Federal Reserve Board. That would be number four. All they do is jack up interest rates and print too much money for the godless spendthrifts in our midst to spend. Number five would be the Department of State. The American people are sick and tired of worrying about the rest of the world. They want to worry only about themselves for a while. Close down the Department of State until we need it again, which might be in ten or fifteen years, depending on how we do on taking care of only ourselves."

Everybody was laughing. Joan had had no idea Mike Howley had a sense of humor. She was delighted. So were Henry and Barbara. Some of my own reporting about Howley's early years bore some surprising results along this line. His regular TV viewers and column readers might be stunned to know that he was known in high school as a cutup and even had a George Gobel stand-up comic routine he did for his fraternity brothers in college.

Barbara, also a person with a performance sense of humor, got into it. She said, also in a deep Meredith-like voice: "And God in heaven knows we can surely do without the Department of Defense. All they do is make war, and God in heaven knows that now that godless communism is no more, we sure as hell is down there do not need to make any more wars. No siree, hallelujah! Except on our own people who are not white and Baptist and self-righteous and male like I am. And we got the pole-leece to do that. Yes siree, hallelujah!"

"The rivers," Henry said, not doing that well in his mock-Meredith voice. "Dam up the rivers. Kill the rivers. All they're used for is for wetbacks to swim across to sneak into this country illegally so they can get on our good Christian Anglo welfare and baby-sit our good Christian Anglo children and empty our good Christian Anglo Porta Pottis and pick our good Christian Anglo fruits and vegetables and wash our good Christian Anglo dirty dishes. Get the government out of the river business once and for all. Out, out, out."

"Hey, hey," said Joan. "I think we have uncovered a hotbed of contempt for David Donald Meredith, and shame, oh, shame on us all!"

"You can say amen to that," Barbara said, mimicking the Meredith entourage's favorite line.

"Is it not so that all Americans who walk with a limp should be shipped out of the country and fried in the flames of Jesus, Mr. Meredith?" Henry said, as if at a news conference. "You can say amen to that," he responded, as if he were Meredith.

Joan said: "We had better be careful. The guy we are mocking and maligning here, friends, is going to be the next president of the United States."

She did it again. It stopped the playing this time.

"When it happens I may have to move to Mexico, from where my forefathers and foremothers, as well as my real mother and father, came," said Henry in his regular voice. And that—emigrating to Mexico, he thought but did not say—would make him the dumbest son of illegal immigrants in the history of the United States of America.

"Africa, here I come," said Barbara in her normal voice.

"I can always go back to Denison, Texas," Mike Howley said in his usual voice. "What about you, Joan? Is there an ancestral home for white women anchorpersons to return to?"

Joan Naylor did not like the question, did not like the way it was asked, and, suddenly, did not like the sunavabitch who asked it. Not funny, Mike Howley, she thought.

In a burst of angry sarcasm, she said: "I was born in a log cabin in southern Illinois, daughter of illiterates who were too stupid not to throw away their girl children and keep trying until they came up with a boy, a male, a man, a real person."

Now the smiles were completely gone from all faces.

"Hey, I pissed you off," Howley said. "Sorry. That was not my intention. We're all going to need each other very much."

"You did piss me off and I accept your apologies," said Joan, intentionally ignoring Howley's last statement. "To get on with the business at hand a bit. The problem, and I mean *the* problem, is thinking—seriously—about what kind of answer such a question about cutting federal agencies would get from Governor Greene. God, watching him and listening to him is painful. So, so painful."

Howley then said: "I may try to write a book about what happened to him. How a guy can go from being a successful, if quiet, governor of a state like Nebraska to a national candidate like him is more than I can understand. Most people rise to the occasion. He has fallen."

"He has the worst set of loser staff people I have ever come across, for one small thing," Joan said.

"I agree and have written same," Howley said.

"You can't blame him on his staff," Barbara said. She swears she said it without her friend-roommate Barbara Hayes in mind. It's not terribly important, but I do not believe her. It may have been unconscious, but I believe her concern for her friend was there.

"The only Hispanic guy in the campaign barely knew who I was," Henry said. "I bet he does now." Then he looked right at Joan and said: "I think you are wonderful on the air and I have always admired you in every way and I am honored to be on this panel and at this table with you, but I must respectfully say that I think asking about the deficit right off the bat would be a terrible mistake. It would put everybody to sleep. The groans all over America would be deafening, I really do think so. Everybody out there cares about the deficit, but they don't want to talk about it anymore. It makes them drowsy. I promise you, it makes them drowsy. It makes *me* drowsy."

Joan Naylor felt her shoulders tighten. She also felt it was time for a little Journalism 105. "We are in the care business, Henry, not the No-Doz business."

"I don't think I think so."

"Well, think again. We are all paid to go out there in the middle of issues and events and people and to decide, in our best judgment, what is important. That is all our job is, when you cut all of the rest away. We are not entertainers, Henry. We are not in the business Meredith was in before he took up politics. We are not out there counting groans, keeping people awake. If we can't stay awake ourselves, then possibly we are not in the right line of work. . . ."

She told me she caught Howley's eyes in a glance his way. They were full of wondering laughter.

But all he said was: "Why don't we go over and look at where it's all going to happen? We can resume this in the morning. There's plenty of time. We'll be fresher then."

Nobody disagreed.

Nobody ever disagreed with Mike Howley.

★

They had their first look at what would later be described as either the scene of a historic triumph or the scene of a historic crime. On that pre-debate Saturday night it was still only a compact auditorium with 450 theater-type seats and a small stage.

Barbara had been in a few television studios, and every time the big surprise was the difference between what they looked like in real life and what came across on the television screen. Big-time talk shows that appeared to be coming from elaborate rooms were actually done in grubby little places not much larger than closets. What looked like thousands of people sitting in bleachers around Phil and Oprah and Maury were really about a hundred or so.

Here it was happening again. Somehow in her mind she had seen a huge hall about the size of Madison Square Garden or a football stadium. After all, this was a presidential debate, by God. No expense, no nothing, would be spared. Huge, it would be. Everything about it would be huge.

Instead it was small. Disappointingly so. Two podiums at angles on either side of a stage for the candidates. For her and the panelists a long table in front with four chairs facing the the candidates. Everything was decorated in red, white, and blue. There was an old-fashioned sign in the shape of an eagle above and behind everyone and everything. It was gold—and it was huge. Yes, it was huge and impressive. But that was about it. Everything else seemed so small, so out of scale with the magnitude of what was going to happen on this stage tomorrow night—in less than twenty-four hours.

Barbara Manning was having these thoughts before she even knew what the real magnitude of the magnitude would be.

Nancy Dewey asked them to sit in their assigned chairs on the stage. And speak into their microphones. She pointed toward the various cameras—there were six in all—that would be shooting the event. She told them never to worry about where the cameras were or which one was actually on at any given moment. "That's our job," she said.

The exception to that, of course, was Howley. He was shown where he should look to deliver his opening and closing copy. A stage manager off to the left would cue him with a hand signal. They rehearsed it twice to make sure Howley and the stage manager understood each other.

Howley put on the earpiece he would wear during the debate. An audio man checked it out to make sure it worked and that the volume was right for Howley. "I'll be in your ear with time cues and other things like that," said Nancy Dewey. "I will be the only one who will be in your ear."

She explained and they rehearsed the signal lighting system that would be used to tell the candidates their time was up for any given answer. As long as the green light was on, they were fine. When the yellow one came on, they had thirty seconds. When it started flashing, fifteen seconds. When the flashing stopped, time was up. The candidates' lights would be on the cameras in front of them. On the desk in front of Mike Howley were three Christmas tree lights on a small metal board that replicated what the candidates would see. Barbara vaguely remembered a problem with lights like these in one of the previous debates. In 1988, she thought. Yes, the first Dukakis-Bush debate in Winston-Salem, North Carolina. The TV guy who was the moderator couldn't see the lights properly and he cut Bush off on an answer before the time was up.

Several local print reporters and television correspondents with their crews were around the auditorium doing predebate prep stories. The big-time national reporters like me were off doing other things. Other things that in the final analysis really did not matter that much. I sorely wish I had been in that auditorium with the four panelists.

Henry Ramirez was asked if he was nervous about tomorrow. "As a cat on one of those roofs," he said, and he was proud of himself for having said it.

Joan Naylor was asked the difference between doing a presidential debate and anchoring a nightly news program. "Like that between a light shower and a thunderstorm," she said, and she was also rather proud of herself and her quote.

A black male reporter from a station in Norfolk asked Barbara if she felt a special burden because of her race. "Should I?" she replied, annoyed at being asked, annoyed at not knowing what to say. The reporter, who looked about fifteen years old to Barbara, smiled a hi-there-Uncle-Tomasina kind of smile and said nothing while the camera rolled.

Nancy Dewey, joined by Chuck Hammond, gave them a complete tour of the setup. She showed them the rooms where the various networks had set up their anchor stations, where the candidates would wait and be made up, where the spin doctors would do their spinning after the debate.

The largest ballroom in the Lodge, the Virginia Room, was being out-fitted with hundreds of tables, television monitors, telephones, and TV lighting spots for the spinning. Howley and Joan had both played in that league before, wading through bodies of reporters and candidates' varied "representatives" right after a debate getting reactions to what had just happened. More reporters and more spinners than ever were expected here tomorrow night. "It's going to be a madhouse, I am sorry to say," said Hammond. "But we all know how 'they' all are."

They, meaning Us, of course, thought Joan, thought Barbara. Henry didn't pick up on the crack. It's a pretty good bet Howley did and proba-bly thought, Yes, Mr. Hammond, we all know exactly how we all are.

Chuck Hammond and Nancy Dewey wished them luck and a good night's rest, and Howley, Joan, Henry, and Barbara walked the hundred yards across a street and through a couple of parking lots to the Inn.

Tomorrow night they would be driven in a limousine back the other way to their appointment with destiny on that small stage under the TV lights of history.

★

Henry asked Barbara if she would like to have a drink at one of the old taverns around Colonial Williamsburg. There were several of them, according to the information Hammond had given them. They had Williamsburg-sounding names like King's Arms, Christiana Campbell's, and Josiah Chowning's.

We young minorities must stick together, he said to her.

Sure, why not, she replied.

A drink of solidarity was really all he had in mind. Yes, he was aware from looking that Barbara Manning was one very attractive woman, and he was aware from listening that she was also pretty smart. A lot smarter than he thought when they met for the first time at five o'clock in Longsworth D. He thought even as he was asking her for the drink that he could not remember a case from high school or college or radio news where a Hispanic dated a black, in any combination of male or female. None he knew or heard about, at least. Now, wasn't that interesting? he thought. There was a lot of mixing of all kinds with whites and blacks, browns and whites, but no blacks and browns. His mother had always said that black and brown blood mixed together came out as mud.

Barbara accepted Henry's invitation without thinking about it at all. She had noticed, of course, that Henry Ramirez was a good-looking man. She had also been impressed as the evening wore on with his smarts. But he was also clearly not her type. And that was that.

They sat at a very small table in one of several dining and drinking rooms in the King's Arms Tavern. It was on the pedestrians-only main street in the historic area. From the back of the menu Henry read aloud to Barbara that there were a lot of King's Arms taverns in the Colonies before the Revolution. But all of them changed their names after 1776, this particular one to Mrs. Vobe's Tavern and eventually to Eagle Tavern.

"It says the big guns in the Revolution—Jefferson, Washington, all of them—came in here to drink and talk about independence," Henry said.

"Terrific," Barbara said. "It's for sure none of them looked like you or me."

"There weren't any of my people anywhere around here," Henry said.

"There were plenty of mine," Barbara said. "They were slaves—in the kitchen, out back breaking their backs."

Henry said: "So here you are and that's called progress."

Both ordered small draft beers. They had walked by several old reconstructed houses and shops to get there. The waiters and waitresses and everyone else who worked at the tavern were dressed as if they were George or Martha Washington. Even the black employees, whose eighteenth-century ancestors really were slaves. Barbara still had problems with being waited on at hotels and restaurants by black people who were older than she. It was particularly bad at places like this where they wore costumes. She always heard a choir from an A.M.E. church humming chords from "Old Black Joe" in the background, and it made her feel like a disrespectful, disloyal little twit.

"You ever had peanut soup?" Henry asked. He was still reading the menu.

"Nope."

"Wonder what it tastes like."

"Probably like peanuts."

Barbara did not want to talk to this guy about what peanut soup tasted like!

Henry decided he would get serious. He would ask Barbara about blacks dating Hispanics. She seemed smart and mature enough to handle such a smart and mature conversation.

"Who in the hell knows?" she said. "Is this your way of coming on to me? If it is, go away. I am here to deal with asking questions of two white boys running for president of the United States before two or three or so billion people, including every Sunday-school teacher and preacher I have ever had, every boyfriend I have ever had, every aunt and uncle, brother and sister, momma and daddy and Gramma Maude I have ever had. Including a lot of redneck whites and jealous other kinds who will be pulling for me to fall right square on my African American face. I am not in the mood or spirit to think about sex with anybody, much less with some Mexican who wants to have a sociological discussion about why we and them don't do it more."

That really made Henry mad. All he wanted to do was to have a serious conversation, to prove to himself and to her that he was serious. All he wanted to do was be a serious person. Jesus!

"You have it all wrong," Henry said, trying his best to be pleasant, to avoid showing how really pissed he was at this smart-mouth girl. "I was only doing my best to come up with something to talk about that mattered. Sorry. Seen any good movies, been to any great rock concerts, read any keen stories in *People* lately?"

Barbara realized that she had been a fool. She had only accepted his invitation to be nice. Now she was being just the opposite. She said to him: "Henry, I am sorry. I really am. All of this is too much for my nerves. I may not be quite ready for this, the big time."

"Not ready? No way. We are ready."

"Speak for yourself."

"I am."

Each took a long swallow of beer.

"Are you worried about your questions?" Henry asked.

"You are damned right I am," Barbara replied.

"I have plenty of questions. Good, tough questions. I will loan you some. How many do you want?"

Barbara was concentrating on emptying her beer glass as fast as she could.

Henry continued: "Just name the categories you want questions in. I have them on everything. On foreign affairs I have several on Mexico, of course. There could be a revolution coming down there in my ancestral home. But I also have a great one on Cuba I could let you have. I have a terrific medical one about strokes and some experiments being done at NIH with squirrels when they hibernate. I have some zinger personal ones, particularly for Meredith. That newfound religion thing of his scares people. I have some questions about the Bible. He says he follows the Bible. Well, depending on how he reads it, that could mean trouble for a lot of people in this country. People don't read the Bible all the same way. I am Catholic. Let's say you aren't. Well, when we sit down to read the Bible, the same sentence can mean different things to each of us."

"Thanks for the offer," Barbara said, trying to keep from screaming at this Mexican guy at the top of her lungs, I know about the Bible! I know people read it differently! I know! I know! So shut up!

And within minutes both of their beer glasses were empty and they were on their way back to the Inn.

Both say when they said good night in the lobby of the Williamsburg Inn it was essentially forever, except for the business of the debate still to come. Neither was the least bit interested in the other. Neither was the least bit curious about the other. Neither had the least bit of a thought about sex with the other.

Neither had the least bit of a thought about anything with the other.

★

Joan Naylor went directly to her room in the Inn and spent the evening there alone. She read up even more on the issues of the presidential campaign and watched television without the sound. No-sound television was a practice she and her husband Jeff had developed. It began quite innocently when Jeff discovered silence was the best way to enjoy *Monday Night Football.* While millions of others were out there being annoyed once a week by Howard Cosell, it was Frank Gifford, a perfectly nice and mild-mannered ex–football player, who did it to Jeff. Gifford seemed to be off in another world from where Jeff found himself on Monday nights. So to avoid going wherever that was with Gifford he turned off the sound.

From *Monday Night Football* Jeff found that all sports events, particularly the big ones like the World Series and the Super Bowl, were much more enjoyable to simply watch, not hear. Jeff and Joan then began watching an occasional old movie that way once they realized they already knew the story and the pictures brought enough of it back to make it make sense. The worst discovery was that some documentary and newsmagazine programming could also be understood and appreciated without the sound. In other words, you didn't always have to *hear* Mike Wallace to know what he was saying. Even parts of most nightly news broadcasts were that way. Much of the news on television, world and national as well as local, was mostly predictable and readily identifiable by eye. A shot of a car and a body being pulled from the Potomac River says all that needs to be known. A shot of a secretary of state standing at a microphone with King Hussein of Jordan does the same. As does the scene at the table in the Rose Garden at the White House, the pictures of civilians running from sniper fire or army tear gas or dying of starvation in Armenia, Angola, Somalia, Sudan, Beirut, Rwanda, Haiti, Tibet, Burma, Bosnia-Herzegovina, or other places along the road to the New World Order.

The major asset of soundless television was that it was less stimulating to the blood and emotions and less occupying of the mind. That made it possible to do other things that required less than a full-blooded emotion or a full mind's attention.

Like doing what she was doing now, which was talking to Jeff and the twins on the telephone. It was a conversation that Joan Naylor herself admits may have played some role—mostly unconscious—in drawing her toward Sunday's fateful decision.

It began innocently enough.

"I haven't done anything much yet, honey," she said to Rachel, or at least she thought it was Rachel. She and Regina not only looked alike, they also sounded exactly the same. They were twelve years old, identically blond, tall, bright, athletic, and full of guilt-inducing, straight-for-the-jugular questions for their famous mother.

"Then maybe they didn't need you to go down until in the morning," said Rachel. Yes. Joan was now certain it was Rachel. Regina had come on another line.

"The movie was terrific," Regina said. "You would have loved it. Except for the arm-sex parts. Dad made us close our eyes when they came on, so don't worry."

"But we didn't," Rachel said.

And they both laughed.

Arm sex?

"Did Dad tell you about the telegrams and the faxes?" Regina said, getting down to the serious business.

"I haven't talked to Dad yet," Joan said. "You answered the phone, Rachel, remember?"

"Every kook and kooky outfit there is has sent you questions to ask tomorrow night," Rachel said.

"Some of them are really off the wall," Regina said.

"You have really got to stick it to Meredith, Mom," Rachel said.

"You really do, Mom," Regina said.

And in alternating sentences, they said to their mother:

"I know how you are about not taking sides, but this is different."

"He's evil, Mom, I really do think so. So does everybody else."

"Everybody."

"Evil like the devil is evil."

"This is different."

"You can't let him be president, Mom."

"You really can't."

"We talked about it this afternoon with Dad and he agrees."

"Dad says Meredith will turn race against race . . ."

"Rich against poor . . ."

"Baptists against Catholics . . ."

"Quakers against Jews . . ."

Joan said she had to resist an interrupting laugh. Regina and Rachel went to Sidwell Friends, a private Quaker school in Washington known for its famous parents and smart faculty, tough academic and public-service requirements. The well-worn Washington joke that came to her mind was the one about Sidwell being the only place in America where Jews taught Episcopalians how to be Quakers.

"Gays against straights . . ."

"Cops against firemen . . ."

Joan could not let that one go. "Cops against firemen? Come on now, girls."

"All right, maybe not that," Rachel said. Joan was sure it was Rachel.

"You know I can't do anything about this," Joan said. "I am but a simple journalist. Put your father on."

"Good night, Mom," Regina said. "Good luck."

"Good night, Mom," Rachel said. "Good luck."

And then Jeff was on the phone.

"How is my own personal Joan of Arc tonight?" he said.

"No comment," she said. "What is this about arm sex?"

"No comment."

"It's bad enough that everybody else in the world is on my case about Meredith," she said to Jeff after a few minutes of light and catch-up chitchat. "My daughters are doing it, too."

"Sorry about that," Jeff said. "I should have waved them off. I should have given them the old Momma-is-a-journalist-not-a-god line. I could have quoted some stuff from Mulvane. . . ."

"It's not a line, goddamn it."

"I know that, goddamn it."

"Do you have the television on?" she asked.

"Yeah. You? An *Equalizer* rerun on some cable channel."

"Is it the one with Pat Hingle in it?"

"Yeah."

"That's the same one I'm watching. I'm having trouble picking up the story."

"Me, too. I remember seeing it before, though, because of Hingle. I think he's a schoolteacher with a problem kid who comes to McCall for help."

"I need to work on my questions and things," Joan said.

"Good night, my goddess of the airwaves."

"Shut up."

"Yes, ma'am."

Within minutes she was back reading a briefing book the CNS bureau had done on reducing the federal budget deficit while also trying to figure out exactly what Pat Hingle and Robert McCall, The Equalizer, were up to.

★

Mike Howley went to the Inn's bar by himself and ordered a nightcap—a Cutty Sark scotch on the rocks. He had taken only a sip or two of his drink when he received a phone call and left the bar.

He spent the rest of the evening in his room, No. 3255, drinking Cutty Sarks on the rocks delivered by room service and talking on the phone.

Among other things.

5

Jack and Jill

The sun rose Sunday morning across Colonial Williamsburg at 6:07, according to the weather-bureau record of that day. It was a magnificent rising, the sun coming up through and behind the trees beyond the Inn like a strip of bright red-orange neon. I can bear my own witness to that fact because I was already up and out at 6:07. This was my first trip to Williamsburg, and I was determined to see a little of it as well as do my job for American journalism and *The New American Tatler*.

I was also determined not to miss my daily jog. Running early in the morning was—is—my way to keep the body and the mind alive and alert. No matter the place or the weather, I run. I always run. Always.

So there I was trotting down deserted Duke of Gloucester, the main street and pedestrian walkway in the restored area, when I came across the second most famous couple in America. Jack and Jill. There they were, running in matching red, white, and green running suits coming right toward me. Any regular reader of *People* and similar magazines would not have been surprised to see them. They also always ran every day, no matter the place or the weather. Always. They ran side by side together. Always, together, Jack and Jill. It was their trademark. It was their life. They most particularly ran together early Sunday morning, the day of their television program, the most popular of its kind on the air.

Here they were like a colored magazine photo, right in front of me. I smiled and said: "Good morning."

"Right," said Jack, not looking at me.

"Amen," said Jill, giving me a quick smile.

They looked like they should have looked, Jack and Jill together there running side by side as they did every morning. Always.

Then in a few minutes there came another jogger my way. It was a man, younger and running faster than Jack and Jill. He caught my eye and stopped dead in his tracks and motioned for me to do the same.

"Hey, sorry, amigo," he said, blowing wind out of his mouth. "But was that Jack and Jill who just went by here?"

"Yes, it was," I said, anxious to get on with my run.

"Damn!" he said. "I figured they'd be out this morning. I wanted to meet them. . . . I'll never catch them now. I missed them."

"Sorry," I said.

The man was young, probably in his late twenties, black hair, dark eyes and skin. He was wearing a gray sweat suit with TEXAS IS HEAVEN ON EARTH emblazoned on the front of the shirt.

"I am Henry Ramirez," he said. "I am one of the debate panelists." I may have imagined it—or been influenced by postdebate events and my later knowledge—but it seemed to me that he made "I am one of the debate panelists" sound as if he were announcing his presence on a throne of some kind.

I told him who *I* was.

"I've read your magazine a time or two," he said. "Most of the stories are too long for me, sorry."

I said nothing and made ready to resume my jog. I was weary of people telling me the stories in the *Tatler* were too long. I knew it and loved it. It was what made the magazine different from all the others. In a world of the short—short attention spans of readers and short visions of media owners—it was also most probably a difference that would not last much longer.

Henry Ramirez was still looking down Duke of Gloucester in the star wake of Jack and Jill.

"Someday I'm going to be one of them," he said, again in the form of an announcement.

Even though I had never met or heard of this young man before in my life, I knew immediately what he was talking about. I knew he meant he was going to someday be a Jack and Jill. And I almost laughed.

It was not a surprise that he aspired to be a Jack and Jill. The remarkable success of their program, *Face to Face with Jack and Jill*, was being heralded as a major development in the fast-moving history of American television journalism. Columbia University seminars and think pieces in various journalism reviews were already authoritatively suggesting that this program was the future, the natural end result of a three-way marriage of the values from journalism, show business, and politics.

How it happened has been thoroughly reported. CNS's thirty-two-year-old *News in the Making*, the mother of all Sunday-morning hard-news interview programs, had fallen to a weak third in the ratings behind NBS's *Review of the Week with General Schwarzkopf* and ABS's *Sunday Morning Ross*, hosted by former presidential candidate Ross Perot. CNS changed hosts four times in three years, sets and theme music three times in four years, and formats five times in four years. It expanded from thirty minutes to an hour, then went back to thirty, way up to ninety, and then back to an hour. The ratings remained the same. The problem, according to a *Washington Post* television critic, was that "CNS is mired in the boring business of seriousness, and until it gets itself unmired it is doomed to third place."

A new management at CNS News, the fourth in six years, took that advice and decided to unmire. They fired all of the real journalists producing and appearing on the program and hired the Chicago clownalist Mark Southern to take over. He said he was going to get rid of the "pencil-neck professors and pundits in Washington talking to themselves" and replace them with real Americans. He said: "Americans are going to be on the show. Lots of people who talk like regular people are going to be talking, and the politicians are going to be listening to them. It's going to be totally different." He and his real Americans made broadcast history. For the first time ever, a major network's Sunday-morning program's rating was BMS—Below Measurable Standards. The *San Francisco Chronicle* TV critic called the premiere program "an embarrassment for the host, the guests, the network, the industry, and real Americans with brains and taste everywhere." Southern was fired the next day, the program was scrapped, and another broadcast-industry record was set. Southern had the shortest tenure of any host of any network news/public affairs program ever. One program.

And—for $3.2 million a year each, according to our "Tatler Media Intelligence" column—Jack Gilbey and Jill Christopher were immediately hired to co-create and co-host another whole new program and approach. Jack and Jill were the hottest public-affairs couple of the moment, possibly of all moments. Jack Gilbey and Jill Christopher had begun their public lives as successful political consultants. Jack worked for Democrats, Jill for Republicans. They worked against each other in one presidential campaign so much, so closely, and so intensely that they fell in love and into the news, the columns, and the magazines. During the campaign, their dates were sometimes covered by reporters and photographers. Their picture appeared on the cover of *Newsweek,* each holding a copy of a nasty press release and videotape cassette as if in a shoot-out at the O.K. Corral. One unimpressed ("He's lying with envy," Jack retorted) critic claimed Jack and Jill got more favorable publicity and attention than either of their candidates. After the campaign they married, signed a multimillion-dollar his-and-her book contract, sold their story to the movies as a natural sequel to the early Hepburn-Tracy sagas, launched a major lecture tour (*Them* magazine said they got $30,000 for a joint one-hour Q & A appearance), and assumed joint ownership of a giant house in Georgetown and a forty-two-foot sailboat at Annapolis.

It was their specific decision to form themselves into a two-person, left-right, one-call-does-all commentary team that led to their Sunday program. All networks, national radio call-in shows, and others competed to pay them money and tribute to come on after presidential speeches and other events to offer instant analysis. Then it came to a head for Jack and Jill, CNS, and America when instead of returning to their original profession, political consulting, when the current presidential campaign began, they chose to remain on the outside in their new world. They offered themselves to all interested parties as a commentary/television team on an exclusive basis. In a fortunate bit of timing, the bids were still being considered when Southern flopped. CNS jumped in, dramatically raising its bid both in money and program potential.

Face to Face with Jack and Jill was not only number one in the ratings from its first week on the air, it had since gone to a full two hours and there was talk of making it even longer. "How long, O Lord, how long will it be before CNS turns over not only all of Sunday but possibly even all of Monday, Tuesday, and Wednesday to them?" asked the *Los Angeles Times* television critic.

As coincidence would have it, when I returned to the Inn from my jog I ran into somebody who was going to be a guest on today's *Face to Face with Jack and Jill* later in the morning. I knew it from my reading through a stack of press releases and Media Alerts that had been pushed under my hotel-room door along with a packet of background clips and other material the *Tatler* research office had FedExed to me.

The person was Joan Naylor, the CNS anchorwoman, who like the young jogger was a debate panelist.

I had never met Joan Naylor, but she was known to be a friend of the *Tatler* because of a long, favorable profile we had run of her a few months ago. I recognized her immediately when I entered the Inn's large Regency dining room, which was filled with flowers, white starched tablecloths, heavy silver, and journalists who were in Williamsburg for the debate. She was at a table for two with a woman I did not recognize. I, for reporting and courtesy—and, yes, bravado—reasons, decided to go over and introduce myself. I was not yet seriously interested in the panelists for my story, of course. I saw it mostly as a social call.

"Happy hunting tonight," I said.

"Thank you," she said. I found her to be as attractive and charming in person close-up as she was from the distance of television and as she had been portrayed in our profile.

"Meet Barbara Manning," she said, motioning to the young black woman sitting across the table from her. "She's also part of the hunting party."

"Oh, yes," I said, and extended my hand. I was struck immediately by the perfectness of Barbara Manning's face and the coldness of her right hand. She told me after the debate that the coldness was caused by the nervousness she had felt that morning when she woke up. She had immediately called Joan and asked if they could meet for breakfast. "I needed a fix of comfort, companionship, company," she told me.

I had no idea of any of that at the time, obviously. I had now, by chance, met three of the four debate panelists. The opportunity to meet the fourth, moderator Mike Howley, was presented to me via a Media Alert I found under my door when I returned to my room a short time later to shower, change, and prepare for my day and night of work.

TODAY'S JOURNALISTS TO QUIZ THOMAS JEFFERSON, said the announcement. Howley and five other reporters would participate in a special nine A.M. press conference with "then Governor Jefferson on the occasion of his departure from Williamsburg with the moving of the Virginia state capital to Richmond in 1780." It was being staged as a fund-raiser for some local Williamsburg charity in the East Lounge of the Inn.

It sounded intriguing, fun—interesting. I figured there might be something there for my magazine piece. And I could possibly meet Howley, too. So I went.

Howley and the other reporters—none of whom I knew or recognized—played their parts well. So did the guy, a professional actor all dressed up in full Colonial regalia that included white breeches and a burgundy frock coat, who played Jefferson. He not only stood tall and supreme the way we would want Jefferson to stand, he also spoke in a voice that was deep and firm and Jeffersonian—or at least Jeffersonian as we would imagine it to be.

Jefferson was asked several questions that were clearly setups. They were about attacks by hostile Indians between the Ohio and Illinois rivers, a Patrick Henry–sponsored bill to collect taxes in support of Christianity, and a territorial dispute with Pennsylvania, among other things. Then for a few final minutes it turned open and freewheeling.

"Did you and your fellow revolutionaries really believe you were going to be able to prevail over Britain when you signed the Declaration of Independence?" a reporter asked.

"There are times in the course of a man's life, sir," said the Jefferson character without missing a beat, "when the price of doing nothing is much higher than that of defeat."

I had no idea if Jefferson ever said anything remotely like that, but the actor certainly made it sound Jeffersonian-authentic.

Mike Howley asked the last question of Thomas Jefferson. "Have you a dream for what this new nation might become in two hundred or so years?"

"Yes, sir, I do. It is a dream I dream most nights, particularly after having spent the day looking out from Monticello, my mountaintop home west of here, at a land and a people that have had the good fortune to be put in the same place at the same time by a benevolent and thoughtful God."

Again, it had the sound of the real Jefferson. I had no idea if it really was and it did not matter.

I went up front afterward and shook hands with Howley. We had the following exchange:

"I guess we shouldn't be expecting any bombshells tonight?" I said. It was strictly a small-talk question.

"Not unless you know something I don't," he said. "I've got to run now, sorry. I want to catch the talk shows and then there's a lot of work still to be done before tonight. . . ."

He seemed relaxed, cool, confident—the way the outside world had come to view Michael J. Howley. Sifting through his words and demeanor after the fact of the debate for any clues of what was to come was fruitless. He gave nothing away that morning to me or to Thomas Jefferson.

I, too, had clippings and background material to read and television programs to watch. It was, in fact, almost time for *Face to Face with Jack and Jill.*

★

Joan Naylor had kept her public mouth very quiet about Jack and Jill. But privately to Jeff and to a few others she held nothing back. She thought they were more than the beginning of the end of network news. They were the end. She had already visualized the scene and heard the words when somebody, probably a somebody she had never met before, called her into an office to inform her that, effective tonight, Jack and Jill would be anchoring the nightly news seven days a week from now until the end of time. Nothing personal, he (Oh, please God, let it be a he, not a she!) would say. We simply are no longer in a financial position to give the people what they no longer want, which is regular journalist-type people doing regular journalism-type news on television.

The awful irony for Joan, one she also mentioned to very few people, was that she thought Jack and Jill were terrific on the air. They were funny, entertaining, and fascinating to watch. It was certainly not journalism, but it was . . . funny, entertaining, and fascinating to watch.

And watching them was what she was doing now in a huge Williamsburg Lodge ballroom CNS had converted into a broadcast studio for Jack and Jill. Joan was waiting with twenty-two other guests for her turn to go on the air.

Their now famous opening came on. It was a double head shot, live, of Jack and Jill from the side, noses almost touching.

Jack said: "Once again you are in a position of defending the indefensible—namely that nonprincipled scumbag candidate of yours."

Jill said: "At least he breathes and he talks, which may be more than can be said for that intellectual and emotional cipher you are supporting."

Jack: "Watch him pull the upset of the century tonight in the debate!"

Jill: "It would take an act of God for that to happen, and He's clearly on *our* side."

They both turned toward the camera and Jack said: "Good morning, Democrats and other correctly thinking Americans, I am Jack. . . ."

Jill said: "And I am Jill. I have a good morning to the real Americans of America . . . the Republicans and those of like right mind who want to Take Back America."

They smiled at the camera, then back at each other as the camera pulled back to show them sitting side by side in red, white, and blue director's chairs while the orchestral rendition of their theme, which sounded similar to "America the Beautiful," played in the background.

After a few credits and commercials, they started through their guests, all of whom were seated facing Jack and Jill in plush movie-house chairs arranged bleacher-style in four rows of six. There were always twenty-four chairs, and there were always only twenty-three guests. The empty chair was always reserved for the president of the United States, the outgoing one being the only public person in all of America—excepting possibly J. D. Salinger and Elvis—who had thus far been asked and refused to appear on *Face to Face with Jack and Jill.*

Jack said this morning, as he did every Sunday morning, that "one day we will look up and that empty chair will be occupied by *a* president if not *this* president."

The twenty-three guests this morning were a typical assortment. The secretary of state, three pollsters, two columnists, two regional newspaper editors, two economists, two senators, two high-school debate coaches, a Southern Baptist minister, a Presbyterian minister, a banker, an Exxon service-station owner, two housewives, the presidents of two university student bodies, and Joan Naylor. The breakdown gender-wise was twelve men, eleven women. Eleven were white, five were black, four were Hispanic, and three were Asian. All were there to speculate, argue, or otherwise talk about that night's debate, the one and only debate of this presidential campaign.

The swift, skillful, fun, and seemingly effortless way Jack and Jill passed the question balls back and forth and among twenty-three guests—any twenty-three guests—was a marvel and the central core of why their program worked. There was nothing else like it on television anywhere. Again, in the words of the *Los Angeles Times* television critic: "Alas, what is left for poor Norman and poor Ross to do but to add guests. They could go to 25 or 27 or 31 or even 50. Think about it. A talk show with 50 guests! Think about it! The tragedy is that somebody probably already is."

They were more than forty-five minutes into the program before Joan was formally introduced and asked by Jack: "I guess you're not going to tell us what you're going to ask these two clowns tonight?"

"That's right."

"Make that one clown, one saint," Jill said. "This is a pretty big deal for you, isn't it, Joan?"

"Pretty big for everyone, I would say."

"You could go down in history with a real zinger question, couldn't you?" Jack asked.

"Remember what Bernie Shaw did with that wife-rape question to Dukakis," said Jill.

"No thanks," Joan said.

"Doug Mulvane said in his op-ed piece this morning that such hypotheticals were 'gimmicks designed to show off the questioner rather than to elicit information from the candidates.' Do you agree?"

"Yes," said Joan. "I think I do. Although some hypotheticals might be all right. Shaw's question did lead to quite a revelation about Dukakis."

"Yeah, that he was a jerk," Jack said.

Jill said: "Mulvane also said you and the other panelists should . . . and I quote . . . 'stand in front of a mirror and say aloud: This is about them, not me. This is about them, not me.' Did you do that this morning?"

"I didn't have to tell myself that," Joan replied. "I already knew it."

"Are you in the market for questions?" Jack asked.

"Sure."

"Well, then, how about this for Meredith? 'Sir, why is it that you are a bigoted man intent on destroying the live-and-let-live philosophy that has helped this country grow and prosper?' "

Jill said: "I have one. 'Governor Greene, is it true that you have not had a fresh idea since the day you were born?' "

Joan, feeling like a fool, smiled and shook her head, first at Jack and then at Jill.

"I assume all of you panelists are dyed-in-the-wool Meredith haters?" said Jill.

"No, no—"

"Is there anyone anywhere in the press who supports the man who is going to be the next president of the United States?"

"Not only not in the press but anywhere else this side of a Take It Back rally or an NRA meeting," Jack said.

"Should we look for anything dramatic tonight, any fireworks of any kind?" Jill asked Joan.

"This isn't about drama or fireworks tonight," Joan said.

"Dull is what it is going to be," Jack said. "Dull as dishwater . . ."

"With a capital W," Jill said.

"W?"

"As in wipeout. A wipeout of Greene by Meredith."

And after a while they turned to the two preachers for a back-and-forth about the proper role of religion and ministers in politics.

Joan got one more brush of attention at the end of the broadcast.

"Again to Joan Naylor of our own CNS family before we go," Jack said. "She is one of the four panelists for tonight's debate. And from here you go back to work with the other panelists to think up some good ones, I assume?"

"That's right, Jack."

"I'd love to have a camera in there with the four of you," said Jill. "Hot stuff, I bet."

"Not so hot."

"Well, good luck, Joan. All of America will be watching and depending on you," Jack said.

"Try to be fair to the next president of the United States," Jill said.

"I always try to be fair."

"Nobody is fair to David Donald Meredith."

"He is the unfair one," Jack said. "He is the one who insults and castigates, distorts and disrupts, disrespects and grotesques—"

"Grotesques?"

"Happy hunting, Joan," Jack said.

"Thank you," Joan replied.

6

The Decision

Henry Ramirez opened the door to Longsworth D for Joan Naylor and closed it behind her. What happened behind that door over the next five hours and forty-five minutes may very well be the most important meeting ever conducted by and among journalists. There had always been talk and charges from the uninformed and angry of the right and/or left about alleged journalistic conspiracies but hear ye, hear ye, here now there really was one.

But first there was some good-spirited skylarking.

"Joan, Joan, she's our girl! If she can't do it, nobody can!" Henry yelled, and he clapped and cheered, and so did Barbara and Howley.

"God, what I would give to be on *Jack and Jill,*" Henry said. "I cannot even think of what I would give to be on *Jack and Jill.*"

"Your soul," said Joan. "Only your soul is required."

"What I would give to *be* Jack and Jill!" Henry said.

"Only your balls in addition to your soul," said Howley. "Sorry. . . ."

A few minutes later they were talking about questions. Henry said: "All of my really tough bad questions are for Meredith. I can't think of any for Greene. But I can't think of any other kind for Meredith. I really cannot. I just put the sight of him in my head and I want to scream."

"You can say amen to that," Barbara said. "We need zingers for Greene, that's all. For Meredith, they're easy."

"Forget the idea that you are really going to zing that man," Joan said. "Nobody handles people like us New Arrogants better than he does."

"He's a menace to this country and all who live in it," Barbara said.

There was a moment of silence, broken finally by Joan asking Mike Howley: "Do you agree, Mike? Do you believe he will be as bad for this country as . . . as everyone else seems to? Everyone but the voters?"

Howley, after a few beats, said: "Yes, as a matter of fact, I do. I have not said it in print or even on the air, but here in the privacy of this room I do say it. I honestly and strongly believe the election of David Donald Meredith would be a devastating development for our country. I wish I did not feel that way, but I do."

"How devastating?" Joan asked. "How bad?"

"I cannot imagine in my worst nightmares anything worse. I honestly cannot. I know I should not be saying stuff like this. But you asked me. There is my answer."

"I agree with you," Joan said.

Henry looked away, out the windows of the room to a small outside courtyard.

"Jesus," said Barbara.

And her word hung there by itself in the stillness of the next few seconds.

"What are you going to do about it?" Joan asked Mike Howley.

"Do?" he replied. "There is nothing I *can* do."

"Don't you owe it to all of those Michael J. Howley readers and listeners to tell them what you think?" Barbara said. "That's what you can do."

"That's not my job."

"Whose is it?"

"Editorial writers. Politicians. Talk-show hosts. Ross and Norman. Jack and Jill. The clownalists."

"What all of them say don't mean sweat compared to what it would mean if you said it," Barbara said.

Joan Naylor was suddenly uneasy, almost scared about what she had started. She decided to call it off, to stop it before it went too far. "There is no point in talking about this," she said. "Like it or not, personal opinions aside and all of that, we have our jobs to do and that is to ask questions at this debate tonight. Let's get on with it."

"Good idea," Mike Howley said.

"Bad idea," said Henry Ramirez.

"Are you thinking what I think you're thinking?" Barbara asked him.

"Sí, sí, señorita. Sí, sí, and amen to that."

"Wait a minute," Joan said. "Don't say it. Don't say it."

Henry said it anyhow. "We all think Meredith should not be president of the United States. We all think he would do heavy damage to our country, the country we all love and cherish. So why don't we do what we can tonight to make sure he does not become president of our country?"

"No!" said Joan.

"Right on!" said Barbara.

"Wait, wait," said Mike Howley. "Don't say another word."

He went over to the television that was in a console along the back wall. He turned it on. "What'll it be, Stormin' Norman or Squeakin' Ross?"

Nobody answered, so he put on General Schwarzkopf's *Review of the Week* on NBS. His show and Perot's *Sunday Morning Ross* on ABS were on at the same time, right after *Jack and Jill,* both having run away in fear of going heads-to-heads with Jack and Jill.

"I thought you checked out everything," Barbara said.

"That was last night," Mike said. He adjusted the TV sound so it was audible enough to thwart electronic surveillance but not loud enough to intrude in their conversations. "Background noise is the perfect use for that crap Ross and Norman thrust on the American people," he said.

Howley chose Norman over Ross. The voices of the Desert Storm commander and his talk-show guests thus became the cover Muzak noise for the planning of America's first major journalism storm.

"Well, as I was saying," Henry said once Howley had returned and sat down. "We are in a position tonight to do something about this awful thing. . . ."

"Sorry, Henry, but I must stop you again," Mike Howley said. "We are about to do some walking on some extremely dangerous ground. If we are going to go on with this line, then I think—I believe, I insist, really—that we should agree on some rules of conversation."

"Like what?" Barbara said.

"Like what I proposed yesterday. Nobody talks about what is said in this room from this point on. Nobody. Nobody does any stories about it for their newspaper, magazine, or television network."

"Radio. I'm in radio," Henry said.

"I'm sorry," Howley said. "I forgot."

"Everybody forgets radio."

"So moved," said Joan. "So moved that we all go to jail and die before we breathe a word about this. Mike is right."

"I think so, too," Barbara said. "Unless we agree otherwise—"

" 'Think' won't cut it," Mike Howley said. "I walk out of here right now if we do not have an ironclad agreement. I do not need a story in *This Week* magazine or on the radio—"

"Thanks," Henry said.

"About the fact that I participated in a serious discussion about rigging a presidential debate, no matter the outcome. Sorry, but I do not need that. I will not have that."

"I hear you," said Barbara. "OK, OK."

"Hearing is also not enough," Henry said. "Mike is right."

Barbara pointed to Henry and said to Mike: "You trust us? Him and me?"

"Good question. The good answer is yes. The honest answer is I'm thinking about it."

Barbara said: "What about you, Joan? Do you trust us?"

"I'm thinking about it, too. One word anywhere about my just being in such a conversation and the network would boot me back to doing Eyewitness weather in Chillicothe."

"Is that how you got your start?" Henry said. "I didn't know that. I'm fascinated with how everybody got their start. Some of the stories are really strange. There is no one way to do it. Rachel Jergens at CNN was discovered by some local news producer selling women's beach accessories outside Miami—"

"It was a joke," Joan said. "I started as a reporter with WFRA in Cincinnati, way down the road from Chillicothe."

Henry joined her and the others in silence. And the only noise in the room for a full forty-five seconds was the muffled one of Norman Schwarzkopf interviewing three pollsters, two political consultants, two senators, three governors, four radio-talk-show hosts, and two late-night comedians about what to expect in that night's presidential debate.

It was Barbara's call and she made it. "It's a deal. No matter what happens, no matter what is said, we do not talk, unless we talk about it and agree to it beforehand. If you've got a razor blade or a pocketknife, cut me and draw some blood."

"Great and olé," Henry said.

"So now, Mike and Joan," said Barbara, "it's up to you two. You've got a lot more to lose than us little minorities persons. The question is whether you trust us enough to place your asses and your other vital important white parts into our little minorities persons' hands."

"Mike, what do you say?" said Joan, asking what must have been the most important question ever asked of Michael J. Howley.

"I'm game if you are," he said. "All we're risking is all."

" 'All We're Risking Is All' would be a great title for my book about all of this that I am hereby swearing with my blood never to write no matter what," Barbara said.

"Repeat after me, amigos," said Henry. " 'All I'm risking is all, amigos.' "

Mike and Joan and Barbara joined him in saying: "All I'm risking is all, amigos."

And they all four laughed. But not very loudly or for very long.

Barbara said to Howley: "Start talking, white man."

And Howley started talking.

He said: "I think it's accurate and fair to say that we might be able to come up with some things to do tonight that might—'might' is the operable word—might throw not only the debate to Greene but also the election."

That was it. Those were the words.

I think it's accurate and fair to say that we might be able to come up with some things to do tonight that might—'might' is the operable word— might throw not only the debate to Greene but also the election.

Those were the words of action and conspiracy, unlike any ever spoken before. Those were the words of Michael J. Howley, one of America's most respected journalists.

"You are saying, Mike," Henry said, "that the four of us, sitting in this room right now, could do it. Just by what we did this evening at the debate, we could—"

Joan, her feet suddenly very cold, interrupted. "We're journalists. If we're going to talk about this, then let's begin with a little reminder of what we are."

"Aren't we Americans first?" Barbara responded. "Isn't the issue whether we four patriotic Americans can sit back and let an evil fool become the president of our country? Isn't the question whether being journalists means we must sit back and watch our country be ruined by some maniac who stands and lives for everything that is wrong in our country? A man who would divide us, rather than heal us—"

"A man who has not one caring or understanding bone in his body," Henry said. "A man who has no idea of community, of the family of all of us different peoples we are supposed to be."

Joan looked at Mike Howley. Say something, please, she said with her eyes and demeanor. Tell these kids what is going on.

Howley took the cue, saying: "I have been at this longer than any of you-all. I have always enjoyed the cover being a reporter has given me. I do not put bumper stickers on my car. I do not serve on committees and commissions. I do not sign petitions. I do not attend rallies or meetings. I don't even vote—"

"What?" Henry said. "You don't vote?"

"I gave it up in the sixties. I was having trouble separating out my own views from my reporting—particularly when it came to Kennedy against Nixon and then Goldwater and the crazies who were around him. . . ."

"They'd look like PTA ladies compared to Meredith and his Take It Back people," Joan said.

"True," Howley said. "At any rate, I decided to keep my own decision making out of it by not voting then. And I haven't since."

"Do you think none of us should?" Henry said.

"Oh, I don't know. It's an individual thing. I was just saying that to make the point that until the last few weeks, days, hours, and now, in this room, minutes, the very idea of doing something like throwing a debate to one candidate or the other would have been in the same league with committing murder. Or with, say, a doctor intentionally letting a patient die, a lawyer throwing a case, a preacher refusing to save a soul. This is very serious stuff to me. That is what I am saying. The most serious stuff there is. I have lived my whole professional life on the other side of that line."

The words made an impact on the other three. They established what Joan described later as "a justification context confirmation." If Michael J. Howley, the purest of the pure, felt compelled to throw over all of his professional journalistic constraints, then it was surely all right, surely justified for the rest of us.

Howley, after delivering the words, took a deep breath and poured himself some coffee from a thermos pot someone had put there on the table along with four cups.

Joan said: "There are all kinds of analogies to dream up. What if you were walking down the street and came across a burning building? A woman yelled at you from the fifth floor to call the fire department. Would you do it or would you just stand there? I'm a reporter. I cannot get involved. Let somebody else call the fire department. I will cover the fire. If they get there in time to save the lady's life, so be it. If not, nasty break. I am a reporter. I am not responsible. My job is to observe, not to act, not to call the fire department, not to sound the alarm. Even if it means people die in burning buildings."

Henry clapped his hands together.

Barbara said: "Amen, sister, praise the Lord."

"Olé, olé," Henry said.

"As the lawyers say, there is precedent for this," Henry said. "Woodward and Bernstein. They didn't sit by and let Richard Nixon screw the country."

Mike Howley said: "Please keep in mind they did what they did as reporters. What we're talking about is a prime-time spectacular. Using our positions as journalists to publicly sandbag this guy in front of the whole world nine days before the election. We wouldn't be acting as reporters. We'd be doing it as actors . . . assassins. The ultimate act by four ultimate New Arrogants."

"You're not backing off, are you?" Henry asked.

Howley replied: "I just want to make sure we all know what we're talking about."

Joan said: "Look, we've gone this far. Let's go a little further. Mike, you said you thought it really was possible for us to . . . I'm having trouble saying it . . . well, rig the debate so Meredith loses it. How? What could we do?"

Mike Howley blew some air out of his mouth, settled back into his chair, and said to his three co-conspirators: "I don't know really. I said that because I assumed we were smart enough to think of something or some lot of things. I had nothing specific in mind. Not really in mind. But let's think. Let's all think about it out loud."

But he said nothing out loud. Neither did anyone else. Barbara, Henry, and Joan were thinking. They were thinking, each in his and her own way, of something specific they might do to dictate a dramatic turn in the debate and the election.

Finally Henry said: "Is anybody else hungry?"

" 'How can you think of food at a time like this?' is the famous line," Barbara said.

"Line from what?" Henry said.

"I don't know, I don't know."

Mike Howley said: "The first thing, and the obvious thing, would be to make sure Greene knew in advance every question we were going to ask and the order in which they were going to be asked. He could get ready for the right things, which would certainly give him an advantage."

"How would we get them to him?" Henry asked.

Mike Howley answered: "Come on, Henry, just think about it. We'd get it to him the same way people get things to us. We would leak it. One of us would tell somebody, who would tell somebody else, who would get it to somebody in the Greene campaign. Secrets flow uphill as well as downhill. It's just seldom done that way."

"I read somewhere that the Nixon people believed with all of their heart and soul that the press panel in the first Kennedy-Nixon debate set Nixon up or got the questions in advance to Kennedy—something like that," Joan said.

"Now think about that as God's work," Barbara said. "Can you think of a better thing to do for democracy than to have tried to keep Richard Milhous Nixon out of the White House? We are confronted with an equally glorious opportunity to help our country, our people."

"I can't even imagine our country without Richard Nixon," Howley said.

Barbara said: "My roommate works in the Greene campaign. She's here in Williamsburg somewhere. It would be an easy go to get her the questions."

"We haven't even talked about our questions yet!" Henry said.

"As a practical matter," Joan said, "I'm not sure giving the questions to Greene would do that much good."

"He'd figure out a way to blow it anyhow," Henry said.

"What if we leaked a phony set of questions to Meredith at the same time?" Barbara said. "He'd spend his time and worries on the wrong ones. . . ."

Howley said: "Whatever we do, if we do anything, we had better decide on it pretty soon."

"I wish you hadn't mentioned food a while ago, Henry," Barbara said. "You made me hungry for a grilled-cheese sandwich. When I get nervous I always want a grilled-cheese sandwich."

"Vegetable soup and mashed potatoes are my nervous food," Joan said. "I had them the night before my twins were born."

"A bean burrito unlike anything you can get in any restaurant is what I always want when I'm tight but can never have unless I am at my mama's café," Henry said.

It was Mike Howley's turn to identify his nervous food. "It used to be nonfilter Camels and a gin martini straight up. Now it's a lean-meat hamburger all-the-way and a caffeine-free Diet Pepsi usually. Something like that."

With great energy and relief each grabbed a menu to see if what they needed was on it.

★

Henry, who handled the phone job of placing the orders, was the only one who did not come close to getting the nervous food he wanted. No burritos, no Tex-Mex food of any kind, fit Colonial Williamsburg's eighteenth-century culinary decor. So he got something called The Tazewell Club, which was a regular turkey club sandwich on something called Sally Lunn bread. He figured Sally Lunn must have been somebody special to have had a bread named after her. He had always thought his mama's burritos sold under the name of Mama Luisa's would make it big.

The room-service woman said the order would be there in fifteen minutes, if not sooner, and she did not lie. Two waiters, both young black men in white coats, and a supervisor, an older black man in a dark green blazer, were there with two rolling carts, smiles, and good cheer in just under thirteen minutes.

Henry said something to them about the wonder of their speed and service.

"You-all are the special people here today, I can tell you that," said the supervisor. "Special to all of America, I guess."

"I guess," said Henry.

Barbara oh, so wished they had sent three white men or three Hispanic men or three anything but black men.

"I'll bet we could make a bundle if we knew what you-all were going to ask those two fellas tonight," said the supervisor as the two waiters went about the work of laying out the food on the round table in the corner.

"Probably so," Mike said.

One of the waiters came over to Barbara with a menu in his hand. "One of the chefs wondered if you-all would mind signing one of our menus for him," he said.

"Me? Just me?"

"No, ma'am, all four of you is what he said. If that's all right."

It was all right. He took the menu from Barbara and then to each of the others.

"You're the one on ABS, aren't you?" the other waiter, also finished with his work, said to Joan.

"Nope. CNS," she replied.

"I'm sorry," said the waiter. She could tell he was absolutely mortified.

"No problem," she said. "People have trouble telling us TV people apart." The words just came out. She looked immediately at Barbara, who was on the verge of breaking up.

"Well, good luck," said the waiter, clearly ready to break into a run for the door.

His colleagues were not that ready to go. "I can't even imagine what kind of pressure you-all have on you," said the supervisor.

"It goes with the territory," Henry said, as if he were a pitcher in the seventh game of the World Series talking to a knothole gang meeting.

The supervisor, still smiling, said to Joan: "You-all sure are tough on the president at those news conferences. Why is that?"

"That's our job."

"Yes, ma'am. But I don't get all of that yelling. Why do those reporters do all of that yelling?"

"You have to yell to be heard over all the noise."

"It seems to me like you-all are making the noise. I don't think people ought to yell at a president. But that's none of my business now, is it?"

Barbara wanted to scream: Get out of here!

"We'll try to do better," Joan said. "Thanks."

"Sorry to do so much talking. You-all are so busy. I can't even begin to imagine the kind of pressure you-all have on you."

"You just said that," Barbara said.

"I did, sorry. Those reporters at the White House are not only loud, they're also kind of snide and nasty. I don't think they should be that way to the president. But that's none of my business either now, is it? Call us when you're through eating and we'll clear everything away."

Nobody said anything else and in a few seconds the two waiters and the supervisor were gone.

"The voice of America," Mike Howley said once the door was closed.

"Not my America," said Barbara.

At first they talked about each of their meals and drinks and the two waiters and the supervisor. And about Pompous Perfect Mulvane's "Open Letter to the Press Panelists" in the *Post*. As Jack and Jill had already pointed out to Joan and their TV audience, Mulvane had advised the panelists to ask simple, direct questions, to avoid exotic hypotheticals, and, most important, to remember the debate wasn't about us, the press, it was about them, the candidates.

That subject plus the simple passing of time and circumstance soon brought them right back to the crushing business at hand.

The television set remained on, but Norman and Ross were long gone. The TV scene and noise had turned now to a stock-car race somewhere where the sun was shining and short sleeves were worn.

And it was only a few minutes afterward that Mike Howley brought the conversation to another major turning point.

"I've been thinking about one overriding truth involved in what we're talking about doing," he said. "I think we have to accept the fact that we can't do it any other way than right out front. Directly, in front of the whole world with the whole world knowing from the beginning what we are doing. The idea of leaking some questions to Greene and then going out there acting like we're playing it straight or whatnot simply will not work. Unless one of you has an idea for a way to do it covertly—covertly, yes, that's the word I was looking for—I don't see it. Forget a covert action. I do not believe it is possible. The only possible way is, like I said, direct, straight. We are throwing off our traditional roles as journalists and acting as Americans concerned for the future of our country, as the ultimate New Arrogants."

Henry put his Tazewell Club sandwich on Sally Lunn bread down on its plate.

Joan dropped her spoon into her bowl of vegetable soup.

Barbara, after swallowing a mouthful of her grilled-cheese sandwich, said again the magic word: "Jesus."

"I hadn't thought it that far through," Henry said.

"I can't believe it," said Joan, "but neither had I."

"Oh my, oh my," Barbara said.

Howley said: "Maybe you-all can think of another way through our questions or whatever to do it on the sly, but I can't. We could go out there and make fools of ourselves and not accomplish a damned thing, particularly not what we really want, which is . . ." He stopped.

"You're still having trouble saying it, aren't you?" Joan said.

"Yes," he said.

"I'm not," Barbara said.

Henry said: "I am now. Now that Mike has said what he said. I had this idea that maybe we could rig the thing in such a way as to cause Meredith to screw up and lose the election, but somehow nobody would ever know what we were up to. You know, that we sat around in here and figured it out."

"Well, I thought that, too," Barbara said. "We all thought that."

"Well, we've gone this far," said Joan. "Can you take it another scary step for us, Mike?"

Howley had managed to eat only one good bite of his hamburger and two or three potato chips. He bit into the sandwich again and then slowly chewed and swallowed it and then took a sip of his Diet Pepsi.

Then he said: "We could go directly at Meredith. 'Sir, it has been widely suggested by members of the campaign staff of your opponent and others that when you were a student at the University of Colorado, you lived the life of a transvestite, that you had a homosexual experience with your roommate while at the same time having a heterosexual one with the wife of the head of the English Department, that you seriously considered moving as a couple with each of them to Nova Scotia so you could pursue your relationships and avoid military service during the Vietnam War. Is that true?' "

"That would do it!" Henry said. "Good-bye, Talk Man Meredith! Hello, President Greene! Hello, America!'"

"Jesus," Barbara said.

"Jesus is right," Joan said. "Where did you get that story? None of our people picked up anything like that about Meredith."

"Come on, come on," said Mike Howley. "That's not true. I just made that up to make the point."

"Too, too bad," Barbara said.

"Hello, President Meredith again," Henry said. "Some story that would be. Some story."

"I made it up," Mike said.

"OK, OK," Henry said.

"So the real question is what are the real questions we really could throw at Meredith in order to do him in?" Joan said.

Do him in. Do him in. Those were the words, the words of action and conspiracy.

"Give us some of those zingers you've been talking about, Henry," Barbara said.

The other three listened while Henry read aloud from a sheet of paper.

"Mr. Meredith, it has been widely reported that you believe the United States is a Christian nation. Does that mean Jews, Hindus, Buddhists, Muslims, and those of all other faiths are either not real Americans or some kind of second-class American?

"Mr. Meredith, is the fact that you have no blacks or Hispanics in your campaign organization a signal of your interest in and regard for blacks and Hispanics?

"Mr. Meredith, what kind of wall would you build along the Texas-Mexico border to keep out people who look like me? Brick, concrete—or barbed wire?"

Howley said: "Good questions, Henry. Particularly the one about the wall."

"Yeah," Barbara said.

"But, with all due respect, Henry," said Joan, "I don't believe they will blow the lid off, so to speak. Most of that has already been gone over. He's already been asked most of those questions in some form or other, and he's managed to dodge and charm and lie his way around them. The American people, I am sorry to say, have sat there and watched and listened and read while he did it. But they still want him as president—if the new poll is right. They want a wall and a moratorium on immigration and all of the rest."

"The poll is right," Howley said.

"He's manipulated the people," Barbara said. "He's in the same league with Koresh and Jones and those other cult fanatics, only he's done it to more people—enough to elect him president."

For a few seconds the only sound was from the television. The stock-car race had now given way to a movie starring Elizabeth Taylor and Richard Burton. It seemed to Joan that there was always a movie on television starring Elizabeth Taylor and Richard Burton.

"Maybe we should forget this whole thing," Joan said. "Maybe the people really do know what they're doing and supporting. Maybe the people have a right to ruin their country. That is democracy, isn't it?"

"We're back where we started?" Henry asked.

"No," Barbara said. "Let's see what we can think of. I had a question for Meredith about civil rights. The bastard really does not believe anybody should have them except white males. He really did say the other day that reverse discrimination is now the real racial and gender problem in this country. Can you believe that?"

They could all believe that. But it clearly wasn't enough. Not to throw the election. Not to do him in.

"It would sure help if Greene was a better candidate," Joan said. "His poll negatives are almost as bad as Meredith's."

"Worse in some areas—like 'leadership,' 'presidential-like,' 'bearing,' 'charisma,' 'breathing,' " Mike said.

"We can't give up," Barbara said. "We've come a long way. Let's not quit now. . . ."

"I'm not sure I'm there yet about laying it out there at the beginning the way Mike said," Henry said. "I think we are smart enough to do it and not leave any fingerprints."

"I disagree," Mike Howley said.

Henry told me his mouth moved into shape to say Yes, sir, but the words did not come.

"Look," Joan said. "I had sketched out a jugular one for Meredith. Let me read it." She looked down at some papers in front of her. "Mr. Meredith, there is a growing consensus in the country about three things. One, that you are going to be elected president. Two, that you will have done so by dividing the American people into their most self-interested groups, by appealing to their worst sides, to their fears and loathings, to what separates them one from the other. Three, that as president you will govern the nation in that same way. What is your comment?"

Barbara clapped. Henry signaled a thumbs-up.

"Right, right on!" Barbara said.

"Now we are talking," Henry said. "Olé, olé, gringo anchorwoman!"

Mike Howley said: "I'd give you an A for content, D-minus for length."

Joan shook her head. "Thanks, one and all. But is it enough? If we could depend on Greene to pick up on it and for all of us to jump in—"

"Without appearing to be piling on," Henry said.

"That's the way it's going to look no matter what, but who cares?" Barbara said.

Again, the other three turned toward Mike Howley. Again, he was the one they wanted to hear from.

He had them now exactly where he wanted them.

There was a knock on the door.

Henry, once again, did the duty, holding a shsssh finger to his mouth and going to the door.

It was the room-service supervisor, the guy in the green blazer. He was holding a huge round tray off to the left side of his head. "Surprise, ladies and gentlemen of the press! Surprise!" He took a ta-dah step into the room. "Hot-fudge sundaes for everyone!"

"I don't think we ordered anything like that," Joan said rather meekly and quietly.

"They're on the house. The management and employees of Colonial Williamsburg and the Williamsburg Inn and Lodge want you to have them as a token of our admiration and good luck."

Henry, still the welcomer at the door, said: "Well, sure. Thanks and olé."

"Is it against our journalist code of ethics to accept free hot-fudge sundaes?" Howley asked.

"At my place the rule is anything worth less than ten dollars doesn't count," Henry said.

"My magazine specifically exempts hot-fudge sundaes from all rules," Barbara said.

With flourish and commotion, the man in the green blazer served a sundae to each of the four. Then he stood back and off to the side as if he were settling in to watch them eat each and every bite. Henry said it was clear he had something else on his mind. And in a few seconds he got it out.

"I have a favor to ask of you, if it is not too much," he said.

"We are not going to tell you our questions, sir," Henry said quickly.

"No questions. A picture. I wonder if I could have my picture taken with you? I have a camera." He pulled a small Canon Sure Shot camera out of his jacket pocket. "I asked one of the waiters to come with me. He is out in the hall. . . ."

Henry looked at his colleagues. "No problem?"

And soon the supervisor in the green blazer was standing against a wall surrounded—two on each side—by Michael J. Howley of *The Washington Morning News,* Joan Naylor of CNS News, Henry Ramirez of Continental Radio, and Barbara Manning of *This Week* magazine. One of the two waiters who had been in the room clicked off three shots.

"This picture will make me famous in my neighborhood," said the supervisor. "Thank you."

Henry, escorting the two men to the door, said: "It was nothing. We love to have our picture taken."

"Ask good questions," said the supervisor.

"Do you have a question you think we should ask tonight?"

"Yes, I do. Ask why they lie about everything."

Henry opened the door. "Good idea. Thanks for the sundaes."

"We'll be back for the dirty dishes."

"No reason to do that. They will not be a problem."

Henry closed the door. "Ain't democracy an olé thing," he said to Howley, Joan, and Barbara.

Howley held up his hand to signal the others. Hush, please. Say nothing. He picked up his ice-cream bowl and looked and felt the bottom. He nodded for the others to do the same. Silently.

Bingo. A small receiver, dull silver the size of a penny, was stuck to the bottom of the bowl Joan Naylor was using. Nobody said a word as Howley took the tiny thing between the thumb and forefinger of his right hand and carried it into the bathroom. There he placed the stopper in the sink, filled the basin full of water, and dropped the little piece of round silver into the water.

It was Henry who said "Jesus" this time.

It put an eerie urgency to the business at hand, which nobody had to restate. Nobody had to restate the fact that time was running out, the fact that they had agreed on nothing, the fact that it had come down to Mike Howley. He had been about to say something when the knock on the door of the man in the green blazer interrupted.

Nobody had to say, Well, Mike, what were you going to say—if anything? Well, Mike, have you got an idea, Mike? Hey, Mike, how *do* we do in David Donald Meredith?

Howley put them through several excruciatingly tense silent dum-ta-dum-dum seconds. He walked back and forth across the room twice, the last time turning up the sound on Liz and Dick. He shook his head from side to side several times.

It was quite an act.

Finally, back in his chair at the big table, he said: "As a matter of fact, I may have a way to do it. Some papers came into my possession right before I left Washington. I didn't take them to a Xerox machine, so I have only one copy of each. If you wouldn't mind reading them one at a time?"

He reached down into a small black canvas briefcase on the floor by his chair and pulled out some papers. He handed them to Joan, who was the closest to him.

They spent the next two hours reading those papers and making the decision that would transform a presidential election, journalism, and themselves.

Part 2

What

7

Twenty-seven Minutes

At 6:01 P.M., Eastern Standard Time, Michael J. Howley took the hand-signal cue from the stage manager. Howley looked at the spot he had been told to look at, grinned slightly, and then said to an estimated ninety-two million Americans and several million other people around the world:

"Good evening. . . . And welcome to the only debate of this presidential campaign between David Donald Meredith, the Republican nominee, and Governor Paul L. Greene, the Democratic nominee. Welcome, Mr. Meredith . . . Governor Greene."

The candidates smiled and nodded. They were standing behind the blue-gray podiums that came up to just above each man's waist. Both were dressed in dark blue suits and white dress shirts. Greene's tie was his trademark shamrock green. Meredith's was his customary dark burgundy. Howley and the three panelists were seated facing the candidates from behind their table. It was the customary look for presidential debates.

Howley continued: "I am Michael J. Howley of *The Washington*

Morning News. I am working tonight with three other journalists—Joan Naylor of CNS News . . . Barbara Manning of *This Week* magazine . . . and Henry Ramirez of Continental Radio."

Joan Naylor looked like Joan Naylor always looked. She was usually described in the personality magazines as that perky, spirited girl-next-door type who was clearly number one in CNS's Doris Day Always Lives Here corps. Joan was blond, blue-eyed, lovable, and she was all of that and more now as the camera went to her when Howley called her name. She was dressed in a dark green silk suit. That was because she had never flubbed a line or done a poor interview after drinking a cup of hot tea with lemon, talking on the phone with her Aunt Grace in Sandusky, Ohio, or while wearing dark green. She had called her aunt before leaving her room at the Inn while sipping a cup of hot tea.

There had never been a personality-magazine story about Barbara Manning. If there had been, it would probably have described her as a natural physical heiress to Lena Horne. She could probably have been a campus beauty queen if she had been so inclined. She was looking down at something on the table in front of her when Howley mentioned her name. The camera missed her facial beauty but not the stylishness of the beige dress she was wearing. Her main predebate problem had been resisting the temptation to tell Barbara Hayes what was coming. When she had gone back to her room from Longsworth D, there was a hotel message slip under the door, and the red light on the phone was blinking. Call Barbara Hayes. Barbara Manning wavered but did not call her back.

Henry Ramirez was as attractive a man as Barbara Manning was a woman. He came to that debate table even more unknown than Barbara Manning. His hair was full and black and combed straight back. He gazed right into the camera and winked when Howley introduced him. He appeared ready, confident. It triggered prize fighter analogies. Henry was wearing his dark blue suit, the one he wore at his Texas A&I graduation and all monumental and solemn occasions since. The shirt had been a problem because he didn't think any of the ones he owned was right. So he had gone to Brooks Brothers on L Street and bought a blue pinstripe oxford-cloth button-down "classic" before leaving Washington. Unfortunately, he had forgotten that new shirts come out very wrinkled from their cellophane and pins. Fortunately, he unwrapped it and discovered his problem soon enough to send it off in the hands of a bellman for a rush press job. He also bought a new tie at Brooks Brothers. It was dark blue with half-inch pink stripes angled across it. He thought he vaguely remembered Phil Donahue—or was it Robert MacNeil?—wearing something like that the other day on television. The last thing Henry had done before leaving his room was talk to his mother in Falfurrias. "Muy bien, my son," she had said. It was an expression he had heard from his mother since the first time he remembered hearing anything. There were no better words to hear.

Howley was dressed in a dark brown suit because that was what he always wore when any kind of serious chips were down. He had worn that suit the last two times on the NBS morning show, and when he got his honorary degree and delivered the commencement address at Amherst College in Massachusetts. ("I beg of you to enter journalism," he said to the graduates. "Come save it from what we're all doing to it before it's too late.") The only physical flaw he exposed to the American people this night was his hair. He had thought about getting a fresh haircut before the debate, but Marengo, his barber in Washington, was away seeing his family in Lebanon, and Howley had neither the interest nor the energy to find someone else. To hell with it anyhow, he must have thought. This isn't show business, this is serious business. So his graying dark brown hair was careening slightly down over both ears and his shirt collar.

He said to the millions: "We are here in an auditorium in the Williamsburg Lodge on the grounds of historic Colonial Williamsburg, Virginia. There could be no more fitting setting for such an important exercise in modern democracy."

There was no TelePrompTer. Howley had worked to memorize the copy, but he looked down at his paper now. The next was the most difficult part, the important part. It had to be said correctly and firmly. It had to resonate, reverberate. . . .

O Jesus, help us as we travel toward the shadow of death, thought beautiful Barbara Manning.

Olé, Mike! thought handsome Henry Ramirez.

From this next moment on, my life will never be the same, thought perky Joan Naylor.

Howley said to the TV camera: "There have been ground rules agreed to for this debate. They called for a back-and-forth between the candidates that was precise in its minutes and order. But the four of us—Ms. Naylor, Ms. Manning, Mr. Ramirez, and I—have decided to dispense with those ground rules."

"No! Mike, no!" came the voice of Nancy Dewey into the earpiece in Mike Howley's ear.

Howley continued: "Earlier this evening I consulted with officials of the National Commission on Presidential Debates. I asked about the commitment of the commission and of the television networks to carrying whatever happens out here on this stage tonight. I was assured that what happens here is what you, the American people, will see. I was told it would be like a thunderstorm—once it begins there is no stopping it. They said no one from either campaign had the authority to pull the plug. The only way it could be stopped would be if one of the two candidates chose not to participate and literally walked away."

In the eighteen months since he had been an active candidate for the Republican nomination and then for president of the United States, David Donald Meredith's face had never been seen by anyone in the outside world in any way other than that of a quiet, amused, friendly, knowing, serenely comfortable man. Now, for just a blink of a second, the four panelists and the American people saw a frown on his face.

"May I ask your purpose?" Meredith said to Howley.

"Our purpose is to get to the real issues of this election in a way that will allow the voters to make a real decision," Howley said.

"I much prefer the more open format anyhow and always have, of course," Meredith said.

"Mike, stop it!" Nancy Dewey shouted again into Howley's left ear. "You can't do this!"

Mike Howley reached with his left hand down to a knob under the table that controlled the earpiece volume. He turned it with a harsh move to the left. He could no longer hear Nancy Dewey in his left ear.

★

Howley could also not hear what was happening in the room behind the auditorium that had been converted into a television control room for the debate.

Jack Turpin and Brad Lilly were sitting in canvas director's chairs on either side of Hammond directly behind Nancy Dewey. She was at the huge console of buttons, levers, colored lights, and TV monitors through and by which what was happening onstage was being transformed into a television broadcast. She had people sitting on both sides of her—a director, an assistant director, and an array of various technical and engineering people, all wearing headsets.

"Stop this program and stop it right now!" Turpin yelled at Hammond the second Howley finished his line about ignoring the rules of the debate. "They can't do this!"

"What is going on here?" Lilly said, also rather loudly.

"I don't know what's going on, but I do know I could not stop it if I wanted to," Hammond said. "I'm as upset and stunned as you-all are."

"Go out there and call a recess," Turpin said. "I must talk to my candidate."

"No."

"You cannot say No to me!"

"Shut up or get your ass out of this control room, Jack," Hammond said. "There's work to be done in here."

Turpin yelled: "You will never work again in media, in politics, in America, in the world, in the universe, Hammond!"

He got up from his chair and took one step forward and leaned over Nancy Dewey. "Shut it down, lady. Shut it down right now!"

Nancy Dewey had learned her craft at the old CBS News under the crazy, smart, tough guys such as Fred Friendly and Don Hewitt. "I'm busy, Mr. Turpin," she said. "Be quiet, sir, or get out. I'm talking to Howley in his ear."

"Tell him to stop it!"

"That's what I just did."

Chuck Hammond stood up. "She's doing her best, so leave her alone, Turpin," he said. "Do it in a count of three or I'll get a cop in here to throw you out of here." Hammond was a large man in muscle but not in height. His great Marine sense of himself must have made him seem even larger at that moment, because when he stood up now he seemed to tower over Jack Turpin. They are the exact same height—five feet ten and a half inches. I checked.

Turpin lowered himself back down in his chair. Hammond sat again.

Lilly said nothing, did nothing. His instincts all told him to remain silent, remain invisible, remain out of it.

"Are *you* OK?" Hammond said to Lilly.

"Go," Lilly answered, as all looked hard at the small television monitors and listened as Mike Howley spoke the words:

"Gentlemen, each of you has the fundamental right and practical opportunity to stop it right now. Do I proceed?"

I was watching this with some two-hundred-plus other reporters of all media and persuasions on one of the many television sets that had been placed up, down, and around the Virginia Room. There had been a slight stirring noise from the beginning, as there usually is in the press at events like this. Suddenly, almost as if somebody had flipped a switch, the Virginia Room got absolutely silent, except for the noise that was coming out of the televisions.

In the control room, Turpin yelled at Meredith in the TV monitors: "No! Say No! Say No! Say No! Get out of there!"

Lilly said quietly to his man in the monitors: "It's all right, Governor. It's all right."

Turpin shot his right hand into a fist and then into the air and screamed: "They're going to screw you! Stop it! Walk away!"

"By all means, proceed," David Donald Meredith said to Howley and to the world.

Turpin put his head in his hands and said: "No, no, no. It's over. It's over."

Lilly said to the monitors: "Go, Governor, go."

★

Paul L. Greene's face had been locked into a worried scowl for the nine months since he declared his long-shot candidacy for the Democratic nomination. Now the panelists and the people saw a real grin, the happy kind people get when surprised on their birthday or when winning the state lottery.

"Proceed," said Governor Greene to Howley and the world.

Howley said to the two candidates:

"Thank you, gentlemen. We believe the central dividing element between you, as with all candidates for president, is that of character. No matter the rightness or wrongness of a candidate, a president, on any given issue or set of issues, the underlying power of that person lies in his or her character. We have come to the conclusion that it is a particularly crucial and cutting issue in your election. That is what we want to discuss with you for the next ninety minutes. We would like to begin with some questions designed to get to some basic attitudes about various subjects and people—and ultimately to the question: What kind of men, people, human beings are you?"

David Donald Meredith must have known now for absolute sure what was going to happen. It might not be the first question, but it was coming. He refused to discuss any of this with me (or anyone else), but it is not difficult to imagine what kinds of questions must have been ricocheting through his mind and psyche at that moment:

Do I stand here and take it? Do I fight? Do I remain here in front of all of humanity and participate in such a despicable and dangerous exercise? Do I preempt these usurpers, these scums, these criminals? Confront them now, right this minute? Challenge them, dare them? Do I storm off in anger, refusing to participate in such a shameful last-minute attempt to steal this election victory? Do I run? Do I stay? Where is the greater risk? Can I take them? Can they take me?

Paul L. Greene told Bob Schieffer in a postdebate interview that he was confused but confident at that moment. There was no panic, no fear. He considered Mike Howley to be a respected, reputable person and journalist. He acknowledged he was no fan of Joan Naylor and he assumed she, like all of those TV showboats, would do anything for a rating point or a point of attention. He knew nothing about the other two. But he was comfortable. He knew there was nothing of a "character" nature they could go after him about. But. What in the hell *is* going on here? What *can* I do? If I walk, I say I am afraid of answering questions about my character. If I stay, I say I am a weakling, somebody who can be pushed around by four journalists making their own rules. But then he realized that he had nothing more to lose. Absolutely nothing. That gave him confidence. That made him calm. Proceed, please. Proceed.

Whatever either may have been thinking, neither Greene nor Meredith said a word or made a move. They were both still standing silent at their podiums when Howley opened the bomb-bay door for the first drop. He said: "We'd like to begin with a series of questions about a character issue that arose only this afternoon. Henry Ramirez?"

Henry said he did not mind going first. Back in Longsworth D he had even volunteered to do so. He said he crossed himself in his mind like the good Catholic that he was, repeated, Muy bien, my son, to himself and then said to Greene: "Governor, does your campaign have a private security firm working for it?"

"No, it does not," Greene answered.

"How do you do background checks on personnel, friends and enemies, the press, and other things like that?"

"We do not do such things. We are not interested in investigating anyone. We have no need for any private detectives."

Henry turned toward Meredith. "Does your campaign employ a security firm?"

"I believe we do, yes. I fail to understand the relevance of such a question, however. Please, Mr. . . . ."

"Ramirez. My name is Henry Ramirez."

"I know your name." Meredith held up a piece of paper. "It's written down right here, in fact."

Henry said he could hear his mother and everybody at the café and maybe a few other places in Falfurrias cheering. *Ramirez. My name is Henry Ramirez.*

He said to Meredith: "The name of that security firm is Nelson and Associates, is it not? Isn't that the one that works for you?"

"I believe they do some security work for us, yes."

"Doing background checks on people?"

"I'm not sure of the scope of their work."

"Does some of their work for you involve electronic surveillance?"

"Certainly not! I am outraged that you would even suggest such a thing." The camera was right on Meredith's face. It was in a full glower as he looked right at Mike Howley. "If this is your idea of asking about the essential issue of this campaign, sir, I believe I can tell you that you have lost your senses, Mr. Howley. This is an outrage. I would remind the four of you that this is a debate about the presidency of the United States, about the future of the United States, the most powerful nation in the world."

Howley responded in a quiet, confident voice: "As I said when we started, Mr. Meredith, you are free to go at any time. You said to proceed. We have done so. If you are now saying, stop, then we stop. It's your call, sir."

"I have never run from a fight and I am not about to start now, particularly one with the likes of you . . . you people in the press, you self-appointed . . ."

It hung there. "You self-appointed . . ." You self-appointed *what*? Nancy Dewey and her director kept the camera right on Meredith's face. What were the words he was considering and discarding until he found the right one? Watchdogs? Arbiters? Gods? Emperors? Dictators? Fools? Idiots? Sinners? Scumbags?

"Yes, sir?" Howley said. "You were saying?"

"Never mind," Meredith sneered, and then waved Howley off with his right hand.

The camera shot switched to Howley. The whole world saw him nod again to Henry Ramirez. Proceed, young man, proceed.

Henry was very nervous at this point. Not only did he have to speak coherently, he now had to move with force and grace. As confident as he was, he was aware of the potential for making an ass of himself and the entire exercise.

He said to Meredith: "I have something here in my hand that I would like for you to look at, sir."

Henry got up from his chair, as he had seen Raymond Burr as Perry Mason, the people on *L.A. Law,* and many another TV lawyer do, and as he had rehearsed in his hotel room many times that afternoon. He walked the ten feet over to Meredith and handed him something too small for anyone watching on television to see and thus identify.

With head up, shoulders back, Henry then walked deliberately back to his seat at the panelists' table and sat down again. He said to Meredith: "Sir, do you know what that is?"

"I do not," said Meredith, the sneer back in place. I would give anything to know what that man was thinking at that very moment. Could he have begun to see his election as president of the United States slipping away?

"Mr. Meredith, that is a miniature microphone."

"Well?"

"We found it this afternoon under a bowl of ice cream that was brought to us by room service at the Williamsburg Lodge."

"So?"

"Did people from Nelson and Associates put that microphone there on your behalf?"

"No! No, no, no. I cannot believe you are asking me that!"

Meredith's face showed some fresh coloring. He turned away from Henry again and faced Howley. He said: "Mr. Howley, please ask your Ms. Manning there about her roommate. Doesn't she work for the Greene campaign? They'd have no need to bug a room. They have their own person working on Governor Greene's behalf right there inside the room."

Mike Howley turned to Barbara Manning and said: "It is true that your roommate works for Governor Greene, isn't it?"

Barbara assumed that the television picture to all fifty states, around the world, and to Mars and all the stars and planets became her distressed face about the time Howley said, ". . . isn't it?" She assumed that the peoples of the nation, the world, and the universe saw in her eyes and mouth and ears and nose the composite look of an assassin, a serial killer, and a child molester. She assumed that the billions of people in the television audience were holding their breaths for the confession, for the ultimate *Oprah*.

She had thought the subject of Barbara Hayes might get raised, but she didn't think it would be this early in the debate. Howley had told her to have an answer ready. "Tell the truth, the whole truth, and nothing but the truth," he had said. So she'd thought about what she might say. And now she was saying it to Howley and the billions. "Yes. Yes, she is my roommate. But I have said nothing to her about anything having to do with what was said by any of the panelists about this debate. We talked briefly the afternoon I was selected for the panel but not about anything other than the fact that I was selected."

Was that the truth, the whole truth, and nothing but the truth? Not quite. She and Barbara Hayes talked about slightly more than just her being selected. Barbara Hayes had made a direct appeal for help in saving the country from the probability of a Meredith presidency.

Howley asked Barbara: "Did you tell Barbara Hayes or anyone else what was said or decided by any one of the four of us during our debate preparations last night and today?"

"No, I did not. I certainly did not. Not one word. The four of us agreed to tell no one and I have certainly kept that agreement."

Howley looked back at Meredith, who said: "And I guess we are simply to believe her? She speaks, we say, Yes, ma'am, whatever you say, ma'am?"

"Believing or not believing, of course, is in the mind of the listener, sir," Howley said.

"I cannot imagine any one of the four of you or anyone else in the press letting somebody like me . . . or even the governor here or anyone else in public or political life get away with such an appearance problem with a dismissive denial like that. The double standards that you people, you—"

"Self-appointed something-or-others, sir? You never did finish that a while ago."

The reporters in the pressroom with me had been stunned into a state of funereal quiet up till this moment. Now somebody yelled out: "Point to Howley!" And there were some quick but thunderous cheers and applause before the room fell—switched, click—silent again.

"The tone and substance of this travesty is beyond all that is considered professional and fair and civil, Mr. Howley," Meredith said.

Howley said: "I take it the Nelson people were the ones who told you about Barbara Manning's roommate?"

"I don't remember who told me," Meredith said. "It's common knowledge."

"No, it isn't!" Barbara barked out.

Another cheer—smaller and shorter—went up in the pressroom.

Howley said to Meredith: "So on the issue of who bugged our meeting room, sir. You are saying nobody connected with your campaign or in the employment of your campaign had anything at all to do with that tiny microphone and the placement thereof in our room—Longsworth D, just down the hall here in the Williamsburg Lodge?"

"That is exactly what I am saying! How dare you speak to me as if you are some kind of prosecuting attorney! I am not in the dock. I am not on trial."

"No one is suggesting you are, sir—"

"If you have any proof about any of this, put it out here now in front of us all so we can see it. Do your Mister District Attorney. Let's have it. Call your witnesses. This is an outrage, a travesty."

"We are going to ask the FBI to investigate," Mike Howley said.

"So you have no proof, is that it?"

"We will leave it to proper authorities—"

"You people of the press love to talk about McCarthy tactics." Meredith found the camera that was on him and spoke right into it. "My fellow Americans, you have seen an example of McCarthyism of the highest order. Here, in front of you, I have been accused of placing a hidden microphone on the bottom of an ice-cream bowl in order to eavesdrop on the deliberations of these four journalists. But when I ask for proof, what do I get? Nothing! I get nothing! This little thing?" He held the microphone up in front of him. "He says this is a miniature microphone. Is it really? I have no idea. What if it is? Where did it come from? He says from the bottom of an ice-cream bowl. Could it have been purchased by one of these distinguished journalists at some neighborhood electronics shop? Or maybe Miss Manning's Greene-operative friend acquired it and gave it to them. Who knows, who knows, who knows? What we do know is that the outrageousness of this is beyond the pale of anything I could ever have imagined. They talk about police states. Talk about the New Arrogants. My fellow Americans, we are seeing here tonight the end result of the New Arrogants' Press State in America. It's our America. We must take it back."

He dropped his head and closed his eyes. He must have assumed— prayed, hoped, imagined, dreamed—that they were cheering for him out there in television land. From the close-up view of his bowed head it appeared as if he could hear them and was, in fact, listening to them. From my perspective in the Virginia Room I had no idea how it was playing out there in television land, but it seemed to me that Meredith had gotten the better of the exchange. I wrote in my notes: "Score—Meredith. Cheap shot—no proof." I was sitting at a table between a young woman reporter from *The San Diego Union-Tribune* and an older man reporter from *The Kansas City Star.* Until this moment not a word had been spoken out loud by any one of the three of us since we had been frozen silent by Howley's opening statement. Now the *Star* man, to my right, murmured: "I feel something serious happening out there." "Me, too," I responded. "Incredible," said the San Diego woman.

Howley ignored Meredith and said: "Barbara Manning will ask the next series of questions. Barbara?"

All right, here we are, Gramma Maude, she thought. Here we are at all of the gates—the gates to hell, to heaven, to glory, to the Promised Land, to life, to death, to happiness, to shame, to immortality, to mortality, to fame, to fortune, to infamy, to poverty, to everything. Watch me, Gramma Maude. Watch me, watch me. Hold my hand, hold my hand. Pray for me, pray for me. Hold my hand! Here I go!

Barbara said to Meredith: "It's been suggested . . . charged, alleged . . . repeatedly during this campaign that you would be a dividing president. That when you look at people with my color skin, for instance, you see—"

Meredith shook his head and held up his hand for her to stop. "Young lady, please—"

"If I might finish my question, Mr. Meredith?" Look at me, Gramma Maude! Hold my hand tight!

"No, you may not finish! I'll tell you what I see when I look at you. I see a troubled and misguided soul. I see somebody who needs help in finding her way. I see neither black nor white, male nor female, liberal nor conservative—"

"Wait a minute!" It was Greene. Governor Paul L. Greene of Nebraska, the Democratic candidate for president of the United States. The other man on the stage, the guy behind the other podium, the one who hadn't said hardly anything yet. His voice was unnaturally loud, firm.

"If I may finish," Meredith said.

"No, you may not finish," Greene said. "No matter what words you weave and dispense now—tonight—the words you have thrown around during this campaign up till now have already offered a full-formed answer to Miss Manning's question. And that answer is a loud Yes. You are a divider. When you look down—and down is clearly the direction you look—at people like Ms. Manning with skin a color different than yours, you see a different and lesser American. You see an inferior person, a person you do not believe is equal to you, your kind, our kind—"

"That is a blasphemous lie!"

"That is a disgraceful truth!"

"Prove it! Prove it if you can!"

"Your own words prove it!"

"Be fair! Be fair if you can!"

Paul L. Greene, the man Joan Naylor and others had suggested was among the worst presidential candidates in the history of American politics, did what Meredith had done a few moments before. He looked right into the camera that was trained on him.

And he said directly to the television audience: " 'Be fair,' he said. Yes, we must be fair to this man. So fair we will be. I just leveled a charge and he answered it. It is up to you to judge the validity and the veracity of our competing thoughts and words. In that spirit—that spirit of basic American and human fairness—I ask you, my fellow and sister Americans of all ages and races and politics, to think through what you have heard this man say during this campaign. Not just now but in stump speeches and in campaign commercials. Think through his position on enforcing civil-rights laws in a way that would all but end affirmative action as a method for redress for all minorities who feel they have been discriminated against. Think about what he has said about there being a cultural war raging in this country between the forces of sin and evil—the Democratic party forces of abortion, murder, gun control, and perverted sex—and his forces, the Take It Back forces of family, love, discipline, prayers, and lullabies that have taken over the Republican party. What is he saying really? Ask yourself that question and then answer it. Answer it honestly. . . ."

"He's alive after all," whispered the San Diego reporter on my left. "He talks, he breathes, he's real," said the Kansas City man on my right. I agreed but said nothing. My head was alive with the certainty that I was watching—along with the rest of the press corps in the Virginia Room and America and the world—the most remarkable event of its kind ever. And what none of us knew then was that the best—or the worst, depending on the view—was yet to come.

"I cannot let this go on!" Meredith yelled. It was a real yell. His voice was loud and ragged and high. It immediately reminded me of the way he exploded during the debate rehearsal back at the Omni–Newport News.

Greene said: "Are you going to bow your head and pray? God cannot help you out of your words, out of the patterns of hate and discrimination and division that you have woven—"

"You talk to me! You attempt to preach to me! The answer to your charges will come on Election Day, Governor. The American people are listening to you, and they have been listening to you. They will provide the answer, not me. I am their servant." Then to Mike Howley he said: "What happens now, Mister Moderator? Do your job, please, or I really will exit myself from this attempt to thwart the democratic process. . . ."

★

In the control room Chuck Hammond took a call from the president of CNS News. Then came calls from executives of all the other networks. The chairmen of the Democratic and Republican national committees phoned. So did the two co-chairmen and three of the seven other members of the debate commission. In each case, Hammond listened to their varied inquiries, messages, and requests and then said, No, I did not know this was going to happen. Yes, Howley asked me about the procedure and I did compare it to a thunderstorm. No, I had no idea why he asked. Yes, it is out of my hands. No one—not even the Republican chairman, John Singletary—demanded that Hammond go out there and stop it.

Hammond received the most significant news from the outside in the calls from the network people. He passed it on to Brad Lilly and Jack Turpin: "The United States of America has come to a screeching halt out there. People are getting out of their cars to run into places and watch it on television. People by the millions are calling networks, radio stations, newspaper offices, to react. To shout, holler, threaten. It might beat *Roots* and the Super Bowl."

Turpin responded to the news in a tone used by the surviving families of mass murders and terrorist attacks: "You will pay for this, Hammond. All of you will pay for this. I mean pay. Do you hear me?"

We of the press in the Virginia Room were also being informed about then of what was happening out in the country because of what was happening down the hall from us on that stage. Young people in blazers moved silently among us, distributing photocopies of stories about the flocking of the people of America to the closest television set.

★

Then came the main event.

Howley said to David Donald Meredith: "Mr. Meredith, do you know a woman named Jonell Jane Hampstead?"

"I'm not sure," said Meredith.

The camera was right up close on his face. I could tell—anyone looking could tell—that here was a man in torment. Clearly, after the fact it is easy to conclude that for Meredith the moment had truly come. He had reached the point of ultimate conflict, of no return. It was decision time. And the presidency of the most powerful nation in the world hung in the decision.

Do I, David Donald Meredith, bring this travesty to a screeching halt? But what does it really halt? If I walk off this stage, these terrible people will have quite a story about that, and they will also simply release their other story to their fellow travelers in the press anyhow. I can't halt anything. They will run it without my comment, my response, my reaction. I will appear to have run from a fight. But if I refuse to play their game, will the people—the real people of America watching this spectacle now—side with me or with them? This is outrageous behavior these four people are engaging in. It goes against everything the press in my America supposedly stands for. If I survive this, I guarantee something will be done about the press in my country. I guarantee it!

Whatever thought route he may have taken to get there, the camera showed the face of a spirit switched to OFF.

Howley moved on. He said: "She is a woman who says she worked for you in your Take It Back headquarters office in Charlotte, North Carolina, as a part-time secretary from May 1986 until June 1988."

Meredith kept his eyes on Howley. With a monumental effort that was actually perceptible to us television viewers, the Republican candidate for president of the United States changed the look on his face as cleanly and decidedly as if he had slapped on a Halloween mask. There, slap, look at me now. Now I am a man at ease with himself, with this situation. I am a picture of serenity and comfort. Look at me and my relaxed state. This absurdity is no problem for me. No problem at all. I can handle these people. I can handle anything. God and the people are with me. It is the godless and the press who are not. *Only* the godless and the press. Serene and comfortable. That is what I am right now. You can see it here in my face.

Again, Meredith said not a word. I do not ever recall even hearing about a few seconds of silence—a full twelve seconds, according to my count from the videotape afterward—that matched those for their shrieking intensity. "Never in the history of American politics has there been a louder silence" was the way the columnist Richard Field described it the next day. The Virginia Room, jammed with more than three hundred people who are seldom quiet, was absolutely noise-free. I had never experienced anything like it, even in personal terms. Postdebate reporting said it happened almost everywhere people were gathered in front of television sets for those twelve seconds. *Click-uh, click-uh, click-uh*, they went, one after the other, as Nancy Dewey and her director, a man named Richard Deutsch, moved back and forth between full head shots of Meredith and Howley. *Click-uh, click-uh, click-uh.* Meredith, Howley, Meredith, Howley, Meredith, Howley.

Howley broke the silence. He said: "She claims in a notarized statement that I have before me now that she observed you striking your daughter Allison, who was then fourteen years old. She said you hit her in the stomach with your right fist after she confessed to you that she had accompanied some friends to a movie called *Last Tango in Paris* starring Marlon Brando."

Howley stopped. It was an opportunity for Meredith to speak. Was he going to take it? Was he going to remain silent? For how much longer?

Meredith's mind must have been racing at full throttle. But it could not be seen in his face, which remained in a state of serenity and comfort. Remain calm, remain calm, he must have been saying to himself. You are calm. Count some numbers. Think of other things. Remain calm. Say nothing. Show nothing. You're on top of this. You're in charge. This godless man of the press will not prevail! He will not get me!

Again, Mike Howley went on. "She said that your daughter left your office bent over, crying. She said that when she—the woman employee— moved to help your daughter, you ordered her to leave her alone. Within ten days she was told that her job in your organization had been eliminated. Then she learned in fact that someone else was hired after her departure to fill it. Would you like to comment, Mr. Meredith?"

I felt I was now about to be an eyewitness to a catastrophe, a tragic, earth-rumbling collision. Two elephants butting heads in an open field at a dead run. Two Metroliners crashing head-on north of Baltimore at speeds of 125 miles an hour. I remembered the debate rehearsal again, but I also recalled something I had just read that afternoon. It was a story in that packet of material the research department at *The New American Tatler* had FedExed to Williamsburg for me. Yes, it was something about Meredith's father in a profile of Meredith in the *Charlotte Observer*. James Grayson Meredith was a car salesman in Rocky Mount, North Carolina, who had dropped dead of a heart attack when he was forty-seven years old. It happened late one Friday afternoon just after a customer had rescinded an order to buy a new blue loaded Ford Victoria four-door sedan. The original sale had put Meredith's father over the top in a Ford Million-Dollar Salesman contest that had as its prize an all-expenses-paid trip for him and his family to New Orleans for Mardi Gras. The shock of losing it after having won it stopped his heart. The *Observer* story said it embedded profound like-father/like-son possibility fears deeply inside Meredith's mother. As a result, she was obsessive-compulsive in preaching to her lone son David Donald about the lifesaving need to be peaceful, easy, serene, comfortable.

"No, I would not like to comment," that son said now to Michael J. Howley and the world. His demeanor and his manner were those of a lone son who had been taught to be peaceful, easy, serene, comfortable. "The shame of what you are doing to me right now is on you, Mr. Howley. It is one that is for you to bear and to wear like a crown of thorns. Your soul will bleed from those thorns, Mr. Howley. I have nothing to say. Not now. Nothing at all."

★

We in the Virginia Room were informed via distributed wire copy that motorcades of angry Meredith supporters were being organized in Norfolk, Richmond, and in the northern Virginia suburbs of Washington to drive to Williamsburg. One of the leaders was quoted as saying: "We will take back democracy from those four arrogant criminals of the press."

In the control room an ABS producer passed on the same information to Hammond. He whispered it to Turpin, who said: "Great. I hope they arm themselves and come in shooting." Lilly barely heard the report. He shushed Hammond. He did not want to miss a word of what was going on out there on that stage. What he was experiencing then made up for every bad or awful thing that had ever happened to him. He found himself several times on the verge of humming out loud "America the Beautiful" and other songs, including offbeat ones such as "Mack the Knife" and "Jesus Loves Me."

★

Mike Howley said: "Joan Naylor will now ask the next series of questions."

Everything had happened with such stunning quickness that I had not focused on the fact that Joan Naylor had yet to be heard since the debate began. Joan Naylor, the most experienced and comfortable of the four on live television, had not said one word.

Paul L. Greene chose that moment to speak. "Pardon me," he said to Howley. "There are two of us up here, Mike. May I comment on what has just been said?"

"Certainly, sir," said Howley. "Forgive me."

Greene turned toward Meredith and said: "I would just like for you, Mr. Meredith, to know that what is happening here now is as much a surprise to me as it is to you. I hope you believe that."

Meredith did not respond. He did not even look back at Greene.

Greene continued: "While I have leveled my criticisms of you on the issues and your opinions and beliefs, I do not believe matters of a personal nature have any place in a campaign for president of the United States. This kind of journalism of the leer that has taken over our airwaves and printed pages is something to be condemned."

★

"Shut up!" Brad Lilly screamed at the control-room television monitors. "For God's sake, shut up!"

Turpin screamed: "Right, Governor! More, more! For *my* sake, more!"

★

Joan thought at that moment that it was over. Paul L. Greene had stopped them in their tracks. She was so focused on what she was going to do that the rightness or wrongness of what Greene said did not penetrate her consciousness. She only saw this man Greene, standing behind a podium directly across from her, as an idiot, a fool, a ninny. Here we are, on the verge of making you president of the United States, and you're trashing us. Take it away, David Donald Meredith. The United States of America is all yours!

She looked to her left at Mike Howley. She had to go through the eyes and around the faces of Barbara and Henry to get to Howley's. Joan saw fear in those kids—even Henry—and she did not blame them. Joan's reading was correct. Done, cooked, in the garbage, was what Barbara thought at that moment. Henry was wondering what it was going to be like picking peaches in the Valley the rest of his life.

But Joan read resolve and confidence in Howley's face. It was just enough to pull her back to the fact that what was happening here was not up to Paul L. Greene. They—the four of them—had made a decision to take direct action to prevent this evil man David Donald Meredith from taking over the United States of America. They had decided the country would not be his. Nothing had changed.

Howley said to her and to the world: "As I said, Joan Naylor will ask the next series of questions. Joan?"

Joan said to Greene: "Are you saying hitting a teenage child in the stomach falls into the category of journalism of the leer, Governor?"

"I am saying what I said," Greene said.

Joan, in a steady voice, said to Meredith: "Another woman, named Yolanda Dinkins, has made a statement concerning your wife—"

"Is nothing sacred to you people?" Meredith said. "Can you not leave my daughter and my wife out of this?"

"No, I am afraid we cannot," Joan said. "Yolanda Dinkins, a former neighbor of yours and your wife's in Charlotte, North Carolina, says in her statement that your wife, Madeline, came screaming and crying to her home one Sunday evening in 1986. She says your wife's face was swollen and red around her left eye. When asked what happened, she said, and I quote: 'David got mad at me.' Do you have a response?"

Meredith bowed his head and closed his eyes. "Dear Father in heaven, forgive these four people of the detestable, arrogant press for the sins against God and the truth and the people and our democracy they are committing. Give the great people of this great country the strength and courage to see this for what it is—a blatant, arrogant attempt to thwart the will of the democratic majority, to wrest from the people their right to decide who shall lead their country and their spirit as president of the United States. In Your name I pray—we all pray. Amen."

He looked up and at Joan. "That is my response, Mrs. Naylor, to your awfulness, to your sins."

Greene raised his right hand. On television it appeared as if he was back in school. Call on me, please. I have the answer. I have something to say.

"Yes, Governor," Joan said. You are called on.

"Lest anyone think otherwise from my earlier comments," he said, "I want to say that spouse abuse, child abuse—abuse of one human being of any kind by another—is abhorrent. I condemn it with all of the energy and strength I can muster."

★

In the control room Lilly clapped his hands and stomped his feet. "My hero," he said. "Greene, Greene, he's our man. . . ."

Turpin was hot again. "Mark my words, everyone in hearing distance of my voice, somebody is going to pay for this atrocity against humanity and decency. Television, journalism, this stupid debate commission, none of you will survive this. None of you. All of you are going to be made to pay by the new Meredith administration. Stand by and bend over, friends. Every single one of you. You had better pray that you have not cheated on your income taxes, harbored an illegal-alien maid, driven five miles over the speed limit, put an unstamped letter in a mailbox—"

"Now, is that any way for the manager of the campaign of God's chosen candidate to speak?" Lilly said. "Surely, what is happening out there is God's will? Can it be anything other than that? Doesn't God will everything? Could this possibly mean God has switched sides? Or is nonpartisan? God, God, he's our man, if he can't do it, nobody can."

Hammond detected a slight inclination toward mayhem in Turpin's body language. It caused him to reflexively stand and face Turpin, as if he were a human shield. He would prevent Jack Turpin, professional campaign manager, from slaying, maiming, or otherwise hurting Brad Lilly, professional campaign manager.

★

Back out on the stage, Joan Naylor said: "Mr. Meredith, I have another statement here from a woman named Bonnie Kerr. She states that she worked for you as an assistant editor at the Take It Back Publishing Company. She says that in a state of rage over her inability to find a particular manuscript, you shoved her against a concrete wall. She badly bruised her back and cracked a bone in an elbow. Do you have a response, sir?"

Meredith said: "Have you absolutely no shame, no ethics? That is my response."

Joan said: "I have a statement from a woman named Terri Anne Cloverdell. She states that you slugged her hard on her left arm after she failed to bring a book to you as quickly as you had asked. She worked as a desk assistant in the Take It Back Reference Library in Charlotte. Did that happen?"

Meredith only closed his eyes and shook his head. The camera was right on him. I was no longer able to read anything from his face. The peace and serenity were gone. That was certain. Nothing else was, though. Was he going to attack, to bolt, to blow? I could not tell.

Howley said: "Now back to Henry Ramirez for some questions. Henry?"

Henry said: "Another statement, Mr. Meredith. It is from René Jeanne Jarvis, who worked as cleaning woman at your home in Charlotte. She swore in this statement before a notary that she watched you—with her own eyes—slap your wife because she failed to have some laundry and dry cleaning picked up. She thinks she remembers it was a dark blue suit you needed to wear that night at a meeting of your Take It Back Foundation board of trustees."

"You are sick people," said Meredith. To the camera, he added: "I ask you, my fellow Americans, has there ever been anything like this in the political history of this country? Can this be America? Can this be our treasured democracy, where four self-righteous members of the press—unelected, unchosen by anyone—decide to lynch a candidate for president of the United States right here before the whole world on national television? Has there ever in all of our history ever been a more egregious abuse of power? Can this be America? Must we also take back our free press?"

"If I may," said Paul L. Greene, not raising his hand or waiting to be called on. "What you say may be true. But it also may be true that this is the first time in history that a candidate for president of the United States is a man prone to violent outbreaks of force and harm to his fellow human beings. I believe that knowing this about a person is a legitimate issue in a presidential campaign. I really do. I see now that these four brave journalists deserve commendations and praise for their courage. I am sure it was not easy for them to do what they are doing here tonight. But they know, as the American people know, no country can be governed by a president who is going to emotionally explode at any moment and start throwing punches at his aides, his loved ones—anyone's loved ones."

A fast, intense cheer went up in the Virginia Room.

Meredith glared at Greene. "You are not even an irrelevant pimple on this dire and atrocious happening, Governor. I have nothing to say to you. Nothing at all." He then turned his face again toward Mike Howley. "Are you through, Mr. Howley? Are you and your three co-conspirators through? Is this unsavory political assassination attempt finished?"

Howley said: "No, sir, we are not through. Barbara Manning has a question." He looked to his right and nodded to Barbara.

She said to Meredith: "I have here the statements of three women who state they lived in the same freshman dormitory with your daughter Allison while all were students at Duke University in Durham, North Carolina. That was six years ago, long before you entered politics—as a presidential candidate, at least. All three of these women claim they were present in the room of your daughter when she told them you had, in her words, 'a tendency to fly off the handle,' end quote. And that when you did so you could, quote, 'get pretty mean and violent.' She showed them some scars on her back and claimed they were from leather-belt beatings you had administered. She said she had also seen you strike your mother, her aunt—your sister—and several other female relatives."

All peace, all serenity, was now gone from Meredith's face. I could feel an eruption coming—I really could. Meredith said nothing. Howley said to him: "I take it you have no comment on these three women's story."

"You may take what you wish, Mr. Howley," said Meredith. He was only a few minutes—seconds, maybe—from exploding. I was sure of it.

"Henry Ramirez," Howley said.

"Mr. Meredith," said Henry, "there are nine other statements from women who claim they either experienced or heard about similar kinds of acts by you. In each case, as in the others, you are alleged to have committed an act of physical violence against someone, usually a woman or a child. And in each case that act of violence came in the midst of an angry fit. Why is it, by the way, that you only seem to hit women and children? Do you never blow your stack at a man?"

Meredith's head was down as if in silent prayer. Not even his eyes could be seen.

Joan, without an introductory word from Howley, picked it up. "I have a statement from a woman who states she was involved in a minor traffic accident in a suburb of Asheville, North Carolina, in 1989. She says her foot slipped off the brake of her car in a rainstorm and she slammed into the rear of a car driven by you. She said she immediately jumped out of her car to express her apologies for what had happened and that you grabbed her by her yellow slicker raincoat, threw her against your car, and kicked her in the right shin. She said you then twirled her around and smashed her head into the rear window of your car. She swears it was you and says she can prove it was you because she kept a Xerox copy of the check she received from a law firm representing you. In exchange for silence and for not preferring charges, she got a check for eight thousand dollars. Did that happen, Mr. Meredith? She says it did."

Meredith said nothing. He kept his head down.

Joan said: "I have another statement here from a woman named Isabelle Anne Mathews. She was working as a passenger service agent for USAir in Charlotte when you came to her gate to catch a flight to New York's La Guardia Airport. She states you arrived a few minutes after the door had been closed, and the plane was about to leave the gangway— already retracted from the door of the plane. She says you demanded that she stop the plane so you could get aboard. When she refused, she claims you slammed your hard-edged leather briefcase against her legs. An airport security officer was called. You were detained but then released. Your comment, sir?"

Meredith still did not raise his head.

Joan said: "Here is a statement from a waitress in the restaurant at the Ritz-Carlton Hotel in the Buckhead section of Atlanta. She claims you turned over a plate of food on the floor and stabbed the empty plate into her groin area because you said the food was not properly cooked. Your comment, sir?"

Meredith was still neither looking nor talking.

Joan was through. Mike Howley nodded to Henry Ramirez.

Henry said: "The question, in summary, Mr. Meredith, is would you care to confirm or deny or comment in any way to the American people at this time on the apparent fact that you have a tendency toward violent behavior—"

Henry did not finish the question because the force of the hatred and loathing that was in David Donald Meredith's face and body stopped him. It leapt out of the television set like a crazed animal. Stand by. Here it comes.

Meredith said: "How dare you question me, you . . . Mister . . . whoever you are, wherever you came from."

"Henry Ramirez is who I am, sir. My mother is named Luisa and she owns and operates her own café in Falfurrias, Texas. She and my father, who was a fruit picker, came to the United States from Mexico as illegal aliens forty-three years ago. They became American citizens and they are Americans. I, their son, am a native-born American who works for Continental Radio News. Now you know who I am and where I came from, sir."

Meredith took the bait solidly in his mouth and hooked himself to political death.

He said to Henry in a manner soaked with contempt: "I already knew all I wanted to know about you and your kind, thank you."

"That I wouldn't argue about," said Henry. "When you looked down at me you saw only a little Mescan, I bet. A wetback, a spic, the very kind of person you do not want more of in this country. What right does he have to be here, to ask me—big-gringo-shot talk-man me—questions about anything? He probably even smells like grease and salsa and corn chips. That is what you knew about me. That is what you thought about me."

I could tell the reporters in the Virginia Room wanted to cheer again. But there wasn't time. There wasn't a way to make any noise, to interfere, to interrupt.

Meredith said: "Tell us about the liquor and health violations that your mother has committed in that café of hers."

★

In the control room Turpin was the only one who spoke. Not everyone heard him, in fact, because his volume was so low. Those who could hear reported his words to be: "No, not that. Don't bring that up. Not now. It's too late for that. No, no, no."

★

"What do you want to know about them?" Henry said to Meredith. I was then only vaguely aware of how old this kid radio reporter from Texas was. But I was struck now with how well he was handling himself in an extremely difficult situation. I could not, sitting there in the Virginia Room at that moment, have imagined a more difficult one.

Governor Paul L. Greene said: "This is getting nasty. Is this relevant to anything that matters?"

Mike Howley ignored the duly nominated Democratic candidate for president of the United States and said to Meredith: "Did the Nelson and Associates detectives provide you that information about Henry Ramirez's mother and her restaurant, Mr. Meredith?"

"I don't know. . . ."

"Please do not tell us it is common knowledge," Henry said.

Howley gave Henry Ramirez a glance that any fair-minded and well-trained observer would have had to describe as intimidating. Shut up, Henry, it said. Howley said nothing to Henry, speaking instead to Meredith. He said: "Is there anything else about any of the four of us you would like to put on the table at this time?"

Meredith waved him off with a flip of his right hand.

"All right then. If we could continue—"

Howley did not get to finish the sentence. Meredith looked up and right at him and said: "I know Joan Naylor's sister had an abortion when she was sixteen. I know you come from a family of deadbeats, Howley. I know *that*! I know about your uncle's bankruptcy! I know everything!"

Here now was one of several turning points in the event. My careful and repeated watching of the videotape of what happened, augmented by intensive and extensive interviews with others, have convinced me that Meredith might have still survived if it had not been for what Howley engineered right then.

Howley did not respond. And with his eyes and body language he kept the other three from doing so, too. The result was a terrible scene for Meredith. There he stood, his anger and rage virtually out of control, contrasted with the four reporters who were silent, calm, and under control. They were the ones of peace and serenity. The contrast and the silent moments that went with it were crushing to Meredith. I felt it watching. Others elsewhere said they felt the same way.

What we all saw was the spectacle of Meredith's face filling up and over with an unbearable, unmanageable hate. It seemed much longer, but by my clock, it was only six seconds before it all came out the top.

Meredith screamed: "Enough! No more!" He sounded like a man with a sword, an arrow, a javelin, a butcher knife, in his chest.

David Donald Meredith shook his right fist, first at Henry, then at Barbara and Joan, and then at Howley. "Each of you will be sorry for this. You will be tried and convicted and imprisoned for an act of revolution, the crime of illegally and immorally seeking to interfere with the legal process of a democratic presidential election. The trial might not be in a formal court but in the court of the American people, the court of public opinion. It will be done. I promise you. Each one of you. I promise that to your faces and to the faces of every person who is hearing and watching this anywhere in this country and in the world." And he bowed his head.

Nancy Dewey's camera went immediately to Mike Howley. I detected—others told me they did, too—a hankering in Howley to respond, to defend, to fight. But it clearly passed. Howley's restraint, his silence, decided the day. He was a Mister Roberts. Meredith was a Captain Queeg.

The camera was on Barbara when she reached her right hand to her right and put it gently on Henry's left. Henry returned the squeeze.

★

Out in the control room there was also silence.

Chuck Hammond found himself thinking about what he was going to say to the press and the commission members and to God and all others when this was over. He had a thought about the certain fact that no matter what finally happened, he and Nancy would from this evening on be known as the two people who produced the Greene-Meredith debate, maybe the most incredible single event in the history of presidential politics, of television, of life.

Jack Turpin at that moment saw himself with an AK-47, spraying shots around this control room, and then around that stage out there, and then in the press "spin" room, in the newsrooms of the networks and America's largest newspapers, and then at people in Safeways and Hechingers, in airports, bus depots, and train stations. He admitted to me that if he had been examined by a team of psychiatrists and psychologists at that moment, they would surely have found him to be insane, to be unable to distinguish right from wrong. He was certain that any jury of his peers would have found him innocent of mass murder or any other crime on grounds of justifiable homicide, if not of temporary insanity.

Brad Lilly was running names through his mind. Names of possible cabinet members for the Greene administration and top assistants he might hire for his staff at the Greene White House. Let's see now, we'll bring Schlesinger back in for Defense, give State to Bradley, put Rohatyn in Treasury, make Cutler attorney general—no, White House counsel. Wonder if I could get one of the old press hands to come in as press secretary. Hey, what about Howley? He'd be terrific. If not him, how about that Joan Naylor? A woman press secretary would be great. That Barbara Manning would be something, too. The first black press secretary. Not bad. Of course, that Chicano kid was pure dynamite. Why not make some history for the Hispanics? Didn't he say he was the son of illegal immigrants or something? Hey, hey, hey. And maybe we could wipe out crime and drug use, eliminate poverty and unemployment, rebuild the education and health-care systems. Hey, hey, hey. Hello, I'm Brad Lilly, the White House chief of staff. President Greene asked me to call you and tell you to do what I say or he will close down all military bases, post offices, and roadside parks in your state. Got that, Senator Helms? Senator Moynihan? Senator Gramm? Senator Kerrey? Senator Nunn? Senator Dole?

And then came the awful ending.

★

David Donald Meredith tore the microphone out of the podium in front of him.

He threw it with force toward Howley, barely missing his head.

Meredith picked up the wooden podium with his two hands and raised it over his head.

"No more of this!" he shouted. "No more!"

He threw the podium at the panelists' table. It crashed to the floor before it got that far and splintered into several pieces.

He screamed: "God will fucking punish all of you for this! You will fucking die! You will fucking perish!"

David Donald Meredith then turned to his left and exited the stage at a dead run.

It was 6:28, Eastern Standard Time.

8

Riots

Barbara Manning later described the stage, the space David Donald Meredith left behind, as airless. "Nobody was breathing in or out—not even Jesus is God Himself."

Every careful listener—including me—picked up a slight quivering in Michael J. Howley's voice when he spoke to camera the closing words:

"Well . . . I told the candidates that each had the right and the power to end this debate whenever he wished. Mr. Meredith has just exercised that right. There is nothing more that needs to be said . . . other than to thank the two candidates and my fellow panelists . . . and to say, from the Williamsburg Lodge in Colonial Williamsburg, Virginia, I'm Michael J. Howley of *The Washington Morning News*. . . . Thank you and good night."

Paul L. Greene, clearly the happiest man in the world at that moment in time, leapt toward the panelists' table. He went for Howley with arms outstretched. Howley stepped to the side in time to deflect an embrace. That was a television and/or still-photo shot he must have decided he did not want sent around the world. Greene ended up only with Howley's right hand in both of his. Greene shook it like it was a handle on an old-fashioned water pump.

"You have changed the course of America here tonight," said the Democratic candidate for president. His eyes were filled with tears. "What you have done is what the Minutemen did at Concord, Jefferson did in the Declaration of Independence, Armstrong did on the moon. I salute you. I honor you. I treasure you."

Greene did the same to Joan's right hand that he had done to Howley's. And then he did it to Barbara's and to Henry's. Nancy Dewey and her technicians had turned off the microphones but not the cameras. All of this was being seen on C-SPAN and several of the other broadcast entities that were carrying the event throughout the country and the world.

"You are American heroes, yes indeed you are," said Greene, as the four panelists pulled themselves away from him and headed for a break in the curtains in the rear of the stage.

Chuck Hammond, Jack Turpin, and Brad Lilly beat them to that spot, coming the other way.

"Congratulations," Lilly said. "You are at this particular moment the four most important people in America."

Hammond, Joan, Henry, and Barbara claim Turpin said: "If it takes me the rest of my life and all life on this planet and the rest of my energy and all energy, rest assured, you four will pay for what you did out there just now. Rest assured. Please, please, rest assured. You are Oswald. Ray. Sirhan Sirhan. You are assassins. You must be punished. You will be punished."

Turpin denies he meant anything he said as a threat to anybody's life.

The four panelists kept their heads and their tongues down. And they walked right on by Turpin, Lilly, and Hammond through the curtain.

Hammond called after them: "In a few minutes the Secret Service is going to open it up back here. A tidal wave of your friends and colleagues in the press is going to come down on this place and you four people unlike anything that has ever been seen. Think about how you want to handle it. You have about two minutes to think. Buzz me on extension four fifty-two. I'm here to serve. I'll set you up a news conference, whatever. . . ."

Mike Howley acknowledged the offer with a smile and a wave and, with the others, kept walking.

Tidal wave. A tidal wave was coming, Hammond said. They all four heard that. A tidal wave was coming in two minutes. What ever happened to the thunderstorm? Henry thought. Is a tidal wave worse than a thunderstorm? Barbara asked herself.

They opened the door of Longsworth D, their room. There was a man inside, there was a man inside their sanctuary, there was a man in there!

"Let me be the first ordinary American to say, simply, Thank you," he said to Howley, Barbara, Joan, and Henry. "Thank you for coming to the aid of your country at its most excruciating moment of need. Not since the Japs bombed Pearl Harbor has there been a moment like there was tonight."

Japs bombed Pearl Harbor? thought Joan. What is this? Who is this?

The man who said this was tanned, old, and dressed impeccably in a dark blue suit, shiny gold silk tie, white cuff-linked shirt, and a toupee of bright red hair.

"Who in the hell are you?" said Howley. He and the others were now inside. The door was closed behind them to keep away the tidal wave.

"My name is Sam. Sam Rhodes. I appear before you four American heroes now as the representative of Harry A. Mendelsohn himself."

Harry A. Mendelsohn?

"The man who made Dawn Now Productions what it is today. . . ."

Dawn Now?

"Harry authorized me to offer the four of you one million dollars each for the rights to your story. Plus a piece of the back end for foreign rights, videocassettes, T-shirts, baseball hats, doll replicas, whatever. He envisions a made-for-TV movie for CNS, a deal I heard him confirm on the speakerphone just now while I was on the other line. They're talking five nights during a sweeps week. One of you can write the screenplay. All four of you can write the screenplay. It's your call. Everything is your call. The whole world is your call. What do you say?"

"We say, Good-bye," Mike Howley said, moving Sam Rhodes toward the door.

"Harry's already got a working title," Sam said. " 'Williamsburg II.' Get it? History was made here once, now twice. The man's a genius."

And then Sam Rhodes was gone. The door was closed.

"How in the hell did he get in here?" Joan said. "Guys like him are always in here," she said, answering her own question.

A tidal wave was coming!

Howley said: "Before another second ticks away, let me say all of you were absolutely fantastic out there tonight."

He shook Henry's hand.

Barbara hugged Joan.

Henry hugged Joan, and Howley hugged Barbara.

And then Howley hugged Joan, and Henry hugged Barbara.

"You were incredible, brown boy," Barbara said.

"So were you, black girl," Henry said.

A tidal wave was coming!

"I can't believe it worked," Joan said. "He blew his cool. He blew it all."

"Just like you said he would, Mike," Henry said.

" 'Might,' " Howley said. "I said he might. If we got lucky."

"We got lucky, all right. 'Fucking.' The man of God and goodness yelled 'fucking.' I could not believe it!"

Henry said: "Three times! He did it three times!"

Barbara said: "How are the Christian-families people going to take that? He's a goner! We did it!"

Howley said: "The question now is what do we do about those awful jackals of the press? Hammond said we've got two minutes . . . less than that now."

"I should call my newsroom," Henry said. "I love the idea of some-body there having to interview me. 'Mr. Ramirez, tell us how you did it, why you did it. . . .' "

Barbara said: "*This Week* is going to want an exclusive, the real story from me. . . ."

Joan said: "My folks are going to be knocking that door down in a minute. . . ."

Mike Howley, still in control, said: "First, do we agree to talk?"

Yes, yes, the other three nodded.

"But nothing about what was said in Longsworth D," Howley said. "Can we agree in blood on that?"

Again, the other three nodded. Sure.

Howley said: "OK, then, what if we let Hammond set up a quick news conference first. Then we can go our separate ways with our own people. . . ."

So agreed. Howley's control remained firm and complete.

Or so he must have believed.

★

Within a second after Howley said his good night the Virginia Room erupted. There was hollering and shouting and people up and running like a mob for the door. The San Diego woman on my left was one of the few who stayed seated. She phoned her office. The *Kansas City Star* man said to me: "Let's go."

"Where to?"

"Who knows? Where everybody else is going."

I followed him out from behind our small table into a narrow aisle. We were immediately hit with the force of moving bodies behind us, almost picked up off the floor and swept away as if by a roaring current of a river flooding out of its banks.

There was a lot of good humor at first as we moved along toward the door. People laughed and there were jokes about pack journalism and feeding frenzies. Then I heard a scream up ahead. It sounded male, frantic. Somebody had been hurt. There was another scream from off in another direction. And another, and another. Somebody yelled: "Stop!" I heard some moans and other shouts of extreme profanity about pushing and shoving and knock it off.

I was caught, immobilized, squeezed in the center of a moving prison of bodies. I remembered the stories about the drunk fans being crushed to death at soccer games in Europe. I wondered how the *Tatler* would handle the story of their man dying in the line of duty, crushed to death by his colleagues in the media. The ultimate irony, the ultimate media event.

The *Star* man had disappeared! He had been right up against and almost in me on my right front, but suddenly he was no longer there. My God! What happened to him? I didn't even know his name. I felt something soft against my right foot and leg and heard a voice shouting: "Help me! Help me!" It was the man from *The Kansas City Star*.

I am thirty-four years old, five feet eleven inches tall, and I have what would probably be described as a medium build. I used all of what that added up to plus a rush of adrenaline to push myself down toward the *Star* man. I got hold of his suit coat with my right hand and pulled up with everything I had. He came up with me and I threw my arms around him in a bear hold. He was about my height, but he was limp. There was blood spewing out of his nose. I said to him: "You're going to be fine. You're all right." I held him and moved toward what I saw as a patch of daylight on my right.

Another man about my age but much bigger than me saw my problem. "Follow me," he said to me. I did. He told me afterward that he was a reporter in the Washington bureau of the *Baltimore Sun.* He said he had been a Navy SEAL in Vietnam and before that played football— offensive left guard—at the University of Wisconsin. He yelled things like "Make a hole! Wounded coming through! Get the fuck out of the way!" as he tossed his colleagues in the press to either side like they were department-store dummies.

In a few minutes we were at the daylight, up against a wall, still in the Virginia Room but away from the moving mob, out of harm's way.

We lay the *Star* man down on the floor. The bleeding had stopped, but he was unconscious.

"You OK here with him?" said the *Sun* man.

"Right, right," I said.

"I'll go find a medic, a doctor, something, and send them over."

And as if he were the Lone Ranger or Superman, he disappeared back toward and then into the moving human mass of media, all of whom I hated and detested at that moment. I saw them as something nonhuman, as animals. I was ashamed to be one of them, ashamed that I had been part of the mob, the riot, the stampede. I was no better than any of them. I was one of them. It was the lowest point of my professional life as a journalist.

I stayed right there until a two-man medical team with a stretcher on wheels came for the *Star* man. By then an army of Colonial Williamsburg security officers and local and state police had restored order by forcing all of the rioters—we distinguished members of the national press corps—back into the Virginia Room and into their chairs.

I went back to my original seat. The San Diego woman was still there. I told her what had happened to the man from the *Star*.

"How can we all cover what happened in here?" she asked.

"I don't know."

"What can we say about ourselves?"

"I don't know."

"I almost forgot about the debate, what happened, what Meredith just did, and screamed—the *real* story."

So had I.

In a few minutes—not more than five or six, to be more exact—Chuck Hammond appeared behind the microphones and the podium on the small stage down in front of us.

"First, let me say how terrible we feel about what happened here in this room," he said. "The injured are being attended to. Initial reports seem to indicate that all of the victims will survive with no permanent or lasting effects. We'll release what information we get here as it becomes available."

"How many were taken to hospitals?" somebody—a woman—yelled out.

Hammond said: "I don't have any exact counts at this point. But I understand it was less than ten."

"Come on!" some other idiot—a man idiot—screamed. "Give us a count or let us out of here to find out ourselves!"

Hammond said: "The Virginia State Police and the Secret Service have ordered us to maintain the status quo in this room for now."

"Status quo? What the hell does that mean?" some male reporter yelled out.

You would have thought that being part of a mob would have caused these people to back off, to calm down. But no. Without so much as a decent interval, here they were back in their attack mode, back to being animals, back in their pack.

Hammond said: "It means none of you is leaving this room until we say so."

There was some grumbling, some profanity.

"Who do you people think you are?" another reporter shouted at Hammond.

Hammond said: "We are the people with the responsibility for keeping you people from trampling or otherwise killing or injuring yourselves."

Chuck Hammond considers that to be the finest moment of his post-Marine life.

Then he said: "We are aware of your reporting needs, and as a way of trying to meet them I have asked the four debate panelists to come in for a news conference."

That triggered a mixture of cheers and boos from the cream of American journalism. Hammond turned to his left rear, the cue for Mike Howley, Joan Naylor, Barbara Manning, and Henry Ramirez to come in and meet the press.

They had watched the press riot on a television monitor in Longsworth D.

Joan's first fear was that of death. Many of those journalists were going to die, and then so would the four of them. She remembered scenes from an Elizabeth Taylor movie—with Dana Andrews, not Richard Burton—about a herd of elephants in Ceylon or somewhere that went wild and trampled people and houses to death and dust.

To Barbara and Henry the shock of watching a group of their heroes—the best of the national press corps—going berserk was beyond description.

Mike Howley had thoughts about how the riot in the Virginia Room confirmed his worst fears about what the American press had become.

Hammond had warned him and the others that most everyone in the Western world with a camera and/or a microphone would be on them live with pictures and audio from the moment they entered the Virginia Room. *Everyone.* And in case there was doubt about what he was talking about, he said it meant the three commercial networks, PBS, Fox, CNN, C-SPAN, MTV, plus the BBC, the CBC, NHK in Japan, and a variety of other foreign broadcasters, domestic independent stations, and cable channels. "Even before the press riot I was sure there'd never been anything quite like this," Hammond told them. "Now it's bigger even than Desert Storm—maybe even Watergate."

Mike, Joan, Barbara, and Henry walked out to the small stage and bunched in a semicircle behind the podium, which was rigged with seventy-seven microphones. (I personally counted them.) I am no master estimator of crowd sizes, but the pros there who are said there were three hundred people with more microphones, video and still cameras, and notebooks.

Joan spied a few familiar faces, but most of them were not only unfamiliar, they also seemed terribly unfriendly. She could not tell whether everyone was out of sorts with her and her three co-panelists for what they had done to Meredith or because of their own disturbance. So this is what it looks like from this side of it, she thought. She was not completely over the unsettling terror that hit her watching the press mêlée.

Barbara's attention was on how few dark faces she saw out there. These white boys and girls look like they want to hang me from a limb of a tree with a rope around my neck. OK now, Gramma Maude, I need that hand of yours again.

Henry felt great up there in front of all of those ladies and gentlemen of the international media. After watching you-all make absolute fools of yourselves just now, I am even more at peace about myself, about this brown boy. Ask *me* your questions and I will tell you no lies.

And then the yelling started. Several voices, a mixture of all genders, ages, and volume, came right at them.

"Mike Howley! Mike Howley! Is it true the idea for this conspiracy was yours?"

"Was destroying Meredith what you came here to do?"

Howley's mouth moved, but it was impossible to hear what he said. It was not impossible to see him shaking his head. No was the answer.

The questions continued at full volume all at once. The press riot continued all at once.

"Are the four of you satisfied?"

"Why did you do it?"

"Is this what the press is supposed to do?"

"Who appointed you four to decide who gets elected president of the United States?"

"Where did all of that abuse stuff come from?"

"We hear you got it from the Greene campaign."

"Did the Greene people pay you?"

"Are any of you going to work for Greene in the White House if he's elected?"

They were pretty good questions. But there was no way to answer any of them. There was not enough quiet space between and among the screamed questions for Howley, Joan, Barbara, or Henry to get even a word in.

Jesus, thought Barbara. Am I one of these?

Shut up, you fools! thought Henry. Let us answer!

Mike Howley held up his hands for quiet.

Trying to read his lips at the time and listening carefully to the tape afterward, I am fairly sure he only said: "There will be no answers under these circumstances."

The yelling continued.

Mike Howley said: "Look, unless you give us some quiet . . ."

A few stopped screaming questions and started screaming at each other. "Pipe down!" "Let 'em talk!" "Shut up!"

Joan knew that Jeff and the twins, along with the rest of the world, were watching. She wanted to tell the twins she was not like the people in this room. Their mom did not screech at people like this. Their mom was a real journalist, one of the old-fashioned kind. The kind who treated people with dignity and respect. These screaming crazies are not journalists! They're not even human!

Howley shouted: "There will be no answers until we and you can be heard. So shut up, goddamn it!"

There were pockets of quiet now. *Shhhhhhhhh*s ricocheted around the room.

"All right, Mike!" boomed a loud male voice. "Tell us who appointed you four people God!"

Howley clearly recognized the voice, and when he found it he recognized the face. So did most everyone else in the room, including me. They were those of T. R. (Teddy) Lemmon, Jr., the lead political reporter and analyzer for *The New York Herald*.

Suddenly, magically, the room was absolutely silent.

Howley waited a few more beats and then said to the room: "Did everyone hear the question?"

That drew a few hundred laughs and/or snickers. Howley said to Lemmon, who was in the middle of the room about eight rows up: "Nobody appointed us God, Teddy. We did not see what we did tonight as playing God, as a matter of fact. If you do, then so be it. Write it."

Jesus, thought Barbara. Mike Howley is one tough sunavabitch. That was Teddy Lemmon himself!

Howley pointed at Tom (Bat) Masterson of *The Boston Globe.* He and Bat had known and liked each other for years. Bat talked, but nobody could hear him in the avalanche of questions that came shouted from all around the room.

Mike Howley held up his hands again for quiet. "Please, let's have some quiet."

There was no quiet. I heard a male voice from over somewhere yell out the question: "Do you bear some responsibility for the injuries suffered in the disturbance in this room a while ago?" I would have loved to have heard an answer to that one. But it did not get answered by anyone.

Howley, on the platform, turned to Joan, Barbara, and Henry. "What do we do?" he asked.

"This is appalling," Joan said, raising her voice to be heard. "Let's get out of here."

She turned to Barbara. "I'm with you," Barbara said.

"Henry?" Barbara said after repeating what Joan had said.

"We're press. How can we walk out of a press conference?" he said to Barbara. He moved in front of her toward the podium. Mike Howley smiled and slapped him on the back, helping him to a place right behind the microphone.

"Hey!" Henry shouted into the microphone. "Everybody in the world is watching all of us! Do you realize what kind of scene you-all are making for them to see? Don't you realize what you already did a while ago?"

"Don't lecture us, Ramirez!" a man yelled back. He was in the front row and thus one of the few who could hear what Henry had said.

Henry turned to face Barbara, Joan, and Howley, and gave them a palms-up what's-the-use gesture.

And they all four walked off the stage and out of the Virginia Room after twelve minutes and having answered only one question.

What they heard as they left were boos and shouts of scorn for having run away.

I could not even begin to imagine at that moment what the American people were thinking about me and the others of their free press.

★

After a state and sound of civilized behavior returned to the Virginia Room, I phoned Jonathan Angel, my *Tatler* editor. He had caught sight of me on television during the press riot. "Are you all right?" was the fourth question he asked me from New York. The first three were: "Are those people nuts?" "Was it as bad as it looked?" "Is it over?"

My answer to all four questions was yes—yes, they *are* nuts, it *was* as bad as it looked, it *is* over, and I *am* all right.

"Jesus," said Jonathan. "Did you hear what Jill just said?"

"Jill?"

"*The* Jill of Jack and Jill. She said the panelists should be indicted for criminal conspiracy. Jesus . . . Let me see what Ross is up to."

I heard the sounds of another set of televised voices in Jonathan's background. "He's got Gerry Ford and Walter Mondale. . . ." I heard a click. "Norman's got a bleacher full of senators. . . . Tom, are you watching this stuff? It's incredible. Look! PNN's got shots of cars full of Meredith supporters turning around in the middle of the highway. They were on their way to Williamsburg. They heard him say 'fucking.' It's unbelievable. They heard him on their car radios. I cannot believe this."

I could see glimpses of Jack and Jill and Ross Perot and Norman Schwarzkopf and their guests and all kinds of other things in the various TV monitors around the room. But I could not hear what anybody was saying.

Said Jonathan: "Jesus. Jack and Jill just announced they were going to stay on the air until they got to the bottom of this thing."

"That's what I want to do, too, Jonathan," I said. "I want to stay on this story. . . ."

"Go, Tom, go. Yes, yes. Go after this story with everything you have. Go until you have everything, until you have every drop, until *you* get to the bottom of it, until you drop."

I was delighted. I said: "Thank you, thank you."

He kept talking. "The earth moved a while ago, Tom. I felt it. We all felt it. The earth movers were those four people out there on that stage. Go get 'em, Tom. Who are they? What are they? Where are they? Jack and Jill said Joan Naylor was coming on their show. Ross and Norman said they were trying to get all four of them. Jesus, think of the questions. Particularly for Howley. Howley! Who would have thought Howley? Why did he and the others do what they did? Who are they? How are they? I want to know it all. Every tiny little detail, Tom. Give it to me. Give it to America. They moved the earth, Tom. Four journalists moved the political earth of America. They got Meredith to say 'fucking' in front of everybody! How did they do it? Go get that story. Go, Tom, go."

Go, Tom, go.

"Jesus, Norman's already gone to the phone calls! He said there's never been so many in the history of the phone! Not just to him but everybody. Everybody's on the phone, Tom! Jesus! Perot's doing something now with Lilly. . . . He's something with Greene."

"He's the campaign manager," I said.

"Right, right. He just compared the four debate panelists to the signers. The guys who signed the Declaration of Independence. Jesus!"

It was time for Tom to go.

I left Jonathan in the hands of his channel switcher and Jack and Jill, Ross and Norman. My intention was to go, Tom, go immediately from the Virginia Room in search of the four earth movers. But the authorities had yet to alter the room's "status quo," meaning they had yet to conclude that the press could be trusted to move about Colonial Williamsburg and elsewhere in the outside world without hurting ourselves or others.

So I moved over to a corner of the room where there were a cluster of television sets. All of them were tuned to some kind of debate-reaction programming. Except on some of the specialized cable channels that ran nothing but old movies or documentaries about icebergs and wolves mating, there was nothing else to watch. Reaction to what had happened on that stage some fifty feet down the hall from where I was then standing had consumed all of television, and through it not only Jonathan Angel and his friends on the West Side of New York, but most everyone in America, too.

And there on the screen of one of the monitors came Joan Naylor on the *Jack and Jill* show. Several of us there in the corner moved right up to the set so we could hear. But in a few moments it was no longer necessary. Miraculously, the Virginia Room got absolutely silent. Everyone— all three-hundred-plus members of the confined press—also wanted to hear what Joan Naylor had to say. They wouldn't listen to her before when she was right there in the room with them, but now they did. Now they would listen.

Jill came at Joan in a full rage.

"I assume the first thing you did after the debate was take a shower?" she asked.

The camera, up close on Joan, revealed without question that she had no idea what Jill was getting at. "A shower?" she said. "I've been waiting down the hall to come on your program. . . ."

"To wash off the dirt and slime of what you and your three co-terrorists did to David Donald Meredith?"

Now Joan knew what was going on. And she was up to it. "He did the worst terrorism on himself. I would think that you and the other Meredith supporters have had reason to take a lot of such showers during this campaign—and another after what he did tonight."

Ms. Perky had decided she was not going to take any shit from the likes of Jill of Jack and Jill.

Jack said: "Great answer, Joan. Absolutely perfect." He sent one of his traditional scowls toward Jill. Then back to Joan, he said: "But. But, but. As much as I abhor Meredith, Joan, and was as repelled as anyone by his profane fit there at the end, I must say the idea of four journalists interposing themselves between the candidates and the voters the way you-all did tonight gives me serious pause. I like the end result—exposing Meredith for what he really is—but I wonder about the means. That is my question."

It was, of course, no such thing as a question. But again, Joan was there. "We did no interposing," she said. "The voters of America will make the final decision on Election Day. They will make their own judgments about the candidates and about what happened here tonight. . . ."

"It was outrageous what you did," Jill said.

"You are welcome to your opinion just like every other voter, Jill," Joan said.

"Whose idea was it? Whose idea was it to take the electoral process into your own hands?" Jack asked.

"We all made it and we made it together."

"Why won't you answer Jack's question?" Jill said.

"She did, darling Jill," Jack said, turning to face his wife/co-host.

"She did not, darling Jack." Swiveling back to Joan, she said: "We hear it was Howley. We hear he browbeat the other three of you into doing it."

"That is not right. We were together. Nobody browbeat anybody into anything."

Jill said: "Are you proud of what you did, Joan Naylor?"

"I don't know if 'proud' is the word. . . ."

"Would you do it again?"

"I don't know."

"Is this the kind of thing we can expect from journalists now? Deciding for the voters who should win or lose?"

Jack said to Jill: "Come on, darling Jill. As Joan said, the voters still make the final decision. Nothing that happened here in Williamsburg changes any of that."

"Wrong, wrong, wrong. Everything changes because of what happened here in Williamsburg."

Jack said to Joan: "I do have one last question. We asked you here this morning if any bombshells were coming tonight and you said no. Why did you tell us that?"

"It was an honest answer," said Joan. "Nothing along the lines of what we did had even been discussed by then, much less decided on."

"What would you say to someone like me who confesses to having a hard time believing that?" Jill said, her voice full of loathing and contempt.

Said Joan: "I would say only that there will always be people—well-meaning, fair-minded, serious people even—who have trouble believing the truth."

Jack thanked Joan. My attention turned to another monitor showing

Ross Perot's program. There came a shot of Barbara Manning and Henry Ramirez sitting side by side. Perot was interviewing them.

"Those women's statements didn't just drop down from the big statement goose in the sky, did they?" Perot asked.

"No gooses were involved," Henry said.

"OK, then, where? How did they get into your hands a while ago to use as bludgeons against Meredith?"

"They came to us from a legitimate source, one we trusted," Barbara said.

"Isn't all that really matters, Ross, is whether they're true?" Henry said. "Do those women exist and do they stand by their stories?" Henry loved calling Ross Perot, one of the richest men in the world, by his first name.

"Good point, good point, good point," said Perot. "In closing, I must say you-all look like a smart couple sitting there together. Have you given any thought to being a team?"

"Football or otherwise?" Henry popped back.

"Otherwise, otherwise, otherwise," Perot said.

"Good," said Barbara, "because I have never played football in my life."

I stayed in front of the TV monitors in the Virginia Room for a few more minutes. I was hoping to find somebody interviewing Mike Howley. But Jack and Jill had gone to a focus group of journalism students at the University of Missouri; Schwarzkopf was doing what they called on his show a "Sea-to-Sea Dialogue" with twelve experts around the country on male-against-female violence; and Perot went back to taking calls on what he called "The Perot People Party Line" about how the electorate was reacting to Meredith's use of the F-word. Nobody was even promo-ing an upcoming interview with Michael J. Howley.

I wondered where he was and what he was doing. And a few minutes later—after we were allowed our freedom again—I left the Virginia Room determined to find out.

I decided to go by way of the scene of the crime. Maybe there was something there in the auditorium and on the stage that I could use later to set a mood or an atmosphere.

Not only were the candidates long gone, but so was most everyone else. There were TV technicians rolling away cameras and unstringing lights. Several men on ladders were taking down the golden eagle high in the back. But the light blue carpet was still on the stage, and so were the table and chairs for the panelists and the red, white, and blue bunting. Greene's podium remained in place. Meredith's was there on the floor in its pieces, right where it landed and splintered. I wondered if someone was going to think of saving it for the Smithsonian or some political-science museum. That is where it belonged. I looked around for the microphone Meredith had tossed at Howley. I couldn't find it.

There were no security or other kinds of people to question or stop me, so I just walked around like I belonged there. I stood where Meredith had stood and looked down and over at the table where Howley, Henry, Barbara, and Joan had sat. What must it have been like to stand here and take what he took? Then I moved to Greene's podium. What must it have been like to have stood here and been given what he was given? I sat in Howley's chair. And then in each of the others'. I looked where each of them must have looked when they spoke the words that threw one candidate for president of the United States into an F-word rage and the other probably into the White House.

I was reminded of a story a Dallas newspaper reporter wrote after he went back to the assassination site at Dealey Plaza well after midnight on the day President Kennedy was shot. The reporter said he could hear the faint sounds of gunshots and screams and motorcycles and screeching tires. And he swears he picked up a faint smell of gunpowder.

In this case, I heard the screaming voice of a wounded candidate for president and I picked up the faint smell of political sweat—and death.

★

I went back across to the Inn in search of Howley. Twenty or thirty people were gathered around a small television set in a corner of the lobby. I heard the voice of Jack and then Jill interviewing Doug Mulvane, the man they called Pompous Perfect. He proclaimed this "journalism's darkest hour," and he called "on every journalist in America who cares about the future of his or her noble profession to stand up, speak up, shout out, and be counted, to condemn what those four people did under the sacred cloak of journalism on that stage in Williamsburg tonight."

A woman at the Inn's front desk said Howley had not checked out, but she refused—politely but firmly—to give me his room number. The doorman told me he had not seen Howley leave the Inn since he returned shortly after the debate ended. But he said there were several other doors besides the big front one here at the lobby. Said the doorman: "Everybody's been looking for him. He's more famous than Patrick Henry around here right now." Spoken, I thought, like a well-trained man of eighteenth-century Williamsburg.

Another person—a source not affiliated with the Inn who must remain unidentified—assisted me in obtaining Howley's room number. It was 3255, down a long hallway on the second floor.

I went to it and put my ear to it. There was no sound of a television or anything else. It was only nine o'clock. It seemed inconceivable to me that Howley could be sitting quietly in his room reading a good book or staring silently off into space. There was simply no way in the world a normal mortal could resist watching and listening to all of the Jacks and Jills, Normans and Rosses, of the world chew over and spit out what they thought of what he had just done across the street to a candidate for president of the United States.

I knocked on the door. I put my ear back against it. Not a sound. I hit it a couple more times. Again, no response. The man was clearly gone or dead. Dead? Was it possible that Michael J. Howley, overcome with profound second thoughts about what he had wrought, had ended his own life? Was that possible?

At that moment I caught sight of a maid, a young woman, working her way with her cart of clean towels, chocolate mints, and the like on her "turn-down" rounds. I ran to her and pulled on her something I saw Richard Widmark do once in a movie.

"Pardon me," I said in my most worried voice. "I left my wife alone in the room a while ago after we had an argument. Now I can't raise her. I'm worried, frankly. Could you quickly open the door to see if she's in there—and all right? I hope she hasn't . . . you know . . . hurt herself."

The woman, easily deceived because she was a caring person, ran with me to 3255 and opened the door with her master key.

It was empty. Not only of Michael J. Howley or any other person, but of any *sign* of Michael J. Howley or any other person. There were no clothes in the closet or in the chest of drawers. There were no toilet articles in the bathroom.

"Oh, my God," I exclaimed. "She's run away. I can't believe that."

"You'll find her and everything will be just fine," said the maid as we left the room together. "I'm sorry."

I thanked her and headed back down the hall to the lobby.

Go, Tom, go.

I had a pretty good idea that the other three panelists—Joan Naylor, Henry Ramirez, and Barbara Manning—were still over at the Lodge, probably being interviewed on somebody's television or radio show or by a print reporter.

I went first to the area where the *Jack and Jill* show was still originating. Private network security people were everywhere, at every door. I went to one of them, a young man dressed in a two-tone blue uniform and holstered pistol, at the main door, and identified myself correctly and then lied about my purpose. I told him I was to be a guest on Jack and Jill's program.

"Through that door," he said, pointing me in the right direction.

Inside the door sat a young woman in a dark red blazer with the CNS logo on the right front lapel pocket. "I'm here with a message for Ms. Naylor about her car," I said.

"She's still in the green room, I think," said the young woman, again pointing me in the right direction.

The green room is what all television organizations call the places guests wait for their turn to go on the air. In this case it was a small meeting room that had been equipped with many chairs and much food and drink. It was teeming with people, most of whom I did not recognize. But there she was, Joan Naylor, sitting over in a corner talking on the phone.

I went to where she was, and when she hung up I reintroduced myself from that morning at breakfast and told her my real purpose. I wanted to talk to her at length about what had happened and why.

She said: "I love your magazine. I feel I owe you for that wonderful story about me. But you'll have to stand in line. The whole world wants to talk to me, it seems. Call me in Washington next week. I'm on my way there in a few minutes myself now."

"Do you happen to know where Mike Howley is?" I asked.

"I have no idea. If he's not at the Inn he's probably gone back to Washington."

She looked off at one of the two TV monitors in the room. Jack and Jill were interviewing four reporters—two men, two women—who had been in the Virginia Room during what they called "the journalists' disturbance." Jack asked them: "Were you scared for your lives?" Yes, a lot, said one of the women. Yes, but not much, said one of the men. The other two said, Not really. "How do you explain that kind of barbaric behavior by people who spend most of their time lecturing other people about theirs?" asked Jill. None of the four had an explanation. One of them, a woman, said: "It served as a good reminder of how human we all are." "Human?" said Jill. "I think that's hardly fair to the rest of us, to paint us all with that brush. I think it is unfair to suggest, for instance, that a roomful of doctors or dentists or candlestick makers would have reacted the same way."

Joan Naylor shook her head and said to me: "This is all too much to take in, isn't it?"

I agreed with her.

"Were you in that room? Was it that bad?"

I told her I was there and it was that bad.

"This is all too much to take in."

And she smiled and picked up the phone to make another call.

Henry Ramirez and Barbara Manning were not in this green room. I was able to gain access to those of Perot and Schwarzkopf as well as those of PNN, PBS, and three others. They had been there, been on the air, but were now gone, and nobody knew for sure where.

I went back into the Virginia Room, thinking it was possible they had gone back there for individual interviews. I thought it might also be well for me to return to the scene of that crime as well, the place where "the journalists' disturbance" had occurred.

There were only a few reporters left at the work tables and computer terminals and telephones. None of them were interviewing Henry Ramirez or Barbara Manning. I looked at my watch. It was now only 9:45.

All of it had happened so fast. The debate began, there was the explosive ending, the mêlée, and the aborted news conference in this room, and now it was over. It really was a thunderstorm.

I went to a phone and had the Colonial Williamsburg operator ring the Inn room of Henry Ramirez. There was no answer after eight rings. I hung up and did the same to Barbara Manning's room. Again, no answer.

I felt they were probably both still in Williamsburg and I had a hunch they were together. That was probably because of the power of the suggestion contained in that little closing with Ross Perot. Otherwise, otherwise, otherwise.

I tried to think where they might have gone to be otherwise or anything together on this important night in their lives. A quiet corner in a quiet bar for a quiet drink? A stroll under the moonlight through the eighteenth century?

Back at the Inn, I left written notes at the front desk for each of them. I said to both that I wanted very much to get together with them back in Washington as soon as possible. I made a plea for their cooperation in meeting my magazine's serious and substantial commitment to "doing your story and doing it thoroughly and well."

★

Back in my room at the Lodge, I turned on the television. Jack and Jill were still on the air. And so were Ross and Norman and it seemed like half of the rest of the Western world. If you were awake, opinionated, voiced, and available, you could express yourself on what the four panelists did and why, on the F-word, on what it all meant for Meredith, Greene, the press, and America, and on most anything else you had on your mind if it was even vaguely related to Williamsburg.

Everyone said afterward that there had never been anything like it in the history of television and news and public affairs and talk, and I do not quarrel with that conclusion. I finally went to sleep at two o'clock in the morning because my channel switcher, ears, eyes, and mind were worn out. So I did not see it all live, but over the next few weeks I did either watch videotapes or read transcripts of just about everything that was broadcast that night.

Jack and Jill, for instance, may not have honored their commitment to stay on the air until they got to the bottom of it, but it wasn't because they didn't try. They did not sign off until 3:22 A.M., Eastern Time, almost nine hours after they went on the air immediately following Howley's debate good night. A world-record 114 guests were heard before it was over, and that did not count the many ordinary people who simply called in to scream something—several only some version of the famous F-word.

Ross Perot was on the air for seven hours and twenty minutes, giving-and-taking with ninety-three guests, most of whom condemned what the press panel had done. Perot himself was also critical of the panelists, after a while calling the whole thing "Debate-gate" and predicting it would do to the press what Watergate, the original "gate," did to Richard Nixon.

Norman Schwarzkopf, the first former four-star general to have his own talk show, did a mere six and a half hours with only seventy-one guests, most of whom were with him in loving what had happened. He praised the four panelists for "taking the bull by the horns," for "going for 'the high ground," for "pulling off a journalistic Desert Storm."

All three of the major shows, as well as the many others on cable and elsewhere, divided the emphasis between the panelists-press angle to the story and the specific charges against Meredith and his behavior on the stage.

Tape replays of Meredith throwing the microphone and then the podium and screaming the word "fucking" and walking off were repeated in various speeds of slow motion time after time after time. Several family, youth, and religious channels on cable bleeped out the bad word in their replays. Pundits on all channels had an awkward time talking about the potential impact of Meredith's profane departure. Some tried to do it without actually saying the word, but not all were so squeamish. David Snider, the PNN analyst, broke new ground and held it by referring all night to it as "the 'fucking' thing."

Psychiatrists, psychologists, and other behavior specialists also weighed in. Some contrasted Meredith's predebate religious and Puritan pose with his debate profanity and the reports of his violent side to conclude that he suffered from a psychic disorder known as Jekyll-Hyde syndrome. Others stood at television monitors with pointers and made clinical observations about what the freeze-framed shot of Meredith's forehead and mouth and fist said about the state of his emotional health.

Much of it was ridiculous and stupid, but it was clear to me by the time I went to sleep that the trend was more than established. Ross, Norman, Jack and even Jill, as well as most of their guests and call-ins, bought the validity of the charge that David Donald Meredith was an unstable man of violence. All of the broadcasts went repeatedly to live feeds in front of the homes, apartments, and hideaways of the various women who had had their statements read by Howley, Joan, Barbara, and Henry. Some declined to be interviewed, so the television reporters interviewed their neighbors, friends, and anyone else they could find in the immediate vicinities who would talk. The scene in front of the duplex of the woman in Asheville who claimed Meredith kicked her after a fender bender was particularly grotesque. The woman insisted that all interviews be conducted with two uniformed Asheville police officers standing on either side of her. "My life is in danger," she said to every interviewer. "The Meredith forces cannot let this stand. You saw him there at the end. You saw what a madman he is."

The F-word politics came into full focus when William Allen Tonapah, the chairman of the American Christian Families Coalition, emerged from an emergency conference-call meeting of his executive council to issue the following statement: "We are outraged over the way those four press jackals attacked David Donald Meredith tonight. But we regret to say that their conduct does not excuse that of Mr. Meredith. We were stunned, disappointed, and repulsed by his use of gutter language. As an organization dedicated to furthering what is clean and Christian, we must withdraw our support for his candidacy. There were young people in that vast television audience tonight. They were looking for moral leadership from David Donald Meredith. They saw and heard the opposite. This is a sad day for America."

That statement helped develop a clear—and obvious—consensus through the evening and early-morning hours among the many varieties and types of pundits. The result of the Williamsburg Debate was going to be the election of Paul L. Greene as president of the United States rather than David Donald Meredith.

There was one important picture and voice and view that was not seen or heard on anyone's program that night. Its absence was noticeable not only to me but to most everyone else. Jack of Jack and Jill, for instance, said at one time into his camera: "Mike Howley, if you're watching us now, call us. We need to talk to you. America needs to talk to you.

"Defend yourself. Speak for yourself."

Part 3

Why and How

9

Citizens First

Michael J. Howley talked to Jack, me, and everyone else in the world the next morning. There across the top of the front page of *The Washington Morning News* was a story under the headline MIKE HOWLEY: "WE WERE CITIZENS FIRST." It was above the main news story about the debate, which appeared under a larger hard-news banner headline: MEREDITH ACCUSED OF VIOLENCE. The subhead under the banner was "Candidate Throws Fit, Cusses."

It was Howley's piece—his own account in his own first-person words—that gave me the first whiff of the scent toward the trail to finding out what had really happened in Williamsburg and why. The smell came not in what he said but what he did not say, what he left out.

The length of the article, in fact, was the first thing that struck me as curious. It was less than two thousand words. Here was the guy who was involved in—led, probably—what even then, on the morning after, was shaping up as a major historical event of American politics and journalism, and *this* was all he had to say about it?

The thrust of his message was contained in one paragraph. He said:

"We came to a joint realization, the four of us, that we were confronted with a searing, crucial choice between conflicting duties and responsibilities. On the one hand were those we had as journalists to remain detached, uninvolved, and on the other those we had as citizens to participate, to take action. We concluded that in this case we were citizens first. Our country deserved and demanded that we act on our informed fears and knowledge."

He said the decision was "agonizing, wrenching, draining, and, yes, in the final analysis, terrifying." He acknowledged that many people—Meredith and his supporters particularly—would probably never understand why it was done. Others might have the same problem, he said, closing with these words:

"I am certain there will also be people with no political axes to grind—many within our own profession of journalism, no doubt—who will also take severe exception to our decision and actions. There is sure to be much debate about the debate.

"Let it begin."

And that was pretty much it. I read his few words three times before what was wrong finally hit me. He had failed to speak to the central questions that the panelists'/citizens' dramatic action raised.

Were the women's charges of abuse against Meredith what caused Howley, Joan Naylor, Henry Ramirez, and Barbara Manning to decide to move against him? Did they conclude that a man so prone to violent outbursts was unsuited for the presidency? Or were there other reasons about political philosophy and beliefs that made him unacceptable first? Were the abuse charges thus only the weapons for the attack and the kill, not the reasons? And then, of course, there were the simple logistics questions. Where did those interview statements from all of those women come from? Who conducted them? How did they come into the possession of those four panelists/citizens in Williamsburg? What kind of fact-checking, if any, was done by the four panelists before using them against Meredith in such a dramatic way? Did they count on his blowing up the way he did? Was that the real point, the real objective?

One of the four people who knew the answers had decided, at least in his article, to simply ignore the questions.

On impulse, I picked up the phone—I was still in my room at the

Williamsburg Lodge—and called *The Washington Morning News.* It was only eight o'clock on a Monday morning, but something told me it was possible, probable even, that on this momentous Monday morning-after Mike Howley would already be at his office.

I told the woman who answered the phone in the *News* newsroom that I was calling from Mr. Howley's hotel in Williamsburg about "something he had left behind." She put me through immediately.

"This is Howley," spoke the voice of the man who had changed the course of a presidential election just fourteen hours ago.

I quickly identified myself, reminding him that we had talked briefly after the Thomas Jefferson press conference in Williamsburg the previous afternoon.

"Hey, goddamn it, she said it was about something I left in my room. . . ."

"I am doing some major reporting for some major stories for the *Tatler* about what you and the other three panelists did last night. And how and why you did it. I cannot do it, of course, without your help and cooperation."

"Sorry, can't help you. What I have to say I will say in my own newspaper. Look, got to go. This is already shaping up as the busiest day of my life—"

"Where did the women's statements come from?"

"Hey, forget it—"

"Was it them or something else that caused you-all to go after Meredith?"

"I'm hanging up, Bob."

"Tom—"

"Sorry. Tom—"

"Did you have any idea he would scream a word like 'fucking'?"

"Good-bye, Tom—"

"I'll be back, Mr. Howley."

I don't think Howley heard that last line. By then I was probably talking into a dead phone.

By the time I pulled my rented Toyota into the Georgetown Inn in Washington three hours later, I had formed a rough working plan for how I would get back to Mr. Howley.

Joan Naylor was the plan, pure and simple. If I could use her friendly attitude toward the *Tatler* as an entreé to get her, a veteran and respected professional, to talk to me in a full and open manner, then I could use that fact to bring in the younger and inexperienced Henry Ramirez and Barbara Manning. Then, with the cooperation of those three, I would go back to Mike Howley.

Do I do my story with only their versions, their facts, their points of view, Mr. Howley? Who speaks for you, Mr. Howley? How can I do a fair and complete job without your slant, your perspective, Mr. Howley?

Go, Tom, go.

★

I could not get anyone on the phone at Joan Naylor's CNS office to tell me one thing about where she was or how I might contact her. I took several stabs at it through various ploys, and after about the fifth time I had the feeling that I was being recorded or that my call was being traced. Something was going on. A man suddenly came on the line—all previous calls had been fielded by women—and started chatting me up. I had said this time that I was with Blue and Gray Motor Freight and we had a leather couch from a furniture company in North Carolina that needed to be delivered to Ms. Naylor. Did Ms. Naylor want it at her office or her home? The instructions we had were not clear, I said. The guy on the phone burst into a small talk about the weather and life on Mondays and I hung up.

What I did not know at the time was that the people who ran the CNS television network had decided Joan Naylor's life was in jeopardy. Their switchboards, fax machines, and mail and message receptacles in both Washington and New York had been deluged with threats to her life and person. CNS hired a private security firm to keep watch over her around the clock, and the chatty guy was undoubtedly part of the crew.

The network also suspended her. "For her own protection," said the written press statement from a network spokesman in New York.

I read this press release when I arrived at the *Tatler* office in the National Press Club building that Monday afternoon. I had gone there to set up shop in the office suite that was used mostly by the magazine's Washington correspondent and a secretary-researcher. But it also had three other small fully equipped offices for staff and freelance writers who came to Washington on assignment.

By the time I got there Jennifer Gates, the secretary-researcher, had already assembled much of what I had called ahead and requested. There on the desk in the office that would be the most important space in my life for the next seven months were several stacks of newspaper clippings, wire-service stories, and transcripts and tapes of television and radio broadcasts. They completely covered the desk. I was stunned at first sight at what they represented in millions of words that had already been generated in less than twenty-four hours.

Chuck Hammond and Jonathan Angel, my editor, appeared to have called it right. Jonathan's feeling the earth moving was real. The early reaction was also bearing out Hammond's hyperbole about the debate being as big as Desert Storm and maybe even Watergate. It had already made television history. The Nielsen people estimated the American television audience to have been 132 million by the time Meredith screamed the F-word and Howley said good night. Never before had that many people watched any single program at the same time.

The Associated Press set the pattern for the coverage of Howley, Joan, Barbara, and Henry. Its first story on their news conference began:

"The four journalists who turned Sunday's presidential debate into an attack on Republican nominee David Donald Meredith stormed out of a raucous news conference afterward.

"They answered only one question about why they had done what they did. Michael J. Howley of *The Washington Morning News,* the debate moderator, acknowledged that nobody appointed him and his three journalist-colleagues God but said, 'We did not see what we did tonight as playing God.' "

The Reuters and UPI stories were similar, the Reuters story calling the news conference "out of control," UPI labeling it "stormy." None of the three major news services explained why the four panelists had left the news conference. None reported the fact that the news conference was raucous, stormy, and out of control because the reporters from their own news organizations and others made it so.

I was stunned, mortified also, by the way the wires handled the earlier "journalists' disturbance" in the Virginia Room right after the debate.

The woman from *The San Diego Union-Tribune* had wondered how we were going to cover ourselves, and the initial answer was clear—poorly. None of the wire services even did separate stories on the mêlée. All three just stuck paragraphs about it into their press-conference stories. UPI, for instance, said only that "five reporters suffered minor injuries as the assembled press corps raced to cover one of the most important stories of the campaign."

The daily-newspaper stories mostly took the same approach on the disturbance. On the news conference, they, too, took the line that the four panelists, apparently unable or unwilling to explain themselves, ran for cover from the *real* truth seekers of American journalism. It was left to a handful of television critics to point out what everybody who watched it all already knew—that a few hundred of America's leading national journalists had made absolute fools of themselves on live television.

"I turned to my wife and children, my dogs and cats, my mice and rodents, and screamed: 'I am not one of those people!' " wrote the *Los Angeles Times* television critic.

Doug Mulvane said similar things in, according to my rough count, a record-setting twenty-seven separate television and radio appearances that first night, morning, and afternoon. From his seventeenth appearance on, he had taken on a line from the Bush administration's rhetoric in launching Desert Storm. "This will not stand," said Mulvane, referring to the new conduct of journalists as "mobsters—to each other as well as to the democratic process."

The New York Times led the print editorial attack against Howley, Henry, Barbara, and Joan. In a lead editorial that Monday morning the *Times* called them "America's first journalistic usurpers" and said there may be evils such as the Holocaust and Joe McCarthy that were so evil that such drastic "journalistic vigilantism" was called for, but the probable election of David Donald Meredith did not qualify. *USA Today* called the four "journalistic felons" and demanded that their employers immediately dismiss them to send a "message to the public and to other journalists that this is not acceptable behavior." The *Fort Worth Star-Telegram* added the recommendation that all four be banned forever from employment anywhere in the business of journalism. "Yes, call it black-listing," said the *Star-Telegram* editorial. "Call it anything you wish—

but do it." Several other papers picked up the Debate-gate theme from Perot.

The condemnation was anything but unanimous. *The Washington Morning News,* while noting the conflict-of-interest fact that Michael J. Howley was one of its own, labeled the four "America's first journalist-activists" and said that a new form of journalism might be in the making. "It may not be to everyone's liking, but neither are such things as rain, thunder, and snowstorms," said the *News* editorial. "But we live with them, we cope with them, we accept them. We can do the same with journalistic activism." *The Washington Post,* the Minneapolis *Star Tribune, The Denver Post, The Atlanta Constitution, The San Diego Union-Tribune,* and the *Chicago Tribune* used terms like "unorthodox," "out of the ordinary," and "precedent-shattering" to describe what had happened. All said one way or another that they wished the four journalists had not done what they did, but having done it—maybe the dire possibilities of a Meredith election justified it. Just this once.

The most amusing sidelight to the print coverage was the variety of ways the large dailies—the family newspapers of America—chose to cope with "the 'fucking' thing." Most never used the word itself. Some—including all eighty-seven of the Gannett papers—wrote it, "f——." Some—including the *Los Angeles Times* and the other Times-Mirror papers—used "f——ing." The truly skittish covered it up altogether in other words, calling it things like "a well-known curse word," "a pornographic expression." The few who used it included most of the largest newspapers—all five New York City dailies, the Washington papers, *The Boston Globe, The Atlanta Constitution,* the *Chicago Tribune,* plus *The Miami Herald* and the others owned by Knight-Ridder. All did so with a variety of Editor's Notes such as the bold-faced one in *The New York Herald* that said: "More than 132 million Americans of all ages, politics, and moral and language standards heard the word spoken by a candidate for president of the United States. His speaking of that word could very well influence the outcome of the election. To deny its existence at this point would be similar to denying the existence of a smoking gun in a dead man's hand."

The New York Times even went to columnist William Safire, its famous language man, to write a straight-faced piece on the origins of the word. According to Safire, it came from *fokkinge*, the Low Dutch word for sexual intercourse, and *fukka*, the Norwegian word for same. First usage had been traced back to the fifteenth century. Safire gave the sailors of the world credit for spreading it from port to port and eventually into the English language.

An overnight poll by Gallup for CNN and *USA Today* showed 57 percent approved of what Howley, Joan, Henry, and Barbara had done in triggering Meredith's anger and use of that ancient word. Thirty-nine percent disapproved; 4 percent had no opinion.

Pro-con seminars, many of them featuring Mulvane and led by Socratic-method law-school professors, sprouted up immediately on C-SPAN and local public-radio and cable-television stations. By that Monday afternoon teach-ins, forums, seminars, and debates-about-the-debate were organized for thousands of college campuses and luncheon clubs all over America.

The *San Francisco Chronicle,* an "f——ing" paper, surveyed the political-science, mass-communication, and sociology departments at the seven major universities and colleges in its area. They found "an interest in the debate-about-the-debate on a par equal to that of a presidential assassination or military coup."

"History is already recording this as the seminal man-made political event of this cycle," said one professor, who was either not asked or the *Chronicle* felt it unnecessary to report what he meant by "this cycle."

The story also predicted it was only a matter of time before heavy seminars featuring linguists, semanticists, and other experts would be scheduled to discuss the "impact such a dramatically public use of the word 'f——ing' may have on public discourse in the future."

I checked in with Jonathan in New York. He was as excited about the story this afternoon as he was last night. His go-Tom-go's were delivered with even more force and intensity. He also—for the record—approved my staying at the Georgetown Inn in a $335-a-night "junior suite" and keeping the Toyota "for the duration." We did not discuss how long that might be.

Another thing I had asked Jennifer Gates to do was get Joan Naylor's home address. She presented it to me in the form of a photocopied page from *The Washingtonian,* a local gossip-type city magazine that regularly ran photographs, addresses, and estimated values of homes of prominent Washington people. TV anchorwoman Joan Naylor and her lawyer-husband, Jeff Grayson, lived with their twin daughters in a three-story white stucco house. The address was 3542 Newark, NW, in Cleveland Park. The estimated value was $1.2 million.

There were two private security guards in uniform sitting in a car in front of the house when I got there. So I kept driving. I circled the block and parked on Thirty-sixth Street, the next cross street, in a way that kept me out of view of the guards but with the help of binoculars made it possible to see the front of the house.

After about forty-five minutes I saw a man come out of the Naylor-Grayson home. He waved and did a thumbs-up in a friendly manner to the two men in the car and walked down the street east in my direction. He crossed in front of me. I waited until he was gone and followed. He was headed toward Wisconsin Avenue, a major business and shopping thoroughfare a block away.

He went into a drugstore on the corner and so did I. He was dressed in classy sports clothes—racing green corduroy pants, a white sweater, and beige buck shoes, all from J. Crew, Country Road, or some other upscale place. This was not a security man. This was Jeff Grayson. It had to be Jeff Grayson.

Go, Tom, go.

He was looking at contact-lens cleaners and other items in the eye-care section.

"Mr. Grayson, please forgive me for accosting you like this," I said. He stiffened. He shrunk back as if I had hit him in the face. "My name is Tom Chapman. I am a contributing editor of *The New American Tatler.* I met your wife in Williamsburg yesterday. I want to help her tell her story and the story of the debate in our magazine. Could you let me talk to her for a few minutes, just to make my case?"

"No way," he said. "She likes you-all—that was a great piece in the magazine about her—but she's laying low for now."

"I know about the threats and the security people."

"How do you know that?"

"The network put out a press release."

I watched the red come from his neck up through his face. "Those stupid bastards," he said. "That only makes it worse."

"They said she was suspended for her own good."

"That is absolute network bullshit."

And in a few minutes we were walking together, past the security men into his house.

Joan Naylor was at first surprised that her husband had brought a reporter back from the drugstore along with the contact-lens saline solution. But after he quickly explained and I made my case for cooperation, she invited me into their library, an old-fashioned room full of bookcases and photographs and dark furniture. We sat down and she talked to me. It was the first of many sessions we had over the next several weeks.

The first thing she and Jeff did was explain the network suspension. Yes, there had been some death threats, which were scary and unpleasant, but there was actually no connection between them and the suspension. Joan said that Carol Reynolds, the CNS Washington bureau chief, talked to Joan late Sunday night after the debate and after Joan had appeared on *Jack and Jill.* She said that the presidents of the network and the news division, plus their appropriate executive vice presidents and other helpers, had decided to "let things cool off." She said that they were troubled by the fact that one of their leading anchors had acted in such an "activist manner," but they did not yet know how troubled they were.

Joan said that Carol Reynolds said to her: "In other words, they might fire you for having disgraced the network and the principles of broadcast journalism in America today, but on the other hand they might promote you and rename the network after you. They just don't know yet whether they should or shouldn't do anything, whether this or that or that or this would help them or hurt them. They won't know what they think until the affiliates and the press and the vibes and the spirits and the gods and the markets and the polls tell them what to think."

Joan said Carol ordered her to go home and stay home and off everyone's air and grant no interviews with anyone about anything until further notice.

She did as she was told—until now, when she started talking to me.

Jeff had stayed home with her to help fend off the outside world of phone calls, of threats and taunts, praise and worship, that came crashing in on their unlisted line at the rate of thirty an hour. They said she was offered everything from rare forms of sex to stock tips and honorary degrees.

They told me about Sam Rhodes, the movie man who had appeared mysteriously in the panelists' holding room right after the debate. He had somehow gotten their unlisted number with all of the others and had called twice today to say Harry A. Mendelsohn was willing to consider doing her story alone if a deal could not be struck with all four of "you Americans of the hour." There were calls from six other people claiming to represent movie and television interests. Another five came from people claiming to represent major publishing houses in New York. Jeff wrote down the information from all of them as well as many of the others. His favorite was a guy in Spartanburg, South Carolina, who wanted to bring out a "Joan Naylor of Williamsburg" line of women's sportswear. There were three other calls wanting permission to put Joan's and the other three panelists' likenesses on sweatshirts and plastic raincoats.

Joan, with Jeff adding comments and information as we went along, then told me about the worst of her Monday. That was earlier that afternoon when the twins came home from school—their private Quaker school, Sidwell Friends.

She said the girls walked into the house like a double storm. They stomped and yelled and then cried. After a while Jeff and Joan were able to settle them down enough to find out what had happened.

Everything had happened. First, it was Meeting Day at school. Following the Quaker tradition and practice, Sidwell students gathered on a regular basis to sit silently in a room until somebody—anybody—felt moved to stand and talk about something—any something. This morning within the first minute a girl—"her dad's something Republican in Congress"—was on her feet.

"I just want to say that I think what those four journalists did to David Donald Meredith last night was unconstitutional, un-American, and awful," she said. "I think they should be disbarred from the profession of journalism and sent to Cambodia."

Rachel Grayson stood and responded: "One of those four, as everyone in this room certainly knows, is our mom. She is none of those things.

She should not be sent to Cambodia or anywhere else except to heaven-on-earth for trying her best to keep that awful man from being president of this country. You saw how awful he is. You heard what he yelled there at the end."

A boy both Rachel and Regina Grayson knew to be the grandson of a former Republican senator and vice president of the United States said: "Nobody elected anybody's mom or any of those other three to decide that kind of thing. They're like fascists or Nazis or communists who think they know what's right for everybody else who is not as smart as they are."

Regina Grayson said: "You call our mom a fascist, Nazi, or communist one more time, and I can tell you and everyone else in here that everything we have been taught here by the Quakers about nonviolence is going to be needed to stop me and my sister from doing to you what ought to be done. . . ."

And so it went all day for Regina and Rachel. Teachers, as well as students, wanted to do nothing but talk about the debate, their mother, the election, violent behavior disorders, profanity in public, and the future of the republic.

Joan and Jeff heard them out and then their own small dialogue began with their twin daughters.

"One of the kids said you ambushed him, Mom," Rachel said. "He said that was not honorable or ethical no matter how bad Meredith was—and what bad things it got him to do. Like saying that word."

"I guess he's right," said Joan. "I guess he's right about it being an ambush. But Meredith knows himself what he did to those women and what his personality is like. The only surprise was that we brought it up during the debate."

Regina asked: "Where did you-all get all of that stuff about his hitting those people?"

"Mr. Howley had it. He shared it with the rest of us. Once we saw it, we felt we could not let this man go on to be president."

Rachel said: "One of the teachers—Mr. Emory in history—said he wondered if you had had the same kind of information on a Democrat, on a candidate who was not like Meredith, whether you would have sprung it on him like that."

Joan said she looked at Jeff at that moment and they read each other's minds. Both were saying, Whose idea was it to send these kids to Sidwell Friends anyhow?

"That is a great question," Joan said to the girls. "I would like to say . . . I would like to think . . . I would hope that we would have."

Rachel said: "Even if you knew it would cost the election of somebody you thought would be a great president?"

I knew what I had by now. I had some great anecdotes about personal anguish, but the real stuff was what she said about where those Meredith abuse statements had come from. Howley. Mr. Howley had them.

I waited awhile before returning to that particular point.

"How did that actually happen? When and how did he tell you he had some dirt on Meredith that involved violent acts against women?"

She held up her right hand and said: "We agreed not to talk about what was said in our meetings. Sorry."

I said I certainly understood. I thanked her profusely for her cooperation and said I would call her again either here—she gave me her number—or at the office to talk again.

No need to push it too far now. There was time to come back to everything. All was well.

Slow, Tom, go.

★

Both Henry Ramirez and Barbara Manning also received threatening calls and messages. Their respective news organizations provided heightened "security awareness" in their respective offices and buildings, but nothing else was done. No security guards shadowed them around. No operatives intercepted their phone calls. Henry said he would not have accepted such services even if they had been offered. "You have to live with what you do, and if that means dying, too, then so what?" he said to me. Barbara's attitude was similar. "I can't worry about stuff like that," she said. "The way I see it, I was closer to dying of fright in Williamsburg before the debate than I am of dying from some Meredith nut's gun now."

I had misjudged Henry Ramirez and Barbara Manning. In my plan, I saw them easily coming along with me down the road of full disclosure. A little nudge with the news of Joan Naylor's cooperation might be necessary, but that was it. I was wrong. I followed a difficult and circuitous path toward getting each of them to talk to me about what I wanted to talk about. They were easy on matters such as postdebate opportunities and reactions but impossible on what had happened predebate inside Longsworth D.

With Barbara I was so wrong that I almost blew the whole enterprise. She had not responded to my initial message back at Williamsburg, and it took three calls to her Washington office on Tuesday before she agreed to talk to me. We met for coffee at the Sheraton-Carlton Hotel at the corner of Sixteenth and K, a block from Lafayette Park, two blocks from the White House.

She apologized for being so difficult to get on the phone, but she said she had been busier than it was possible for any one normal human being to be. Her life-after-Williamsburg was suddenly there for me to see myself. Within minutes after she sat down, four people came over and asked for her autograph. Three others simply walked over and expressed their approval. "Right on, Barbara Manning," a man said. "You're a national treasure," said a woman.

After the place calmed down and got used to her presence, she recounted to me a litany of offers and proposals similar to Joan Naylor's. She said, for instance, all of the late-night talk shows—Leno, Letterman, Limbaugh, Koppel, Miller, Rose, Rivers, Russell, Costas, O'Brien, Wholey, Matalin and Wallace, Shields, Snyder, Quayle, and Harding—wanted her as a guest. So did Donahue, Oprah, Maury, Ricki, Jenny, Hugh, Geraldo, Ruth, Kathie and Regis, Sonya, Meg, Lefty, Bryant and Katie, Joan and Charlie, Harry and Paula, Laura and Eric, Roger and Ginny, and everyone else who talked to people on television for a living during any other time of day or night.

Magazines, including several that competed directly with her own, wanted interviews and/or photo sessions. So did newspapers from all over the country and the world. So did lecture and appearance agents and representatives. So did that man Sam Rhodes and many others with movie, book, and TV nibbles. So did product and service pushers, including several from clothing, cosmetic, and hair-care lines. There had already even been some sniffs of job offers, some of which, she said, were absolutely amazing. There was one in particular that was particularly amazing that she could not yet talk about.

"I can't honestly tell you that I did not consider the possibility beforehand—there in our meetings before the debate—that we would draw attention like flies for what we were about to do," she said, "but I can honestly tell you I had no idea it would be anything like this."

I moved in on that statement and I did so too fast, too forcefully. I told her I was interested in what led to their decision to go after Meredith the way they did.

"I understand Howley had the statements from the women," I said. "Is that right?"

Her mouth puckered, her shoulders snapped backward, her whole body became a red flag. "Who told you that?"

"I have my sources," I said, much too glibly, stupidly.

"We all agreed not to talk about what happened in that room. I keep my word, all right? No more questions about that. I cannot believe any of the others told you a thing about that. You're fishing, aren't you? Yeah, that's it. Well, go throw your line into somebody else's pond. They ain't biting here."

I had my plan. Thus the name of Joan Naylor was in my mind, in my mouth, and moving right for my lips. I was about to say something like "Joan Naylor is cooperating with me. I had a long session with her yesterday, in fact, with more coming." Something kept those words from actually being spoken. Something I sensed and reacted to by reflex must have arisen in me at that moment to shut my mouth. Thank God for it.

Instead, I asked about her life, her career. We talked for another twenty minutes and she agreed to talk to me again as soon as she could, as soon as her life "returned to dull."

I told her it was possible it never would.

"I'm beginning to think that, too," she said.

★

Henry Ramirez, like Barbara, had not responded to my initial message in Williamsburg. When I finally got through to him Tuesday afternoon, he said he was sorry and that he remembered me from our jogging encounter on Duke of Gloucester Street. "I was panting after Jack and Jill," he said. "Now they and everybody else are panting after me."

I pressed him for an appointment at any time of day or night as soon as possible, and he said he really had no time, none at all, in the next many days.

I asked him if he jogged every day.

You bet, he said. Around a track at a school in the neighborhood.

What if we run together? I asked.

Sure, he said.

And so the next morning at seven there we were running side by side around a high-school cinder track in Arlington, Virginia, the next-door Washington suburb.

After my experience with Barbara Manning the afternoon before, I went more cautiously. I began with questions about what Williamsburg had already done to his life, and he detailed the calls and the offers. Sam Rhodes had gotten through to him, too. He told me how he had gotten his wish to be interviewed at length by one of his own colleagues and about the reaction of his mother in Falfurrias, Texas. She had told him that she thought her son was the best person on that stage. She told him that everybody in the Valley, even some of the Anglos, agreed. She said there was already an effort under way to rename the junior high school in Falfurrias after Henry. That morning he had been faxed a letter inviting him to make the commencement address at Texas A&I at Kingsville, his alma mater. It was only after several minutes of chat-up like this that I backed in to Williamsburg.

"I never had a chance to look at those women's statements you-all were reading from," I said. "What did they look like?"

"Look like? They looked like white pieces of paper with black typed writing on them."

"I'd give anything to see them," I said.

"You came to the wrong man, amigo," Henry said. "There was only one copy of each and they left with the man who brought 'em."

"I don't guess Howley said where he got them, did he?"

We had been running for about twenty minutes and were now on our sixth go-around on the quarter-mile track. Like Barbara at the Sheraton-Carlton coffee shop, Henry had also been hailed and hollered at by newly won fans. I was struck by his open happiness. He loved being recognized. He loved being Henry Ramirez. He loved talking to me.

"Nope" was his answer.

"What did he say about them when he threw them out on the table in front of the three of you?"

"Forget it, amigo," he said, not missing a step or a breath. "We're not talking about any of that."

"I understand Howley and Joan Naylor came to Williamsburg with this plan already worked out," I said. It was another tried-and-true trick of the journalist trade. Say something outrageous, forcing the source to correct it and, in doing so, reveal what you are really trying to find out.

"What plan, what are you talking about?" Henry said.

"They came with the statements. They came to get you and Barbara Manning to agree to go after Meredith, to get him to blow up the way he did."

"That's taco bullshit."

"How do you know that?"

"I was with them. I know them. It's taco bullshit."

"The old foxhole line?"

"Now what are you saying?"

"If you've been in a foxhole with somebody, you know them."

"OK, OK. Call it that. Call it anything you want. I know them. They would not, did not, do that."

"How did it come up?"

"Forget it, amigo. I have a very important breakfast to go to. Big job prospect. Big secret."

He wouldn't say anything more about the big secret, but he talked straight and openly about his problems with Continental Radio. He told me the story about how the president of the network threatened to take him off the panel in the first place.

"What does he think about it now?" I asked.

"He loved me not, now he loves me," Henry said. "He wants to give me my own show maybe. He wants me to come to dinner with his fancy friends in Georgetown, he wants me to speak to the annual convention of the affiliate stations, he wants me to marry his daughter, who knows? He thinks I am wonderful, just like my mama does."

"That must really piss you off after what he said before the debate," I said.

"No way, José. Nothing can piss me off right now. Nothing."

We said our good-byes, but he, like Barbara and Joan before him, did agree to see me again when I and their schedules were ready and could mesh. In the notes I wrote after he was gone, I said: "Ramirez—comfortable, at ease, charming, real."

★

That breakfast Henry was hurrying off to turned out to be one of the most important of his and Barbara Manning's lives.

They were invited through intermediaries to meet with Joshua L. Simonsen, the president of the ABS television network, and Bob Lucas, the president of ABS News. They met in a dining room of a private suite at the Four Seasons Hotel in Georgetown.

"There are some things that cry out to be discussed honestly," said Simonsen right at the beginning of the breakfast.

"We believe we spotted a potential in the two of you as a team to revolutionize Sunday-morning television," said Lucas. "Revolutionizing television, one time slot at a time, is what we are up to at ABS."

"We are interested in the possibility of the two of you, as a team, taking over our Sunday-morning slot," Lucas said. "The approach we have there now is running third behind the other two programs in that slot. We are used to being number one in all slots, and we are used to doing what it takes to be number one in any and all slots. And we believe that it might be possible that what we need to do now to be number one in that slot is to put the two of you there, as a team. What do you think?"

"The first thing I think is that Ross Perot is not going to like that," Barbara said.

"He is *our* problem," Simonsen said.

"You mean you'd just up and fire Ross Perot?" Henry asked.

"Ross comes from the business world," Simonsen said. "He understands that products and people who do not produce are replaced by people or products that do."

"Nobody fires Ross Perot," Henry said. "He'd come after you guys with everything he's got. It would not be pretty."

Lucas said: "Look, I appreciate your concern for and about Perot. He really is our problem. We want to know the level of your interest."

Barbara and Henry exchanged large grins—possibly the largest of their lives up to that point. "For discussion purposes, let's say we might be interested," Henry said to the two ABS men. "What happens next?"

"We would move this discussion to the venue of agents and lawyers and see what can be worked out," Simonsen said.

"We don't have agents, but we'll get a couple," Barbara said.

"Well, well, this went a lot easier than we thought it might," said Lucas.

"We were afraid you had been deluged with offers and opportunities since Sunday," said Simonsen. "That is why we moved so quickly."

"We have," Henry said.

Both Henry and Barbara told me they had not laid eyes on each other or exchanged a word in the two days since Williamsburg. Both had been approached with "feelers" about potential job offers, but this ABS thing was the first and only joint-venture proposal. In other words, Ross Perot had cast the seeds of his own departure from his own job with his parting comment to Henry and Barbara about their looking like a team sitting there across from him.

Now, as they went from one course in their white-coat-delivered-and-served meal to another, it became clear that Simonsen and Lucas, the men who would fire Ross Perot, had some wrinkles in mind.

"Do you always use the name Henry?" Lucas asked Henry over a cherry danish thing.

"Yes, sir, I use it because that is what it is," Henry replied.

"Would you have any problems being called Hank?"

"I have never been called Hank in my life."

Simonsen turned to Barbara. "Does Barb as a nickname have any resonance for you?"

"Nope."

"What are you getting at?" Henry asked.

"We're getting at the potential attractiveness of a program titled *Sunday Morning with Hank and Barb*."

"As in 'Jack and Jill'?" Henry said.

"In a way, yes," Simonsen said. "Fight fire with fire, you might say."

Barbara fought back an urge to laugh out loud, to giggle, to scream.

Henry talked to himself, saying: Hank, Hank, Hank. Hello, I'm Hank Ramirez of *The Hank and Barb Show*. Hank, Hank, Hank. Hello, Mama, this is your son Hank. Hello, America, this is Hank Ramirez, the nation's first son of illegal-alien parents to be a Sunday-morning talk-show co-host.

"In the interest of further honesty," Simonsen said, "a romantic link between the two of you might also be helpful."

"Oh, come on!" Barbara said. She thrust her white linen napkin down on the table a little harder than she intended. "This is getting ridiculous."

"Are you saying you have no interest in me as a man?" Henry said. "Am I only a journalist to you, only someone you can ask questions at debates with?"

There were smiles everywhere now.

"We just wanted everything on the table now, right up front," Lucas said. "The crying out for honesty is still being heard."

Barbara said: "Look, I am as ambitious as the next little African American girl. But this is stupid . . . and embarrassing."

"Sí, sí," Henry said. "You can't negotiate something like a romantic interest, for God's sake."

Simonsen said: "We realize that, believe me we do. But please, think about it from our point of view. We have a Sunday-morning slot problem because of Jack and Jill. How do you compete with Jack and Jill? You come up with your own Jack and Jill. But one with a different slant, so to speak. A Jack and Jill who are Hank and Barb, who are young, who are minorities, who are the most prominent celebrities in American journalism at this moment in time. Think about it from our point of view."

Lucas said: "Would you be interested in simulating some romantic interest?"

"Simulating?"

"What?"

Lucas said: "It could always be our secret."

Simonsen said: "You might say it was our un-dirty little secret."

Barbara said she moved her chair away from the table. She was out of there.

Henry said he moved his chair away from the table. He was *adelante mucho.*

Simonsen said: "We are prepared to offer you two-year, no-cut contracts that pay each of you two million dollars annually, plus guaranteed monthly bonuses tied to ratings performance. Obviously, the twenty-four-hour limo, New York and Washington apartments, and other usual network perks would apply."

Barbara moved her chair back to the table.

Henry moved his chair back to the table.

They stayed for more coffee and a new life.

10

Go, Tom, Go

Election Day came to America that Tuesday as a foregone conclusion. The result in the race for president of the United States was considered a solid sure thing by the time the first in-person ballots were cast
in that small town in New Hampshire where the polls open at 6:00 A.M.,
Eastern Time.

The opinion polls and the pundits of all stripes and persuasions had
Governor Paul L. Greene winning by a landslide—by more than 10 percent of the popular vote, by a huge margin in the electoral votes. The
debate did exactly what Mike Howley, Joan Naylor, Barbara Manning,
and Henry Ramirez had in mind. It transformed the race for president of
the United States.

Not only did every probable voter in America see and hear what happened, so did an extra few million nonprobables. The Nielsen ratings,
which said that an estimated 132 million Americans watched all or part
of the debate, also reported that most hung in there for the Virginia Room
disturbance and news conference as well as many of the Jack and Jill,
Ross, Norman, and other reaction broadcasts afterward. The Election Day

turnout nationally had been projected to be only about 105 million. So, as the *New York Newsday* television critic observed: "Obviously some kids and convicted felons who couldn't vote also loved the show."

The total effect was an astonishing reversal in the horse race. Within hours after the debate, the Hart-Divall poll of 1,789 homes showed Greene making up 15 points on Meredith. The other major media polls all reported similar dramatic ocean-liner-turning-on-a-dime change, with Greene rocketing within seventy-two hours to an 11-point—on average— lead over Meredith from a position 12 points—on average—behind him before Sunday's debate. Every leading political pollster in America said it was historic, incredible, unbelievable. Nothing like it had ever happened before.

The debate had also turned Paul L. Greene into a whole new person and candidate. In the words of Teddy Lemmon on the front page of *The New York Herald,* Greene "came away from Williamsburg about as born-again as it was possible to get." A new forcefulness came into his speeches. New crowds came out to hear and to see and to touch him. The post-Williamsburg news stories referred to him as being "previously underrated," as "the stealth candidate," "the man from nowhere Nebraska who was suddenly somewhere everywhere." Long "second-look" profiles appeared in print and on all kinds of air, and so did the first stories ever about the possible makeup of a Greene administration.

Since the debate, there had been little said that was favorable about David Donald Meredith, the man who had everything going for him nine days before the election. The initial reports and my own reporting since bear out that he left Williamsburg in an acute, advanced state of livid that he never got over. There was angry red around his eyes, angry spit around his words, angry motions around his every gesture.

At an airport news conference in Newport News that Sunday night and at every campaign stop through the Midwest the next day, he called on the American people to join him in a national day of prayer to draw strength and guidance from God to rise up against what "those four scum who dare call themselves journalists" have done. He denied the accuracy of the individual statements read during the debate and of the general allegation that there was a violent side to his personality. By the end of the day he had to also furiously deny that his call to rise up was a camouflaged call on some fanatic supporter to murder Howley, Joan, Barbara, and Henry. He said nothing about his use of the F-word and his violent departure from the debate stage.

Meredith continued to campaign, but the crowds were small, the rhetoric sour and high-pitched. He was seen by the reporters who traveled with him as a "mortally wounded candidate," "a member of the walking dead," "a shrinking giant," "a destroyed, decaying figure," "a morose man of tragedy." He never again submitted to questions from any reporter about the debate, the F-word, or anything else.

The polls and the frenzied follow-up reporting showed that the abuse allegations against Meredith, reinforced by his own conduct at the end of the debate, had sticking and staying power. As Jack and Jill and the others discovered on Sunday night, most of the women who were found and interviewed confirmed what they had said in their statements. Even critics who saw the four panelists as villains saw Meredith as a bigger one. "Emotional instability of this kind in a president is simply unacceptable," said *The Detroit News* in its editorial. *The Wall Street Journal* was the most prominent holdout. It had been almost alone among newspapers, large or small, in strongly supporting Meredith and everything he stood for before the debate. It continued its lonely stand postdebate by calling the abuse charges "an irrelevant diversion" and the cussword outburst "an understandable slip of the emotional tongue." Women's groups accused the *Journal* of endorsing violence against women, while Christian-right groups accused the *Journal* of endorsing public profanity.

Every poll, and even every radio call-in host, reported the public believed the accusers but mostly believed their own eyes that saw Meredith lose control of himself on national television. "The sound of those bad words and the crash of the podium may go down as the loudest and most critical sounds ever heard in a presidential election," wrote David Broder in *The Washington Post*. David Donald Meredith, less than a fortnight away from being elected president of the United States, had been destroyed, shot completely and forever out of the political water, by four journalists and himself.

The arrival of Election Day was seen by most people in and out of politics and journalism almost as a form of mercy killing. Meredith had been kept alive by artificial means since that Sunday night in Williamsburg. It was time to pull the plug, to put the sad, mean creature and the rest of us who had to watch him out of our misery.

But for the Greene and Meredith people and others closely connected with the campaign, the cat was by no means in the bag. The conventional wisdom that political polls are gospel to political pros is mostly wrong. I found that they sweat them and talk obsessively about them and use them to make points, but in the final analysis most of them don't really believe the polls. They particularly don't believe any that show anybody winning anything by an overwhelming margin.

So the operatives in both the Greene and Meredith campaigns and at the two national committees, and the reporters and editors and producers at the networks, wire services, and newspapers, started their day as they did all Election Days. At full expectation, at full edgy.

It was not until almost noon, Eastern Time, that the first of the exit polls began to come in from New York, New Jersey, Florida, Massachusetts, and the other New England states. It was then that it became real. The election most pundits, editorial writers, and political scientists had already called "the Greatest Turnaround in American Election History" was clearly going to be "the Greatest Turnaround in American Election History." The sweeping nature of what had happened to Meredith was made dramatically evident when exit polls from Virginia, North Carolina, South Carolina, and Georgia showed Greene way ahead.

As always, the networks and the wire services said not a word about the exit polls so as not to discourage people from voting later in the day. The stories talked only about turnout—which was heavier than expected—and what the pre-election opinion polls had predicted would happen.

It was not until 9:01 P.M., Eastern Time, that the anchorpeople on all three commercial networks declared Governor Paul L. Greene of Nebraska to be the projected sure winner of the race for president of the United States.

Greene came out to a cheering crowd in the ballroom of the Park Plaza Hotel in Lincoln, Nebraska, a few minutes later to claim victory.

"I am overwhelmed by the show of confidence the people of this great country have placed in me on this historic day," he said. "I am not overwhelmed by the task ahead. I will do it. I will do it in a manner that will

give no one who voted for me today any reason to ever regret their votes—
no matter their reason for so voting."

That line about reasons was as close as he came to acknowledging
the extraordinary circumstances that had caused him to win this election.

David Donald Meredith became the first presidential candidate in
modern times not to make a public appearance on election night. A crowd
of his closest followers gathered at the Sheraton in downtown Charlotte,
but they had nothing to celebrate, nothing to cheer. The networks did
only fast brushes past their red-white-and-blue-decorated ballroom.

There was not even any definitive word on exactly where Meredith
was. In the last three days of the campaign he had canceled all of his
planned national television commercials and made only a handful of perfunctory campaign appearances. There had also been stories of massive
layoffs and a possible shutdown of the entire Take It Back operation in
Charlotte.

As David Brinkley said on television that night: "David Donald
Meredith's demise gives real meaning to the term 'defeated.' Never has
any candidate for president been so thoroughly and completely defeated."

★

Joan Naylor, still under suspension "for her own good," watched the
returns with Jeff and the twins in their Cleveland Park den.

Barbara and Henry had planned to get together for a late-night drink
among the ferns in the lush bar at the Four Seasons. But it did not come
off, because both ended up having to spend the evening in their respective newsrooms. Neither had a real assignment other than to simply be
there in their new famousness and watch it all on television with their
less famous colleagues. Their deal with ABS was still a deep secret, but it
was very much in the works and only days from being signed and
announced. Each felt spending the evening at their old office was the
least they could do before becoming Hank and Barb.

Mike Howley watched the returns by himself in the front room of his
town house. His only companion was a bottle of Cutty Sark scotch.

He and the other three heard what was said on television after the
9:01 calls and every few minutes from then on. Pundit after pundit,
anchorperson after anchorperson, campaign official after campaign offi-

cial, said this election had been historic, incredible, unbelievable. Nothing like it had ever happened.

Both Brad Lilly and Jack Turpin made the rounds of the network election-night programs. Lilly spoke glowingly of what the four panelists had done at the debate, comparing them to "all warriors who have risked their bodies and souls for their country." He was less glowing in describing his candidate, the president-elect. The world was to find out a week later what caused the restraint. Brad Lilly would not be going to the White House with Greene, as everyone had expected.

Turpin's anger with Howley, Barbara, Henry, Joan, and the press generally had not abated. He said they were "the political equivalent of war criminals," "no more than thugs who used words instead of guns." He was asked about the state of mind of Meredith, but he could honestly say he had no idea. Meredith had fired him as campaign manager right after the debate.

Mack McLarty, one of the twenty-seven pundits appearing on ABS, spoke for most of his fellow pundits when he summed it all up at the 12:30 A.M., Eastern Time, sign-off this way:

"History is replete with times when the press of America was accused of deciding the outcome of a presidential election. This marks the first time such a charge is absolutely one hundred percent accurate, directly on the mark, and thus a remarkable milestone in the political and journalistic history of our still-young nation. Paul L. Greene was elected president of the United States today because four journalists made an unprecedented decision to act in an unprecedented fashion. I think, for the record, it is well to repeat their names. Michael J. Howley of *The Washington Morning News*, Joan Naylor of CNS News, Barbara Manning of *This Week* magazine, and Henry Ramirez of Continental Radio. Some are tonight, no doubt, calling them patriots, journalism heroes of a new kind. Others are calling them arrogant un-patriots, journalism villains of a new and scary kind.

"Whatever, those four individuals, as individuals, go to bed on this election night knowing that what they did was something momentous, something they must know with certainty will be the subject of debate—the debate about the debate—for a very long time. Maybe for all of time."

Henry Ramirez told me that McLarty's words, as well as others spoken on election night, only reaffirmed his belief and pride in what he had done.

Barbara Manning said she sat there in the Washington bureau of *This Week* in front of Mel Renfro and all of the other white boys and cried and cried and cried.

Were they tears of joy or pain? I asked.

"Both," she replied.

Joan Naylor said her twins hugged her and said how proud they were of their mother. Jeff said the same thing. She admitted to me that it was late, more than two hours after they went to bed, before she went to sleep.

"I didn't have second thoughts, really," she said. "Call them dawning thoughts. It truly dawned on me at 9:01, Eastern Time, what I had been a party to. I had participated in the changing of the course of this nation in a way that most people as individuals never have the opportunity to do."

Should four individuals have such power? I asked.

"Thinking about that was what kept me awake," she replied.

I asked Howley what was in his mind at 9:01. His answer was dismissive. "I don't recall having anything in particular," he said.

I considered it to be a stupid and completely unbelievable thing to say.

No real or sane person in Michael J. Howley's position that evening could have avoided having a lightning storm of conflicting thoughts crashing, cracking, smashing, banging around in his head.

★

My first major breakthrough concerning Mike Howley came two days after the election and from a most unlikely source—Jerry Rhome, the executive editor of and Howley's boss at *The Washington Morning News*. I called him that Thursday morning almost in a perfunctory checklist way, not really expecting anything but stonewalling and difficulty. I was stunned when he took my call within seconds, said he knew and respected Jonathan Angel and his magazine, and then without hesitation agreed to talk to me.

He told me to meet him in the lobby of the *News* building in a couple of hours—at one o'clock—and we could walk a bit and then eat some lunch.

"They're waiting for Howley," he said as we passed a covey of television crews waiting on the sidewalk outside the *News* building. "Everybody's waiting for Howley."

Instead of turning left in the direction of Lafayette Park and the White House we went to the right, toward Massachusetts Avenue. We crossed Sixteenth Street at Logan Circle and passed right in front of the headquarters of the National Rifle Association. Jerry Rhome raised the middle finger of his left hand high in the air in the direction of the building.

"I despise those bastards," he said, almost by rote.

We cut across Rhode Island toward Herb's, the restaurant in the basement of the Holiday Inn on the corner of Rhode Island and Seventeenth Street. Rhome said Herb's was a hangout for writers and others in what passed for the working arts world of Washington. He said it was his favorite place to have lunch because the noise, the company, and the price were all right.

"I hate being interviewed," he said as we sat down. "The only thing I hate more are people like me—people in the business—who refuse to be interviewed."

We were given a table—I had the feeling it was his whenever he wanted it—in a corner of a room with walls covered with autographed photographs, framed theater posters, and paintings and sketches by local artists. The table was right next to a large glass-enclosed bookcase full of books by Washington writers who came here for lunch. Two of Mike Howley's "Campaign Diaries" books were in there along with the one he had co-authored with Pat Tubbs and five of the more recent and more famous ones written by Tubbs alone.

Rhome ordered Cobb salad. I ordered a turkey club sandwich on toasted wheat bread, and he asked me where I wanted to begin. He was a straightforward man of charm and edge, the kind most of us—particularly those of us in journalism—would love to be. I had no trouble understanding why he was admired, feared, and mythologized by the people who worked with, around, for, and against him.

I told him I wanted to start at the very beginning, with the decision of the *News* to change its policy on debates.

"Mike said he had been invited to moderate Williamsburg. I heard him out and we changed the policy," he said. I then asked for and he gave me the details of his long walk to Lafayette Park with Howley.

"Did you know he was going to go after Meredith the way he did?" I asked.

"Hell, no, I didn't!"

"He didn't call you or talk to you to clear it with you?"

"Mike Howley does not clear things like that with me."

"Do you wish he had?"

"I don't know."

"What would you have told him if he had asked for your OK?"

"I don't know. Jesus."

Our lunch arrived and his relief was obvious. I could tell that here was a man who was uncomfortable, who was doing this in much the same way he would have corrective gum or open heart surgery.

"After the fact now, what do you think of what he and the other three did?" I asked after we ate a few bites accompanied by some irrelevant small talk.

He said: "I think it could change journalism forever. I think the idea of people like you and me, Mike and those others, deciding the people don't know what they're doing is dangerous as hell. We're accused of doing it all the time, but it took something like Williamsburg to make me realize we really don't do it very often. I've got to think about it some more, to tell you the real truth. I really do. I've got to wonder if the pants were on the other legs, if Mike and them knew all of that about a good guy, would they have sprung it on him like that a few days before an election? I know the argument. I know no two cases, no two elections, no two candidates, are the same. Meredith really was a prick who definitely should not have become president of the United States. I might have moved to Venice or Paris, in fact, if he had. He was more than a prick, he was a menace to the country. He was all of those awful things all of us who have ever covered politics always worried would come along. Here in this one person were all of the worst traits of Perot, North, both Jesses, Farrakhan, Limbaugh, Dole, Brown, and Zhirinovsky, all rolled into one. I know all of that. But I wonder. I've got to think about it some more. . . ."

I tried to read what he said for anything more, any hidden agendas—personal or otherwise. I could find none. I had the feeling that he was merely answering a difficult question as truthfully as he could. I continued to be very impressed with Jerry Rhome.

"Is there an official *News* position on what Howley did?" I asked.

There was a flicker in his eyes—they were green—that signaled trouble.

"Sure," he said. "It was in our lead editorial the next morning."

"I mean on a more personal basis, say, with the Gerrards."

There was another flicker. This time the message was clear. Oh, shit, it said.

Herman Gerrard was the owner-publisher of the *News*. His two sons, one niece, and two nephews worked for him as vice presidents and assistants to the president of the holding company that owned the *News* plus a discount bookstore chain, a discount beauty-shop chain, seven neighborhood health spas in northern Virginia, a flock of Wendy's hamburger restaurants, and the Washington area's largest charter and tour bus operator, called Vision Lines.

Rhome said: "Look, it was what you would have expected. At first they were appalled along with most everyone else, and then they were confused, and finally, now, they are proud. Right on, Mike, and God bless America."

I asked what Howley's status was with the *News*. He told me what I already mostly knew from reading the clippings. Howley was not allowed to write anything about the election between the debate and Election Day. The ban was ordered, said the announcement, to "avoid potential appearance problems." It applied to straight news stories, analytical pieces, and even his column. He also agreed to a management request to avoid all outside interviews on television and radio as well as all print outlets. This meant he did not even take his regular slots on the NBS morning program or the opinion food-fight program on Saturday night.

"What happens now?" I said.

"He has a job at *The Washington Morning News* as long as he wants it."

"Does he want it?"

"I'm sure he does."

"You haven't talked to him?"

"Not lately."

"Where is he?"

"None of your business."

The green eyes were full of play and mischief now. Anything else, young man? they said to me.

Yes, I had something else.

"Where did that stuff about Meredith come from?" I asked.

There was no change in his expression or eyes. He said: "If I knew I probably wouldn't tell you, but I don't know so it isn't even a problem for me."

"Have you asked Howley?"

"Nope."

"Why not?"

"Because I didn't want to know."

Now he was mad. Not at me, I didn't think, but at somebody else. Howley? Yeah, it had to be Howley. Why, why, why? Then I had the answer. The obvious answer.

I said: "I guess you must have wondered the same thing I did. If it came from Howley, then why hadn't it all appeared in *The Washington Morning News* before that night in Williamsburg?"

"I'm not talking," he said.

"One can't help but wonder why he saved it for the debate instead of writing it up for his own newspaper."

I had Jerry Rhome on the horns of several dilemmas. He took a long swallow of iced tea and fooled with a black olive on his plate and looked off at the bookshelf at Howley's, Tubbs's, and the other books.

I said: "I'm willing to go on background, if you wish. I use it but not attributed to you."

"I'm a goddamn newspaperman, Chapman, not—to use Meredith's word—the fucking deputy under assistant secretary of state for bilateral governmental intercourse or something. I don't go on background with anybody."

I shut up and let him fool with his napkin and rearrange the salt and pepper shakers and the saucer of little pink packets of sugar substitute there in the center of the table between us.

The waiter came and asked if we wanted some dessert and coffee. We both said no to dessert, yes to coffee. It bought Jerry Rhome some more time. I knew what he was doing. As a journalist himself, he was try-ing to imagine how what he was tempted to say would look in the cold type of *The New American Tatler* magazine. It is one thing to say some-thing to somebody in a relaxed setting such as this, but he knew from his own hands-on experience on the other side that cold-type print is trans-forming. Innocent words can become something very different.

Finally, he spoke: "I am not going to dodge it. OK? Sure, I got hot watching that debate. I didn't understand why with all of the great god-damn reporters we have working for my great goddamn newspaper we didn't get that story. It doubled—tripled—the hot when I'm listening to *the* story of the presidential campaign being thrown out there in Williams-burg by my leading political reporter, a man who works for me, a man who draws a nice salary from me, a man who I thought understood that I get first dibs on all stories he comes across in the course of his exciting work as a famous journalist of our times. OK? I said it. OK?"

He said it, all right. But it didn't make sense. Something did not add up.

"So I guess you really jumped Howley about that, right?" I asked.

"Nope, not really. Whatever I said is none of your business anyhow."

"I'm confused."

"Good."

The coffee came and Jerry Rhome changed the subject. To me. He asked me questions about how I got into magazine writing and about Jonathan Angel and the *Tatler*. He told me how Jonathan had worked for him as a kid reporter and how he always read our magazine. Rhome was doing to another what he as a reporter had probably had done to him many times by people skilled in handling reporters. I am sure there is a rule among the smart, experienced interviewees: No reporter can resist the opportunity to talk about himself.

I resisted—almost. I told him only a little bit about growing up in Connecticut and going to Williams College. I said almost nothing about Jonathan and the magazine.

Then, as we walked out—he insisted on paying the check—I resumed my business.

"There is no real doubt that those statements were brought to Williamsburg by Howley, is there?"

"I have some doubt."

"I don't."

He looked at me as if to say, OK, bud, stop it there. If I want to know anything more I'll ask. We walked in silence back across Rhode Island. Rhome again shot the finger to the NRA building, and we headed toward his newspaper.

As we got closer to the *News* I realized that while with some of the others on my master interview list there might be second, third, and even fourth or fifth chances for follow-up and cleanup questions, this was probably it for Jerry Rhome. I either got it now or I didn't get it.

I said: "So where do you think Howley would have gotten those statements?"

"*If* he had them, you mean. If he had them, he could have gotten them from the Greene campaign or from some other troublemaking Democrat. There are lots of places he could have gotten them."

"But wouldn't he have brought them right to you or somebody else at the *News* if it had happened that way?"

He closed his eyes, shook his head. We were past the waiting-for-Howley TV crews now and were only seconds away from parting. He was only seconds away from escape. I was only seconds away from getting a scrap of information that I was certain—still without knowing what it was—would be extremely important.

"I hear you," he said. "But that's all I do."

"Could somebody from the *News*—another reporter, say—have given them to him?"

"Not and kept his balls if I ever found out about it." His eyes reinforced his words. There was no question he would have personally de-balled such a person.

I walked away from Jerry Rhome convinced that he had either already found out about it or had a damned good guess about it. It meant, if my reading was right, I now also knew how those statements got to Howley. All I had to find out was the name of the *News* reporter who did it—and how and why it was done.

Go, Tom, go.

★

There was a man waiting to see me when I returned to the *Tatler* office that afternoon. It was the man from *The Kansas City Star*. I knew from reading accounts of the Virginia Room riot that his name was Richard Fisher and he was fifty-nine years old. He was holding a cane by his right side when he stood up to shake my hand, but otherwise he looked fine.

"I don't think it's exaggerating to say that you saved my life, Tom Chapman," he said. "I came by just to say thank you."

He gave me a copy of the first-person account of his experience in the Virginia Room that he had written for his newspaper. The headline was A SCRAPE WITH DEATH BY PRESS-ING.

In the story he gave full credit to me as his savior. He did not mention the former football player–SEAL from the *Baltimore Sun*. He said he didn't know about any of that because by then he was completely out of it, but he would find the guy and thank him, too.

I liked Richard Fisher. Maybe the foxhole rule is real. Maybe difficult experiences do bond people together quicker and firmer than all others. Whatever, I found myself talking to him like we had known each other for years.

After a while he asked me what I was up to and I told him. I told him all about my assignment, all about how I was trying to piece together the many parts of the what, how, and why of the debate. I talked a lot more than I should have and revealed a lot more than I should have, violating a working-press rule against telling another reporter anything you would mind seeing in/on that other reporter's newspaper, magazine, newscast, or whatever.

But with this man, this man whose life I had saved, I forgot myself. I told him about my need to find out where those women's abuse statements came from. Richard Fisher, without a second's hesitation, said: "Ask them."

"Who?"

"The women. Somebody had to approach them and interview them."

In retrospect, I think it is fair to say that it is more than likely that I would have eventually arrived at that simple—and obvious—approach on my own. But sitting there at that moment in my office, I saw the man in front of me, Richard Fisher of *The Kansas City Star*, to be a journalistic genius of some kind.

The way I saw it at that moment, he had returned the favor. He had saved *my* life.

★

Richard Fisher of *The Kansas City Star* was barely out the door before I went to work with Jennifer Gates and our ever mounting files of clippings, transcripts, notes, and other material. We assembled a list of fourteen names of women, mentioned during the debate directly or by apparent inference, who had made statements of one kind or another about the violent outbursts of David Donald Meredith.

Seven, according to what we could glean from picking through the reams of follow-up interviews and other material, lived in the Charlotte, North Carolina, area. Another was in Asheville, North Carolina, and the rest were spread around the country.

Within an hour we had phone numbers for several of them, and I asked Jennifer to stay on the task of finding the numbers of the others while I placed the first call. It was to Jonell Jane Hampstead of Charlotte, who allegedly saw Meredith strike his then fourteen-year-old daughter.

The phone was answered on the second ring by the recorded deep voice of a man with a very southern accent. He said: "Hello, this is Kenneth L. Dixon. I am an attorney here in Charlotte. I represent Mrs. Hampstead. If you are calling about something personal, by all means, leave your name and a number after the beep and someone will get back to you. But if you are from the news media or otherwise involved in inquiries related to the Williamsburg Debate, then I would ask that you call my office. My number is area code 704-555-3556. My secretary's name is Norma. Thank you."

I dialed the number for the second woman on my list. She was Terri Anne Cloverdell, who alleged Meredith slugged her for being slow to retrieve a book. She also lived in Charlotte.

On the second ring I heard: "Hello, this is Kenneth L. Dixon. I am an attorney here in Charlotte. I represent Miss Cloverdell. . . ."

He was also there for Yolanda Dinkins, a former Meredith neighbor with the story about Mrs. Meredith's crying after claiming she had been hit by her husband, for Isabelle Anne Mathews, the USAir employee who claimed Meredith struck her with his briefcase, and for three others on the list in Charlotte.

So I called Kenneth L. Dixon. Norma told me Mr. Dixon was "dictating" but would be back to me as soon as he could. "Is it urgent, Mr. Chapman?" she asked in a voice that was a female version of Dixon's. I assured her it was urgent.

Dixon was back to me in a few minutes. I told him that I wanted to ask his clients some questions about their statements concerning Meredith.

"Well, so do a lot of other people, Mr. Chapman," he replied. "There are so many people who want to talk to them, in fact, that we have had to set some circumstances for such talk."

Circumstances? I wasn't following him. I said: "All I want to know are a few details about who talked to them in the first place and took their original statements," I said. "It won't take more than a couple of minutes for each of them."

Kenneth L. Dixon laughed. "How many times have I heard that in the last few days?" he said.

"What do you mean about circumstances?" I said. "What must I do in order to talk to them?"

"Well, for one thing, you must keep in mind that these women are working women. The time that they spend talking to you is time they are not spending doing their work and thus not generating income."

Now I was following him. "They want to be paid for their interviews, is that it?"

"That's it, Mr. Chapman."

He gave me the price list: $1,500 for each interview of under fifteen minutes, $2,500 up to thirty minutes, $4,000 for thirty minutes. Anything more was "to be negotiated."

"I promise you I will not need more than five minutes for each," I said.

"Sorry, friend," said Dixon, "but it wouldn't be fair to all of the others to violate the minimums."

"What others?"

"The other reporters who have come before you and will come after you."

"How about some kind of package rate for doing all seven?"

Kenneth L. Dixon, an operator, was with me—probably even ahead of me. "What's your offer?" he said.

"Five thousand for five minutes from each of the seven."

"In person or on the phone?"

"What difference does that make?"

"It's easier and we can make sure it's a real five if it's on the phone. We just hang up when the time is up."

"Phone."

"Deal. Payable in advance."

Within minutes I got an OK from Jonathan Angel and he authorized wiring $5,000 to Kenneth L. Dixon, Esq., Charlotte, North Carolina.

Then the next morning beginning at ten, in accordance with a schedule his Norma worked out with Jennifer Gates, I called all seven of the women on the Charlotte list.

I asked each only about how they came to give their original statement, the one referred to in the Williamsburg Debate. The only two consistencies in their answers were the timing—all were interviewed the previous May—and the fact that each was asked to maintain absolute confidentiality about having given her statement.

The first said that the original contact came from a woman identifying herself as a "friend of the Meredith family" who was interested in "mending some family fences." The interview itself was done by a second woman, "dressed like a lawyer," who said she "took statements for a living."

Number two said that a man, flashing a badge the words on which she couldn't read, said he was trying to run down for dismissal an old "rumor of assault against Mr. Meredith." She assumed he was a policeman or FBI agent—maybe even with the CIA.

The third was interviewed by an older man who carried a small black bag and "looked like a doctor." He said that he was a psychologist looking for answers to questions about what prompted "violent behavior in men of power."

The fourth woman, a Catholic, said that a man in his mid-thirties dressed as a Catholic priest did the contacting and talking in her case. He said he ran a ministry in Raleigh—the capital of North Carolina—that "helped women recover from violent abuse."

The fifth, the wife of a Republican member of the North Carolina legislature, said only that she gave her statement "to somebody who lied to me about who he was." She refused to say anything more.

The sixth and seventh were even less forthcoming. One said: "It happened and it's true. What else matters?" The other said: "I am not answering those questions. You ought to ask Dixon for some of your money back."

I had already had a similar thought.

This transaction, of course, as well as several others of mine, has set off barrages of condemnation and censure from Howley (see Appendix) and others in the self-anointed "responsible" press. They accused me of practicing checkbook journalism, a charge to which I plead guilty and do so without remorse or apology. Please, please, answer me this: Why should those women in North Carolina give away their stories to reporters like me and our conglomerate-owned media employers who then use those stories to make money and careers? We do not force farmers to give away their wheat to bakeries to turn into bread and money. Why do we expect news makers and sources to give away their commodity?

But at that moment the problem for me was not defending myself from the self-righteous and double-standard-ed. It was sorting through what the women of Charlotte had told me in search of coherent clues or scents. The sorting left me mostly questions.

★

I carried the questions with me like a low-grade fever wherever I went.

I returned to Williamsburg for three days and two nights. I walked the halls of the Inn, the Lodge, and the other buildings that had been part of the greater debate stage. And I was not the only one. Officials at Colonial Williamsburg, the masters of creating a view into eighteenth-century life in America, had been forced to set up special entrance and tour arrangements to accommodate the crowds of people who also wanted to see the auditorium and the other specific places involved in a more modern piece of history.

I spent more than an hour in Longsworth D, imagining what it must have felt like to sit in there and eat and drink and, finally, plot an unprecedented attempt to influence the outcome of a presidential election. The Virginia Room, scene of the famous riot of American journalists, was full of people again. But this time they were there to participate in a forum on American antiques. I had meals at the King's Arms and the Josiah Chowning's taverns. I even ordered and ate some of the food the panelists did during their time together. All in the name of research, of course.

I talked to many Colonial Williamsburg employees, the people who played the important parts of extras in the debate drama. They were friendly and helpful except for one important thing. None would talk about anything having to do with anything they might have seen or heard that concerned Howley or any other particular guest. Not even my offers to pay for some of the details changed any minds. As one of the room-service waiters, who I am sure could have used the extra money, said: "A person ought to be able to come down here and not worry about people like me talking about them."

But I was able to find a person—not a Williamsburg employee—who had a piece of important information. He/she told me of a conversation with a person who talked to a Williamsburg Inn room-service waiter. That waiter had made two separate trips to Howley's room that Saturday night before the debate after Howley had suddenly left the Inn bar. The man said he delivered a Cutty Sark on the rocks to Howley's room each time. The waiter told my source's source that he saw papers, some of which looked to him like official documents, strewn all over the room. He also reported that he had the following exchange with Howley when delivering the second drink:

"My, my, you are working hard tonight," said the waiter. "You are going to really pin those two candidates against the wall tomorrow night, I guess."

"Only one of them," the waiter quoted Howley as saying. Howley, according to the man, was looking around the room at all of the papers when he said it.

There is little question that those papers were the women's statements about Meredith's various outbreaks of violence.

I also picked up an important piece of information concerning Howley's phone calls that Saturday night.

All I knew before from the bartender at the Williamsburg Inn was that Howley had taken a call in the bar that caused him to hurriedly desert the bar and his freshly poured Cutty Sark on the rocks. Now I got the number of the caller. Once back in his room, Howley placed two calls to the same number. One call lasted forty-five minutes, the other fifty-seven minutes. It was an area code 202 number—Washington, D.C.

In order to protect the innocent, it is important that I explain how I got this information. I went to a non–Williamsburg employee involved indirectly in the phone billing system at Colonial Williamsburg. I told the person I was a Bell Atlantic fraud investigator checking a series of calls on the night of October 14 to and from the Williamsburg Inn that had been billed without proper authorization to an AT&T MasterCard account. I am not particularly proud of my methods, but the search for truth is not always pretty.

Back in Washington, I quickly discovered the number was unlisted. But I figured it would probably turn out to be that of a woman friend or somebody else who had love or some other kind of personal business to discuss with Michael J. Howley that Saturday night. I handed the job of tracing the number to Jennifer Gates while I went on with my interviewing.

★

I had long sessions with Chuck Hammond, Nancy Dewey, and several other staff and members of the debate commission. At first most were reluctant to say much, but they gave in after realizing—correctly—that the magnitude of this event made keeping secrets impossible. The public's interest and right to know every tiny scrap of detail overrode all natural and man-made secrecy agreements and inclinations. This is the driving force that makes it possible for outsiders to write insider books about Nixon's final days, the Supreme Court, the CIA, and Desert Storm. The larger the event, the larger the need for all involved to tell their individual stories—for the record, for history, for their grandchildren. I believe this force, in fact, helped Henry Ramirez, Barbara Manning, and Joan Naylor decide eventually to cooperate fully with me.

That force had no effect, interestingly enough, on two members of the news media—Jim Weaver of Continental Radio and Carol Reynolds of CNS News. They were no Jerry Rhomes.

Weaver refused all of my requests for an interview about his predebate threats against Henry Ramirez. He finally agreed to receive questions in writing. I submitted seven questions that were based on Henry Ramirez's account of what was said in the phone conversation and afterward. What I got back was a faxed statement from somebody named Jeffrey Walling, who identified himself as general counsel for the Continental Radio Network, West Hollywood, California. Here is that statement in its entirety:

"Jim Weaver acknowledges that he expressed his displeasure with Henry Ramirez's failure to consult with his supervisors in regard to the Williamsburg Debate panel invitation. Mr. Weaver categorically denies the tone and substance of everything else. The issues raised concern sensitive personnel matters that cannot be discussed without violating the privacy standards Continental Radio considers essential to a healthy and delicate employee-employer relationship. Mr. Weaver and all others at Continental Radio have the utmost respect and regard for the professional capabilities and personal attributes of Henry Ramirez. He is a credit to our network and to America."

Carol Reynolds would not speak to me about anything, including the process that led up to Joan Naylor's selection for the panel. She acknowledged only that she was involved. "The rest is privileged inside information," she said. I asked her how she as a professional journalist would react to someone who said that to her as a justification for not answering a legitimate inquiry. "I do not consider yours legitimate," she replied.

I spent an important afternoon with Brad Lilly.

We met in his tiny half-furnished office in a large suite of offices on K Street in downtown Washington. The sign on the main door said FOUNDATION FOR THE STUDY OF AMERICAN POLITICAL HISTORY.

"This has all the looks of a CIA front," I said to break the ice.

Lilly was in no mood for any jokes about his current station in life. "It beats sleeping on the grate outside," he said.

Then, speaking mostly in a tone of annoyed resignation, he told me everything I wanted to know. I took him through the panelist-selection meeting, the control-room chaos during the debate, and all of the other small predebate events with Greene that I thought were pertinent. I was impressed with his memory for detail, his feeling of responsibility toward helping to keep "the historical record straight."

I was surprised by his willingness to tell me how he was fired. He said Greene did it to him during the ride in the limo from Williamsburg to the Newport News–Williamsburg airport right after the debate.

He said Greene's first words to him after the limo started moving away from the Lodge were: "I don't want you to get on the plane with me. I want you out of this campaign, out of my sight."

"I was crushed beyond belief," Lilly told me. "Here we were, the favored recipients of the most glorious gift in the history of presidential politics. I was higher than I had ever been before in my life. Political and personal sugarplums were dancing in my head like Roman candles. And here he hits me—bam! It's all over. Good-bye, sugarplums. Good-bye, everything."

Lilly said he asked Greene why and he got a one-sentence answer: "I want no more of your loser mentality."

Greene would not even respond to Lilly's protest that it was him—Greene—who had the loser mentality before the debate. "Let's not talk about it anymore now or evermore," said Greene.

Lilly appealed to Greene's decency and sense of fair play, saying: "This will humiliate me in front of the world. I will be ruined forever."

Greene did not respond. Lilly said he suddenly knew what it felt like to drive a Volkswagen into a six-feet-thick concrete wall. This man was not budging. There had been a crash and he—Brad Lilly, professional political campaign manager—was the crash-ee. So he turned to the details.

He said to Greene: "What will you say to the press about me, about my leaving?"

"I will say I want to take the campaign in a new direction."

"A new direction? The debate just did that! 'Fucking' just did that!"

"You are a hired gun. Hired guns are hired and they are fired. And, please, don't think I have forgotten about your book. Write what you want.

You were going to anyhow. You were going to write that I was a loser, a fool, a whatever. Well, now you will be writing about the next president of the United States, so it will definitely improve your sales."

Then, Lilly said he said to Greene in a fit of anger and stupidity, "You can't fire me."

Greene said: "After what happened back there tonight, I can do anything I want. Out, go."

Out, go. After a good two to three minutes of absolute silence between them, Lilly said he came back with what he admitted to me was nothing more than the plea of a desperate man.

"Governor, could you give me some time—until after the election? I will stay out of the loop, out of command, out of everything, if you wish."

"How about out of my sight?"

"It's a deal."

Lilly said Greene honored the commitment and he was saved the jarring humiliation of being fired right then on the spot, but it leaked, as everything does, and he was, in his words, "only half humiliated instead."

Then I decided to toss a phony grenade. I said: "I would love to know any details you can give me on how you-all got on to Meredith's violent side, how you found the women, got their statements, passed them on to the panelists—all of that—"

Lilly did not let me even finish the question. "You must think I am some kind of idiot, Chapman."

"Well, I know it's confidential stuff, but it's all over now. Why not give me a lead or two at least?"

"Here I sit in this shithole closet of an office because I had nowhere else to go. My guy won. But he fired me, disowned me, ruined me—my network-commentator possibilities, my book contract, my consulting opportunities. I took this because they were willing to give me the use of this tiny desk, this phone, and this fifteen-year-old computer if I would write them a paper on the campaign. Now you come in here insulting my intelligence, screwing around with me. Please, buzz off. I have enough problems."

The man was clearly upset. I said: "Are you saying you did not know about those statements until they were read during the debate?"

"Yes, goddamn it. Yes. That is what I am saying. I can promise you they would have gotten out a helluva lot sooner than they did if I had.

We had heard the same rumors everyone else heard about Meredith's so-called violent side. But we never had the interest or the resources to run them down. The governor didn't believe in that kind of campaign stuff anyhow. Go ask Howley or somebody who knows. Leave me alone."

I told him Howley had thus far refused to talk to me, and the other three panelists—again, thus far—had said they did not know where the statements came from.

"Have you asked Turpin?"

"Turpin? How could he know?"

"He had those Nelson thugs working for him. He knew everything."

Turpin had reluctantly agreed "in principle" to an interview at some unspecified time in the future but had turned down all my approaches since. I made a note of Lilly's suggestion but without much faith in its value. First, it made no sense that Turpin or any other Meredith people would have had anything to do with acquiring those statements from the women and/or giving them to Howley for the debate. Second, if they knew who did, they would be screaming bloody murder about it on *Jack and Jill* and all the other shouting spots on all the other networks from sea to shining sea.

If I had been doing a different kind of book, one that concentrated on the candidates and the campaign rather than the debate and the panelists, I might have said something more to Lilly. I might have said it must be an unbearable hell to have come as close as you came to the ultimate prize in American politics and have it snapped away. Tell me about it.

I didn't say any of that. I simply asked a last question: "I guess it would not make sense to ask if there is any way you might be able and willing to help me get an interview with Greene?"

"You're right," he said. "It makes absolutely, one thousand percent, all the way, full house, shithouse no 'fucking' sense."

I thanked him for his cooperation and left his tiny little office and future.

★

Within two days Jennifer Gates produced a recording of a recording that she thought I ought to hear. She said various cross-checking and cross-referencing and other attempts did not produce a name to go with that unlisted phone number I had given her. So she took direct action. She simply dialed the number. After the fifth ring an answering machine took over. She hung up and called it back with her phone on RECORD. That made it possible for me to now listen to an arrogant male voice say:

"Hello, this is Pat Tubbs. Neither Mary nor I am able to take your call now. Leave a message at the tone and we'll get back to you. I promise."

Pat Tubbs. *The* Pat Tubbs of *The Washington Morning News.* Pat Tubbs, one of the richest and most famous investigative reporters in America. The man who ran presidential candidates and cabinet officers and Supreme Court nominees and all kinds of other public figures back to where they came from—or to jail.

Why was Mike Howley talking to Pat Tubbs so long on that Saturday night before the debate?

I decided to call Pat Tubbs right then and ask him. I assumed he would not take a call from me, so I told the woman who answered his phone that I was Alan Greenspan, the chairman of the Federal Reserve Board. I had read in one of the gossip columns that Tubbs was working on an "inside the Fed" exposé book and Greenspan had thus far refused to talk to him.

He came on the line immediately and I quickly told him who I was and asked my question.

"What were you and Howley talking about that Saturday night before the debate?"

"I do not *answer* questions, you lying asshole, I *ask* them" was his answer, delivered in the gruff, arrogant style that was his famous trademark.

Then he hung up the phone with a loud smash, another of his famous trademarks.

11

Historic Firsts

The birth of *Sunday Morning with Hank and Barb* was announced in the ballroom of the Ritz-Carlton Hotel on Massachusetts Avenue. It was a Washington news conference–cocktail party pageant catered and attended by the most expensive of their respective kinds.

There were an army of well-dressed waiters, many baskets of flowers and trays of drinks, finger sandwiches, hot snacks, and sweets fit for a prince and princess—if not for a king and queen. The nation's print and electronic press sent its top radio-TV, media, show-business, feature, and gossip people. One television critic, speaking most satirically, called it "another eye-watering, momentous development in television, that electronic marvel that remains the greatest potential for good ever invented." The network spokespersons and press releases, speaking seriously, called the teaming of an African American and a Hispanic on a regular national program "a historic first."

Barbara Manning and Henry Ramirez had been dressed and otherwise prepared by a network team of designers, makeup experts, and others from New York. Henry wore a dark blue double-breasted suit—the first double-breasted suit he had ever had on his body. Barbara, her hair sparkling and perfect, wore a light blue suit.

There were several to-the-point questions asked of them and the network executives on hand.

"How do you know it'll work?" was the toughest.

"We don't," Henry said. "But I agree with the people here who hired us—it is sure worth a try."

"Seriously," said a reporter, "what makes you two think you can whip Jack and Jill?"

"We're not out to whip anybody," Barbara said. "We're just going to do our best and hope and pray we don't make fools of ourselves."

That brought some laughter from throughout the room.

"Are you really worried that might happen?" somebody asked. "That you might make fools of yourselves?"

Barbara was afraid she had already made a fool of herself just standing there in a thousand-dollar suit. She honestly believed there was every good chance that she and Henry—Hank and Barb—would last one Sunday and one Sunday only, just as Mark Southern, the original clownalist, had done.

Henry answered the question. "Barbara is the modest one on this team. Obviously, we know we can and will do this, and do it successfully, or we wouldn't be out here now, and out there beginning two weeks from this Sunday."

Henry swore to me that was not just talk. He really did have a terrific feeling about what he and Barbara were going to do. "It seemed as natural as music with salsa," he said. I resisted the urge to say I had always believed it was chips, not music, that went with salsa.

Henry and Barbara and all of the others who stood on a small stage for the brief question-and-answer period declined to say how much the new team was being paid or disclose anything else about their contracts. Neither Henry nor Barbara would give *me* the details either. All I knew—know—was what came out at that first Four Seasons breakfast about two million dollars a year guaranteed for two years, no matter what, and a lot of limo and apartment perks. Not only did Henry and Barbara clam up on the details in my later conversations, the agent from William Morris who ended up negotiating their final ABS contract wouldn't say anything either. Neither would the people at the network on an official basis. But I was told unofficially by someone who claimed to know that the contract had what this person called "an unprecedented ratings escalator." If Hank and Barb caught and overtook Jack and Jill, the amounts of money that would go to Henry and Barbara, according to my source, were of "Sawyer-plus dimensions." I asked if a figure even as high as ten million was out of the question. The answer was a simple no.

There were several questions at the Ritz-Carlton announcement event about Henry and Barbara's personal relationship. They were astonishingly direct and personal, a reflection of how direct and personal matters had gone in some areas of American journalism.

"Are you two lovers—or what?" somebody asked.

"Come on, now," Henry replied. "What ever happened to privacy?"

"How many times have you slept together?"

"Please," Barbara said.

"More than twenty or less than ten?"

"Please!"

"Have you *ever* slept together?"

Henry said: "What kind of question is that?"

"Is that a yes?"

"Do you practice safe sex?"

Both Henry and Barbara just shook their heads.

"Seriously, do you use condoms or not?"

Both Henry and Barbara just shook their heads.

"All right, then, describe your relationship in your own words," said a reporter.

Barbara and Henry looked at each other and then back at the assembled gossip-showbiz-TV press of America. With a smile, Henry said: "I would describe our relationship as one between two people who like and respect each other very much, who have decided that it is professionally to each of our benefits to join hands and forces every Sunday morning on the ABS television network."

He reached over and took Barbara's left hand with his right.

Barbara said: "The man said it and he said it right."

"So you're not lovers?"

Both Barbara and Henry only smiled.

I was convinced all of this was some kind of a charade—but I was not sure what kind. By the time of this news conference I had already had four separate interview sessions with each of them about the lead-up to the debate, most particularly about what happened in Longsworth D. But neither Henry nor Barbara, no matter how I came at it, would reveal anything that rang true about their real relationship. I honestly did not know if they were mad, passionate lovers or two partners in a business enterprise that required them to fake something.

"Is it true that Ross Perot is thinking of getting revenge by buying your network?" was the touchiest question asked of network president Joshua Simonsen at the news conference.

The answer: "Ross is an old friend who has done great work for us and for America. We understand his concern over what has happened, but we are sure it will pass. He is a man of business who understands the need for hard-nosed business decisions."

"You really think he's going to take this with a smile?"

"No question about that at all. He has given us assurances of a smooth and graceful transition. He will continue to do the program for the next two Sundays—and do it with full vigor and dedication and professionalism—until the new team takes over."

As the whole world found out the following Sunday, Ross Perot had something other in mind than a smooth and graceful transition.

He threw a historic first on-air fit. After promising the network—according to the network, at least—that he would not say or do anything but his regular program the following Sunday, he opened the program with a squeaky, fiery speech about the awfulness of the people who run the ABS television network and all of network television.

His best lines were: "I've been asked if I might hit back by buying this network. Forget it, friends. I've got a lot better things to do with my money—which, by the way, I didn't get by investing in the dying and the past. I'm not starting now. These people aren't long for this world anyhow. I understand a merger with the Disney Channel is in the works. Makes perfect sense. One Mickey Mouse outfit deserves another."

He talked for twenty-two minutes like that right to the camera and then walked off the set. The network's Capitol Hill correspondent, who happened to be in the newsroom that Sunday morning, was rushed into the studio to finish the program dressed in blue jeans and a sweater.

At a news conference outside in the ABS Washington bureau parking lot on upper Wisconsin Avenue, Perot denied he ever promised not to say anything about his "public beheading" and then took some more parting shots. His best: "These people aren't qualified to run a toilet concession at a roadside park on the information superhighway."

"What do you think of Hank and Barb?" he was asked by a reporter.

"I don't think about dirty cartoons about little boys and girls trying to act like grown-ups," Perot answered.

★

Jack Turpin. Source after source told me this man had gone into a hate fit because of Williamsburg, and that that fit consumed his mind and his spirit—his very being. That was allegedly why he had done only a few interviews and why only a few scattered quotes from him showed up in our massive postdebate clipping and transcript file.

Then one day I saw a story—by accident, really—in the *Washington Post* sports section. It said Turpin, who spent two years right out of college as a catcher in the Detroit Tigers organization, had been hired as a special assistant to the commissioner of baseball. The commissioner was a Northrop aviation heir, lawyer, and former Republican governor of California who had once been a minor-league pitcher in the Houston Astros farm system. Turpin, said the story, had worked on one of the commissioner's gubernatorial campaigns. Turpin's special task now for baseball would be to improve the public image of The Game, to design a public-relations campaign that would, in the words of "a source close to the commissioner's office," reestablish baseball as America's number one pastime. What was common knowledge but unsaid in the story, of course, was that the well-publicized and competing greeds of the owners and of the players had finally begun to drive people away from baseball. Two days later Jennifer Gates brought me a computer printout of a piece by the great sports novelist Dan Jenkins that had appeared in the *Fort Worth Star-Telegram* and other papers. He wrote about Turpin's coming: "Anybody who could turn a jerk like Meredith into something semi-attractive might have a chance of doing the semi-same for the jerks who run and play baseball. But let's not cheer him on, OK? The problems are not about image, they're about real."

I called the baseball commissioner's office in New York City. After being treated to about nine full innings of runarounds, I was able to determine that Jack Turpin was, in fact, already on the job and in the office. But it took a couple more tries before they would put me through to his secretary, and then he would not take my call. He finally did only after I told somebody that I was a representative of David Donald Meredith and I had some awful news for Mr. Turpin.

"What news?" Turpin said when he came on the line.

I told him who I was.

He said in a firm but unfrantic way: "Goddamn you. I should have known it would be one of you people. The idea of lying, of getting somebody on the phone by false pretenses, is a way of professional life for you and your kind. I have nothing to say to you now about anything and I never will. So you might as well quit calling me. I do not turn the other cheek. I do not forgive and forget. I do not do any of that crap."

I felt he left me no choice but to play a bit of reporter's hardball. It was now or never.

I said: "I have been told you were the source for those statements that were used and read during the debate. Can you confirm?"

Turpin's voice remained controlled. He said: "That is a goddamn lie. You print that in your childish excuse for a magazine and I'll end up owning your childish excuse for a magazine. I did not sabotage my own man. I would never sabotage my own man. You have just spoken a blood libel. Say it again and you are in a court of law. Who told you that? Did Meredith tell you that?"

Our conversation ended a few moments later, and the next morning I caught the 6:50 A.M. Metroliner Express from Washington to New York to keep a 10:00 A.M. appointment with Jack Turpin. The train, the only way Jonathan Angel and the other civilized people I knew ever traveled to and from New York, arrived on time at 9:25. And I was in a room with Turpin at 10:05.

The room was one of several conference rooms at the commissioner's office on the seventeenth floor of an office building at 350 Park Avenue. Its walls were covered with photographs of pitchers who had played and starred in the majors. The first one I saw was one of Robin Roberts, the great Philadelphia Phillie.

"I know you don't really believe I leaked those statements," Turpin said within seconds after he closed the door behind him. "Don't think I fell for your high-school *Front Page* trick."

I said: "Who did then?"

"How in the hell would I know? What is this? They were sprung on us like killers in the night."

"I thought maybe you—the campaign—made an effort to find out after the debate."

He looked away from me, then back. "Look here, Chapman, do you not understand that I was one of the victims of that public assassination? Do you not grasp the obvious fact that the perpetrators of this crime are the ones you should be talking to? They are the ones who must be interrogated, must be forced to tell all to the people of the United States. If you want to know where the assassination weapons came from, for Christ's sake, ask the assassins. The victims are seldom in a position to have such deadly information, much less make it public."

I told him the truth up to that moment. That three of the four panelists had told me they did not know the source of the statements and that I believed them. That left only Mike Howley, who clearly did know but was not talking—yet.

It kept Turpin in the room. He had appeared ready to end the conversation and escort me to the door and an elevator. Now he was listening, at least. So I asked: "Did you know about those allegations before the debate?"

Jack Turpin was probably on some kind of quieting drug. I am not a drug user myself, but I have been around many in the magazine-journalism world of frantic deadlines and never-stop production, writing, and editing sessions. There was something—I could not explain what, exactly—about his eyes and his movements that led me to suspect some kind of quieting, moderating substance. He was probably on a pill that kept his anger in check, that made it possible for him to function—even in difficult situations like this.

What he did now was blink and say to me: "What's the point? What are you trying to prove?"

"I do not know where it will finally lead," I said, again, telling the absolute truth. "But I am interested in how those statements came into the hands of Howley and, frankly, whether it was all cooked up beforehand."

"By whom?"

"That's what I want to find out."

"Why?"

"Because . . . well, because I think the public has a right to know."

"Oh, please, spare me that sanctimonious crap. You want to know because it will sell more magazines."

"Whatever," I said, still doing my best to tell the truth.

"Forget it," he said. "I have nothing to say." But I could not help but notice that he made no effort to get up from his chair. Go, Tom, go!

"What about on an off-the-record basis? Or on background. All I want to know is whether you-all in the campaign knew about those charges before they were read on television that night in Williamsburg."

"Why should I tell you or anyone from the press anything? Why should I trust you or anyone from the press?"

I decided not to try to answer that.

I looked behind Turpin at a photo of Sandy Koufax and Don Drysdale, the two great Los Angeles Dodgers pitchers. Then I looked down at my own two hands and pulled a handkerchief out of my rear pants pocket and blew my nose.

Jack Turpin was making a decision that mattered very much to me— more than I even realized at the time.

He said: "Yes, I knew."

"How did you know?"

"Somebody came to us, claiming she had been hit by Meredith. She was one of the people named by one of those thug-panelists during the debate. I asked Meredith about it. He gave me an answer that was more movement than fact. Alarms went off in my head and soul. So I had our security people do some checking. They dug up several more women with such allegations to make about my candidate. Most of the ones Howley and his hooligans read that night sounded familiar to me. They must have all been in there."

"In where?"

"The material our security people gathered."

"What did you do with that material—those statements?"

"I showed them to Meredith. Again, he gave me some motion but very little else. At my urging—insistence, really—we decided to act like nothing had happened. I shredded all the statements and even the file folder in which they came."

"Nobody else saw them?"

"Nobody."

"No copies were made."

"None."

"Are you certain?"

Turpin grinned for the first time ever in my presence. The corners of his mouth actually turned up like they do on most normal people when something strikes them funny. He said: "As certain as I was nine days before the election that David Donald Meredith was going to be elected president of the United States, before four journalist-muggers decided they knew better than the people what was best for our country."

He was still grinning, so I asked him if he knew—or thought—it was possible Meredith himself had somehow kept copies or told somebody else about the charge.

"That is about as possible as it is for me to ever see people like you as anything other than the enemy."

I thought at first that the medicine was wearing off and I was soon going to be out of there. But there remained a pleasantness in his face. This man was obviously fulfilling a need to get something off of his chest. This had suddenly turned into a therapy session for this angry man.

So I asked him: "Had you ever heard Meredith use words like 'fucking' before? Was he a closet cusser? The image you-all put out was just the opposite—"

"I was as surprised as anyone by his outburst. Not once did he even say as much as 'shit' in front of me. Not once."

"How important do you think it was that he said 'fucking' that night?"

"Important enough to cost him the election. Without that word he might have made it. We could have attacked the credibility of the abuse charges, fought back—and possibly made it. The word made recovery impossible."

I glided into asking him for his version of the debate-panel selection meeting and other predebate meetings and happenings about which I had already talked to Lilly, Hammond, and many others. He was direct and full of detail, but in several instances—the panelist selection meeting in particular—also full of bald-faced lies. I am no expert on polygraphs, but I had a feeling Jack Turpin was one of those people who could beat any of those machines. He could lie and it would never show.

As Lilly had done before him about his dismissal by Greene, Turpin also laid out blow-by-blow his firing by David Donald Meredith.

It happened the morning following the debate after the end of the First Light meeting in the education room at the First Baptist Church of Decatur, Illinois, where Meredith had spoken to a late-night downtown rally the night before. This morning he and his staff were to go over the details of the National Day of Prayer they were halfheartedly attempting to organize.

Turpin said Meredith's opening prayer was the shortest ever. "O heavenly Father, give us the might to fight and to be right," he said. "In Your name we pray. . . . Amen."

Then there was the news, all of it bad. Turpin said he and the others reviewed the instant polls, the editorials, the commentaries, the phone calls that had come from voters to Meredith for President offices all over America. None of it was good except for those who condemned the press. But the reaction to the abuse allegations and to Meredith's anger and F-word performance was almost universally and resoundingly negative.

He said he and Meredith received each tidbit of awfulness as a spear to their hearts and souls. He said the redness around Meredith's eyes and in his face got redder with each new criticism.

When the meeting was over, Meredith asked for a few private moments with Turpin. They walked together out of the church building toward a far corner of the parking lot, in the opposite direction from where the Meredith motorcade was waiting with about twenty limo, van, police-cruiser, and motorcycle motors running.

Turpin said he had no idea what was coming. His own thoughts were all of rage at others—at those four panelists, at those women accusers, at the Jacks and Jills and others who commented about it all night on television, at even God Himself for letting this happen to His man, His candidate.

Meredith waited until they were in the corner, way out of earshot of any possible eavesdroppers, before saying to Turpin:

"You gave those statements from all of those women to the enemy, didn't you?"

Turpin said he almost fell over. He said the charge was so unexpected and so powerful he really did almost fall. He said he yelled: "No! In the name of all that is right and true, no!"

"You wanted me to lose. You are the true agent of the devil, Jack Turpin. The Democratic devil sent you here to do his work, to destroy me."

"That is simply nuts, sir. Simply and unquestionably nuts."

"You were the only one who had those statements."

"I believe in you. I have worked my ass off for you. I am your friend, your everything."

"You are my nothing."

Jack Turpin said he realized that he was standing there shouting at a crazy man. What had happened last night had sent David Donald Meredith up, over, and out. And why not, for Christ's sake? What person could go through having the presidency of the United States snatched out from under him this way and emerge anything but up, over, and out?

Turpin said he then spoke what he thought would be words of comfort and help to Meredith: "Sir, I think it might be prudent for you to consider the possibility of your withdrawing as a candidate. Larry Ward could be affirmed quickly as the party's presidential candidate. I have checked the law. The Republican National Committee has the power to do that, almost over the phone. If you do not wish to do that, you could tell the voters that if elected you would immediately step down in favor of Ward. He is already in place as the vice presidential candidate. The convention affirmed him in that spot. You have said yourself many times that he is ready and able to be president. I am not saying you should do either now, but I am saying that you might want to begin to think about something along these lines. Clearly, the tide has been turned against you in a way that I do not believe it is possible to reverse. I also believe you must, you simply must say something—an apology, an explanation, anything— about 'fucking'. . . ."

Turpin said he saw Meredith's right fist coming in time to deflect it with his own left arm and duck away. His work behind the plate as a baseball catcher helped.

"You are the enemy!" Meredith screamed at Turpin as he broke into a run for his limousine. "You will burn in hell with the fucking rest of them!"

Turpin told me those were the last words David Donald Meredith spoke to him.

"That's why I took that phony call from you yesterday," he said. "A message from Meredith was worth taking."

He said he knew nothing about Meredith's whereabouts, except what he had read in the papers after the election. What those stories said was that the former Republican nominee for president of the United States had left his family, dissolved Take It Back, and gone to live in a fortified commune in the Ouachita Mountains of southeastern Oklahoma. It was run by a strange conservative religious sect that believed all communication with God and Jesus, as well as humans, should be musical. Nobody there talked or wrote. They only sang, hummed, or played an instrument. Only certified true believers were allowed into the place, which had few creature comforts but lots of pianos, violins, saxophones, drums, and sheet music.

"I understand why he ran away," Turpin said. "I almost did myself."

"I guess there is no way I could get you to help me get an interview with Mr. Meredith?"

"You guessed right. I couldn't help you if I wanted to and I do not want to. The man has suffered enough at the hands of people like you. So have I."

The smile was gone. He stood. So did I. It was a few minutes after noon. We had talked for two hours. I left with so much, much more than I'd ever dreamed was possible to get from this terminally angry man.

★

The three-hour Metroliner ride back to Washington gave me a chance to assess what I had and where I was. But I did not need that much time. It was clear by the time the train had come and gone from its first stop at Newark, New Jersey, that the next stop in my search for the truth of Williamsburg was the security firm that worked for Turpin and the Meredith campaign.

Nelson and Associates was its name. Sidney Robert Nelson was its founder and president. The regular *Tatler* Washington correspondent helped me discover that within the practical political world Nelson was known as an honorable man who ran an ethical and honest operation. Meaning, apparently, if you believed it was honorable to bug Longsworth D or anybody else's meeting, telephone, office, or bedroom, or have someone's intimate personal life and secrets investigated, then Nelson and Associates would do it well and do it in a way that might not turn your stomach or get you found out and indicted.

According to the national registry of licensed private security and detective agencies, Nelson and his fourteen full-time associates—investigators/counselors, they were called—were all former FBI and Secret Service agents. Nelson had been FBI agent-in-charge in Seattle, New Orleans, and Chicago before becoming the assistant director for internal security, the bureau's chief spy hunter. Jennifer Gates turned up only one small seven-year-old *Washington Post* story about Nelson in the Nexis computer file of past news stories. It said he left the bureau over a policy dispute with an unnamed assistant attorney general. The story said there was an unconfirmed report that the assistant attorney general had "requested FBI action on an intelligence-gathering matter" that Nelson refused to do. I made a note to ask Nelson what that was all about—if I ever got a chance to talk to him.

The word among the political operatives was that Nelson was politically nonpartisan. He would work for anybody who had the funds, payable in advance. If the Turpins and Lillys of the world were hired guns, in other words, Nelson was a hired spy. That was a hopeful sign because it was likely that he was not a Meredith fanatic, that he did the Meredith assignments for money, not love. But there was the additional word that Nelson never talked about any client or any work he did for them. That was a trademark. He was a secure security man.

After much deliberation and back-and-forth argument with myself, I decided the direct approach would probably not be the way to go. Nelson would likely decline to take so much as a phone call from Tom Chapman of *The New American Tatler,* as he would from anybody else from any other news or journalism organization. He clearly did not get where he was by spilling his guts to reporters. And in a matter like the Williams-burg Debate, he was likely to have an even safer lock on his mouth and secrets.

So. I would have to do it the hard way.

I put on some old clothes and sunglasses and began watching Nel-son go about his business day. I watched him drive his car, a black Mer-cury four-door sedan with three radio or telephone aerials whipping in the breeze, into the underground garage in the small building at the cor-ner of Van Ness and Wisconsin in northwest Washington where Nelson and Associates was headquartered. I watched Nelson eat lunch, usually with men who looked just like him, at restaurants in the neighborhood. And, most important, I watched Nelson enter the Tenley Health Club just down the street from his office every evening shortly after six P.M. and then come out again forty-five minutes later.

The health club was where it was going to happen. I bought a spe-cial introductory thirty-day Tenley Health Club membership for $125 and showed up at 6:15 one evening in a sweat outfit that I normally wore for my morning jogs. I chose an old sweatshirt with an American flag and the symbol of the 1988 Olympics. You never know what might help break some ice.

I found Nelson in the machine room on a turbobike. Our eyes met. I nodded and climbed on the bike next to him.

Nothing happened except that I rode my bike and he rode his.

I knew from my reporting that Sid Nelson was fifty-seven years old, but close-up in shorts and a T-shirt—it said IOWA STATE on the front—he looked forty-seven or even younger. I knew he had been a star athlete in high school and college and was the fourth child born from the marriage of Sarah Field Nelson, high-school guidance counselor, and Frank Peter Nelson, high-school basketball and track-and-field coach, in Davenport, Iowa. He looked like the son of a coach. His body was solid and lean. It wasn't long before I saw why. Nelson's legs pumped the pedals on that turbo with no apparent effort or sweat. I was in pretty good shape myself, but it was obvious that this man next to me was in a whole other physical league.

After more than twenty minutes of pumping and nothing, I decided to make my move. I said: "I'm a new member."

"Congratulations," Nelson said.

"Thank you."

"Time for the whirlpool," Nelson said.

And without another word and before I could utter one myself, Nelson was off the bike and gone.

I saw it as a beginning.

★

There was no splashy press event to announce Joan Naylor's historic first. Her moment in the announcement sun was badly botched by and for all concerned.

Don Beard, the famous CNS anchor, took a call one morning in his New York City network office. It was from a reporter on the New York *Daily News*.

"We hear you are being replaced by Joan Naylor," said the reporter.

"Wrong, wrong, bullshit, bullshit," said Beard. "She isn't even back to work yet."

A few minutes later Beard took a call from a reporter for *New York Newsday*.

"Somebody at the network just told me they have decided to put Naylor in for you. True or false?"

"False!"

There was another call on hold from a guy at *Variety*. And Beard then listened to the same question for the third time and gave the same answer for the third time.

But this time Beard—he was my primary source for all of this— walked immediately and quickly and angrily out of his office, through the CNS newsroom where everyone was staring in silence at him, to the office of Calvin Hill, president of CNS News.

Without a word to Hill's secretary, who sat outside Hill's office, Beard opened the closed door and walked in. Hill was sitting around a coffee table with five other people, all of whom he recognized as vice presidents and public-relations officials of the network. They were looking at a piece of paper in the center of the table.

Hill and the others sat straight up as if they had been goosed, or maybe caught playing with matches or showing one another their private parts.

"Is it true?" Beard shouted at Hill.

"Yes . . . I'm afraid it is. Don, Jesus . . . Yes. I'm sorry. I was just on my way down to talk to you about it. I'm sorry, Don. We're working on the language of a press statement now. The damned thing leaked. . . ."

Beard returned to his own office, grabbed his suit coat and raincoat off a coatrack, and, without a word to anyone, walked out to the elevator, rode it down to the first floor, exited the CNS Building on Columbus Avenue, and went home—never to return.

He had his personal effects collected the next day by a paralegal in his lawyer's office. That lawyer also from that day on did all of Beard's communicating with CNS, which under an anchor-only contract had to continue to pay Beard an estimated $5.7 million a year for three more years.

Joan Naylor, who was already in New York holed up secretly in a suite at the Ritz-Carlton, anchored the *CNS Evening News* that night and has been doing so Monday-through-Friday ever since.

The written announcement said it was another "historic first for women" in that Joan had become the first sole woman anchor of a major-network nightly news broadcast. Several lines about Beard's "monumental contribution" to the development of television news in America and at CNS were left in, but a reference to his moving on to do "special assignments for the news division" was deleted. Hill and the others apparently concluded that Beard's dramatic departure was pretty good evidence their ex-anchorman was not about to do anything else for them.

The going of Don Beard was front-page news in all major American newspapers. He had been anchoring the *CNS Evening News* for fourteen years and, according to most polls, was among the most prominent human beings in America. He was no Walter Cronkite, but he was at least what *The Philadelphia Inquirer* TV writer called "pretty much beloved." But even those who did not like him at all liked even less the way the network booted him. The handling of the dismissal was the principal subject of many radio call-in shows and of editorial writers and commentators. "Shameful," "barbaric," "stupid," "uncaring," "dumb," were some of the words used. "Forcing a man like Don Beard to hear about his firing from some reporter shoots the callous-imbecile needle all the way to the top," wrote an editorial writer in *The Oregonian.*

The network's statement and all of its words that followed, interestingly enough, never said why the change was being made, why Joan Naylor was given Don Beard's job. Since Beard was only fifty-nine years old, there wasn't even a retirement cover available. Joan in for Don, that's it. Time for a change. Life on the information superhighway moves on for Don, as it did for Ross. And for basically the same reasons. But while the obvious conventional wisdom was that it was done because of Joan's new star prominence from Williamsburg, no network release or official even mentioned the fact that she had been one of the famous Williamsburg Four.

The conventional wisdom, in this case, was absolutely correct. Williamsburg was the sole cause of what happened. Ten days after the debate, with her suspension still in effect, Carol Reynolds, the Washington bureau chief, came to Joan's house. She told Joan the verdict was in and she—Joan—had won. The tide had made a permanent turn, according to the public-opinion polls and the calls and letters that had come to the network and everywhere else they had checked. Joan and her three panelist-colleagues were solid American heroes—by a good 70 to 30 percentage points on average.

"So, as usual, our powers-that-be at the network want to go with the numbers," Carol Reynolds said. "They want to make you America's first solo woman principal network anchor."

They want to make you America's first solo woman principal network anchor. Those were the cumbersomely arranged words Joan Naylor had worked toward and dreamed most of her adult life about hearing, words she thought she probably never would hear. Some other woman might hear them in a few years, but not her.

It meant moving to New York, Jeff practicing New York rather than Washington law, the twins finding another good Quaker school. But life is tough, even for the relatives of those on the information superhighway.

Her lawyer-agent negotiated what she said was a "terrific deal," but she would not tell me what it contained. And I have been unable to find out from anyone else. Some newspaper accounts on the day Beard took his booted hike put Joan's salary at $2.5 million a year. That sounds way too low to me, but I have only the sound to go on.

Joan had no illusions about what had happened. She said to me: "In a perfect world, I would have preferred that this had happened through the normal course of professional events and accomplishments rather than as a result of the Williamsburg spotlight. But television news is not a perfect world and never will be. I feel badly for Don Beard in the way it was handled, but, again, nobody said it was going to be an easy and thoughtful world either. I am sure when the time comes for me to go, something similar will happen. Live in the fast track, die in the fast track."

★

I returned to the Tenley Health Club two nights later at six. I thought being there the very next night might be a little obvious. My T-shirt, a gift from a friend, said MISSISSIPPI UNIVERSITY FOR WOMEN.

"How long have you been coming here?" I asked Nelson after a few minutes of side-by-side pumping on the turbobikes.

"Quite a long time," he replied.

"I hope to come here for a long time, too," I said.

"Good for you," he replied.

And that was pretty much the way the dialogue went over the next four side-by-side pedalings over the next eight working days.

He pleasantly answered my stupidly inane questions with two or three words but with no interest and no questions in return. But for no reason—he neither said nor did a thing that was relevant—I became obsessively certain this was indeed my man. Sid Nelson knew what I wanted to know. Sid Nelson could tell me everything I ever wanted to know about those Meredith statements. I also became a fan of Sid Nelson. There was something about him that I envied. He was the kind of man most other men wanted to be—if only for a few minutes at a time on special occasions. The polite tough guy of few words who could, like Superman, stop powerful trains with one hand, fly faster than a speeding bullet, slay madmen and giants with the flick of a finger.

On that sixth evening with him I also became convinced that I could spend quite a long time on a turbobike at the Tenley Health Club next to Sid Nelson and never get there. I would never get on a friendly enough footing to take a subtle first step such as opening the conversation a bit to a discussion of the Washington Redskins or the deficit and then maybe ever so gently suggesting a drink or dinner, and on and on, small step by small step. I had the sudden feeling that we could both grow old and die here side by side and nothing would ever have happened.

So, my legs still pumping away, I simply decided to get on with it. We had been together less than five minutes. The only words spoken were those of our customary brief exchange when I came in. They were about the weather, which was cold and rainy, a typical winter day in Washington.

Now I said: "Mr. Nelson, why did you give those statements about Meredith to Mike Howley?"

He had a smile on his face when he spoke. "We had an office pool on how long it would take you to ask," he said, not even cutting down on his pedaling speed. "I just lost. I said eight. This is six. I can't remember off the top of my head who has six. Miller. Bob Miller. Right. He'll be delighted. Two and a half is not to be sneezed at."

"Two and a half what?" I said.

"Dollars."

"It must have been a very small ante."

"A quarter apiece. We are but hardworking men of law enforcement, please remember."

"So you know who I am?"

"Thomas Blaine Chapman. Thirty-four, white Caucasian, no known physical handicaps or distinguishing scars or marks. Born in New Haven, Connecticut. Only child. Father: law professor; mother: sociology professor. B.A., American studies, Williams. Single. Divorced. Straight. Sexually active. Light drinker, no drugs. No arrest record. Worked on three different newspapers as a reporter. Now contributing editor of *The New American Tatler* under assignment to write the definitive work about the four panelists in the Williamsburg Debate. Who are they and why did they do what they did? Income: approximately a hundred and twenty-five thousand dollars per annum. Resides Tribeca section, New York City. Rents. AA credit rating. Speaks no foreign languages. Personal politics unknown. Parents: both registered Democrats, no record of activism."

He was still pedaling. So was I. In my brain as well as with my legs. My God, my God. I kept pedaling.

Have they been following me? Do they have a tap on my phone at the office? What about the hotel room? Have they bribed Jennifer Gates at the office?

I kept pedaling.

"You might say, yes, we know who you are, Mr. Chapman," he said.

I said: "When did you get on to me?"

"When you first appeared across the street in that homeless sunglasses outfit."

"You guys are good, no question about that." My God, what an understatement!

"What kind of tradesmen would we be if we did not keep a good eye on our own backsides?"

My mind was still throwing and fielding questions and accusations about my stupidity and naïveté and the fact that my life was probably in danger. Maybe he's going to kill me now. Right now. Or if not now, tonight in the hotel. Or tomorrow at the office.

But I went on with it. I said: "Are you going to tell me anything, sir?"

"Time for the whirlpool," he said, stopping pedaling and getting down off his bike.

It was over. He had exposed me to myself as a fool and this was the end. So long, Thomas Blaine Chapman, thirty-four, single, college-educated, sexually active.

"I need your help, sir, if I am going to tell the American people the truth of what really happened," I said.

Nelson was two steps away from our bikes when he turned back to me and said: "The truth?"

"Yes, sir. Will you help me? I'll take it on deep background. I'll never mention your name."

Nelson wasn't moving. I said: "I'll be more than glad to pay you for the information. I know what you know is a commodity as valuable as if it were a jewel, a fine diamond. . . ."

That moved him. And I thought there was a chance—a real chance—that the next story anyone was going to come across about Thomas Blaine Chapman was his obit.

Nelson came back over to me. I stopped pedaling as he grabbed the bar across the front of my bike and leaned into my face. In a voice that sounded about as menacing as any I had ever heard, he said: "There are some things that are too important to buy and sell, and the truth is one of them, Mr. Chapman."

And he left. I saw only one silver thread lining his departure. I was alive.

Which was much more than I could say about my story.

12

Inauguration

There was no choice but to launch a full-court press on Michael J. Howley much earlier than I had planned.

Howley was the hero-villain and thus the central figure in this remarkable story. I knew almost from the beginning that eventually I would have to confront him, but I had hoped that when the time came I would be there with some direct and telling—I have here in my hand!—evidence of exactly what he did and possibly even why. That had not happened. Without some solid material from Nelson or someone else on the origin of those abuse statements and how they got to Howley, it was unlikely Howley would drop on his knees and confess his sins to me. All I could do now was embellish and carefully word what I had from the other three panelists and see if I could at least put him on the spot. And if I got lucky I might pry something loose.

I called his office at the *News* every morning and afternoon for five straight days. I played no games. Each time I identified myself and reminded the message taker to remind Howley that he and I had talked before and what I was doing for *The New American Tatler*.

I was never put through to Howley and he never called me back.

I escalated the approach. On day six I told the person who answered his phone—it was a woman—that I needed to confirm "the origin of some videotapes." No response. The next day I added the phrase "of someone giving someone else a folder of women's statements." Nothing. Day eight brought the additional line: "There is also some sound on the tapes." Still nothing.

I called Jerry Rhome. At first I thought he was going to brush me off, too. But eventually—on the fourth call—he came on the line.

"Hey, Chapman, what I know is what I told you," he said. "I ain't got nothing more to say."

I told him it was imperative that I talk to Howley and explained my problem in getting his world-famous employee to even return a phone call. "He's a free man in a free press in a free country," said Rhome. "If he doesn't want to talk to you, he doesn't want to talk to you. So be it. Besides that, he's on some Greek island right now."

"What Greek island?"

"None of your business."

I waited an hour and then had Jennifer Gates call the *News* and ask for Howley. I told her afterward that she definitely could have made it as an actress. She clearly convinced the person at the *News* that she really was Mike Howley's neighbor, and water was running out from under his front door. "Obviously there has been a break in his water pipes. What should I do? Who should I call? The firemen are here. They want to speak to the owner. I didn't know where he was. I don't know what to do. . . ."

The island was called Santorini. He was staying in a rented house.

Something heavier than a phone call was called for. I drafted a letter and then sent it Federal Express—three-day delivery guaranteed.

It read:

Mike Howley:
I now have a full accounting of your predebate activities. I know where the statements came from and how they got to you. I feel you are entitled to give me your version of the events, your intentions and motives. All I want to do is get it right. Please call me at

202-555-5421—collect—at your earliest convenience. This is urgent. My magazine's deadline approaches with the speed and force of a Metroliner from New York.

Sincerely,
Tom Chapman

And I waited for the phone to ring.

★

Inauguration day turned out to be as important a day in my professional life as it did in Paul L. Greene's.

For him, there was still a Christmas-morning surprise element to it. The people of the United States of America had had seventy-nine days, from November 4 to January 21, to get used to the idea that Paul L. Greene of Nebraska was in fact going to be their next president. But, according to the polls and the anecdotes, there was still an aura of fairy-land disbelief to the whole thing. Here was a guy who had been so far behind, so counted out, that to read the flood of stories about "President-elect Greene" and his family and cabinet and all the rest had a fictional or dream quality to it. Someone said it was as if Michael Dukakis had defeated George Bush, Barry Goldwater had come from nowhere to suddenly cream Lyndon Johnson, and George McGovern had done the same to Richard Nixon in 1972.

There he was, this man Greene, this man they were now calling "a quiet, steady man with Lincolnesque possibilities," standing in the bitter cold on the stage in front of the west side of the Capitol taking the oath of office.

Joan Naylor, alone behind a glass-enclosed and heated booth a hundred yards away, was anchoring CNS's coverage of the inauguration. She looked and sounded terrific, as she had every Monday-through-Friday evening since she replaced Don Beard on the nightly news broadcast. Since she took over, *The CNS Evening News* had risen from its customary third place in the weekly Nielsen ratings to tie ABS News four times for second place. She told me the network brass were so excited the first time it happened that they sent cases of champagne and strawberries and chocolates to both the New York and Washington newsrooms. "We're hoping they'll give us all Rolls-Royces if we ever win second place outright," she said.

Henry Ramirez and Barbara Manning, now the famous Hank and Barb, were part of their network's coverage. They were broadcasting from a huge suite at the Willard Hotel, around the corner from the White House, where they were to make comments and interview celebrities while the inaugural parade passed by and under them on Pennsylvania Avenue. They had become huge celebrities themselves, of course, and much of it had to do with their "America's favorite love story" image as partners on the screen and in bed.

It was after they cut their first AIDS public-service commercial for safe sex that urged the use of condoms that I decided once and for all to determine what was really going on. In the commercial, they stood there together, grinning first at each other and then at the camera. Henry held up a condom and said: "There is only one way, and this is it. Right, Barb?"

"Right, Hank," said Barbara.

I felt there was an issue of credibility and honesty involved here that had nothing to do with any prurient interest in sex.

The breakthrough came from a pharmacist at a drugstore near Henry's apartment in Arlington, the close-in Virginia suburb. With some words and other inducements I got the man to tell me that Henry, a man he recognized from the debate, had purchased a package of condoms. "He even gave me a smile and wink and said, 'Watch my smoke, amigo'—something like that," said the pharmacist. I matched the date of the purchase with those given to me by waiters and doormen and determined—circumstantially, at least—what I wanted to know. Henry bought the condoms during the early evening of the same day that he first took Barbara back to her place and spent the night. But there were only three condoms in the package and, according to the pharmacist, Henry did not replenish. "He came in the store many times after that, but he never bought them again," said the pharmacist. Henry also went back to Barbara's place many times after three times, most particularly after they became Hank and Barb. She also accompanied him to his apartment several times. It is possible, of course, that he had another supplier of condoms or that they had decided to truly one-up Jack and Jill by having a "love child." I doubted—doubt—that. But in their new world anything was—is—possible.

There were no unknowns about the professional side of their relationship. *Sunday Morning with Hank and Barb,* after only fourteen broadcasts, had gone up .4 in the ratings to within .1 point of second-place Schwarzkopf. There had already even been some blind quotes in the trades about the possibility of the Holy Grail—of overtaking Jack and Jill. *The Washington Post*'s television writer, Jack Carmody, quoted an anonymous network executive saying: "That sound we hear under our feet over here is that made by the noisy young on their way to vanquish Jack and Jill." The next morning Carmody had a counterquote from an executive at another network. "Despite their skin colors, Hank and Barb are Jack and Jill 'light,' and that is what they will always be. One Sunday they will be gone, and nobody outside of their immediate families and the network will even notice," said the unnamed executive.

★

I will always remember that inaugural day for reasons that have nothing to do with anything that happened on the west side of the Capitol, on Pennsylvania Avenue, or on Joan Naylor's, Hank and Barb's, or anybody else's network television program.

That was the afternoon it happened to me. That was the afternoon a messenger in a motorcycle helmet and goggles brought an unsigned note to our *Tatler* office. It was addressed to "The Man from Mississippi University for Women." The note, carefully typed in the center of a three-by-five index card, consisted only of the name of a restaurant, an address, and the words "Tonight, 8 P.M."

The excitement I felt driving through the heavy post-inaugural traffic north from downtown that night to my rendezvous was unlike any I had ever had before. It could be difficult—and maybe crazy or even scary—but I knew I was going to come back with the goods. I just knew it.

The restaurant was called Richard's and it was in suburban Maryland on a busy four-lane road of neon, auto dealerships, and strip shopping centers called Rockville Pike.

Richard, of Richard's, was just inside the door. Both he and his place were marvelously dark and musty. There were gaudy travel posters from

Alitalia and Air France on the walls, gaudy people behind the bar and waiting tables under the direction of Richard, the most gaudy of all. His hair was coal black, over his ears and down to his collar in back. He had rings on his fingers and a double-breasted dark gray pinstripe suit on his body, which appeared to be as lean and solid as Nelson's.

"You must be Mr. Chapman," he said before I said anything. "I recognize you, but I don't, if you know what I mean." I had no idea what he meant.

" 'Come with me to the Casbah,' " said Richard.

I followed him through the kitchen, which was inhabited by several black-haired men of all ages and by the powerful smells of gurgling tomato sauces and the sautéing parts of fish and veal.

The back room was nothing more than the wine cellar with a table and four chairs. The table was set for three people. Sid Nelson was sitting at one of the three places. He motioned for me to sit down at the one directly across. That left a place between us.

Who was coming? Matters, along with Richard's sauces, were thickening.

I said something about the mysterious ways of Richard. I was looking for small talk. It was what popped out. I said: "Wonder what he did before he went into the restaurant business."

"Would you really like to know?" Nelson said.

"Sure. But it doesn't matter. . . . I'm just making noise. Idle curiosity."

"He was a killer, an assassin. One of the best we ever had. I don't have any exact figures, but I'd say he's probably got fifty scalps on his belt. And that's conservative."

The best *we* ever had? Who in the hell is *we*? Jesus.

Nelson was still the same soft-spoken tough guy from the turbobike. But in this place, this back room, this Casbah, he seemed much more sinister.

I felt a slight breeze of fear. I really did. I thought it was perfectly possible that somebody, probably Richard, would come into the room, hold up a silencer-equipped pistol, and blow out the brains of Thomas Blaine Chapman of *The New American Tatler*. I thought it was also perfectly possible that after taking a bite of whatever I was about to eat, I might feel a pain in the stomach, a tightening in my throat, and then keel over stone dead. I could see my head facedown in a plate of pasta with tomato sauce coming out of my nose like blood, like in the mob movies. I was scared. I was not only not coming away from here with the goods, I was not coming away with my life.

I looked desperately into Nelson's face for a clue, a flicker of something—anything. There was no change. He was still the man on the turbo who had done nothing but make the smallest of small talk.

"Working on any interesting cases?" I said. I was frantic for some kind of sign of normal life.

"You journalists are the ones with the interesting cases," Nelson said.

"How did you happen to get into law enforcement?" I asked. This was crazy, but I couldn't help it.

"I can't imagine your really being interested in my resumé," Nelson said.

I asked the question about what it was that caused him to leave the FBI. He said it was because the assistant attorney general wanted him to put a tap on the private phone of the British ambassador. Nelson could see no legitimate national-security reason for the tap and suspected some kind of personal reason. The tap was never placed.

"But the assistant AG had friends in higher places than I, so I left and went into the private security and investigation business," he said. "If I had known how nice it is out here in the private world, I would have left one helluva lot sooner."

"What do you think of the way Greene is doing so far?" I asked.

"He just went to work today."

"Right, good point. Right. Was the FBI a good place to work?"

"Sometimes it was. Sometimes it wasn't."

I knew he was going to sit there and let me babble on as long as I was willing to babble on. It was a form of torture, something that clearly came naturally to the likes of Nelson. I knew it, but I could not stop it.

I asked him about his family. He said he had one—a wife, two grown sons, and three grandchildren. One of the sons was a lawyer in New York, the other a Secret Service agent assigned to the White House protective detail. The agent-son had gotten a bachelor's degree in law enforcement at the University of South Carolina.

"I'll bet he could tell some stories," I babbled about Nelson's son.

"Nelsons don't tell stories," Nelson said.

Then why are we sitting here? Have you brought me here to kill me? Is that it? If no stories, what, for Christ's sake?

Finally, finally, finally. He said: "Why did you accuse me of handing over the statements to Howley?"

At last.

"Process of elimination and deduction," I said. "Nobody else had access to them. Nobody I could identify, at least."

"Did you talk to Turpin?"

"Yes."

"He could have passed on the statements."

"He convinced me he didn't."

"You're easy, Mr. Chapman."

"He had no motive."

"Yes, he did."

"What?"

"The same one everyone had—including Howley and his three colleagues."

"Please. Not the patriotism and love-of-country bit. . . ."

I wanted those words back in my mouth, and the tone that went with them. Sid Nelson clearly was not a man who appreciated snide cracks about patriotism and love of country. I didn't really mean it to come out snide either. I didn't mean anything.

For a few seconds I thought I had really blown it. If Nelson had in fact come this night to give me the goods, he would not do it now. I watched his face turn from friendly to loathing. "I spent twenty-seven years in the FBI dealing with people like you," he said. "Is being a holier-than-thou smartass, a smug judge of all morality, part of the qualifications for employment in the field of journalism, or is it something that is taught on the job?"

"I'm sorry. That came out wrong. I believe . . ."

Nelson looked away. Forget it, Chapman, and shut up.

I forgot it and shut up. And held my breath. In a few seconds he started talking again. The worst was over. It had passed.

"Why do you want to know about those statements, Mr. Chapman?"

Oh, shit. What does he think I am doing? Obviously, I want them for the stories I am doing for *The New American Tatler.* Obviously. What in the hell do you think I want them for?

I had no option but to make a speech. I said: "I believe, sir, that it is an important part of the total story—the story of how the outcome of a presidential election was changed by the actions of four journalists in getting a presidential candidate to blow up and drop out of the race. The weapons they used were the statements. I see following the trail of those statements the same as it would be . . . well, following the trail of a pistol into the hands of a killer."

"Killer? Weapon? So that is how you see this case—what happened in Williamsburg?"

"I don't know what I think, sir."

"Yes, you do."

Yes, you—I—do. The man was right, of course. I knew exactly what I thought. Yes, you do.

"My working thesis is simply that Mike Howley came to Williamsburg with those statements, planning to manipulate the other three panelists into using them. . . ."

"Are you an honorable man, Mr. Chapman?"

"Yes . . . certainly, I am." It was a question I had never before been asked.

"You said that with some hesitation. Honest men usually do. There is no single honor code for all, Mr. Chapman. You have one. Howley has one. I have one. It is possible that all three are different, but each of us sees our own as the only one. We measure ourselves and others by it—and only it."

I was not expected to comment, react, or interrupt in any way. So I didn't.

He continued: "Let me tell you, Mr. Chapman, directly and without hesitation or ambiguity, that I very much endorse what Howley and the other three did that night in Williamsburg. They acted honorably, according to my code. They did something for the good of their country—my country. I don't know why they did it, but what they did was right. I admire that and I respect that."

He paused. It was a signal that I was now free to speak.

"I respect your opinion, sir."

"No you don't. You're not wearing a wire, are you, Mr. Chapman?"

"No, I am not, Mr. Nelson. Are you?"

Nelson reached under the table and came out with a small voice-activated microcassette recorder. "This is for me, not you," he said.

"Can I buy a copy of the tape afterward?"

I thought for a split second he might smile. But no.

Nelson said: "I am going to tell you a story, Mr. Chapman. I am going to tell it in the third person. If you hear it being told in other voices, then so be it. I cannot prevent that. I will ask that you not interrupt while I tell the story and not ask any questions after I am finished."

I nodded my agreement.

"Once upon a time there was an investigation done of allegations against a man in public life concerning his fitness to hold the highest public office in the land, that of president of the United States. It followed reports to his campaign hierarchy that the man had a violent temper that sometimes got out of hand. So out of hand that he actually lost control of himself in ways that caused him to hurt people—including members of his own family. The investigation was conducted by a group of highly skilled and extremely discreet investigators. They posed as social workers in some cases, insurance adjusters, priests, or law-enforcement officers in others. They took written statements from more than thirty people who had some information, direct or indirect, about the violent side of this public man. Some of it was minor, but all of it was damning. The man in question clearly had a problem that had been kept pretty much secret. The reason for this was simply that until now this man had not sought public office and thus had not had the scrutiny that goes with running for office. Also, most of the people with information about the man's violent acts were members of his family or were his strong supporters. The others were unaware that there were others and they looked upon incidents involving them or their knowledge as isolated events. Why cause trouble? most said to themselves. Everybody flies off the handle occasionally. He hadn't killed or permanently maimed anybody.

"But this man clearly had a problem that was much more serious than an occasional tendency to fly off the handle. The investigators took their findings to their client, who was the campaign manager of the man himself. The campaign manager read the material, said he was shocked and appalled, and told the investigators something would be done about it.

"But nothing was done. As the date of the presidential election got closer and closer, one of the investigators began to believe that nothing was going to be done. This emotionally unstable man was going to become president of the United States.

"So the investigator, without consulting or even notifying his investigator colleagues, decided to act unilaterally in his capacity as a citizen. He decided not to sit by while this happened. It was not that he supported the beliefs and politics of the man's opponent—quite the contrary, in fact. It was simply that he did not think the country could survive the presidency of a man given to violent fits of anger. The investigator believed an unstable conservative was worse than a stable liberal, to put it in the cleanest of political terms.

"The investigator had a relative with good cutout protection—something like in-laws once removed because of divorce. And so the story ends."

"Ends?"

"Ends."

"Who was the cutout?" I asked.

Nelson shook his head.

"Was it somebody at Howley's paper? Was it Tubbs?"

Nelson made no reaction.

"I don't get it."

"Yes, you do," Nelson said.

Nelson stood up in such a way as to leave no doubt I was expected to do the same. This little meeting was over.

Dinner? What happened to dinner? The third person. What happened to him? Or her?

I looked at that third empty place at the table. "Who was the no-show?"

"Nobody. I had that place set to add some mystery and intrigue," Nelson said.

"It worked." Nothing had come my way in our background check that said Sid Nelson had a sense of humor. Surprise!

We were headed for the kitchen now.

"The *real* Richard story?"

"He was the FBI director's lead chauffeur for twenty-five years. More mystery and intrigue for you, Mr. Chapman."

Thank you, sir, for scaring the shit out of me. You bastard.

We went through the kitchen and back through the restaurant, past loud and gracious good nights from Richard and out into the suburban-strip lights of Rockville Pike.

"I have to ask you one question," I said. "Just one."

I chose to ignore Nelson's shaking head. "Why did you tell me this story? You didn't even ask for money."

Nelson held up his right hand. I blanched. He saw it and smiled. "I am not going to hurt you, Mr. Chapman. I don't hurt people. I protect them from hurt."

I waited for him to answer my question. Why, sir, why?

"I have spent most of my professional life doing things that mattered to others, Mr. Chapman. This was something that mattered to me."

"My stories may turn you into a celebrity . . . of sorts, you know."

His face turned into that of a man who had been hit by something and hit hard. "What?" he said through what was now a narrow opening in his mouth.

"Well, get ready for the talk-show invites—"

"You said you would not use my name!" A chill went with those words. A very cold chill.

"There were no ground rules invoked or agreed to when we started talking . . . not here, just now," I said.

"Ground rules? You told me that if I talked you would not use my name."

"When did I tell you that?"

"At the sports club—the last time we talked."

"That doesn't count. The ground rules have to be arrived at before a specific conversation. That is how it works. You did not invoke 'deep background' before we started talking at the table. That is when you had to do that. Each conversation is considered a separate transaction. . . ."

"You are despicable, Mr. Chapman." The words were spoken quietly, but there was rage behind them.

I was not pleased with myself, but I really was playing by the accepted rules of the game. This was not some innocent little kid I was talking to here. I also knew the value of the story would be diminished considerably if I had to pin it all on anonymous sources. I had the goods. I was not about to turn around and give them back—and away. Not if I could help it.

Nelson said: "Clearly, you are not an honorable man according to my code."

"I doubt if you are according to mine either," I said. "I did have one last question. . . ."

He was moving away from me now. I said: "Did the FBI ever talk to you about that little thing Howley and them found under their ice-cream bowl? The bug. I never heard anything more about that. . . ."

"Good-bye, Mr. Chapman."

"Was there one there before the ice-cream bowl?"

"Good-bye, Mr. Chapman."

He was gone.

★

Nelson had said the statements came through a cutout, "something like in-laws once removed because of divorce."

Jennifer Gates and I got right on it. But after three days we could not identify any such person in Tubbs's life or in the lives of anyone else close to Tubbs or Howley.

The key part of Nelson's statement was clearly "something like."

My mind turned to thoughts of a Greek island named Santorini.

★

But before Santorini something else happened. It was personal, sticky, and somewhat embarrassing, but I feel compelled to include it because of what various so-called media watchers have already said and are likely to say in the future.

It's the story of how no articles by me about the Williamsburg Debate came to be published in *The New American Tatler*—or any other magazine.

I was on the phone to Jonathan Angel, my *Tatler* editor, within minutes after returning to my hotel room that night from my rendezvous with

Sid Nelson. I detected a less than enthusiastic tone in Jonathan's reaction to what I was saying. It was most uncharacteristic and surprising, but I dismissed it on grounds that he was distracted, probably by a roomful of dinner guests.

"Jonathan, I need to go to Greece to confront Howley," I said.

"I'm coming to Washington in the morning," he said. "We'll talk about it then."

I had no idea until that moment that he was coming to Washington, and when I went into the office the next morning I discovered I was not the only one. Neither did Jennifer Gates or any of the other bureau staffers.

Jonathan arrived around eleven o'clock. He was wearing his usual uniform—a long white canvas cowboy overcoat over tailor-made bleached blue jeans, square-toed black boots, a white tux shirt unbuttoned halfway down his chest. His dark brown hair was long and tied in a ponytail. He was thirty-five years old and probably thought his getup made him look twenty-five. Not so. He resembled an old hippie, and all of them are at least forty-five.

He went around the office spreading a few seconds of joy to each of the others before he came into my office and closed the door behind him.

"I'm killing your project," he said.

"No!" I screamed.

"We'll pay you a fifteen-thousand-dollar kill fee—double the usual—and then we zip it all up. You give me your notes and tapes and everything else. We flush them down the toilet of journalism and move on to other things—and back to the asshole basketball coaches, I should say."

There was an item in the "Media Whirl" column of *The Washington Post* under the headline WRITER DRAWS EDITOR'S BLOOD that said I slugged Jonathan and "grabbed him by his ponytail and slung him against a wall." That is not true. It is true that I was angry and I expressed that anger physically. But all I did was throw a softball at him. The ball, left over presumably from somebody's office softball game, was there in an ashtray on the desk I was using. Without really thinking, I picked up the ball and hurled it right at Jonathan. Unfortunately, we were only ten yards apart. I threw it too hard and the ball hit Jonathan in the forehead. He fell backward over a chair, hitting the back of his head against the sharp-edged corner of a metal file cabinet. A tiny bit of blood did come out of a tiny wound, but it was nothing serious. Within minutes he was safe and calm, I was calm, and we talked it out.

The specific words between us are not important. What matters is that he adamantly refused to give a reason for canceling the debate assignment other than "It's a matter of priorities."

I said it had to be a matter of some kind of politics, that Howley or somebody like him had gotten to him or the magazine. Jonathan kept denying that, and I kept saying I did not believe him and he kept saying he did not give a shit what I believed, those were the facts.

Various other stories since the original *Post* item have distorted what happened even more. The New York *Daily News* said five of Jonathan's teeth were kicked loose when I "stomped him in the mouth as he lay on the floor." One of the grocery-store tabloids said I attempted to throw Jonathan out the window of our office to a certain death seven floors below. Another said the real hostility between Jonathan and me resulted from a "gay lovers' quarrel"—despite the fact that neither of us is gay.

Although I did not need it, the entire episode provided me another lesson in how grossly irresponsible some elements in the press of the United States of America can be these days. They write and speak lies about people—even about journalists, people of their own kind.

The truly important purpose of my scene with Jonathan for me was making sure nothing disappeared down any toilets of journalism. I refused the extra kill fee and insisted that I felt bound only by our regular contributing editor's contract language. That stated that if a commissioned article was rejected by the magazine on completion, then I would be paid a $7,500 kill fee and then be free to sell the article or other articles based on the material to another "outlet." In all of my six years as a contributing editor at the *Tatler,* nothing like that had ever happened. They commissioned, I completed, they published.

"I'll see you and double that," said Jonathan when I stated my contract case.

"Double what?"

"I'll pay you thirty thousand dollars for the right to flush," he said.

Since the agreed-to fee for the completed and accepted work was only $50,000, it was clear to me that something was going on. And it was also clear to me that whatever it was meant very much to somebody, somebody with access to Jonathan, *The New American Tatler,* and a lot of money.

I declined the offer.

"All right," said Jonathan, "we pay you the full fee as if it had been accepted."

"The full fifty thousand dollars?" I said.

"Yes."

"Maybe I don't want to."

"Maybe you don't have any choice."

He was right. The contract was clear on that. If they paid the full price it was theirs and only theirs. Except for the book rights.

I nodded my agreement and he said: "This means the end of our relationship—yours and the magazine's, you know."

I knew. "I keep everything I've done on the coaches' story."

"Bullshit. That belongs to us, too, and I want it."

It was worth a try.

Within a week three things happened:

- My agent had arranged a book deal with Random House.
- *The New York Times* had a source story about Herman Gerrard, the owner of *The Washington Morning News,* Howley's paper, and all of those other things such as a health-spa chain and a Washington tour-bus company. The story said Gerrard was "reportedly President Greene's choice for the plummiest of the plummy diplomatic posts—ambassador to Great Britain, to the Court of St. James's."
- I was on my way to the Greek island of Santorini.

13

Chapman v. Howley

My imagination went before me to Santorini. By the time I actually set foot on the place, my mind was already soggy with questions and answers, my soul was already marked by the scars and dripping with the juices of the battle. I had seen myself in triumph. I had seen myself in defeat. I came, I conquered; I came, I failed. I rose to the heights. I fell on my face. I, the hero; I, the defeated.

I spent the night in Athens after the flights from London-Heathrow and Washington-Dulles so I would arrive on Santorini as rested as possible. But my racing mind allowed no rest. I was too fully consumed by the Chapman *v.* Howley—ta-da-ta-da!—coliseum-like dimensions of what I was about to do. It was so bad that I almost didn't pay any attention to the island of Santorini, or Thíra, as it is also called.

It was only during the last few minutes of the forty-minute flight from Athens on a small two-engine Greek-airline plane that I even looked down and out of the window. What I saw first was the sparkling blue of the Aegean Sea and then a treeless island of dark red, green, and brown volcanic ash with white buildings scattered over it.

One of the white buildings was my hotel, the Santorini Palace, which was in Fira, population two thousand, the island's major town. The ride in a twenty-year-old Mercedes taxi from the small-everything airport took less than ten minutes. It was at the hotel-room window that I began to realize what this island was all about. Fira and I were perched together on the top of a cliff. The water of the Aegean was out there in all directions, but it was also straight down, *way* straight down at the end of a sheer several-hundred-foot drop. The view down as well as out to sea and to several other even smaller islands was absolutely spectacular.

But I was not here as a tourist to view spectacular sights. It was eleven o'clock in the morning, the air was hot and dry, and I was ready. I went off to find Michael J. Howley.

★

All I had was Howley's address. The young man at the hotel's front desk, who spoke excellent English and said he had uncles and aunts who made and sold beautiful gold jewelry, gave me directions. It turned out to be a short, easy walk down a narrow street that paralleled the edge of the cliff. I paid little attention to the jewelry and souvenir shops and the open-air restaurants and bars on both sides of the street that I passed on the way to the residential area where I would find and confront Michael J. Howley.

What if he isn't there? What if he went back to Washington? Or Istanbul? Or Kalamazoo? What if he is there but won't talk to me? What if I have come all of this way physically and emotionally for nothing? What if he gets mad? What if he throws something—a softball, maybe— at me? What if he throws *me* off of this cliff?

There he was.

Michael J. Howley. There he was in front of me and down to the right. Michael J. Howley, in person. He was not in Washington, Istanbul, or Kalamazoo. He was here. Exactly where I wanted him to be. There he sat in a white folding chair on a balcony patio of a house that jutted out from the cliff below the path where I walked. He was reading something, a book, something. He was dressed in white pants and a short-sleeved light blue polo shirt. Everything I had seen here thus far was either white or blue.

I went off the path to a small retaining wall and peered over at him. I was now less than fifteen yards away.

"Hello, Mr. Howley," I said.

He turned around and saw me—my head, at least—from over the wall. "Oh, shit!" he said.

"Sorry," I said.

"Leave me alone, Chapman."

"Can't do that."

He stood up and faced me. The look on his face was not a pleasant one. It was as if he had been smacked hard.

"Stay away from me," he said. "I really do mean that."

"I have come a long way to talk to you," I said. "I will not leave until I do."

"My sister said you called her. And she talked to you. I can't believe she talked to you."

"Everybody's talked to me, Mr. Howley. Everybody but you."

Howley turned back the other way. His view in that direction was the same one of the Aegean and some islands I had from my hotel room. Then back to me he said: "I have nothing to say to you. Absolutely nothing. If the *Tatler* is stupid enough to spend big money sending you to Greek islands on wild-goose chases, I cannot help it or feel responsible for it."

"The *Tatler* is out of it now," I said. "I am doing a book."

"I'm sorry to hear that," he said.

"You hoped the *Tatler* had killed the story for good, didn't you?"

Now he was looking right at me.

"I know nothing about people who do your kind of journalism," he said.

"The kind that tries to find out about why four journalists would take the electoral process into their own hands and decide who should be the next president of the United States?"

"The people voted, goddamn it! We didn't interfere in the goddamn electoral process! I am tired of hearing that crap!"

I bit hard into my tongue for several critical seconds. The silence paid off.

"We can't go on yelling at each other like this," he said to me. "Go on down the path. You'll come to a shiny brown door with a small painting of a man-in-the-moon on it. I'll let you in."

I then drew in and expended my first real breath since I'd seen Howley there before me.

He let me in, but he did not offer me his right hand or even a casual word of greeting. I followed him through a sparely furnished sitting room.

The microphone! There was the microphone! The one Meredith had thrown at Howley. There it was lying on an end table. Howley had obviously taken the microphone as a souvenir—a trophy. I wanted to stop and pick it up and hold it. But I kept moving behind him through a small dining room and then a wide-open glass door to the balcony where he had been reading.

The microphone! There was that microphone!

He walked to the far edge of the patio, the one opposite the water, the islands—and the drop. I came up to his right side.

"A whole civilization was destroyed here," he said.

"Where . . . what?"

"Do you know about the Mycenaeans?" he asked.

"No, not really," I replied.

"They lived around here way, way back—more than a thousand years before Christ. They had a language and they made pictures . . . and then there was an eruption of a volcano over there." He pointed down and away in the direction we were facing. "It caused death and destruction as far away as Crete seventy miles from here. The people on Thíra—Santorini—must have known it was coming because no bodies were ever found here."

What is this he's telling me? I am not here to worry about lost civilizations and volcanic eruptions. I'm here for Chapman versus Howley!

"I love watching the people on the donkeys," he said.

Donkeys? I had no idea what he was talking about. But I looked down and saw them. Several donkeys with people or boxes of things on their backs were slowly going up or down the side of the cliff, to and from the water and the port below, to and from the town of Fira on high.

"That's nine hundred feet from here down there to the water—the port," Howley said. "Eight hundred or so steps if you walk it with the donkeys. There's also a cable car. You must have come in on a plane."

"I did."

"You missed the best part of being here."

I hope not, Mr. Howley.

"Why did you come way over here to live?" I asked after realizing that I should take advantage of this small-talk opportunity to ease the hard way that might lie ahead. "How did you know about this place . . . ?"

"My wife and I came here for three days on our honeymoon. We sailed and walked through the islands here on the Aegean. Started in Athens, ended up in Istanbul."

Started in Athens, ended up in Istanbul. I liked the sound of that. I was about to say something pleasant to that effect, but I never got the chance.

"You don't take silence for an answer, do you?" he said suddenly, roughly.

"No, sir. You of all people should understand that."

"Why me of all people?"

"You know what it's like to be onto a story."

He shook his head as if to shake off a fly or a mosquito. He clearly did not like my attempt at identifying the two of us together. He clearly thought he was something I was not. He saw me as something beneath him. He was a real journalist. I was something less than that. Much less than that, no doubt, from the exalted place from which he peered down at people like me.

"I'll give you an hour," he said. "One hour by the clock. You can ask anything you want and then you get the hell out of here and away from me. Is that a deal?"

"No . . . hey, wait a minute. No. I need more time than that."

"One hour or nothing. Take it or leave it, Chapman."

Obviously, I took it. It was an opening, a beginning. One hour could naturally and casually grow and grow and grow. It was an offer I could not refuse.

There were several other white folding chairs there on the patio. He motioned for me to grab one and put it on the other side of a small table from his chair. "I'll be right back," he said. I thought maybe he was going for some coffee, tea, or something pleasant like that.

I got the chair and sat down. He returned in a few moments with a portable alarm clock. There was no coffee, tea, or something pleasant like that.

He said: "Watch me, Chapman. It says it is now eleven forty-five. I am going to set the alarm on this thing for twelve forty-five. When it goes off, *you* go off. OK?"

Sure. I was not concerned. Once we were going, we were going.

"May I tape this?" I said, reaching into my small black canvas valise for a microcassette recorder and my large spiral notebook that I had filled with more than two hundred separate questions.

"No problem," he said. "When I was your age we only took notes."

That's right, and you misquoted people, I resisted saying. That was the old journalism, Howley, the old journalism of inexact quotes and approximations and coziness with the powerful, I also did not say. We in the new journalism, Howley, keep our distance and we tape.

He did what he said he would do to the clock, sat down, and said: "The clock is running, Chapman."

I had rehearsed and lived the opening line of questions as much as the tough, dramatic, jugular ones that I planned to build to for the thundering climax. All interviews develop a tone, a mood, a style, a life of their own. I felt it was important to establish at the beginning a tone of easygoing friendliness and then over time let it grow more confrontational and heated. The need for a soft takeoff seemed even more necessary now that I was in a position of having to work and con my way past an alarm on a clock.

"I guess Williamsburg has changed your life a lot?" I said. It wasn't really a question. It was grease.

"That's why I had to get away, why I came here," he said. "It's been incredible."

"Tell me about it, if you don't mind," I said.

He did not mind. He seemed almost grateful even for the opportunity to talk about what Williamsburg had brought and wrought to him personally.

He said: "From that Sunday night on, there were at least three television crews and another five or six other of what now pass for reporters staked out in front of my house around the clock. The new ghouls of

American journalism. I had always ranted and raved about this barbaric vulturism, and here I was a victim of it myself. They even had them lying in ambush outside the *News* offices. These tabloid assholes—no offense, Chapman . . ."

"None taken, Mr. Howley. I am not a tabloid asshole." I said it softly, but I said it. There was a limit to what I was prepared to take from this arrogant man in exchange for this interview!

He continued.

"These people yelled questions like—'Hey, Howley, did you ever take a swing at *your* wife?' 'Hey, Howley, have you ever said "fucking" in public?' 'Hey, Howley, are you going to pick twelve disciples and start wearing sandals and a robe?' 'Hey, Howley, is it true the Greene campaign paid you a million bucks to do it?' 'Hey, Howley, is it true you were drunk that night?' 'Hey, Howley, are you on Prozac?' Hey, Howley, you scum, you crook, you jerk, you thug, you bastard."

He said the volume of calls, E-mail, faxes, mail, and other messages to and about him to the *News* was heavier than anything anybody could remember since the outpouring of emotion after the Kennedy assassination. "They brought it all in in huge gray canvas bags and tall stacks of pink call slips and audiotapes," he said. "Our personnel department hired twenty-five people from some temp office to deal with it."

He told me about Sam Rhodes—Henry, Joan, and Barbara had already told me all I needed to know about this man of Hollywood—and how he was now pushing a miniseries based on the Michael J. Howley story. It would begin with his early life, "wherever and whatever that was," Howley quoted Rhodes as saying. The working title was "The Reporter." Howley said he also listened to a voice-mail message from a man claiming to be Oliver Stone, a man Howley said he personally believed to be a Big Lie propagandist of Joseph Goebbels proportions and standards. "He said he wanted to make a movie about how most everything that happens to all Americans in all walks of life is controlled by seven or eight highly paid, highly visible people in the press like me— Mike Howley. He said he was sure he could get Costner to play me. Why Stone wasn't laughed out of business years ago I do not understand."

I bit my tongue again. Stone, lying propagandist or not, had a big following among people my age and younger. They believed his wild conspiracy theories, whether people such as Howley liked it or not. But I did not come all this way to have an argument with Michael J. Howley about Oliver Stone.

Howley said he put the alleged Stone call in the same category with those about sweatshirts and requests to name everything from sandwiches and lawnmowers ("the Williamsburg Ripper") after him. He, like Joan, also had many serious proposals for sex, talk-show regularity, books, lectures, and honorary degrees, among other things.

He said one of the most unusual was from a men's hairstylist in Beverly Hills who wanted permission to develop a "Howley cut" based on the way Howley wore his hair that night in Williamsburg. Howley said what the guy didn't know was that he wore it that way because his regular barber in Washington, an Armenian from Lebanon, had gone back to the old country for a family vacation.

"I created a monster and it was me," he concluded after an extremely long recitation of his post-Williamsburg annoyances and opportunities.

"On lectures," I said, "I guess Williamsburg changed the rate for you in a major way?"

"My lecture-bureau guy told my secretary I can now get seventy-five thousand dollars a pop—maybe more," he said. "Can you imagine being paid seventy-five thousand dollars for talking for less than thirty minutes about life inside the Beltway or some other such crap? It's goddamn amazing."

It was indeed. "That puts you in the high brackets with Ronald Reagan," I said.

"No comment," he replied. I could tell he hated the idea of being likened to Ronald Reagan. Too bad, Mr. Howley.

"Why is it all right for journalists to take large speaking fees from conventions and interest groups but not OK for members of Congress and politicians?" I asked.

"Good question."

"What's the good answer?"

"We need the money. They don't."

"Is the real answer—journalists think they are better and purer than politicians and cannot be bought like politicians?"

Howley glanced down at the clock on the table. So did I. Did I want to spend my valuable time here at the beginning in a discussion of journalism ethics? It was 12:10. Twenty-five minutes had already gone by. But ethics were important. They were part of the story. An important part of the story.

But I had to move on. I would return to ethics later in the interview.

I said: "If I could take you now back in time before the debate. Would you mind telling me where you were and how you were told of the invitation to moderate the Williamsburg Debate?"

I felt smart and extremely pleased when Howley seemed to let off even more steam and tension. He leaned back in his chair and, again, continued to talk fully and in detail.

He went through his lecture appearance in San Antonio, the flight back from Texas, the exchange with the American Airlines flight attendant, and his thoughts about 1980 and the press-plane obits. He even remembered what he ate and drank on the flight from Dallas to Washington National.

He told me about how and where he spent election night and a little bit about his late wife and how much he missed her and how he was sure she would have enthusiastically endorsed what he had done at Williamsburg. His description of the Majestic Theater in San Antonio, where he delivered his predebate lecture, was effusive. "It was built just before the Depression, right on the Main Street of town. The great 'atmospherics' theater architect of the time, John Eberson of Chicago, designed it with a Mediterranean plaza in mind. It had three balconies, total seating of twenty-five hundred, blinking lights like stars in the ceiling, which was sky blue, a cloud machine, a huge pipe organ, walls that were elaborate plaster replicas of Spanish and Moorish villages. The theater fell on bad times and some developer was going to tear it down, but the city of San Antonio—the mayor, I think it was Cisneros then—kept that from happening. They spent fifteen million dollars in city and private money to completely restore it, and they converted some old office space above it into apartments. The building is nineteen stories high. . . ."

I interrupted him. I simply did not care that much about a restored movie theater in downtown San Antonio, Texas.

There was so much to cover, to ask, to confront.

I moved him on to his phone conversation with Chuck Hammond of the debate commission and then to Jerry Rhome. The answers got much shorter when he talked about his walk and talk with Rhome. It was clear to me that Howley was annoyed when it became clear through my questions that Rhome had talked to me.

"Why did you want to moderate that debate so badly that you asked Rhome to change the *News* rules to permit it?" I asked.

"It was not a case of 'want.' It was simply that I felt I should," he said.

"But why?"

"That's my answer."

"What's your answer?"

"I felt I should."

"For love of country?"

"That's it, Chapman. You got it."

Rhome had already told me about their final laugh over Rhome's order to make sure "Meredith loses his ass."

I asked Howley how he took that crack.

"The way it was intended—as a joke," he replied.

"How did you know it was a joke?"

"Because I am an experienced listener to jokes."

I asked if he met with or talked to any of the other three panelists before going to Williamsburg. I knew the answer, but I wanted his confirmation and I wanted to ask him:

"Why not? Why not at least call them?"

"There was no real reason to call them. There was nothing special to talk about. The debate format the commission and the candidates signed off on was the simplest—the most controlled. I thought about giving them each a call to welcome them to the foxhole, but I got busy and didn't do it."

"Busy doing what?"

"Doing my job, for one thing. I work for a newspaper, remember?"

"Do you still work for that newspaper?"

"I'm on a long vacation now."

"For how long?"

"For as long as it turns out to be."

The enemy was approaching. The battle was now just over the ridge.

I felt the quickened beat of hearts, the flow of sweat on arms and necks, the smell of gunpowder and quinine. Charge!

I asked my first attack question. I did so gently, almost offhandedly. "Didn't you think the other panelists had a right to know beforehand that you had something very special in mind for the format and the candidates?"

"They would have had a right if that was, in fact, the case. But it was not, in fact, the case. All of that happened later, after we got together."

All right, all right. It was only a quick, light thrust, a pat—in and out. Only the beginning. A taste of what was to come.

I asked him if he recalled his first reaction to learning the names of the three journalists who would be on the Williamsburg panel with him.

"I knew Joan Naylor—I saw her as a pro, no problem. I saw the other two as nonentities, selected no doubt because of the color of their respective skins."

"Did that bother you?"

"Yes."

"Did you raise that point in your conversations with the panel?"

Howley snapped his head away from looking at me toward the direction of the sea. "I am not talking about what happened in Longsworth D," he said.

"Why not?"

"Because what happened there is private."

"Not anymore it isn't."

The darkness that I had seen in his face when I showed up now returned.

"I do not believe any of the other three talked to you," he said.

"You are free to believe whatever you wish."

"Thank you, asshole."

Now I looked away toward the sea. OK, OK, he called me an asshole. Twice now, he called me an asshole. So what. I am here to do a job. I am not here to take offense at being called an asshole. In fact, the madder he gets, the more I might get from him.

So. Do I press this Longsworth D point now? That is the question. Do I completely give away the fact that Joan and Henry and Barbara opened up to me on what happened in Longsworth D? No, I decided. Not now. I'll come back to it later. Let him believe for a while longer that he might be safe on exactly what he said that Sunday afternoon in Williamsburg to get the other three to go along with his scheme to change the outcome of an election for president of the United States.

But it was time for another thrust—something more than a soft pat.

"Where did you get those women's statements?" I asked.

"Who says I was the one who got them from anywhere?"

"I know you got them, Mr. Howley. All I want to know is where you got them."

"No comment."

"How can you say, 'No comment'?"

He leaned across toward me and said: "Read my lips. 'No comment.' That's how I can say it."

"I assume you brought them with you to Williamsburg that Saturday afternoon?"

"You are free to assume anything you wish."

"By the way, how did you come to Williamsburg?"

He told me about driving his own car and listening to tapes and CDs during the ride down from Washington. I asked him what he did on Saturday night and he brushed me off with a simple "Nothing worth mentioning." It changed the tempo, at least, for a few seconds. But only a few.

I was right back at it. "I know who took the statements from those women."

"Good for you."

"They were taken by people on behalf of one of the campaigns."

Howley shook his head and smiled. "Forget it, Chapman." He glanced again at the clock on the table between us. "You've got less than five minutes left."

There was no way I was stopping in five minutes. Maybe not in five hours.

"Was it Tubbs who gave them to you?"

"I said, forget it. There is no gold down that hole, Chapman."

Like hell there isn't, Howley.

"I know you talked to him that Saturday night before the debate."

"Who?"

"Tubbs."

"How do you know that?"

"No comment."

Again, he was pissed.

I said: "Somebody—and I know who because he told me—from one of the campaigns gave those statements to somebody who gave them to you. It was Tubbs, wasn't it?"

"Why is this so important to you?"

"This is not for me. It's for . . . well . . ."

"The public? The American people? Give me a goddamn break."

"Did you or did you not go to Williamsburg with a plan in mind to use the debate to derail Meredith by driving him crazy enough to lose it there in front of everybody?"

" 'Did you or did you not.' Forget it, Mister District Attorney. I am not on trial."

"Yes you are."

"I *was* on trial. But the trial was over on Election Day. The American voters were my judge and jury. They saw and listened and they did not vote for Meredith. That is what this was all about and *all* it was about."

"What were your thoughts when you opened that debate that night?"

"I don't recall having any."

"Not one second thought?"

"Nope."

"Do you have any idea now of the magnitude of what it is you did?"

"Yes."

"The outcome of a presidential election was changed because of what you did."

"Right."

"Are you proud of what you did?"

"Yes."

"Journalism. What about what you did to your profession of journalism? Are you proud of what you did to it, too?"

"It was already headed over the cliff, thanks in part to people like you. All I did was give it a last-minute good purpose before it sailed off a cliff and died."

"Died?"

"Died. Gone. Deceased. Passed away. Expired. Journalism, as something good little boys and girls should devote their dreams and lives to, died. What we are part of is the slimy rigor mortis that is setting in. You more than me, but I am part of it, too, with my lecture fees and TV appearances. We're no better than the big-buck anchors who are treated as movie stars, not as journalists. They read 'lines,' not the facts. They are not expected to inform, only to be entertaining or sexy—"

There was a loud metallic buzzing sound. The alarm. The goddamn alarm was sounding!

Howley reached out with his right hand and turned it off.

"Don't stop," I said. "You were saying about your own role in journalism—"

"This interview is over, Chapman."

"No, no, come on."

"Yes, yes."

He stood up. "Get your ass out of my house and out of my life."

"We have just begun." I did not stand up.

"We have just ended. Beat it."

"You can't be serious."

"Never more so in my whole life, Chapman."

I still did not move.

"I'm going to call the Greek cops," Howley said. "I'm going to tell them you offered to sell me some crack cocaine that you smuggled into their country from the United States. I am going to tell them that when I said I did not want your poison and that I was going to call the police, you tossed your evil merchandise over the cliff in the direction of the donkeys. I will tell them that I hope the donkeys, bless their burdened but noble souls, do not by accident chew on a bite of crack cocaine. That would be terrible because it would probably affect their nervous systems and cause them to toss people and goods off of their burdened backs to their deaths or damage. . . ."

He started laughing. "Crack-crazed donkeys," he roared. "That's what you people were like after the debate."

"You people?"

"You people in the pressroom. Crack-crazed donkeys."

He had *that* right, but I had another problem right now. I said: "You really would call the police?" I had heard all of the stories about the Greek and Turkish police and drugs. He had my attention.

"You bet your ass I would. They throw people in prison for twenty years without parole simply for possessing drugs in this country."

Now I was on my feet.

"I have many, many more questions," I said.

"Out, Chapman, out."

"I am authorized by my publisher to pay you for your story, Mr. Howley."

"You bastard! Go!"

"Seriously. Why shouldn't you be paid for your story? You earned it the hard way."

"Keep talking, Chapman, and I may throw you down to the donkeys where you belong."

"Fifty thousand dollars—in cash."

"No!"

"I can have it here in less than twenty-four hours."

"Go!"

"Seventy-five?"

He made a move toward me. He really did. A step and then another. I decided to shut up. I had seen the men and women—the crack-crazed donkeys—of the American press at their violent worst in the Virginia Room. I had been known to throw an angry softball at an editor myself. There was seriously no telling what this man coming toward me now might try to do to me.

I said: "How about lunch? I'll buy."

"Out! Good-bye!"

Out, good-bye, it was.

Chapman *v.* Howley. I had imagined a round-the-clock marathon of strong, hot, smart words and emotions that would tax civility and intellects. I had expected to be spent, to be exhausted, to be used up, but to be bleeding joy and triumph, as did the warriors who battled in other times, in other places over other things.

Instead, it was over in an hour to the sound of an alarm clock. And I had been thoroughly defeated. He had wasted precious time off the clock with all of those details about that goddamn theater in San Antonio, the plane ride, and other irrelevancies. I thought I could push back the time. I started soft. I threw away my time. He was smarter than me.

He won.

★

I did see and do a few more things on Santorini before I left on the noon plane for Athens the next day.

I walked the eight hundred or so steps that zigzagged down the side of the cliff to the port, had a cup of espresso and a pastry in an outdoor café. The waitress, a Greek woman in her forties, told me in rough English that I was actually sitting on the edge of a volcano. "It's down in water somewhere," she said. "It blows, we blow, happens many times." Back at the hotel I read in a brochure even more about what Howley had told me out on his deck. The monumental volcanic explosion thirty-five hundred or so years ago caused the center of the island to drop into the sea, creating the cliff where Fira and the rest of Santorini was now. Archaeologists have been hard at work since the 1930s unburying Akrotiri, a complete, once-prosperous city on the southern end of the island that was buried in that first big eruption. They still had not found any bones or other signs of human or animal bodies. There had been several other destructive eruptions since, the worst being in 1956.

The brochure said the island was occupied by the Germans and Italians during World War II. I wondered why the Germans and the Italians thought this place was necessary to occupy? How did the people here get through such a horrendous experience? Were there any collaborators? Did any of the Germans or Italians stay here after the war? Was there any intermarrying between the occupiers and the occupied? The whole story of Santorini sounded fascinating, and I thought vaguely that someday—a better day—I might even become interested in finding out more.

I rode a donkey back up to the top of the cliff, a twenty-minute trip made memorable mostly by the flies and the smell of donkey doings. As I went into several of the many shops on the main, pedestrians-only street, I paid some attention to the people this time. All were dark-skinned, made that way naturally by God at birth or since then by being out in the hot Greek sunshine.

I didn't buy any gold jewelry, the apparent specialty of Fira, or any-thing else. The only item that tempted me was a pair of white duck pants I came across in a tiny clothing store. I decided against them because I knew I would never wear them, because every time I put them on I would think again about what happened to me where I bought them.

Chapman *v.* Howley. I came, I failed. I fell on my face. I, the defeated.

★

There now remained on my interview list two central figures in the Williamsburg drama. They were the new president of the United States, Paul L. Greene, and the man he defeated, David Donald Meredith. They were the ultimate victor and victim of Williamsburg, and thus their most detailed personal memories of that Sunday night on that stage were cru-cial to painting the full and complete picture of the event. So were their thoughts and opinions about Howley and Barbara and Henry and Joan and what they did.

I was determined to get interviews with both Greene and Meredith before I rested—and wrote. The story would never be complete without them.

I had begun working on a Greene interview almost immediately—within forty-eight hours of my return from Williamsburg following the debate. The people who replaced Lilly and the other campaign people simply and politely put me off. Nobody ever quite said yes or no, and everyone I talked to was encouraging, hopeful, helpful, pleasant. But there was no interview. Transition problems were cited. Later, they said. Later, later, later. Let him get a cabinet and a government together. Then he will gladly sit down and ruminate about Williamsburg. I came back again and again through everybody I knew or could cultivate within the transition team and entourage. Nothing. The man's got an inaugural address to write and deliver, they said. Let him get that behind him. Later, right after he's there in the Oval Office. Later, later. You're at the top of the list. He really wants to talk to you, they said. Patience, please, is all we ask. Let him get situated and comfortable. Patience, please. Later.

The day after my return from Santorini I zeroed in on Thelma Jordan, the new White House press secretary. She had come to Greene's side from her job as chief Washington correspondent and political editor of the *Omaha World-Herald,* the leading newspaper in his state. She came with a reputation for tough, straight talk.

She finally agreed to see me and I came to the White House one day during what for most people was lunch hour. For her it was clearly just another hour of the day. On her desk in the cluttered West Wing press secretary's office was what looked like a bowl of brown-colored soup and a wheat-bread sandwich of some kind. Neither look sipped or nibbled on.

Thelma Jordan's age had been reported to be fifty-three. I believed it. Her graying black hair and her dirty white face were both uncared for by her and her maker. Her lips were red, I assumed from the application of lipstick, but I was not sure. There were no other signs of makeup. But there were also no signs of masculinity. From my advance reading, I had expected to discover that "tough" was actually a code word for a sexual orientation. Not so. There was something appealing and sensual about this woman that fit the other part of what I had read about her. That she had been the drum major in her Beatrice, Nebraska, high-school band, had been married to the same man—an archaeologist who specialized in the diggings of ancient Troy in Turkey—for twenty-eight years, and was the mother of four sons.

"The debate came and it's over," she said. "He's got nothing to say about it."

"It was a monumental happening in his life," I said. "He must have very much to say about it."

"Whatever, he doesn't want to talk to you about it." She pronounced "you" in much the same way she would have spoken about a dreaded disease.

"Why not?" I said.

"One of the great things about being president is that you never have to answer the question 'Why not?' "

I pointed out the need for our children and grandchildren to know the full story of Williamsburg. I said the record could never be complete without the impressions and recollections and thoughts of the man who benefited the most from what happened.

"The people of this country benefited the most," said Thelma Jordan.

I moved on to make the case for the historians. I had read about her husband's line of work. "Look upon this as a form of contemporary archaeology," I said. "Why wait until the story of the Williamsburg Debate is buried under layers of time and dirt?"

"What a stupid argument for an interview," she said. "But all right, you've got ten minutes."

"Ten minutes? I can barely say hello and good-bye in ten minutes." I wondered if the president of the United States, like Howley, would use an alarm clock to make sure I didn't go over my time.

Thelma Jordan, who had yet to sit down, said: "Look, I understand the drill. You want to be able to say in your book that you talked to the president. OK, you got it. You can talk to the president."

"When would it be?"

"Now."

"Now? I need to think about my questions. . . ."

"Now or never, Chapman. Follow me—to the Oval Office or out the door to the street."

Now or never, Chapman.

I followed her across the hall and down another hallway past a couple of Secret Service agents standing watchful and protective.

Thelma Jordan knocked on a half-open door and stuck her head and body inside. "Mr. President, I have Mr. Chapman, the man who is writing the debate book."

I heard the familiar voice of Paul L. Greene say: "Come in, come in."

I stepped inside the Oval Office. Thelma Jordan stepped aside, and the president came around from his desk and shook my hand. "Welcome," he said.

I wondered if the ten-minute clock was running.

He escorted me to a sitting area across the room. I wanted to look around the place, so I could later describe the office in detail. But he clearly had not moved many of his own things into the office. Hadn't I read something about there being a whole new paint and remodeling job coming?

At any rate, I was not looking around the Oval Office, the most important and famous office in the world. I was looking at the most important and famous man in the world and thinking of how best to spend my ten minutes with him.

Thelma Jordan and I sat down across from the president. I did take note of how he was dressed. A dark gray suit, blue button-down-collar shirt, and a green tie. Always a green tie. The joke already was that there were fears the president's head would become detached from his neck if he did not wear a green tie. There seemed to be no other explanation for his always wearing a green tie. Always. A campaign gimmick had become an obsession.

"I see you have on a green tie, Mr. President," I said. It just came out.

"That's right, Mr. Chapman," said the president of the United States. "It is indeed a green tie."

I dared not even glance around at Thelma Jordan. I could imagine the great-question-you-dumb-ass smile that must have been on her face.

"Mr. President, do you still believe those four panelists did the proper thing at Williamsburg?"

"I do indeed," he said. "I said it then and I say it now—they were as much American heroes as were the Minutemen at Concord."

"But doesn't it set a pattern for journalistic activism that might be harmful for the country?"

"Not necessarily."

Not necessarily?

"Sir, could you tell me what was going through your mind once you realized what was happening out there—you know, with the reading of the statements and all of that?"

"I remember being shocked at what was in those statements. I remember then being delighted that this information was being made public."

"Delighted?"

"Delighted."

"How did that delight manifest itself?"

"I felt good."

"You felt good?"

"I felt good."

"Do you believe you would have been elected president if there had not been Williamsburg?" I asked.

"No."

"Why not?"

"Because I do not believe the people of the United States would have had an opportunity to truly discover the true nature of the two candidates."

"How important was the big scene—the big use of the . . . you know, the big bad word there at the end?" I asked.

I did not say the word itself. I was in the Oval Office, after all. I was talking to the president of the United States, after all. Although I was fully aware of the fact that the big bad word was known, by tape and anecdote, to have been fully and often spoken in the Oval Office by most recent presidents themselves.

President Greene said: "Frankly, I doubt that it had much to do with the final result."

"There are many who think otherwise, sir, as I am sure you know."

Paul L. Greene, his face pleasant but serious, said: "A cussword did not elect me president of the United States. The people did."

Yes, sir.

I continued. "Everybody is still marveling about how you seemed to 'come alive' as a candidate, so to speak, after the debate. What happened?"

"You just said it."

"You mean, you just came alive?"

"That's right."

"So it was there all the time?"

"That's right."

I felt Thelma Jordan standing. I did not look at her. The president was still seated.

"How do you like being president?" I asked.

"I am really enjoying it so far," Paul L. Greene replied. "Thanks for asking."

He stood and now I stood. We three moved toward the door.

"Thanks for coming by," said the president of the United States.

"Thanks for allowing me to, sir," I said.

We shook hands and suddenly I was back out in the hall with Thelma Jordan and the Secret Service agents.

"Well, you've got your scoop, Chapman," said Thelma Jordan just before she left me to return to the West Wing lobby. "President Wears Green Tie—Again! Read all about it!"

I asked if it might be possible to come back for a longer session sometime, but she simply waved good-bye and left my presence.

According to my watch, I didn't get anywhere near my full ten minutes. It was more like three or four.

★

The woman on the phone at the Music of the Messiah Life and Living Center in Tashobi, Oklahoma, was even less cooperative than Thelma Jordan. Even before I had a chance to identify myself, she said that David Donald Meredith would not come to the phone now or at any other time as long as any of us shall live. I could have imagined it, but I thought I heard a slight musical quality to her words and voice that resembled a piece of almost-singing dialogue from an operetta.

So I had no choice but to go to Tashobi, Oklahoma, myself. No offense to anyone in or from Oklahoma, but honest journalism forces me to report that it was almost as difficult to get to Tashobi, Oklahoma, as it was to get to Santorini, Greece. It took me more than ten hours by the time I flew from Washington to Dallas, Texas, back in the direction I came from on a short flight to Tulsa, Oklahoma, and then drove in my rent-a-car down to the Ouachita Mountains of southeastern Oklahoma.

Another similarity to Santorini was the beautiful sights. But instead of a blue sea and high volcanic cliffs, there were majestic pine and fir trees atop a magnificent and unspoiled range of small mountains. I had imagined Oklahoma to be a place of cowboys, flat red land, and oil wells. I saw some of all of that on the road south from Tulsa, but I was stunned by what I saw when I got to the Ouachitas. I had no idea there was a mountainous area of Oklahoma that resembled what I had seen west of

Denver in Colorado and even up in the White Mountains of New Hampshire.

I also knew that getting here was probably not going to be the major difficulty of this adventure. Driving up to a gate and declaring, "Hello, I'm Tom Chapman. I'm writing a book about Williamsburg and I've come to interview Mr. David Donald Meredith," would probably not produce what I had come all of this way to get.

There was a gate. It was at the end of a narrow two-lane dirt road at the base of a mountain. I could hear I was there before I could see it because of the music. There was the enormously loud sound of some people that had all the noise and power of the Mormon Tabernacle Choir singing a religious song of some kind. It seemed to be coming from speakers mounted somewhere out there in the trees.

The gate was small—barely the width of a full-sized car—and was made of old and rusted scrap metal. It was almost dark, but a floodlight exposed not only the gate but also, on a bar above it, a huge cross that was made of what looked like two huge truck bumpers.

I got out of the car and went over to a small squawk box on a wooden post that in an earlier life was probably a lead pipe. There was a red button on the box with the words PUSH—TALK above it.

I pushed the button and said: "Hello there. I am a music producer and talent scout for New World Records in New York. I have come to see if you good people of God might be interested in cutting some recordings for us. We could release them on CDs, tapes—the whole multimedia bit."

I let up on the button. Nothing but silence came out.

I pushed the button again and said: "All I have to offer you are fame and money. I realize that this is not what you-all are all about. But isn't there some charity, some good work somewhere in your world of concern, that could use some extra cash? We have lots of it, you know. We've been told you-all make all kinds of sounds for all kinds of people and age groups and musical tastes. . . ."

The gate swung open.

I dashed back to my car and drove on through. The road, pure dried mud, seemed to get smaller and rougher and more rutted the farther I went. I figured it must be virtually impassable when it rained.

The music was louder. And it had switched to a country-western version of a song about Jesus. A female vocalist was yelling something about "You are my only love, Jesus in heaven / I am ready to be with you when you are." I swear that was what she said.

After almost two miles by my odometer and fifteen minutes by my watch, I came into a clearing where there were several cars and pickups parked. Directly across the clearing I saw a large log cabin that seemed built along the lines of a split-level home or lodge. Several smaller log cabins were out in the trees on both sides.

I drove up to the main house. There was a man on the porch. He was dressed in a white Stetson hat, black cowboy boots, and a shiny red, white, and green spangled outfit right out of a Roy Rogers or Gene Autry movie. He had a guitar strapped around his neck and down on his chest and stomach.

I opened the car door. I heard the strum of a guitar. The other music had stopped.

"Hi there!" I yelled to the man on the porch.

He strummed his guitar. And he continued to strum as I walked up some steps to the porch.

"Hi," I said to the man once I got in front of him. "I'm the man from New World."

The smiling, clean-shaven face under the white hat seemed to be that of a man in his late forties. He was tall and skinny and he was not David Donald Meredith.

"The language of the Messiah was music," said the man to the strum of his guitar. "We only speak that language here."

"Good, great," I said. "I love music. Music is my life."

"How much will you pay us to record our music?" he asked, speaking almost normally. There was no strumming.

"That depends," I said, realizing that my cover story was going to be a problem if this man or anyone else around here actually knew anything about the finances or anything else concerning the music-recording business. I knew absolutely nothing. "It would be on a royalty basis," I said.

"We get paid only after each record or tape or CD of our music is sold?" he said.

"That's right, sir."

"Forget it," he said. He strummed his guitar. "The Messiah prohibits speculating."

"Maybe we could work out a cash-advance arrangement of some kind," I said, making it up as I went.

"How much cash?"

"That would be subject to negotiation."

"Let's negotiate."

I had to slow this thing down. "You bet," I said, "but first I wonder if I might use your rest room. It's been a long drive through the mountains from Tulsa."

"You should have come by horse."

"From Tulsa?"

"Horses were good enough for the Messiah. I will take you inside to the toilet. Inside that door here only the language of the Messiah is permitted. If you speak, sing or hum the words. Do you play an instrument?"

"No, sir," I said.

"Do not call me 'sir.' Only the Messiah is 'sir.' "

"Right."

I followed him inside to a room that resembled the lobby of a rough-and-ready Holiday Inn. There were several people around, some of them talking—singing—to each other. None of them resembled David Donald Meredith.

My ears picked up the sounds of a male operatic tenor in conversation with a female responding in soft rock, a guttural-voiced C-and-W man speaking to another man who was answering in a form of talk-song. And off in the distance somebody was playing the piano, and somebody else was on what sounded to my untrained ears like a French horn.

Nobody paid any attention to me and I followed my guy in the cowboy outfit to a door marked HALLELUJAH!

"In there, pa'dner, hallelujah, hallelujah," he said to the tune of something that sounded vaguely familiar. Was it from *South Pacific*? Or was it an old hymn I remembered singing in the Methodist church when I visited my grandmother in Vermont?

The rest room, I hereby report, was nothing special. By now I expected everything to be special—strange. It would not have surprised me, for instance, to have found urinals in the shape of violins and cellos and to have heard Bach sonatas blaring out to accompany the sounds of toilets flushing, faucets running.

Back outside with my cowboy a few minutes later, I realized it was time to act. Again in my reporting life, it was now or never, Chapman.

"Would you mind giving me a tour before we do our business?" I crooned à la Sinatra to the tune of "My Way."

"There is nothing to see but happy singing, humming people," he responded to the tune of "The Tennessee Waltz." "Let's go back outside."

"Have you got an extra sandwich or something for a hungry soul?" I crooned to the tune of something along the lines of "Hello, Dolly!" "I haven't eaten a bite since Tulsa."

" 'I Haven't Eaten a Bite Since Tulsa,' " he repeated. "That has the ring of a good song title. You have the spirit. You have the music."

"Thank you, sir."

I looked into the man's face—he still hadn't told me his name—for a sign of suspicion. There might have been a flicker of something but nothing serious. Not yet. But I clearly had to be careful. It was an additional strain I did not need. All of the music-madhouse noise and this thinking and talking in the musical language of the Messiah was already making it difficult enough.

The man strummed his guitar, motioned for me to follow him, and sang some words about food and life to a tune I did not remotely recognize.

We walked back through the lobby. I got a better look at and listen to the people of Music of the Messiah Life and Living Center. None of them were David Donald Meredith.

We came into the kitchen and there he was. His face was covered with a beard and his hair was long, but there was no doubt this was the man I had come to see. This was the man who came within twenty-three days, four journalist-panelists, and three "fuckings" of being president of the United States. Now there he stood cooking pots of what looked and smelled like a stew. There he stood dressed in a white T-shirt with the words THE SOUNDS OF JESUS on the front.

We made eye contact. But I managed—it was the most difficult thing I had thus far done in my reporting on this story, I promise you—not to smile or in any way show anything. I felt it was absolutely imperative that he not know that I had recognized him.

There was another man in the kitchen dressed in a similar T-shirt. He was Meredith's fellow cook, apparently. To him, my host and guide said to the tune of "Jesus Loves Me": "Feed this man a sandwich, brother."

A few seconds later I casually turned back to the big stove where Meredith was—and he was gone. I hoped that maybe he had left for a minute to run an errand, to go to the "Hallelujah," to do something other than to be really gone.

The other cook threw a piece of ham and some lettuce and tomato on a slab of white bread, splattered it all with both mustard and mayonnaise, and handed it to me on a simple white plate.

"Thank you," I sang to no particular tune.

"Thank the Messiah," he sang back to no particular tune.

"Thank you, Messiah," I sang.

My cowboy friend suggested we take the sandwich outside, but I insisted on eating it right there in the kitchen, right there just standing up. "It will only take a few minutes," I sang.

Where did you go, Meredith? Come back here!

As I bit into my sandwich—it actually tasted pretty good—and chewed and swallowed, I tried to come to grips with the task before me. I was fairly happy with myself. I had gained entrance to this weird place. I had established the fact that Meredith was here. Now what?

There he was again. Meredith had returned! I had not scared him off. My hope had proved right. He had only stepped out for a few minutes. This time I intentionally avoided any eye contact. I did not want to spook him or scare him away.

I was eating too slowly. My cowboy friend was getting impatient. And, I assumed, it would not be long before suspicion would replace that impatience.

OK, I sang to myself. Go, Tom, go. Now or never, Chapman.

I wiped my mouth with the piece of white paper towel the cook had provided and walked quickly and smartly to Meredith. The cowboy was caught off guard. I was there in front of Meredith before he or the other cook could react.

I said to no tune: "Mr. Meredith, I am Tom Chapman. I am doing a book about what those four devils of American journalism did to you on that stage in Williamsburg. I want to help you tell your story, to help you take retribution against them by offering you an opportunity to punish them—"

David Donald Meredith's face went red. He put his hands over both of his ears. Then he used them to grab the handle of the huge iron skillet on the stove in front of him. He threw the skillet off to his left as hard as he could. The skillet and the stew went splashing and crashing. I halfway expected him to accompany it all with a few "fuckings," but he said not a word.

And he ran from the kitchen.

I took two steps in pursuit and was stopped by the cowboy and the other cook. One of them grabbed my left arm, the other my right.

In a minute or two they were joined by four or five other men, and within another minute I was carried like a shackled prisoner across the porch and down the steps and placed in the front passenger seat of my rent-a-car. The cowboy got in the driver's seat, and two of the other men got in the backseat.

We burned some rubber on the dry dirt of the parking area and bumped and jarred and lurched down the road back to the gate.

I had never heard somebody cuss the way that cowboy man and his two companions did. By the time we got to the gate I had been called every vile name in the book to the tunes of a most wide and varied medley of melodies.

But at least it was over. There was nobody else left to interview. My story may not have been finished—but my work was done.

Or so I thought.

14

Carl Bob

$\mathbf{I}$ had not counted on having to deal one more time with Michael J. Howley.

He had come almost right behind me from Greece to Washington. Just ten days later he flew the same flights I did on Olympic Airways from Santorini to Athens and then on British Airways to London and on to Washington-Dulles. I have not been able to trace all of his movements, actions, and words once he arrived back in Washington. I know he stayed in his own townhouse in Georgetown and I know he went to the *News*. Did he talk to Pat Tubbs there or on the phone? Did he yell at Jerry Rhome for having talked to me? Did he raise hell with somebody for not killing my book contract, too? Did he line up some $75,000-a-hit lectures and talk to a literary agent about writing his own book? There's a good bet he did all of that, but I do not know for sure.

What I do know for sure is that he was in Washington for five days and six nights. I know that he spent one of those evenings with Joan Naylor, Henry Ramirez, and Barbara Manning in an attempt to shut them up.

He had worked his manipulative magic on them once in Williamsburg. Now he came from Santorini for a return engagement in Washington.

Their Longsworth D this time was a soundproof back room at Donatello, an Italian restaurant on Pennsylvania Avenue at the east end of Georgetown. It was a place, my reporting afterward revealed, where Howley had eaten many a Caesar salad and linguine with pesto and drunk many a bottle of the no. 27 wine, an Italian red that came in a dark bottle with a black-and-gold label.

He had it all again that night. Joan Naylor went for a scallops dish. Henry Ramirez ate veal scaloppine. So did Barbara Manning.

I was back home in New York hard at work writing the night of the dinner, and I did not hear about it until several days afterward. Joan was the first to mention it at the tail end of a quick call I had made to her to double-check a small fact. She told me some of what was said among the four of them, and I was able to get more from Barbara and Henry. It was not easy, but I am fairly sure I got most of what mattered. I attribute to Howley the initial hesitancy of Barbara, Henry, and Joan to speak in much detail. He came to intimidate them into silence and he came close to succeeding.

Barbara, Henry, and Joan said Howley phoned out of the blue and suggested a reunion of what he called "the Famous Fabulous Williamsburg Four." None had heard a word from Howley since that Sunday night in Williamsburg. All three told me they jumped at the idea of getting together. A reunion of some kind had, in fact, occurred to each of them, and there was delight over Howley's having taken the initiative to get it organized and done. Everyone said they could hardly wait to get together to swap hugs and pats and to compare notes, new lives, and jobs.

The Famous Fabulous Williamsburg Four together again. Five months and three days after they had done what they had done in Williamsburg to David Donald Meredith, to the election, and to journalism.

The evening began in the lighthearted spirit of a reunion. There was some happy updating about what had happened to each of them since Williamsburg, much of which everyone already knew.

Henry led a cheer for Joan, the first woman in history to anchor a network nightly news program all by herself. Joan! Joan! She's our girl! If she can't do it, nobody can!

There was little need for Henry and Barbara to do much updating on themselves. Americans everywhere—even on the Greek island of Santorini, no doubt—knew about *Sunday Morning with Hank and Barb.* Americans everywhere followed in the gossip and TV columns every move they made off the air, too.

"Is the romance stuff right?" Joan asked.

"No comment," Barbara replied.

"We don't talk about that," Henry said.

Joan found that strange. No comment? We don't talk about that? What in the hell is going on? That was the question Joan wanted to ask Henry and Barbara but did not. She really did not know the two of them that well. Or Mike Howley, either, for that matter. She was struck at that moment by the fact that their real time together was only one Saturday evening, a Sunday day, and a Sunday evening. How little time to have locked themselves together so tightly for the rest of their lives. It caused her to remember something she had read in a World War II memoir— was it by William Manchester?—about Marines in combat on Tarawa or some other Pacific island. Two minutes together under intense fire meant a lifetime together afterward if you survived. Williamsburg was a form of two minutes under fire. But they really did not know each other.

I pointedly asked Barbara and Henry afterward about their "strange" answers to Joan. Neither would do anything but deflect me. What in the hell is going on? was my question, too.

Howley had actually called their hand: "You're working a scam, is that it?" he said to Barbara and Henry.

Joan told me that neither answered the question with words. But their silence said it all. Yes. They were working a scam.

I was already there myself by then, of course. They were still doing condom public-service commercials and going hand-in-hand to dinner, to cocktail parties, to the movies, to the Kennedy Center, to charity benefits and other public events. But it was all show, all for business and image. From what Barbara said to a friend—a source I have pledged never to reveal—an unexpected class problem developed for her. Henry, for all of his common sense and fun, was not as smart as she was. His knowledge of and interest in literature, art, music, philosophy, and similar subjects was all but nonexistent. Their different interests made for a great combination on the air but not anywhere else. I learned from more than one source—also of a confidential nature—that Henry also had a problem that caused him some shame. He apparently could not get his mother's line about black and brown blood making mud out of his head every time he was with Barbara in a personal or intimate situation.

The Famous Fabulous Williamsburg Four moved on to more comfortable subjects, like how being recognized everywhere had changed their lives, how being able to buy anything you wanted had changed their lives, how being the subject of countless seminars and Ph.D. theses, of constant attacks and abuse from a permanent class of press-activism attackers, had changed their lives.

They talked for a while about the opening weeks of the Greene administration. Not bad, was the consensus. Greene had gone to a few of the older Democrats for secretary of state and some of the other key cabinet offices, but there were some fresh and diverse faces as well. He had blundered a few times, but nothing that was fatal to him or the country.

Henry and Barbara told Joan and Howley about how each had been contacted separately—before the *Hank and Barb* show started—about the possibility of coming aboard as Greene's White House press secretary. Talk about an appearance problem, Barbara said. I would have hated it, Henry said.

"I woke up a few nights worrying that if Greene turned out to be a really terrible president, then you know who everyone—now and forever—would blame," Joan said.

"Wash that kind of thought from your mind," Barbara said.

There was not much to say about David Donald Meredith. He had disappeared into that Oklahoma commune and off the face of the political and public earth.

"Nobody will ever get me to shed a tear for that crazy sunavabitch," Barbara said.

Everyone agreed with her. Whatever doubts and second thoughts any of them might have had, there were absolutely none about the unfitness of David Donald Meredith to be president of the United States of America.

They compared stories on the mountains of mail, the speaking and autograph requests each had received. The offers of love, sex, and companionship ran second for all four to opportunities for financial investment.

And they laughed about the latest poll results. A Hart-Divall poll done two weeks ago on a variety of current issues asked a sampling of 1,128 Americans: "After further reflection, do you believe the four journalist-panelists in the Williamsburg Debate were correct and justified in doing what they did?" The results: 64 percent answered Yes; 22 percent, No; 14 percent, No Opinion.

"How could you have no opinion about us?" Henry said.

"I don't believe there are fourteen percent without one," Joan said. "I think it's a hundred percent with opinions and I have heard from all hundred percent of them."

You can say amen to that, said everyone.

It was when they got around to talking about movie and TV miniseries offers that Joan realized what had happened throughout their high spirits and give-and-take so far. In nearly two hours of talk between and among bites of food and sips of wine, Mike Howley, the man who had organized this dinner, had been almost silent. She and Henry and Barbara had been doing most of the talking.

And as she continued to pay attention to that fact for a few minutes, she thought she caught a whiff of something, of something dark, of something that needed to be gotten on with. Mike is clearly not in the same heigh-ho reunion spirit as the rest of us, she thought.

Barbara and Henry also had gradually become conscious of Howley's quiet, dark presence.

It was Barbara who finally got it out there. "Hey, Mike, we haven't heard much from you," she said. "You have taken a leave of absence from the paper?"

"Right."

"You're living where?"

"An island in Greece."

"To write a book?"

"Maybe."

"Not about us, I hope," Henry said.

There. That was it. A book. Joan was certain by the look on Howley's face that this was his destination for the dinner. He had listened and waited patiently until it was time. Now it was time.

"I want to talk to you-all about a book, that's right," Howley said. "But not mine."

He's going to jump us, Barbara thought.

We're in trouble, Henry thought.

So much for the happy reunion of the Williamsburg Four, Joan thought.

Howley said: "We agreed in Williamsburg that we were free to tell the story of what we did as long as we did not go into specifics of what each of us said in that room and as long as we used good judgment and all of that. Do we all remember our agreement?"

Joan, Henry, and Barbara each felt like a little child about to get whacked by Mother or the principal. The chocolate-chip cookies are missing from the jar, or the cigarettes are missing from the top of Daddy's chest, and they know I took them. Somebody poured white paste into the mimeograph machine, and they know I did it. A dead mouse was found in the drawers of my sister or in the drawer of my English teacher, and they know I put it there.

We all remember our agreement, Joan, Henry, and Barbara signaled with slight movements of their respective heads. You bet, we remember. No problem, no problem.

"I have honored that agreement," Howley said.

He waited for any one of the other three of the Famous Fabulous Williamsburg Four to say the same thing. He waited in vain.

"A tabloid creep named Chapman paid a call on me several days ago in Greece," he said. "It was clear to me that he knew most everything that was said by the four of us in Longsworth D."

(Joan, I think mostly to protect my feelings, said Howley said "reporter" instead of "creep." Henry said it was "creep." Barbara said she couldn't remember exactly, but she thought it was either "creep" or "asshole.")

Howley paused again, waiting for a volunteer to speak. There were no volunteers.

So he looked right at Henry and said: "Did you tell Chapman what was said in Longsworth D?"

Henry's mind was on fast play. He's got me, sure. Did Chapman, the creep, tell Howley I talked? Only one way to find out. "Yeah, I told him a little bit," he said.

"So did I," Joan said quickly.

"Me, too," Barbara said almost at the same time. "Chapman clearly already had most of it by the time he got to me."

"Right, right, same with me. He already seemed to know most everything," Henry said. "He said he wanted to check the facts with me to make sure my quotes were correct. . . ."

"That's what he said to me, too," Barbara said.

"Me, too," Joan said. "I assumed Henry or Barbara was telling him, so why play games?"

"You-all were Woodward-ized!" Howley said angrily, referring to the all-I-want-is-to-get-it-right approach made famous by the famous Bob Woodward of Watergate and other reporting fames. "You let him play you one off the other, acting like he already had more than he had, sucking each of you in."

True.

"I didn't tell him much about the last part—when we worked it out about who was going to ask and say what and all of that," said Henry.

"Me neither," Barbara said.

"Same with me," Joan said.

True.

Henry told Howley how he had come to trust me and that he felt I was not out to hurt anybody—particularly the four of them.

"All he wants to do is tell the story," Barbara said.

"He seems well-motivated and hardworking," Joan said, admitting to me that she had wished she had come up with something slightly more dynamic.

"He's motivated by money," Howley replied. "He's doing it for money, pure and simple."

"Unlike who exactly in this room?" Henry said.

"We did not do what we did in Williamsburg for the goddamn money," Howley said.

"But look at us now."

"I'd rather not, frankly," Howley said, making obvious his distaste for his three nouveau riche colleagues—and himself.

"What exactly is your problem, Mike?" Joan asked.

"You three people—each and every one of you—broke your word, that is my goddamn problem."

"So what?" Henry said. "I am proud of what happened in Williamsburg, and if the public is interested in how we came to do it—so what? Tell them."

"Yeah, yeah," Barbara said. "What's the harm?"

"If I have to tell you what harm is done by going back on your goddamn word—"

Joan said that watching Howley catch himself in time, before he went too far, before he said too much, reminded her of how her father would grab her to spank her legs but then stop.

Henry was thinking, Can we get on with it? It's almost ten o'clock already!

Barbara felt a draft.

Henry decided to lighten things up. He said to Howley: "Hey, Mike, you forgot to check this room for bugs. Don't you want to do it before we say anything else?"

Howley almost smiled and said: "I had this place swept with dogs this afternoon. We'll check the ice-cream bowls later. That one in Williamsburg turned out to be faulty, by the way. It didn't work. Somebody went to a lot of trouble to plant a bug that wouldn't bug."

"How do you know that?" Henry asked.

"I know," Howley replied.

Joan, Henry, and Barbara almost smiled. None could remember anything being said for a long time—several seconds.

Then in a slow, deliberate voice, Mike Howley said:

"First, I hereby confess that my purpose tonight was more than a reunion. I came to tell each of you to your face what I think of your violating our Longsworth D agreement. There may be honor among thieves but clearly not among journalists."

"Wait a minute, Mike," Henry said. "We don't have to take this taco shit—"

"Shut up, Henry," Howley said, still not raising his voice. "I have come a long way. I will say what I have to say and you will goddamn listen."

Barbara tried to calm and hush up Henry with a slight wave of her right hand. Let the man talk, so we can get out of here!

Henry read Barbara's hand signal, all right. He also caught a similar message from a frown on Joan's face. Cool it, Henry.

He cooled it. Howley went on.

"I want each of you to know that I will never forget or forgive what you did. If you were paid by Chapman, if you did it for the money—"

"No!" Joan yelled.

"We weren't paid!" Barbara said.

"I didn't get a dime," Henry said.

"OK, OK, OK," Howley said. "You weren't paid. I have said what I wanted to say about what you did—"

"Fine, then," Henry said, standing up. "Hasta la vista, Mike and girls."

Howley gestured him back down. "One more thing, please. I came all this way to be with you here tonight to talk about one more thing. It has to do, I am sorry to say, with those statements we read from during the debate. It has to do with where they came from. . . ."

Joan felt some kind of invisible force behind her. Get out of here, Joan, said the force as it pushed on her.

". . . I am sure you all remember what I said about those statements. I said they came from a source I could and would vouch for. I said I felt I was locked into a situation that prevented me from telling you my source. You—all three of you—went along with it, and we went out there and did our thing. The fact of the matter was—"

"Wait a minute," Henry said. "Maybe I don't want to know any more than I know. I don't know how Barbara and Joan feel, but I am just fine not knowing a damned thing. What I do not know I do not have to lie about, put out of my mind, go to jail about, worry about spilling to Chapman, or do anything else with."

"I agree—I think," Barbara said.

"Why *are* you telling us now?" Joan said.

"It is clearly what that creep Chapman is trying to build his career on," Howley said. "How and why those statements got into Longsworth D is his story."

"I didn't tell him where they came from because I didn't know," Joan said.

Henry and Barbara said that was true for them, too. They knew nothing about that, so they had nothing to tell.

The room was quiet.

"Are you absolutely certain you do not want to know how they came to me?" Howley asked. "I have come from Greece to talk about this—to tell you anything you wish to know."

"Tell me nothing, I tell no lies," Barbara said.

"I am with my partner," Henry said.

Joan said: "Did they come from the Greene campaign, Mike? That's all I really want to know."

"Not from them to me, they didn't. I am not sure of their origin. I got them from somebody who clearly got them from somebody else—who, for all I know, got them from another somebody else. Chapman told me in Greece they came originally from one of the campaigns, as I am sure he has told all of you."

Barbara, Henry, and Joan said then to Howley that, no, Chapman had not told them anything like that. They asked me afterward why I had not. I told them that the information had only come to me—I did not mention Nelson—right before I went to Greece to talk to Howley.

There was a knock on the door.

"Does anybody want an after-dinner drink?" asked Howley. "Sambuca, cognac . . . something like that?"

It had been a while since a waiter had been in their private room. Howley had told the restaurant people beforehand to keep intrusions and service to an absolute minimum. And he told them to knock before entering.

Joan normally had a liqueur only after meals of special distinction on special occasions. "A sambuca would be great," she said to the waiter now without a second's hesitation. Barbara, who could not remember the last time she had a liqueur after dinner, said: "A brandy, please."

Henry was not a liqueur drinker. He ordered a beer.

Howley asked for a scotch on the rocks.

And in a few minutes the drinks were delivered, the door was again closed, and Mike Howley was again talking.

"I would hate to think that we were used by the Greene campaign. If it happened, then it was my fault. I certified those statements to the three of you because I trusted the guy who gave them to me. I did not press him on where he got them, just like you did not press me on how they came to me."

He stopped. Joan asked: "What are you worried about, Mike?"

"I am worried that Chapman runs a story which says we were the tools of the Greene campaign, that I was the conduit from them to Longsworth D—and the three of you."

Henry was shaking his head. "Maybe I'm slow or Mexican or something, but I don't follow the problem. It's what those people said in those statements; what it caused that bastard to do and scream out there on that stage is all that counts. What difference does it make whether that stuff came from Greene or from Mars?"

Joan said: "Henry's right. If it turned out to be untrue, if those women had been figments of somebody's imagination . . . well, I don't even want to think about what might have happened to us. I still have nightmares sometimes thinking about how we didn't make one call to check out anything. We just took them and walked out there and used them. It's amazing, really. But it turned out all right. It was all straight stuff. The women existed. They stood by their stories. It was a close call, but no harm was done."

Barbara said: "In those immortal words—I'll say amen to that. We got away with it."

"Nobody ever needs to know how close a call it was," Henry said.

"Good point," Joan said.

"A really good point, 'Hank,' " Barbara said.

Henry, according to Joan, gave Barbara a look that would have fried a bean in his mother's restaurant. "Thank you, 'Barb dear,' " he said.

No wonder they don't want to talk romance, thought Joan. There ain't nothing to talk about.

Joan had something to talk about—again. The nightmare. She said: "The one thing nobody will ever understand is how we took those statements the way we did, checked out nothing, and just went out there and used them. My own husband doesn't even understand it."

Barbara said: "You just said that, Joan."

"I know. And I am saying it again. I think back on that and I shiver and shake and sweat. We walked right out there and read those things on television. . . ."

"Our fear of Meredith made us do it like that," Barbara said.

"And our trust in the great Mr. Howley here," Henry said.

"I still can't believe we did it," Joan said. "Not a one of us made even one call—"

"Right, right, but look, the only point now is that it worked and the hour is late," said Henry. "I need to hit the road to the hay."

"Not quite yet, Henry—or do you prefer 'Hank'?" Howley said.

Joan had also begun to think Jeff and the twins would be sending the cops out before long. But then she knew nobody was going to be going anywhere anytime soon. She saw a look of pure hostility on Howley's face. She hoped it was the Italian wine, of which he had had much, and the scotch. Whatever, Mike Howley was going to be heard.

"Henry," said Henry. "And I am out of here, OK?"

"You are not out of here, OK?" Howley said. "I have a couple more things on my agenda—"

Henry, on his feet, held up his right hand as if to direct traffic to stop. "Alto, amigo. I ain't hearing no more from you, OK, hombre?" Henry took a step toward the door.

"Sit down and listen to me, goddamn it!" Mike Howley screamed.

Joan leapt to her feet and put her hands on Henry's shoulders. "Hear him out, Henry. We owe him that."

"I don't owe him one tiny little piece of a corn-husk wrapper from a mildewed tamale."

Barbara, still in her chair, said: "Forget it, Hank boy. If it hadn't been for Mike, we'd both still be nothing."

"*I* was never nothing, Barb girl."

According to Joan, Henry's stare at Barbara matched for hate and loathing anything Howley had managed up till then. The match made in television heaven was clearly a product of hell. The hell of a network contract that made them household names and multimillionaires.

Howley said to Henry: "Hey, I'm sorry. I should not have yelled at you like that. That was out of line."

Henry waved him on and sat back down. Henry was seriously afraid if he hadn't, Howley might have gotten out of hand. He, like Joan, didn't know if it was the drink or what, but this was a man in a state of serious agitation. So, all right, all right, late or not, he would hear him out.

Howley asked if everyone wanted another round.

Everyone but Joan said yes. She wanted coffee. Then Barbara changed her order to coffee. Henry stuck with beer. Howley stuck with scotch.

And after all those drinks were on the table in front of them, Howley continued.

"I want a new covenant of silence," he said to Joan, Barbara, and Henry. "And this time I want you three to keep it."

"Chapman's already finished with his interviewing," Joan said.

"Right, right," Barbara said. "He doesn't have anything else to ask us. . . ."

"He told me he was through except for some quote-checking stuff," Henry said.

Mike Howley's light blue eyes got small. He said: "No more talking to Chapman about anything, OK?"

Joan said that no one responded. Not her, not Henry, not Barbara.

"Mike, please," Joan said. "I already told you that I have told Chapman everything I have to say."

Barbara and Henry said—again—that was true for them as well.

Howley said: "When I left that room that night in Williamsburg, I thought I had an agreement with three people I could trust to keep their word. I find that they did not keep their word. They spilled their guts like little kids at the first interview. They got so carried away with being stars, with people out there kissing their asses and giving them money, they couldn't even resist the offers of a sleaze jockey from some shit-pot magazine—"

Henry was back on his feet. He said: "Whatever happened to make me, whether you approve or not, I am Hank. Hank don't have to take this shit-pot stuff from you, Howley. Whatever, whatever. Hank and Henry both say, Good night. And adios—for tonight and forever. OK, amigo?"

Howley stood. So did Joan and Barbara. Joan motioned for Henry to hold on a minute and said to Howley: "What exactly do you want from us?"

"I want each of you to look me straight in the eye—"

Henry interrupted. "What in the hell is really going on, Howley? What are you trying to hide? What are you really trying to protect? Your own ass? A little more truth than you can—"

Barbara said: "Shut up, Henry!"

"Orders from you I do not take either, Barb."

"Everybody now, cool it," Joan said. "And I mean it. You, Henry, you, Barbara—you, Mike. Hush, all of you." Then back to Howley she said: "You want us to raise our right hands—"

"Like Boy Scouts, yeah," Henry said. "Well, it'll snow in Laredo before that happens."

Joan stared him quiet.

Howley said: "I want each of you showboats . . . Sorry. Each of you—"

To Joan, Henry said: "No more. If he wants to see me, he can see me every Sunday morning at nine, Eastern Standard Time, along with the rest of the millions."

To Henry, Barbara said: "I cannot believe what you have become."

"There are two of us, remember. You and me, me and you."

Joan said to Howley: "I hereby look you straight in the eye and give you my word." Then to Barbara she said: "Say it and let's get out of here."

To Howley, Barbara said: "I don't know . . ."

"Henry?" Joan said.

"Maybe. Maybe anything to get out of here. Here we are, the four most famous journalists in America, swearing to keep things from the American people. It stinks."

"I need no lectures from you on journalism, 'Hank,' " said Joan.

"Easy, lady," Barbara said.

Easy, lady, indeed, thought Joan. Easy, everybody.

Barbara said to Howley: "We can break a glass, cut ourselves, suck a sip of each other's blood, Mr. Howley, and promise to die before we ever say another word about anything having to do with us and what we did. And it will not matter. Not one drop of that blood, will it matter. It will eventually get out. Everything will eventually get out. If Chapman doesn't get it, somebody else will. Somebody else always does. You know that, Mr. Howley. You know that probably better than any of the rest of us just because you have been doing what we do longer than the rest of us. So, I swear, you swear, everybody swears, and it don't mean shit. Now can we go?"

Henry admitted to me that he was not proud of what happened next. He said he must have had too much beer and wine. He was now as pissed at Howley as Howley was at him and the others. So why not make some mischief?

He said: "Wait just a minute. We are reporters, let's not forget. Muy Bueno Son knows better than this. We have to tell the full story to Chapman and anybody else who asks. We can't sit on our own story. Reporters don't sit on stories. Reporters don't participate in cover-ups. They uncover cover-ups. Cover-up! Did I really use that word? Yes, I did. Cover-up. The great Mike Howley is asking us to be a party to a cover-up."

"It's not the same thing as a cover-up, goddamn it," Howley said, "and you know it."

Henry said: "Doesn't that Jerry Rhome you work for have all kinds of rules of journalism? Wasn't one of them—the sixth or seventh—something like 'Never Do Anything You Can't Defend'?"

Barbara said: "Where's the check? Let's go. . . ."

"This is on me," Howley said.

"God knows, we can all afford it now," Barbara said.

Henry wasn't through. He said: "Here we are, the Williamsburg Four, semi-heroes and rich for having already violated the most important journalism rule of all about crossing over the line. Now our leader here is asking us to engage in an even larger conspiracy? Suppressing our own story? A conspiracy of silence. I say, let's vote and then be bound by the majority vote. It's the only way to decide it."

Barbara said: "Sure, fine. Let's vote."

Joan said the term "cover-up" was stuck in her throat now. She wondered how the vote would have gone if Nixon had asked for a show of hands from Haldeman, Ehrlichman, Mitchell, Dean, and the rest. What about it, guys? Do we cover up?

She wondered if the Reagan administration decision to sit on the Iran-Contra story was made like this. Would everyone in favor of Ollie North's lying to Congress please raise your right hand and keep it there until we have had time to count them? That's how they did it in school. What about on cover-ups?

Barbara reminded herself that she was only twenty-nine years old. She wondered if there could ever be any life for her after what she had been through. Already, she had participated in the most monumental, precedent-shattering seizure of power in the history of American journalism. Now she was also participating in a possible decision to cover up, to not talk anymore about that monumental happening in her and their and the country's lives.

Henry, still full of the joke that the others were clearly taking very seriously, said: "Let's do it. Mr. Howley, as the moderator, do you want to preside over the vote?"

Joan said Howley's demeanor and body language were no longer shouting anger. The message now was one of droop, sag, drop, fall. He was as over as this evening. In a voice that was empty and weak and pointless, he said: "Everyone in favor raise your right hand."

Henry could not leave the silliness of it alone. He had to make it even worse. "Secret ballot!" he said. "Democracies do their voting by secret ballot."

He pulled a piece of paper from his inside suit-coat pocket. He turned the paper over to its blank side and carefully folded and tore it into four equal pieces.

"Write a big Y for yes—yes, we cover up; a big N for no—no, we don't," he said to the others. "Fold it over and put it in the middle of the table."

They all did as they were told. Joan said it was one of the most uncomfortable moments of her life. What is this charade? What kind of fools are we? Why are we playing like this?

"You mix them up," Henry said to Barbara. "And you, Joan, open them and read them out loud. Hank and Barb, as in *the* Hank and Barb, working with Joan, *the* Joan, the first solo woman network anchor, working together in a democracy."

Barbara was in a state of confused, sad misery. But she mixed them.

Joan read: "Yes . . .

"Yes . . .

"No . . .

"No."

Howley and Joan cast the two yes votes, Henry and Barbara the no's.

Henry said: "The vote being two yes, two no, we must now figure out a way to break the tie."

"Where's Al Gore when we need him?" said Joan, a reference to the Clinton vice president, who cast a record forty-two tie-breaking votes in his capacity as presiding officer of the U.S. Senate.

"I say forget it," Howley said, his voice bulging with resignation and loathing.

Not one more word was said by anyone.

In a matter of seconds they left the soundproof room together. There was no hugging or handshaking or vowing to get together again at least once every few months or years for as long as they all should live.

Then they were outside on Pennsylvania Avenue waiting in silent awkwardness for the valets to bring their cars around from a lot behind the restaurant.

Henry and Barbara, Hank and Barb, were brought theirs first and drove away, Barbara in a new midnight blue Mercedes-Benz convertible, Henry in his new mahogany brown Porsche.

Joan expected Mike Howley to say something to her now that it was just the two of them, now that the two kids were gone. She tried desperately to think of something she wanted or needed to say herself. Nothing came to mind.

She was so grateful when she heard their cars coming down the alley.

"What have we done, Mike?" Joan then asked.

Her new white BMW four-door arrived. Howley's five-year-old dark green Saab convertible was right behind it. Their arrival got them both off the hook. He didn't have to answer. She didn't have to consider what she meant by the question in the first place.

★

I still was not finished.

There was one more happening after the Donatello dinner. Despite several silly aspects of the event, I think it was important because it helped tie up some critical loose ends and bring my reporting to a real and satisfying conclusion.

The beginning came in a box of chocolate-covered toffee candies delivered by messenger to my apartment in New York City. They came two days after a small item in the "Book Notes" column of *The New York Times* reported the fact that the movie rights to my book—the one you are reading now—had been bought by Dawn Now Productions and that a serious bidding war was under way for the paperback rights. The candy box was carefully wrapped in pages of that particular section of the *Times*.

The box was about ten inches square and an inch deep. In the center, wrapped in cellophane among the candy, was a 3.5-inch floppy disk. On the front a handwritten block-printed note on a blue Post-it said: HERE IS THE REAL SWEET.

I knew enough about computers to expect either nothing—or absolute confusion. The computer industry still has not latched on to the fact that there are millions to be made from all of us out there in consumer land who are not interested in becoming computer nerds or whizzes. We just want to use them to write things.

I stuck the disk into my computer, prepared for all kinds of signals and messages in computer gibberish about incompatibility and other stupid problems that would make it impossible to ever read what, if anything, was on the disk. It could be because I used WordPerfect 5.1 software in my computer and the disk was written in WordPerfect 4.2— or something idiotic like that.

But no. I hit all of the proper LIST and other keys, and in a few seconds I was staring at the following message:

```
Mike Howley received the women's statements from
Pat Tubbs. Tubbs got them from a journalist at
another major news organization. That news organi-
zation, working in safe-house security under the
high pressure of the approaching deadline of the
election, decided against using them.
    One of the people involved disagreed with the
no-use decision. He/she gave the statements to
Tubbs. The he/she source assumed Tubbs would get
```

them published in his paper, *The Washington Morning News*. Tubbs had just received them when Howley was chosen to moderate the Williamsburg Debate. Tubbs decided that there was no way he could get them into the *News* on such short notice either, so rather than offer them to his own paper he called Howley. Howley took them to Williamsburg and used them.

    more to kum

    Carl Bob

My knee-jerk distrust of computers—I expect them to eat everything I write—caused me to do something smart. I immediately hit the PRINT key on my computer, and in a few seconds I had the printed text of the message. A few seconds after that the words disappeared from my computer screen. I tried to call them up again, but nothing happened. Somebody had obviously sent me a message that was programmed in some mysteriously nerdy way to self-destruct off the disk after a certain amount of "read" time had elapsed.

Now, on that printout at least, I finally had it. The goods. I had the goods.

Nelson, or someone who worked with Nelson, gave the statements to somebody at a news organization other than *The Washington Morning News*. That was why I could not find the relations cutout Nelson talked about. I had checked only Tubbs/Howley possibilities.

But, of course, I really had nothing. Once I got over my initial euphoria, I came to my senses. The fact that I had read and printed this off a floppy disk did not make it any more believable or credible than if it had come in an anonymous phone call. In fact, that was all it was. The computer equivalent of an anonymous call or letter.

But it had the ring and read of truth to it. It really did. It made common sense. I had it. I knew I had it. Almost.

But there was nothing I could do with what I had. I certainly could not put it in the book—I was already hard at work on the final draft—without some further confirmation. I had to have names—of the organization and the people involved. More, more, more. I had to have it all. And how could I get that? Walk into *The New York Times* and *Time* and

Newsweek and *The Wall Street Journal* and *This Week* and NBS News and all the other major news organizations and announce that I was here on a raid? Everyone up against the wall! Now, tell me if you are the organization that had those statements! And, if so, who gave them to Tubbs of *The Washington Morning News*?

I immediately did the only two things I could think of to do. I again called Tubbs. It was no surprise that he refused to talk to me. And I put in a call to Sid Nelson. He, too, would not speak to me. The exact words of his secretary, however, were: "Mr. Nelson told me to tell you that the only Tom Chapman he knows is a dishonorable man, and he does not talk to dishonorable men." I did not believe I had that coming. I still don't.

So I had to wait for "more to kum," the old newspaper term for telling the typesetters and others that the story is not yet finished. "Carl Bob," where are you? *Who* are you?

The very next evening I found out the answers to both of those questions.

★

I went with a woman friend to the new Lucille Thomas play, *My Tornados*, at the Roundabout Theatre at Broadway and Forty-fifth Street. Curtain time was eight o'clock. My friend and I arrived at 7:45 and went upstairs to the lobby bar for a drink. In the course of sipping my glass of cheap chardonnay at the bar, I noted the arrival across the room of a famous person. That person was famous because of his/her work as one of America's leading and most recognizable journalists.

A few moments later he/she walked my way, our eyes met, and he/she dropped his/her program in front of me. He/she stopped and leaned down to pick up the program. So did I. While our heads were down and close, he/she whispered: "Carl Bob." He/she let me pick up the program and he/she walked on.

Inside the program was stuck another 3.5-inch floppy disk.

I told my woman friend that a "journalistic emergency" had arisen and that I had to leave. I told her to enjoy the play without me and I would join her before the final curtain. She was furious, but there was nothing I could do about it. It was easy come, easy go, for us sexually active types anyhow.

Back at my place several minutes later, I again turned on the computer. This time I hit PRINT at the same time it came on the screen.

All that came was a phone number. I immediately dialed it.

After the third ring a woman said: "Yes?" There was the noise of talking and laughing and music and glasses being emptied and filled in the background.

Was it a bar? A restaurant?

I said: "This is Tom Chapman."

"So?"

"Is Carl Bob there?"

The woman said: "Go park your car on the second floor down in the garage between Eighth and Ninth and Fifty-ninth and Sixtieth."

"I don't have a car."

"Figure it out."

I figured it out, all right. I took a taxi to the parking garage and simply walked in via the ramp from the Fifty-ninth Street side. The place was full of cars, attendants, and a few people picking up or depositing their cars. On the second level down, where there were no people and few cars, I came across a parked dark blue BMW four-door sedan. It looked new and expensive. There was somebody sitting in the driver's seat. I recognized the person as the famous journalist I had seen an hour ago in the bar at the Roundabout.

He/she, apparently having watched me approach in a rearview mirror, got out of the car and motioned for me to follow him/her over to a far and obscure corner of the parking level.

"You know who I am, I assume?" he/she said once we had stopped and faced each other.

"Yes."

"This meeting never happened. We have never talked. I am a source that will never be revealed no matter what. Do we understand one another?"

"No," I said. "I cannot agree to that."

"Fine," he/she said. "Good-bye."

And there before my very eyes, the person who had the information that would put a capper on the story of Williamsburg—*my* story of Williamsburg—began walking out of my life.

"Wait a minute, please," I said.

He/she stopped. "Talk, Chapman."

Talk, Chapman. People were all the time giving me orders or warnings. Go, Tom, go. Now or never, Chapman. Talk, Chapman.

"It's a deal," I said. "I want your story more badly than I want to identify you."

He/she came back to me. "I need a way to enforce the deal, though, don't I, Chapman? It's not a matter of trust, it's one of simple precaution. Call it a source condom, if you will."

I had no idea where he/she might be headed. I was only listening.

He/she said: "If you reveal my identity to anyone—not just to your book readers and thus the world—I will make you sorry the thought ever entered your mind."

This person—this most famous person—was threatening me. Reveal him/her as the source for the story and I will be punished. How will I be punished?

I asked: "How will you make me sorry?"

"If I told you that, you could turn from here now and claim in a separate story that I had threatened you. I have made no threats. I have only made you a promise. Screw me and ye shall be screwed, so help me God."

Now those were words to live by in the profession of journalism. Or any other profession, for that matter.

"OK, OK," I said.

"Spell it out."

"I will never reveal your name."

"Or organization."

"Or organization."

"Directly or even through oblique suggestions or references."

"OK, OK," I said.

"No tape recordings."

I had stuck my trusty little Sony microcassette recorder into a trouser pocket before leaving my apartment. I had clicked it on when I walked into the garage.

"Empty your pockets, please," said he/she now.

I emptied my pockets there on the fender of a car parked by us. The contents included my recorder. He/she looked down, saw the recorder was running, and switched it off.

Then he/she told me the story:

This person's news organization killed the story for themselves on grounds of timing. There would not be time for their reporters to personally and completely verify each of the statements. There were heated arguments at the highest levels of the organization about the public's right to know this about a presidential candidate and the duty of journalistic organizations to tell the public. One group argued that not "running full-blast" with the story amounted to a dereliction of duty comparable to treason. The other argued that to go with a story of this magnitude this close to an election was tantamount to "an assassination." The final decision went to the very top man of the conglomerate that owned the journalism organization. He said, Kill it. He gave orders that the one copy of the statements in the possession of the organization be destroyed. That destruction was assigned to two employees, one of whom managed to make copies before the destruction took place. That employee then took the statements to the person now telling me the story. What should I do? asked the colleague. My source said he/she went into a rage when told that a corporation executive with no journalism background or experience or feel had made such a decision. He/she told his/her colleague that he/she would take charge of getting the story out before the election. Through what he/she described as a "carefully designed series of triple cutouts," the statements were transmitted to Tubbs. And the rest is history.

Yes, it was history. But as he/she finished, I realized it wasn't that much of a story without the names and faces that go with it. I said that to this person and then I asked for his/her own motivations for telling me this.

"Why bother?" I asked. "The material got out during the debate. Meredith was stopped dead and now Greene is president."

"I think what happened at our place should be known," he/she said. "I think the American public should know what has happened to their journalism."

I told him/her I was not sure I knew what he/she meant.

"They should know that corporate CEOs are the ones making the journalism decisions these days," he/she said.

I resisted saying what I was thinking. That some people believe the American public should be more concerned about what journalists like him/her are doing to journalism these days than what corporate CEOs are doing.

His/her story was not in the hot-commodity category that I had hoped for. But it did tie up some important loose ends.

I asked the Carl Bob person why he/she went through the elaborate computer-disk and other Woodward-Bernstein/parking-garage antics to get this story to me. A simple telephone call to make an appointment for a simple lunch somewhere off Columbus Avenue would have done the trick, I said.

"I was trying to feed the need to make it sound good," he/she said, "and give you something to write about instead of me."

It worked.

And said the famous person: "It was also a form of precaution. If this blew up and you decided to identify me, no one would ever believe you. No one would ever believe *I* would do anything as stupid and childish as putting floppy disks in candy boxes and having meetings in parking garages."

That worked, too.

★

I had to take one last pass at Pat Tubbs before I finally rested.

The book that had transformed him from being a famous and respected newspaper writer to a famous and rich nonfiction book writer was *The Administrator*. It was the true story of Richard Dennison, the Vietnam War fighter-pilot hero who became the administrator of the Federal Aviation Administration. He was blackmailed into helping a group of international financiers and swindlers deal in used airliners—mostly 707s and 747s—with confused, falsified, or shady ownerships. A couple of the conspirators turned up dead in Paris with ropes around their necks, and three of the planes crashed under mysterious circumstances, and eventually, under Tubbs's relentless pursuit, so did the scheme. Gene Hackman played Tubbs in the movie. Richard Gere was Dennison.

According to his book, one of the techniques Tubbs used to get an early interview with Dennison was what he called "the friendly stalk."

For two and a half weeks, every public place Dennison went, Tubbs went. At lunch, at dinner, in the grocery store, in church, on Capitol Hill, in hotel meeting rooms, at FAA hearings, at news conferences, Tubbs was there for Dennison to glance up and see. Tubbs was even there when little nine-year-old Amanda Dennison played in a Saturday-morning soccer game on a rain-soaked field in Bethesda, Maryland, the Washington suburb where the Dennisons lived. Tubbs eventually got his interview.

After four unreturned phone calls to Tubbs, I decided to employ the friendly stalk on him. For two days I was there at restaurants and other places every time Tubbs looked up.

On the third day I followed him to Herb's for lunch. Tubbs joined a man I did not recognize at the same table where Rhome and I had eaten our lunch. I now got a table across the room from it—but in full view of Tubbs.

It wasn't long before he was standing there in front of me.

"Who in the hell are you?" he said, acting, it seemed to me, as if he were Gene Hackman, rather than the other way around.

"Tom Chapman."

"I should have known."

"I'm doing a little friendly stalking, Mr. Tubbs. I very much need to talk to you. Some new information has come my way which pretty much proves you were Howley's conduit for those statements—"

"Good-bye forever, Chapman," he said.

Tubbs walked out of Herb's before I could pay my check, and he disappeared.

He was not at any of his usual spots the next day or any of the next several days, and I have not laid eyes on him since. All calls to his office and to his house have drawn either an answering-machine or voice-mail response.

All I know to do and to say is:

Come out, come out, wherever you are, Mr. Tubbs. If you're reading this now, Mr. Tubbs, please call me. I would still like to interview you. It's not too late. We can include what you have to say in the paperback edition, Mr. Tubbs.

Or in the movie.

15

In Summary

Here now are my conclusions.

Michael J. Howley decided that David Donald Meredith should not be president of the United States. If Howley had been a wealthy person or labor leader or someone of political power and influence, he would have backed that belief with his own resources and/or he would have sought to rally those of others. But Howley was a journalist, one of our nation's leading and most respected. He had no money or campaign troops to send to the front against Meredith.

What he did have was the force of his journalism. It was a force that he had always tried to exercise in a fair and evenhanded manner, as if the outcome of any story—any election—was irrelevant to him personally. But David Donald Meredith, to Howley, was different. Howley had come to believe the election of this man would be a catastrophe for the country. He had had similar feelings in past elections—particularly about Reagan in 1980—but the Reagan fear was nothing like the Meredith fear. I think it is possible that he considered using the force of his newspaper columns and television appearances to warn the public about Meredith and then concluded that he would not have made that much difference. Not by himself in a newspaper column and a television commentary. It would take a lot more than that to keep David Donald Meredith out of the White House.

I believe it began to come together for Howley on that flight back from Texas—the appearance in San Antonio, his depressed thoughts about himself and journalism, the word on the poll showing Meredith about to surge ahead of Paul L. Greene, and the probable coming of the invitation to moderate the Williamsburg Debate. I think he disembarked from that American Airlines 757 at Washington National having made the decision to see if he could turn Williamsburg into an event that would change the outcome of the election.

Meanwhile, on another conspiracy track came others who wanted to do the same because they knew the secret of Meredith's violent side. They included a Meredith security man and journalists in another news organization. Pat Tubbs was the last link, the intermediary who brought the two tracks, the goods with the means, together. By then Howley had already forced Jerry Rhome into changing the *News* policy so he could moderate the debate. All he had left to do was to manipulate his three debate panelist-colleagues into doing what he wanted. He got that done behind the closed doors of Longsworth D.

And now Paul L. Greene of Nebraska sits in the White House instead of David Donald Meredith of North Carolina.

My conclusions, obviously, are interpretive in nature. I was not in Mike Howley's mind on that airplane or at any other time while he went about the business of preparing for the debate. But I believe there are supporting facts. Howley's denials of a predebate plan look feeble and wan compared to the healthy evidence on the other side of the theory. Nelson and "Carl Bob" supplied the route the women's statements took from Nelson and Associates to Tubbs and, finally, to Howley. There is no question about what Howley said and did in Longsworth D. A careful reading of his words and actions leads unambiguously to the fair conclusion that he came into that room to turn his colleagues into a journalist strike force against Meredith. He did it skillfully, letting it build, letting even the other three believe—and they mostly still believe—that it happened naturally as a joint action.

Tubbs's and Howley's refusals to talk about any of this are also indicators of a desire to keep a secret. Why won't Howley tell the American people where he got those statements? What does he have to hide? The fact of his plotting and planning and manipulating is one thing he has to hide. Are there others? What did Tubbs and Howley talk about for so long that predebate Saturday night? Was going for a Meredith blowup Tubbs's idea?

I had one further contact with Howley after Santorini. It came a week after that movie/paperback item in the *Times*. I received a faxed one-sentence handwritten note from Santorini.

Chapman: I hereby demand the right to respond to your libelous trash before it becomes a book. Howley

I called him a few days later from New York. He screamed at me, and I screamed back that with his silly alarm-clock trick he passed up the chance to have his side of the story fully told. There were several back-and-forths with my book editor and Howley's agent. Finally, we agreed to send Howley the galleys of the final manuscript so that he could write a formal response of not more than thirteen hundred words that would be published at the end of this book as an appendix. It was an unusual way to do it, but this was an unusual event. Fairness toward Howley, to be completely straight about it, was not our principal motivation. My publisher thought such an approach would also enhance advance media interest in the book—a gimmick, pure and simple.

And as you will see for yourself when you read it, the statement works only as a publicity gimmick. Howley does not deal in any serious or direct way with the specific factual questions raised by my reporting. He mostly vents anger and issues blanket, general denials.

His anger with Barbara Manning, Henry Ramirez, and Joan Naylor is understandable—from his point of view. But I would urge it be taken with a grain of salt—and perspective. Barbara, Henry, and Joan cooperated with me, I believe, because they felt the public had a right to know what happened. Journalists have a special responsibility to tell what they know, and those three people met that responsibility. Howley's attempts to organize silence, I believe, were motivated by a desire to protect himself. He wanted them mute about Longsworth D for his own sake. He did not get his way and he's angry. So be it.

I concede, however, that the Donatello business is slightly different. It was difficult and there was some unwillingness at first, but eventually all three did talk to me some about what happened there, as they had before about Longsworth D. For my own selfish reasons, I am glad they did. I understand the uneasiness this kind of thing triggers among those who wonder about where we have arrived in our world of keeping our words and secrets, of telling lies and secrets.

I am not suggesting that Joan and Henry and Barbara are all pure in motive and action. All three have benefited enormously from having been part of the Williamsburg Four. But I found no evidence that any one of the three went to Williamsburg with any kind of plan to showboat or stunt his or her way that night into a special limelight of celebrity. Joan was—is—an extremely able combatant in the extremely competitive world of network anchors, and being on the Williamsburg panel helped her position—even if she really wanted to be the moderator. Henry came with a packet of tough questions all aimed at showing the world what a tough interviewer he was. Barbara came determined to do as professional a job as she could. But I picked up nothing in what was said in Longsworth D or anywhere else that points to any ulterior or hidden agenda by any of the three.

I—and many others, I am sure—share Joan's confessed astonishment at the casual way she and Henry and Barbara decided to use those statements against Meredith. I find it amazing that three professional journalists, trained and committed to the precepts of fact-checking and fairness, would do nothing to verify even the fact of the women's existence. Somebody—if not Howley, somebody else—could have simply manufactured the women and their stories. I believe they were blinded and dumbed by a combination of their hate for Meredith and their faith in Howley. That is an explanation, but it is not a justification. Based on what was said at the Donatello dinner and my own conversations with Henry, Barbara, and Joan, I am still not sure they realize even now how close they came to falling from the ridge of fame and fortune into the valley of professional death and destruction.

Some of the most vociferous supporters of Meredith continue to harp

on the race angle, citing Henry Ramirez and Barbara Manning as the ultimate examples of "affirmative action run amuck." They charge that no
two whites with their qualifications would have come anywhere near to
being on the debate panel and then taking over the Sunday-morning show
on ABS. That is probably correct. But I tend to agree with those who
argue, What's the problem? Henry and Barbara, alias Hank and Barb, at
least have *some* journalism experience, which is more than Jack, Jill,
Ross, and Norman can say. They are also not clownalists, as defined by
Mulvane. Not yet, at least. Barbara and Henry also have perspectives as
a result of their respective races that ought to be part of the Sunday-
morning mix.

But I will leave these kinds of questions to the great seminars of the
great worriers to sort through while I continue the hard and important
work of detecting and exposing and disclosing lies and secrets. In that
regard, Howley's anger at having his secrets revealed has a slight
double-standard stench to it. What I did to him is only what he and his—
our—profession have been doing to nonjournalists since the beginning
of First Amendment time. As I pointed out earlier, I have felt stings
myself from some irresponsible reporting, and I am sure there is more to
come from Howley and others. There is no question about the fact that
they hurt.

There are more than stings involved, of course, in assessing the
impact of Williamsburg on American journalism. First, Williamsburg was
probably the last debate. It is likely no debate commission or group of
journalists will ever be handed the responsibility of running such a
debate again, because no candidate for president or political party would
ever take a chance on another Williamsburg.

Within just the few months after that October Sunday night, there
were several nonnational copycat incidents. Three print and two television reporters in Houston made their own headlines when they took turns
at a news conference saying, "That's a lie," after various statements by
the mayor. The reporters called what they did "a Williamsburg act." Four
press panelists on a regular Sunday-morning "Governor Meets the Press"
program on public television in Arizona read from the governor's income-
tax and financial statements in what they said was "the spirit of Williamsburg." A local television anchor in Denver used the same phrase in

introducing a special "I-Team Scandal Scope" on the twenty-year-old "love-appearing" letters a prominent—married, with two children—Methodist minister in the city had written to another man. A radio reporter in a small town in Louisiana had even said he was "only doing a Williamsburg" when he was caught stealing a murder-investigation report from a file cabinet in the local sheriff's office. There have been other incidents, and there will be others now until the end of time. Journalistic terrorism, as it has been called, has arrived and is now being condemned or praised as an accepted part of our world.

If so, the reasons are obvious. First and foremost, what the Williamsburg Four did was seen as successful and noble. It worked. A man deemed emotionally unsuited and unfit to hold the highest office in the land was prevented from doing so. Meredith's bizarre behavior on the stage that night and afterward helped confirm the wisdom of what the four had done. So have the early returns on Paul L. Greene's presidency. Every poll shows great—and increasing—support for him and for the four patriotic journalists who put him where he is.

The other simple and influencing fact was what happened to the Williamsburg Four. Henry and Barbara became Hank and Barb and rich and famous. Joan Naylor became the first woman solo anchor on a nightly network news program and rich and famous. How could anyone interested in making it to the top in journalism anywhere not have concluded that a whole new path had suddenly been invented. Go, Baby Tom, go!

I agree with Howley that the revolutionary changes in American journalism did not begin with Williamsburg—the debate itself as well as the riot and the other embarrassing conduct of the reporters covering it. His statement to me on Santorini that journalism was already headed over the cliff with the donkeys had a ring of sincere disgust and alarm to it. From the old journalism perspective of the Mike Howleys and the Pompous Perfect Doug Mulvanes, there was much to be disgusted by and alarmed about. The blight of what they called "checkbook journalism," actually paying people money instead of column inches and airtime for their stories and information. The tabloidization of syndicated and cable-television magazine programs had already slopped over to network television and become the new standard of all television news, which had already adopted dramatic re-creations, stagings, and other entertainment techniques as their own. The widespread use of anonymous sources, begun with Watergate, had consumed the straight reporters on even the largest and most mainstream print and broadcast outlets. Opinion and personal attacks were no longer restricted to editorial and op-ed pages. Gossip about sexual and other personal matters was no longer found only in gossip columns. All of it was everywhere. The coming of the star syndrome to network news—the one that transformed Henry and Barbara into Hank and Barb and promoted Joan to sole anchor—was already there and spilt over all of journalism. Print people, in order to make it in print and on the lecture circuit, had to have a television outlet and star persona, too. So they went on weekend programs and yelled at one another, all in the interest of drawing attention to themselves and increasing their incomes. Lines between reporting, analysis, and opinion became invisible. Snideness toward everyone in public life was the norm. The once unheard-of practice of television anchors and interviewers acting as if they were equal, if not superior, to the people they interviewed had already become common practice. The recent and celebrated interview Jock Reynolds of NBS News did with President Greene four weeks after the inauguration, according to Mulvane, set another standard for "the New Arrogants in journalism." (At one point in the interview, Reynolds said to the president of the United States: "Well, I hear you, but what if I said that answer is simply not acceptable to those of us who follow the European security issue. You clearly are not well-informed at all on that—if I may be so bold as to say so.")

So it was no wonder that Michael J. Howley, from his high perch, saw much in his profession that embarrassed him that predebate October. His way of journalism was going, going, going—and soon it would be gone. I believe him when he says he was as annoyed and upset with himself as he was with others. From his perspective, not only had he not done anything about it, he had participated. He had smelled the money of the stars and followed the odor.

There are those who reject much of his Old Journalism whine out of hand. I am one of them. We argue that a more vigorous, more pressing, more aggressive, more penetrating, more visible press is exactly what this country needs. Why shouldn't reporters be the well-paid stars of a democratic open society? They still don't make as much as basketball players and corporate CEOs. Why shouldn't they give their informed opinions about the subjects on which they report? Don't they know more about them than anyone else? Why should people be expected to turn over news and information to reporters without compensation? Because it's a public service? Aren't *The New York Herald* and *The Washington Morning News* and ABS News and *World News* magazine profit-making organizations? Why shouldn't the most personal details about everyone in public life be known? Why shouldn't a television correspondent take on the president of the United States as an equal? Wasn't this country founded on a non-royalty idea of national leadership? Doesn't the incontrovertible list of evasion and lying at the highest levels of government—Vietnam, Watergate, Iran-Contra, Whitewater, etc., etc.—make it imperative that the press never take the first answer as given? Why shouldn't the makers of television news programs employ the best techniques of their craft to tell a story? It is a visual medium, you know, and the competition for viewers is terrific.

Back and forth, old *v.* new, the argument has gone.

I happen to believe, though, that even at the time of Williamsburg it was essentially already over. The new way had already become *the* way, and the likes of Howley and Mulvane were whistling against the wind. What Williamsburg did to what was left of the discussion was comparable to what that volcano did to Santorini. And the eruption came accompanied by some exquisite ironies. Mike Howley, from the old school, engineered what some have argued was the ultimate new-school operation. Wasn't what those four reporters did on that stage simply a natural, heroic, and noble next step down the road of good clean aggressive journalism in the new world?

Within journalism itself there is probably nobody left at any level or position who has not been asked that question since that October night. At the rate the polls are being taken, it may not be much longer before there is nobody left *outside* journalism at any level or position who also has not been asked.

My answer, for what it is worth, is no. It is a close call for me, but I do not believe it was justified—or natural, heroic, or noble. I do not believe the Williamsburg Four acted properly or in a way that is good for the United States of America. Power abused is power abused. No matter how well-meaning or in what name it is abused, the end result is an abuse of power. The demolition of the original, traditional power of the journalist to inform and influence the people in a democratic society could be the end result of Williamsburg, the most dramatic abuse of journalistic power in our history. To call it "New Journalism" is to mislabel. What happened on that auditorium stage really was a form of press terrorism. So was what happened afterward among the "donkeys" in the Virginia Room. One was organized and controlled, the other was not. Neither should be considered acceptable by any of us—old or new.

Howley ended his front-page postdebate piece in *The Washington Morning News* with the words: "Let the debate begin."

I would submit that the debate about all of this, having begun, will—and should—never end.

Appendix

Statement by Michael J. Howley

I was given thirteen hundred words. I have taken them all.

I think this book should be titled *Confessions of a Trash Journalist*. All of the dirty and unethical tricks of the trade are here in how-to detail: lying to hotel maids, telephone operators and record-keepers, security guards, secretaries, and even singing Jesus cowboys; coercing and paying people to betray friends, colleagues, customers, and confidences; dishonoring ground rules and playing "transaction" con tricks with people in order to use their names, to burn them as sources. I found the proud, matter-of-fact recitals of Mr. Chapman's fabrications, duplicities, and deceits astonishing—and disgusting.

His presentation of scenes and dialogue as straightforward fact without attribution or sourcing carries the practice of "Journalism as Novel, the Novel as Journalism" to a new and despicable extreme. So do his entrances into the minds of others—me in particular—to imagine what they might have been thinking, not only about the debate but about more personal matters. Nothing is out of bounds, off limits, or too much for him and his kind.

Even a casual reader of his account will notice further that when the fact-going got rough for Mr. Chapman, he went to an anonymous source. I would suggest that it is most likely that some are probably more than anonymous—they are nonexistent. I doubt seriously, for instance, that those scholars who are lucky enough to gain access to Mr. Chapman's "tapes and notes" in fifty years will find anything to verify that any of that "Carl Bob" stuff happened. Anyone who now believes it did, please contact me. I have some bridges and uranium stock I would like to show you.

Mr. Chapman has also presented us with a near perfect example of "personal journalism" run amuck. The I-pronoun appears more in this I-the-reporter-hero book than in the average book of I-the-rock-star-hero memoirs. Why would Mr. Chapman believe it is in the reader's interest to know about his jogging habits, train rides, and rent-a-car and hotel receipts? What caused him to think reporting on the blowing of his nose during his session with Jack Turpin was relevant?

But the most important question is about accuracy. Did he get it right? The answer is No. No, he did not. This book is full of inaccuracies, large and small. They are the end result of a reporter who was either too careless, too lazy, too sloppy, or too biased to do the hard work required to get it right, or of a reporter who was simply unable to penetrate the right sources of information and/or gather the right perspectives on what information he did get. I have no idea what exact combination of professional failures were at work here. I know only the failures of the end product.

But I have no interest in doing a line-by-line corrective edit. That should have been done by his book editor(s). I also have no desire to use these thirteen hundred words as a vehicle to tell "my side" of the Williamsburg story or to defend in any way what we did that night. The time and place for that may come, but this is not it. No, my central purpose in writing this response is only to set the record straight on one of the book's overriding premises.

Let me say it directly, cleanly: I did not go to Williamsburg with a covert master plan to trigger an explosion in David Donald Meredith that would destroy his candidacy for president of the United States. I had not worked out in advance, in my mind or anywhere else, what we, the panelists, might do that night. I did not set out to manipulate my three panelist-colleagues toward the decision we finally took. It came about through spontaneous combustion and consultation among the four of us in the Longsworth D room of the Williamsburg Lodge.

Those are the facts. That is the truth. Inferences, allegations, and whatevers from Chapman to the contrary cannot change them into anything else. I would point out that none of the other three panelists has endorsed or taken up Chapman's charge of manipulation against me. I also believe that even any fair reading of Chapman's own re-created account of what happened and what was said in Longsworth D—full of inaccuracies as it is—supports my position of combustion, not his of conspiracy and manipulation.

I would also like to say—for the record—that I had absolutely nothing to do with the decision of *The New American Tatler* magazine to take a large pass on Mr. Chapman's mischief. I applaud them for their wisdom, but I cannot take credit for it. To suggest there might be a connection between that decision and that of the president to appoint my publisher the U.S. ambassador to Britain has the laughable smell of a conspiracy hallucination to it. This is Oliver Stone stuff. I'm sure Stone has an 800 number Mr. Chapman can call to offer it up for screen treatment. If he sticks a serial killer or a child molester into his hallucinatory mix, one of the prime-time network magazine lovelies might even bite. Go, Tom, go.

I was appalled and saddened to learn through the reading of this book the full extent of the separate decisions of Henry Ramirez, Barbara Manning, and Joan Naylor to violate our agreements on what we said about our private conversations in Longsworth D. I consider what they did to be a serious breach of professional ethics and to be a most grievous violation of my right of privacy. It is no less of an offense than the crime the Meredith campaign and its former-FBI-agent thugs tried to commit with their electronic bugs.

But I reserve my most extreme distaste and outrage for the talking they did after our Donatello dinner. I am perfectly willing to dump some of the blame on Chapman and his coercive tactics, but he did not put a gun to their heads. He did not have the power to force them to talk. Chapman claims my anger at Ramirez, Manning, and Naylor is motivated by some sinister desire to protect myself. Nonsense. It is motivated by the quite normal revulsion with three people who can't keep their mouths shut. If they are the new faces and minds and souls and spirits of American journalism, then it will be out of sight over that cliff with the other donkeys even sooner than I feared. They and Chapman make a perfect quartet.

They also exemplify the new order in American public life. There are no secrets, no confidences, anymore in government or anywhere else. Everyone in the Oval Office, in the cloakroom, in the boardroom, in the cafeteria, in the bedroom, in the closet, talks. And talks and talks and talks. Bill Clinton was correct, in my opinion, when he finally blew his stack and fired everyone around him—The Shut Up! Massacre, as it was called—after all of those "inside the Clinton White House" books came out.

I do not dispute Chapman's opening and persistent line about the impact of Williamsburg on the practice of journalism. I will assume whatever responsiblity/blame I deserve. But I would submit that at least the point of our exercise in the debate was prompted by a noble and serious purpose. Rightly or wrongly, we really did believe what we were doing was for the good of our country. I wonder what those fools—those crazed donkeys—who rioted in the pressroom thought their purpose was. And I wonder what Mr. Chapman thinks his is when he pants after the condom scoop that will reveal the real sexual relationship between the newly famous Hank and Barb.

By my count, I have only one hundred and sixty words left before the thirteen-hundred alarm sounds.

I loved what I did to Mr. Chapman with my alarm clock on Santorini. I loved the way he let me fritter away his time talking about the Majestic Theater in San Antonio and similar matters. He thought he was going to con me. He was wrong. Would I really have called the Greek cops? You bet.

I did not listen to CDs on the trip down from Washington to Williamsburg. My car does not have a CD player. I listened to an audiotape of Robert Duvall's reading of *As I Lay Dying* by William Faulkner. I have always been a great admirer of William Faulkner's work, and I am indeed thinking about writing a novel myself. A *real* novel. It is one of the few things this awful travesty of a book—the one by Chapman you just read— got right. I am considering several possible story lines for my novel, one of them being a multilayered epic based on the Williamsburg Debate. Maybe in that book the real and complete truth can be told. It sure as hell hasn't been told in this one.

Time's up.

—Michael J. Howley
Santorini, Greece

ABOUT THE AUTHOR

JIM LEHRER, co-anchor of *The MacNeil/Lehrer NewsHour,* has worked in daily journalism for thirty-five years. This is his ninth novel. He has also written two books of nonfiction and three plays. He and his wife, Kate, live in Washington, D.C. They have three daughters.

ABOUT THE TYPE

This book was set in Bodoni, a typeface designed by Giambattista Bodoni (1740–1813), the renowned Italian printer and type designer. Bodoni originally based his letter forms on those of the Frenchman Fournier, and created his type to have beautiful contrasts between light and dark.

9/15

$23.00

DATE			

SR   AL

Apr

Wall

BAKER & TAYLOR